MEET THE MENAGERIE . . .

MR. DOYLE . . . Sorcerer and alchemist. A man of unparalleled intellect. When evil threatens to consume the world, he gathers those who will fight.

CERIDWEN . . . Princess of the Fey. Solitary and beautiful, she holds the elemental forces of nature at her command.

DR. LEONARD GRAVES . . . Scientist, adventurer, ghost. He exists in both life—and afterlife.

DANNY FERRICK . . . A sixteen-year-old demon changeling who is just discovering his untapped—and unholy—powers.

CLAY . . . An immortal shapeshifter, he has existed since The Beginning. His origin is an enigma—even to himself.

EVE . . . The mother of all vampires. After a millennium of madness, she seeks to repent for her sins and destroy those she created.

SQUIRE . . . Short, surly, a hobgoblin who walks in shadows.

Praise for
The Nimble Man
A Novel of the Menagerie

"The most nimble aspect of Golden and Sniegoski's book is the combined imagination of its authors. *The Nimble Man* is full of rich, inventive stuff, with a new surprise on every page."

—Jeff Mariotte,
author of *Witch Season: Summer*
and *Angel: Love and Death*

continued . . .

STONES
UNTURNED

A NOVEL OF THE MENAGERIE

CHRISTOPHER GOLDEN
AND
THOMAS E. SNIEGOSKI

ACE BOOKS, NEW YORK

THE BERKLEY PUBLISHING GROUP
Published by the Penguin Group
Penguin Group (USA) Inc.
375 Hudson Street, New York, New York 10014, USA
Penguin Group (Canada), 90 Eglinton Avenue East, Suite 700, Toronto, Ontario M4P 2Y3, Canada
(a division of Pearson Penguin Canada Inc.)
Penguin Books Ltd., 80 Strand, London WC2R 0RL, England
Penguin Group Ireland, 25 St. Stephen's Green, Dublin 2, Ireland (a division of Penguin Books Ltd.)
Penguin Group (Australia), 250 Camberwell Road, Camberwell, Victoria 3124, Australia
(a division of Pearson Australia Group Pty. Ltd.)
Penguin Books India Pvt. Ltd., 11 Community Centre, Panchsheel Park, New Delhi—110 017, India
Penguin Group (NZ), Cnr. Airborne and Rosedale Roads, Albany, Auckland 1310, New Zealand
(a division of Pearson New Zealand Ltd.)
Penguin Books (South Africa) (Pty.) Ltd., 24 Sturdee Avenue, Rosebank, Johannesburg 2196,
South Africa

Penguin Books Ltd., Registered Offices: 80 Strand, London WC2R 0RL, England

STONES UNTURNED: A NOVEL OF THE MENAGERIE

An Ace Book / published by arrangement with the authors

PRINTING HISTORY
Ace mass-market edition / October 2006

Copyright © 2006 by Daring Greatly Corporation and Thomas E. Sniegoski.
Cover art by Christian McGrath. Cover design by Judith Lagerman.
Interior text design by Kristin del Rosario.

The Edgar® name is a registered service mark of the Mystery Writers of America, Inc.

ISBN: 0-441-01446-1

ACE
Ace Books are published by The Berkley Publishing Group,
a division of Penguin Group (USA) Inc.,
375 Hudson Street, New York, New York 10014.
ACE and the "A" design are trademarks belonging to Penguin Group (USA) Inc.

PRINTED IN THE UNITED STATES OF AMERICA

10   9   8   7   6   5   4   3   2   1

For Necon's first family, the Booths,
who always make it feel like home
—C.G.

For Dan Davis,
the real live Danny Ferrick.
—T.E.S.

ACKNOWLEDGMENTS

Love and grateful appreciation to Connie and the kids, to my parents, and to Jamie and Erin. Thanks are due, as ever, to Ginjer Buchanan for her tireless work (and fashion wisdom), the Cabal, and the members of the Vicious Circle for moral support, and to Amber Benson, Jose Nieto, Rick Hautala, Tim Lebbon, Wendy Schapiro, Bob Tomko, Liesa Abrams, the Wicked Street Team, Allie Costa, and so many others for friendship and constant encouragement. Special thanks to Deena Warner, Tim Brannan, and Steve Vernon for assistance above and beyond the call.

—C.G.

As always, my loving thanks to LeeAnne and Mulder for being so freaking patient with me. Special thanks are due to Ginjer Buchanan (Queen of the Simian League of Evil), Dave "YIPPEEEE!" Kraus, Eric Powell, Don Kramer, Greg Skopis, Mom and Dad Sniegoski, Liesa "The Angel of Editing" Abrams, David Carroll, Ken Curtis, Jean Eddy, Lisa Clancy, Kim and Abby, Bob and Pat, Jon and Flo, Pete Donaldson, Jay Sanders, Timothy Cole, and the Red Shirts down at Cole's Comics.

Thanks for putting up with the nonsense.

—T.E.S.

ACKNOWLEDGMENTS

PROLOGUE

SOMETIMES Cully Frayne heard music inside his head, beautiful songs from his childhood days in Tennessee. The songs might be just about anything from top-forty radio that made him remember specific days of his youth to the sweet lullabies his grandmother sang to ease him off to sleep when he was just a babe.

Lately, the music had fallen silent, and all he heard was the voice.

On this cold night in Boston, Cully wanted nothing more than to hear the music again, to remember the warm summer days of his past.

"Runaround Sue" would be nice, he thought, as he shuffled down Boylston Street, zipping the stained windbreaker he'd been given at the shelter up to protect his neck from the chill. He tried to remember the words to the song, muttering to himself, attempting to ignore the sharp bite of the cold, November wind.

"Here's my story, sad but true. It's about a girl that I once knew. She took my love, then ran around, with every single guy in . . ."

The voice made his brain bleed—at least that's what it

felt like. Needles, hundreds of needles sticking into the soft, gray matter.

Cully stopped, gasping. Leaning against the cold metal of a light post, he promised he'd be good, if only the voice would make his brain stop bleeding.

The voice agreed, reminding Cully that it didn't care much for Dion and the Belmonts. It preferred the Four Seasons.

Cully pushed off from the pole as the pain inside his skull began to subside. He was tempted to tell the voice that Dion had recorded "Runaround Sue" solo, but why take a chance of pissing it off again. *No,* he decided. He'd keep the musical trivia to himself.

At one time or another, everyone in Cully's family had heard the voice, but he was one of the lucky ones. The voice hadn't bothered him like it had his grandfather or his cousin Jacob down in Georgia, who had killed himself by parking his truck on the train tracks. No, Cully was lucky. The voice hadn't bothered him much at all. Its only effect had been the sweet music in his head and the tender memories that happily dangled behind the tunes like the tail on a kite—until recently.

The voice intruded again. *It must be a fat one tonight.* No explanation, only the order, *a fat one.*

The shelter on Pine Street was up ahead, and by the looks of the crowd gathering in front, it was going to be a busy night inside. Cully usually didn't go to the shelters, preferring to rough it on his own. He didn't want to depend on anyone.

Brief, hurtful images of a woman he'd known as *wife* flashed before his mind's eye, a shrieking harpy tossing a bottle of little, blue pills at him and demanding that he take one. The medications were to help him, but all they'd done was dull his thoughts and take away the music. Cully couldn't live without the music, didn't *want* to live without the music. Knowing that they wouldn't understand, he had pushed away the people in his life that supposedly cared so much for him. Now, thinking about it, he almost laughed out loud. Yeah, they loved him so much they wanted to take away the only thing that made him happy.

No, Cully Frayne didn't need anybody but himself. Not as long as he had the sweet, sweet tunes inside his head. At the moment they were gone, but they would be back soon. All he had to do was finish this errand for the voice.

He stood across the street from the shelter, looking over the crowd with their *stuff*-filled shopping carts. With the heavy blankets draped over their shoulders they looked like desert nomads. He could feel the voice peering out through his eyes, searching. Then he felt it focus near the head of the line on a guy known as Little Tommy. The name was supposed to be ironic, because Little Tommy was pretty damn big, both tall and fat. He'd been on the streets since he was just a kid, and nobody could figure out how he stayed so fat. The story going around was that anyone who went missing had been eaten by Little Tommy, and that was how he stayed so big.

Cully didn't want any part of this guy; he was wild, unpredictable, and he was also at the front of the line to get into the shelter for a warm bed and a hot meal. Wild horses couldn't drag the son of a bitch from the front of the line on a night like this.

But of course, that was exactly what the voice demanded. The voice wanted Little Tommy, and it wanted him now. By way of incentive, it let the music out for a bit—a show tune, from *Oklahoma*—and then violently yanked it away. Cully knew he would do anything for that music.

Slowly, he crossed the street and made his way through the line, racking his brain for a way to get Little Tommy to leave his spot in line. He knew many of the guys. Some called out to him, others acknowledged him with a barely perceptible nod. Little Tommy was sitting on his big, blue duffel bag, talking with some old guy that Cully didn't recognize. He stopped near the big man and waited, thoughts racing. He still hadn't come up with a plan.

Must I think of everything? the voice growled, and then an idea was there, almost as if Cully had created it himself.

He motioned to the big guy, but Tommy wasn't budging.

"What do you want?" the big guy growled, an unmistakable expression of annoyance on his round, dirty face. He looked like an angry baby—a giant, angry baby.

"I . . . I need your help with something," Cully stammered. "C'mere."

"Forget it." Tommy waved him away. "They're serving meat loaf tonight."

"I got a chance to make some money," Cully continued, glancing at the others standing there in line. They weren't paying attention, probably dreaming about meat loaf. "But I need some muscle."

Cully could tell he had grabbed the large man's attention by the way his fleshy brows scrunched together.

" 'Course if you're not interested, I'll—"

"How much?" Tommy asked, lifting his massive bulk off his duffel bag.

"Twenty bucks, maybe more," Cully replied and watched the fat man's eyes twinkle.

Tommy told the old guy to hold his place and lumbered closer to Cully.

They certainly do grow them big on the streets these days, the voice commented, and Cully had to agree as he tilted his head back to look up at Tommy's face.

"You better not be fuckin' with me, man," the big baby growled.

"No." Cully shook his head. "I wouldn't do that."

"What do we gotta do?"

Cully's lips moved, anxious to wrap themselves around an explanation, but nothing came. The voice was silent.

"I told you not to fuck with me," Tommy bellowed, grabbing Cully by the front of his windbreaker and giving him a violent shake.

That's it, the voice cooed. *He's perfect, so full of vio-*

lence. I wonder how many lives he's taken since living on the streets?

"Some rich kids from Brighton," Cully said as the words came unbidden to his lips. "They want us to buy them booze—for a party. Said they'd pay me forty bucks."

"Pay *you* forty," Tommy said, pushing him away, causing him to stumble backward. "What the fuck you need me for?"

Cully smoothed out the front of his coat, glancing down to make sure the zipper hadn't broken. "There's five of them, and only one of me. I don't want 'em to think they can screw me over. They'd think twice before screwing with somebody like you."

Tommy started to smile. "They'd have to be fucking crazy to screw with me."

"Exactly."

"Where are these rich kids?" the big man asked, looking up and down the street.

"They're waiting up on Shawmut. They want to drive to a packy down on Mass. Ave. You in?"

"Thirty for me, ten for you," Tommy said, his smile getting crueler.

Tell him yes, the voice demanded.

"Ten's better than getting my ass kicked," Cully agreed. "You better bring your shit, though." He pointed to the duffel bag on the ground behind the man. "I don't know how long this is gonna take."

Tommy gave him one last look then retrieved his belongings, and the two of them headed toward Shawmut Avenue through the biting wind. Tommy talked on and on about what he was going to do with the thirty dollars, something about Kentucky Fried Chicken and a big bottle of Jack. But Cully was finding it difficult listening to the big guy while the voice was whispering directions inside his head.

He's good, the voice purred excitedly. *An absolute perfect choice; couldn't have picked better myself.*

"Where the hell are these guys?" Tommy finally asked, starting to sound a bit winded.

Cully hesitated, and then the voice ordered him to turn onto Tremont Street. "Down here," he told his companion.

He was just about to pass the mouth of an alley when he felt the tug. It was as if somebody had put a rope around his waist and pulled it taut, halting his progress. He stopped, gazing into the dark alley.

"They down here?" Tommy asked, shambling up beside him.

"Yeah." He didn't need the voice's confirmation this time.

"What the fuck we waitin' for then?" The big man headed down the alley past two large dumpsters. "Let's get our forty dollars."

Cully followed.

Up ahead there, the voice whispered. *Just past the manhole cover.*

For a moment, Cully Frayne saw through the eyes of his passenger. Through the perspective of the presence in his mind, the area just beyond the manhole looked to be surrounded by writhing black clouds, like the ink injected under water by a frightened octopus. The effect disoriented him and then passed a moment later. In his gut, Cully knew that something had happened on that spot, something so bad that it had seeped into the very substance of the street, and not even the heavy spring rains or the grueling New England winters could wash it away. It was a bad spot, and if what he suspected was true, it was about to get a whole lot worse.

Stop him, the voice commanded. *Don't let him get too far.*

"Hold up," Cully called after the big man.

Tommy stopped and turned to face Cully. "Well?" he asked, looking around the alley. "Where the fuck are they?"

Cully could hear the spark of anger in his voice.

That's it, make him good and mad. Get that heart pumping.

Cully always knew that something like this would happen, but still had hoped that he was different. Nobody else in his family had ever heard the music before; just the voices that made them do things.

"They're not coming," he said sadly. "They never were—I made it up."

Tommy's eyes began to bulge, his fat face seeming to swell up to twice its size.

The voice had tried to tell Cully that his family was blessed—that they were some of the last of their kind, sensitive to those who lived on the other side. Cully gathered that at one time, long ago, there were many more people with the gift, but as the years wore on, fewer and fewer were born with the ability to hear. And for the first time he could remember, Cully Frayne actually envied the deaf.

Tommy dropped his bag to the alley floor, reaching out with gigantic hands to grab hold of Cully. Cully did nothing, letting himself be pulled toward the monster of a man, watching with a cold detachment as Tommy hauled back his ham-sized fist.

Cully saw an explosion of color as the blow landed, and pain exploded in his face. His legs went out from beneath him, and he sat down hard on the street.

Excellent, crooned the voice.

"I warned you not to fuck with me," Little Tommy screamed, lumbering toward him.

Cully made no effort to stop the man from taking hold of him by the front of his jacket. Little Tommy hauled him to his feet. He stuck his tongue out from the corner of his mouth, tasting the warm saltiness of his own blood, and he prepared to be punched again.

He has to be brought to the brink of madness—to the brink of murder—before the time is right.

Little Tommy hit him again. One of Cully's front teeth broke off, sending a spike of excruciating pain up into his brain. Cully rocketed backward, his momentum stopped only when he collided with the metal surface of one of the dumpsters.

"I'm gonna take thirty dollars out of your ass," the man growled, any semblance of humanity leaking away. His face was a blistering shade of red, glowing in the dim light cast by the distant streetlamps.

Cully was drifting away on a wave of pain, pulled beneath the black, cold waters of unconsciousness, when the voice violently dragged him to the surface.

It's time.

The behemoth that was Little Tommy stood over him, fists pounding down upon the dumpster lid, making sounds like the crashing of thunder. "Why'd you fucking do it?" he screamed, the words blending together to create more of a primal scream than spoken language.

It was time.

Cully stared up at Little Tommy, hot blood running from his nose and mouth. His tongue flicked over the jagged break where one of his front teeth used to be, and he gestured with a curling finger for the big man to come closer.

"Do you want to know why?" Cully slurred through bloody, swollen lips.

Tommy bent down, bringing his face close, the filthy stink of the man filling Cully's nostrils.

"Tell me!" he screamed. "Tell me before I rip your fucking head off and shit down your—"

Now.

The voice was like a starter's pistol, compelling Cully's hand to pull the homemade knife from inside his windbreaker pocket. The knife felt warm, like it was somehow filled with life, but that was crazy—wasn't it?

It had come from the wreck of a car in which an entire family had died: mother, father, little girl no older than six, and a newborn baby boy. They had been killed by the miscalculations of a drunk driver coming home from a company picnic. The lush had been trying to change the station on the radio, completely unaware that he had crossed over into oncoming traffic.

The blade had been cut from a piece of the car floor, where the family had died—where the greatest amount of blood had pooled—and filed to a nasty point. Its grip was made from strips of material from the dead baby's pajamas.

The knife glided through the air with wicked precision, plunging into the soft tissue of Little Tommy's throat, severing the carotid artery with its first strike. It was like holding on to a deadly snake, the blade seeming to strike out on its own, stabbing the man's throat three more times before the big man had time to react. Cully could see that he wanted to scream, but was too busy trying to keep the blood from squirting from his neck.

He wasn't doing a very good job.

Don't waste it, the voice commanded, urging Cully to his feet. He had to get Little Tommy over to the designated space. With a nervous tremor Cully recalled what he had seen there earlier, the swirling black mist that somehow signified that that particular patch of alley was tainted.

His head swam as he stood, lunging toward Tommy, driving the monstrosity of a man across the alley with his attack. He plunged the still-hungry blade into Tommy's girth over and over again, stealing away his strength and driving him to his knees.

The dying man fell forward onto his stomach, flopping around on the floor of the alley like some gigantic fish hauled gasping from the sea. But Cully saw that Tommy was at least two feet away from where the voice needed him to be. Furious, face spattered with the huge man's blood, he got a grip beneath Little Tommy's arms and pulled him to the special spot, muscles shrieking with the effort.

Yes, that's it, the voice urged. *Almost there.*

The man weighed a ton, but the blood leaking from the stab wounds acted like a lubricant, helping Cully slide his massive bulk across the ground. When he reached that black, tainted spot on the alley floor, Cully let go of the man and stepped back to catch his breath. His face ached, and one of his eyes was nearly swollen shut from the beating.

"Serves you right," he spat, staring down at the barely twitching body of the man who had beaten him so badly. For a brief moment Cully thought the music had been returned to him, but realized that it was still the voice he was hearing, only now it was humming.

Little Tommy's blood drained out in multiple crimson streams. It was strangely mesmerizing, watching the pool of blood around him expand in size, the flickering streetlights at the far end of the alley causing a strobe that made the gore shift in color from fire-engine red to nearly black.

Dragging his gaze from the pool, Cully realized that Tommy wasn't moving anymore and that the blood had pretty much stopped flowing from his body. The humming had stopped as well, and he began to grow anxious. He listened intently, waiting for a sign that he wasn't alone.

It wasn't long before the pooling blood began to bubble. Cully stepped back. Every instinct screamed at him to run, but he couldn't bring himself to act. Not yet. The voice had yet to do what it had promised—Cully was still not hearing the music.

"Where are you?" he asked, watching as the blood bubbled and frothed. "I did what you wanted—give me back my music," he said, his voice growing louder, tinged with panic. "Do you hear me?"

The roiling pool of gore exploded upward in a roaring fountain, covering him in a fine, gory mist that filled his nostrils and mouth, stinking and tasting of metal.

Cully stumbled back, temporarily blinded by the blood in his eyes. As he frantically wiped at his eyes, trying to clear his vision, he sensed that he was no longer alone.

"I can hear you just fine," said a voice that made Cully remember every bad thing that had ever happened to him.

As his vision cleared, he saw its body glistening wetly

in the flickering fluorescent lights from the mouth of the alley. Its long, spindly arms moved as if conducting the Boston Symphony. It was far more, now, than just a voice.

Far, far more.

1

THERE'S still a music to this place, Arthur Conan Doyle thought as he strolled into the woods behind the small cottage he had acquired in Cottingley. The forest glowed with autumnal colors and the warmth of the fall sunshine. Yes, things had changed much since the last time he'd visited, but the music was still here. Faint, but here nonetheless.

He breathed in the cool, November air, his mind traveling back to the year he'd first visited this quaint English village, situated between the larger towns of Shipley and Bingley in West Yorkshire. It had been warmer then, the gardens and forests lush with summer growth. Conan Doyle smiled at the pleasant memory.

With all the recent supernatural threats to the world and the knowledge that somewhere out there in the cosmos, the ancient evil known as the Demogorgon was even now traveling toward Earth, Ceridwen had convinced Conan Doyle that he needed to recuperate, to rest and rejuvenate himself. Neither of them could think of a better place to do that than Cottingley. It had been here, after all, that Conan Doyle had first encountered the world of Faerie.

He had met seventeen-year-old Elsie Wright and her

younger cousin Francis Griffith in 1920 and found himself captivated by the photographs they had taken, and which had caused an uproar among the local populace. Of course, he had known they were forgeries, these fanciful photographs, showing the girls interacting with tiny fairy folk and gnomes, but he played the part of the gullible old man. Conan Doyle had been in his sixties then, his studies of spiritualism and magic beginning to garner far too much attention. He had needed more privacy to continue his studies, and what better way than to be branded a credulous old kook.

Yet his strategy had had unexpected consequences. The trip to Cottingley had been all for show. The last thing he had imagined was that he would encounter actual mysteries in the woods outside the village, or that the playful hoax of two young girls would lead him to a real encounter with the Fey. But he stood now not far at all from the very spot where he'd had his first encounter with creatures from Faerie and discovered in an impossibly hollow tree an entrance into a world beyond his imagining.

The voice of his lover stirred him from his ruminations of the past. Ceridwen had gone on ahead, anxious to view the Cottingley Beck again, the narrow brook fed by a cascading waterfall that ran between two steep banks. That was where Elsie and Frances had chosen to compose their fantastical photos, and the beauty of the place made it simple to understand why.

Ceri called his name again, and he quickened his step. There was a tension in her voice, not one that implied danger, but certainly something had upset her. Conan Doyle conjured a quick defensive spell and felt the magic swirl around his fingers as he carefully descended an embankment that led down to the stream.

He found the princess of Faerie standing beside the stream, not far from the falls, her back to him as she scrutinized her surroundings. Conan Doyle was again struck by the way she was dressed. Her usual couture consisted of silken gowns and wraps in the colors of earth and ocean.

Ceridwen was an elemental sorceress and felt most comfortable in the hues of nature.

The colors she wore today were no exception, but rather than a silk gown, she wore stylish khaki trousers and a sky-blue blouse. As breathtakingly beautiful and elegant as she always was, it lifted his heart to see her this way, to have an aspect of his home world accepted by her, even if it was something as inconsequential as fashion. Ceridwen had not confirmed it, but Conan Doyle felt certain this was Eve's doing—she had such a taste for style—and he made a mental note to thank her when they returned to the States.

"What is it, love?" he asked as he approached.

Ceridwen cast a worried glance over her shoulder at him. Her thick, golden hair was pulled back and knotted. Her alabaster skin glowed in the faint sunlight of the autumn afternoon. In that moment, her beauty would have stolen his breath, if it hadn't been for the sadness in her eyes.

"Ceri, what is it?" he asked, hurrying to her side. "What's wrong?"

She'd dropped the basket they had brought with them for a picnic repast. It had fallen on its side, its contents partially spilling out onto the riverbank.

"Look what they've done, Arthur."

He placed his hands gently upon her shoulders, attempting to see through her eyes—through the eyes of a being inherently connected to the elements.

Where there had once been none, there were now homes built on either side of the stream. Beyond them he saw a fence, likely erected because somebody believed that the site was potentially dangerous for public access, even all these years later. Even though the girls' claims were debunked so thoroughly.

Conan Doyle sighed, wrapping his arms lovingly around her from behind. "It's awful," he said softly. "But we can't expect them to leave it as it was. To *them*, this is progress."

Ceridwen stiffened in his arms.

"Progress?" she spat. "They're killing it."

She spoke of Cottingley Beck as if it were a person, and to the Fey, that was precisely how it was perceived.

"Houses practically built atop one another, their pollutants finding their way into the stream . . . and somebody actually put up a fence," she said, stabbing a finger toward the offending structure. "A fence, Arthur."

He held her tighter, trying to calm her angry spirit. "This wasn't the purpose of coming here," he said. "To make you angry and bring you that much closer to declaring war on humanity."

She scoffed at his attempt at humor. "And you were appalled by what my race calls your world."

"The *Blight*," Conan Doyle said, the word sounding incredibly ugly as it left his lips. But true.

"When I see something like this," Ceridwen said, turning in his arms to face him, "it makes it so difficult not to wish them ill will."

Conan Doyle told himself he knew how difficult it must have been for her to leave Faerie in order to be with him in this often cold, ugly, human world. Yet he knew he could never understand the true extent of her sacrifice. It must have been torturous, but here she was, standing by his side. The time that he had spent living in Faerie was no sacrifice at all, in comparison. In truth, he had gained far more than he had lost while residing there. Often he had questioned his decision to leave Faerie and to leave Ceridwen behind. She had refused to come with him, and he had been unable to stay. Now he wondered how he had ever had the strength to turn his back on their love.

That they had been brought together again, found the love growing between them once more, was a greater gift than he had ever deserved. Silently, he vowed to himself that he would never let her go again. No matter the cost. Yet looking back, he knew all too well that had he not made that decision to leave Faerie, humanity would likely have met its demise by now. The world of his birth would have been swallowed up by some horrific preternatural threat if not for his efforts and those of his special operatives—his *Menagerie*.

He put his mouth close to the delicate shell of her ear and whispered, "Even though it has changed, it is still the place that brought us together. That is what brought us here, Ceri. And even with the way the woods have changed, it is still a beautiful, autumn day. Are we going to allow it to go to waste?"

She wrapped her arms tightly around his waist. "I hope not, Arthur. Somehow I know you'll do your best to ease my mind."

Ceridwen did not wait for his response. She pressed her lips tightly to his in a passionate kiss, her hands leaving his waist to cup his face. He responded in kind, pressing his body tightly against hers.

It wasn't long before they lay beneath the trees, their passions inflamed, and fumbled with their clothing. Conan Doyle could feel the environment around them responding to his woman's pleasure. To the magic in her. The grass grew tall around their entwined bodies, the air filled with the sound of insects and the chirping of birds.

Ceridwen sat astride him, her rhythmic movements sending wave after wave of intense pleasure through them both.

"Though the world may change around us," she breathed, "what we now have together . . . this is something that will forever remain untouched."

She leaned down to kiss him again, her hair brushing his face as their bodies moved together.

A delicious overture, before the inevitable storm.

"SO when do the lovebirds get back?" Julia Ferrick asked her son from the stove, where she was currently putting together their evening's meal of Texas chili.

Danny loved his mother's chili, and his empty stomach rumbled just thinking about it. Seated on a stool behind the marble island in the center of the large kitchen, he inhaled

the delicious smells of her cooking. The lovebirds she re-
ferred to—though the expression made him wince—were
Mr. Doyle and Ceridwen, gone to England to spend some
private time together.

"I think sometime tomorrow," he said, picking strips of
dead skin from around his fingernails. His body was continuing to change, becoming more and more . . . *demonic*.

"Don't pick," his mother scolded. Julia chopped up an
onion on the wooden cutting board, as four strips of bacon
popped and sizzled in the frying pan on the gas burner. The
air was filled with the delicious aroma of cooking meat.

"It's just dead skin," he said, paying her no mind. His
nails had become long, curved, and thick, growing to nasty
points, and when he tensed the muscles in his fingers, the
nails distended, reminding him of a cat's claws. *They could
do some serious damage in a fight,* he mused, recalling the
scrapes he'd gotten into since coming to live in Conan
Doyle's Beacon Hill brownstone.

"I don't care," his mother replied. "It could still get infected. Leave it alone."

Danny glared at her. "Have you fucking looked at me
lately? An infection is the least of my problems."

Using tongs, his mother flipped the bacon over in the
pan. "Language, Danny, please. I didn't let you talk that
way in my house, and I don't want you to talk that way
here."

He laughed. "Everybody talks that way here."

"Talks how?" asked a voice, and the temperature in the
kitchen dropped considerably. The ghostly form of Dr.
Leonard Graves slowly materialized.

Danny shrugged. "Y' know, cursin' and shit. Everybody
does it."

"Well, I don't, and neither does Leonard," his mother
said, sliding the pan over to an unused burner. Using the
tongs, she moved the bacon to two sheets of paper towel.

"Your mother's right," Leonard said, in that low voice
that somehow managed to be both creepy and comforting
at the same time. "There's no reason to speak that

way . . . unless you want people to think that you're an un-educated cretin."

Danny chuckled, pretty certain that he'd never been called a cretin before.

Julia came over to them with the bacon on the paper towel, placing it down in front of him. She didn't use the actual bacon in her chili recipe, just the grease. He helped himself to a piece; it was crispy, cooked just the way he liked it.

"I'm making chili," Julia said to Graves. "I'd ask you to join us, but I know you don't eat." She gave a small laugh, smiling at the ghost, as her hands played with her hair.

There it is again, Danny thought, chewing slowly on his bacon. His mother had been acting weird around Dr. Graves lately. Different. Almost nervous. He'd entertained the notion several times that his mom was flirting, but dismissed it as too crazy. Now he wasn't so sure. Did his mother actually have a thing for the ghost of a guy who'd been dead since World War II?

How fucked up is that?

"Thank you, Julia," Graves said. "I'm sure it's delicious. I wish I could try some, but it's just beyond my reach."

With a sympathetic look, she returned to the stove and began to scrape the bacon grease into the large, cast-iron kettle that she'd brought from home.

"Well, you're welcome to hang out with us, of course," she said, turning the flame on beneath the kettle and placing the dirty pan in the sink, filling it full of warm, soapy water. "We've got an exciting evening of Battleship and a showing of . . . what's the name of the movie again?" she asked Danny.

"Old Boy," he said. "It's Korean, supposed to be a killer."

"Yeah, that's it," she said, smiling again as she wiped her hands on a dish towel. "Like I said, you're more than welcome."

Danny felt himself becoming perturbed; this was supposed to be *their* time—just him and his mom. It pissed him off a bit, her inviting somebody to hang, when it was just supposed to be the two of them. He dug at a particularly itchy patch of skin on the back of his hand, drawing blood. The crimson liquid slowly oozed to the surface of the torn, yellowed flesh.

His mother slid two packages of ground hamburger into the iron kettle. It hit the hot bacon grease, and the sound and aroma of it sizzling in the pot filled the air, distracting Danny from his anger. Once the meat was partially cooked, she'd add the tomato paste and then the spices. His mouth began to water, and his gums to itch, another new trait of his continued transformation. Whenever he got hungry, or even thought of food, his teeth grew longer. Danny flicked his tongue over the pointed tips of his prominent incisors. They were sharp, and he had to be careful not to slice his tongue.

"Thanks for the invitation," the ghost said. "But I'm afraid I have some pressing business that must be attended to."

His mother turned from the stove, continuing to stir the cooking beef and spices around in the pot. "Is everything okay?"

Dr. Graves seemed agitated, more distracted than usual. Danny had grown able to read him pretty well. They'd been spending quite a bit of time together lately. Danny couldn't go to school, and so Dr. Graves had been tutoring him a little. He didn't understand what the point was of continuing his education—after all, it wasn't like he was going to have a normal life. But Graves had been able to make him understand that knowledge wasn't just something to be used to impress a prospective employer or a college interviewer . . . it was a weapon. The right piece of knowledge at the right time could mean the difference between victory and defeat, between life and death.

On that level, Danny understood. So he went along with the whole tutor idea, most of the time.

The more he learned about Dr. Graves, the more

amazed he was at how much the guy had experienced and all the knowledge he had accumulated in his lifetime. Hell, he was still accumulating it, even after his death. Yeah, it was freaky to have a ghost for a teacher, but that was only appropriate, considering he himself was a total freak. He doubted the faculty over at Newton South would be up for teaching a kid with skin like an alligator, claws, and horns growing out of his head.

The anger was back, this time over the changes that were twisting his body. And that in itself was another change. Lately he'd found himself getting angry more often, the littlest things making him want to tear something apart—or tear some*body* limb from limb. He grabbed another slice of bacon, shoving the whole thing into his mouth.

The ghost had hesitated, and Danny could see storm clouds of trouble in his eyes.

"Dr. Graves?" he ventured.

"To be honest, everything is not okay," the ghost said. "And it's high time that I devoted my full attention to dealing with that."

"Sounds serious," Julia said, turning the flame down low beneath the kettle, so the contents could simmer a bit before she added the last of the ingredients. "Anything we can do to help?"

"Yeah, what's up?" Danny asked, refocusing his anger into concern for his tutor.

"I haven't spent a lot of time talking about it, but I know you're both aware of how I died. It was murder, and the mystery of my death has never been solved. I think I've waited long enough for answers, don't you?"

Graves didn't talk about this part of his past very often, but Danny couldn't blame him. He couldn't imagine how fucked up it must be to still be around after . . . to know what it's like to be murdered.

"Isn't Mister Doyle supposed to be helping you with this?" Julia asked.

The ghost chuckled, but there really didn't seem to be

much humor behind it. "Yes, yes he is. In fact, the entire reason I've stayed here so long, in his house, and taken part in his war against the darkness—been a part of his *Menagerie,* as he likes to call us—was as payback for his help in finding the solution to my murder."

Danny tore off the end of a piece of paper towel, using it to staunch the seeping wound that he had scratched in the top of his hand.

"All the time you've been working with Mr. Doyle and still . . . ?" he asked, looking into the ghost's nearly transparent eyes.

Graves nodded. "Exactly. It's been a very long time, and I'm still no closer to answers."

Julia returned to the stove, lifted the lid, and stirred what was inside. "Why is that, do you think?"

"I can't be certain," Graves said, shaking his head slowly. "There has been the occasional lead over the years, followed with a thorough investigation, but in the end—"

"The big donut," Danny said. "Nada. Don't you think it's sort of weird that somebody as smart as Conan Doyle—he created Sherlock Holmes for fuck's sake— couldn't dig up at least a little something that would be useful in solving your case?"

Danny watched as Graves slowly crossed his arms, hovering a good six inches off the kitchen floor. "One would think. To be honest, I've let trust and friendship and sometimes despair get in the way of asking that very question. But after all this time, I'm not sure the answer even matters."

Julia pulled a blender out from beneath the counter, setting it down and plugging it in. A deep frown creased her forehead as she turned to stare at them.

"Are you two implying that Mr. Doyle is purposely not helping? Because if that's the case, I think you're both being ridiculous."

She poured into the blender the contents of another pan that had been boiling on the stove. Bright red chili pods bobbed inside the plastic container. Julia hit one of the buttons on the blender, and the clear water inside turned a dark, churning red, as the peppers were pureed.

"Regardless," Graves said over the roar of the blender. "I can't wait anymore, can't divert so much of my attention to other things. I'm going to start the investigation from scratch."

The kitchen went suddenly silent, as Julia switched off the appliance. "You're leaving?"

Again, Danny saw it in his mother, this affection for Graves.

"If I'm going to do this properly . . ." Graves's voice trailed off.

Though he was only a ghost, a transparent, shifting apparition of ectoplasm . . . not even really there, when you thought about it . . . he seemed weighted with regret. Danny stared at him. It was crazy enough to think that his mother had feelings for a dead man, but now Danny had to wonder if the ghost had feelings for her as well.

Julia detached the pitcher from the blender, taking its contents to her kettle. "How long do you think you'll be?" she asked casually, apparently not wanting to appear upset, but Danny could hear it in her voice.

If there was one thing he'd learned about his mother, it was how to read the tone of her voice.

"I don't know," Graves replied. "And I'm sorry. I know I made some promises about keeping up with Danny's tutoring—"

"It's cool," Danny said, batting a rolled and blood-stained piece of paper towel back and forth between his hands. "Do what you have to."

"And once you solve this case, your . . . your murder, what then?" his mother asked.

Graves was silent for a moment, drifting in the midst of the kitchen, moving as if struggling against a breeze Danny couldn't feel.

"I've . . . stayed here because of this, because I had unfinished business. Wandering spirits find it difficult to move on to whatever awaits after life, because they can't rest yet, because something remains to be done. Once I have the answer, once I know who murdered me, and why, the reason for me to haunt this world will be gone. Gabriella, my fiancée . . . she died during the years that my spirit was wandering aimlessly, before I was able to focus as a ghost. Somewhere on the other side, she's waiting for me."

His mother's hands went to either side of the sink, as if supporting herself. There was that smile again, and the slow nodding of the head.

"It would be nice for you," she said. "Finally getting to . . . to rest and . . . to be with your fiancée again."

"Yes, it would," the ghost replied.

"I hope you know how much you'll be missed," she told Graves, and it was painfully obvious to Danny that she wanted to say more, but couldn't bring herself to, maybe because he was sitting there.

From that point on, his mother was silent, going about the business of finishing dinner as if nothing was wrong.

"Will you be all right?" Graves asked, and Danny wasn't sure if the ghost was talking to him or to his mother.

"I'll be fine," he finally answered, wanting to fill the void of silence. "It's all good."

But it wasn't.

It wasn't good at all.

THE rest of the evening had been a disaster. He and his mother pretended that everything was fine, but he could see that she was distracted by what Dr. Graves had told them, and the anger inside him continued to fester.

They'd eaten pretty much in silence, neither of them feeling very hungry in the end. After dinner, they put on the movie, but Danny found he couldn't really get into it. Eventually he pretended to fall asleep, and noticing this, his mother shook his leg, saying that she was tired, too, and was going to call it a night.

As far as he was concerned, she couldn't have left soon

enough. It was taking everything he could muster not to lose it. Directionless anger and frustration boiled up inside of him, just looking for a target. He'd been feeling this way a lot since getting back from Greece the previous month—since his body had changed even further. It was worse at night; his skin would start to itch, and his temper was like a ticking bomb.

It was best that his mother left Conan Doyle's house and headed home, especially after the kind of night it had been.

Now Danny was lying on his bed, trying to calm down. His head buzzed like he'd drunk five Red Bulls. He was even desperate enough to have attempted some of the relaxation techniques the psychiatrist he used to see had tried to teach him, but it didn't do a damn bit of good. All he could think about was the headshrink's gorgeously blond receptionist, sitting behind her desk, and what he would have liked to do to her.

Vivid images filled his mind, loaded with sex and violence—heavy on the violence. Danny recoiled, the scenes appearing in his head disturbing even to him.

Whoa, where'd they come from? he wondered, sitting up in the bed, the sights inside his skull gradually beginning to fade, but not fast enough.

He guessed that this was all part of the transformation—of becoming what he was—and tried to play it down. Eve and Graves had been telling him all along that whatever his origins, he could choose to be whatever he wanted. Hell, Eve was a pretty damned good example of that.

He scratched vigorously at an extremely itchy patch of skin in the center of his chest. It felt even weirder than the thick, scaly hide usually felt, and he got up from his bed and walked across to his bathroom. Flicking on the light, he winced. Bright light was starting to hurt his eyes. On the other hand, his night vision was awesome.

Danny squinted, adjusting to the brightness of the bathroom, and was finally able to look at himself in the medicine cabinet mirror.

What a piece of work, he thought, gazing at his reflection with a mixture of disgust and awe. Every time he looked, there seemed to be something different. For example, he was certain that his horns had gotten longer since that morning.

The irritated patch of flesh on his chest called attention to itself again, and he lifted up his *Reservoir Dogs* T-shirt to get a look. Every inch of his exposed body appeared dried and irritated. It seemed like he was sloughing off his skin at least once a week, but the spot on his chest looked different somehow.

What's up with that? He leaned in closer to the mirror as he poked and prodded at the area with a clawed finger. Something was growing in the center of his flesh. It was small, about the size of a grape, and if it weren't for the ridiculous itch, he probably wouldn't even have noticed it. It felt different than the rest of his changing skin; squishy, like it was filled with fluid. Danny was tempted try and tear it open. He pressed one of his claws into the little nodule, but then became distracted.

Distracted by a smell.

Danny tilted his horned head back and breathed it in. The scent wasn't from within the house. It came from outside. Leaving the bathroom and forgetting all about the weird growth on his chest, the teenager stood in the center of his room, the enticing aroma luring him. He walked to the door and stepped out into the hall. It was eerily quiet in the house. As far as he knew, nobody else was home.

Danny squinted, realizing that he could actually see the scent writhing in the air like smoke curling from a cigarette. He followed it to another set of stairs that led up to the brownstone's roof and began to climb them. The closer he got to the roof, the stronger the smell became.

Unlocking the heavy wooden door, carved with all manner of bizarre ancient symbols that he couldn't begin to decipher, Danny emerged onto the rooftop. A gust of cold,

November air blasted him, but he was undeterred. The scent was even stronger now, and he followed it across the rooftop. He sprang up onto the wall that ran around the roof perimeter, perching there, head tilted back, like some kind of living gargoyle.

The scent came from across the way, from a building on Mount Vernon Street, and more specifically, from her.

In the darkness, Danny smiled, feeling the teeth within his mouth grow. The cute girl that he'd seen a few times going in and out of the building over the last few weeks was standing on the steps down below. She was dressed in a leather jacket and a short black dress and was clutching a tiny purse. Waiting for somebody to pick her up, he imagined.

"Ain't it a little late to be goin' out now?" he asked the night, watching as she pulled up the sleeve of her coat to check the time.

Danny inhaled sharply, differentiating between all the different smells that filled the night air of Boston, until he found the one that he was looking for—the scent that had pulled him from his room onto the rooftop.

He had smelled the girl before—a mixture of perfume, body soap, and shampoo—but this was different. The other scents were all still there, perhaps even a bit stronger than usual, almost as if they were there to cover something up. But he could still smell the odor underneath it all, pungent and sharp. It took him a moment to realize exactly what it was.

The smell of blood; a woman's blood.

Danny smiled again, amused by what his heightened senses had revealed to him. He'd wanted to talk to the girl from the first time he'd seen her, but knew it was impossible. The way he looked, she'd probably start screaming the minute she laid eyes on him.

He saw the scenario play out in his head; him going out on the street to just say *hi,* and suddenly she'd be screaming, running into the house and slamming the door. By the time he made it back to Conan Doyle's, the sound of police sirens would be coming closer.

"Fucking bitch," he growled, the ever-present ball of anger inside him increasing in size as he raked his fingernails over the granite of the wall he was perched upon. He was tempted to jump down there; knowing full well that the fall wouldn't hurt him. It gave him pleasure just imagining the look on her pretty stuck-up face as he came at her, letting her know that he could smell her stink from inside his house.

The muscles in his legs tensed as he prepared to actually carry out what he was thinking, but a silver-gray BMW came roaring down the street, traveling way too fast, and came to a screeching halt in front the girl's house.

She stood on the steps for a bit, arms crossed, pretending not to notice that her ride had arrived. The guy opened the door, coming around the car to escort her to the passenger side. He was pulling her close to him, whispering in her ear, and kissing her neck. Danny couldn't quite make out the words, but he heard her call him an asshole. The guy just laughed, returning to the Beemer's driver's seat.

As they pulled away from the curb, tires squealing just to show anybody around how cool they were, Danny came to the conclusion that he didn't like them—the girl or her boyfriend—and had the overpowering desire to share that with them.

In a move that seemed perfectly rational to him at the moment, Danny leapt from Conan Doyle's brownstone, landing in a hunched crouch in the middle of Mount Vernon Street.

Pretty good jump, he thought, sniffing the air, finding what he was looking for.

And he began to follow their scent.

2

EVE let the music of the dance club fill her, the rhythmic pulse of the loud, techno beat acting as a kind of surrogate heartbeat. It wasn't anything like having the real thing, throbbing around inside your chest, but in her situation, it would have to suffice.

It was hot inside Sultan's, the hottest new club on Lansdowne Street. Three hundred or so sweaty bodies moved to the music on the dance floor, and she was in the middle, pretending she was one of them, acting like she belonged. And for moments, here and there, as she allowed herself to get caught up in the music, she could almost believe.

But eventually something would come along to screw it up. Something always did.

Eve saw him across the room, an island of absolute stillness in a turbulent sea of gyrating bodies, and he was watching. She closed her eyes, wanting to lose herself in the pulsing beat, wanting to be part of this microcosm of humanity, even if it was just for a little while. Maybe he'd go away if she ignored him.

"You dance beautifully," said a cold, soft voice that somehow managed to be heard even over the blare of the club's sound system.

She opened her eyes to see that he was closer, less than two feet away. Eve doubted that the others could see him, but they still gave him space as he moved across the dance floor, unknowingly moving out of his path.

Jophiel. He was part of the heavenly host, one of the Cherubim. Eve had not seen him since they had run into one another at a symposium in Tel Aviv on the forgotten books of the Old Testament. That had been five years ago, and the time before that . . .

Eve turned her back to him and tried to lose herself in the moment, hoping the physical act of dancing would keep the painful fragments of her memory at bay. It did not. In her mind's eye she saw Jophiel as she had the first time, so very, very long ago, wearing armor that seemed forged of the sun, brandishing a sword of fire. The beating of his powerful wings as he chased them out of the Garden had sounded like the end of the world.

And in a way, that was precisely what it had been.

"What do you want?" she asked the angel, continuing to dance.

Several people around her shot confused glances in her direction—obviously believing she was talking to them— and they moved away, allowing Jophiel to glide closer.

"It amuses me to see you here—among them." The angel smiled, and it was the most hideous thing she had ever seen. "What would they say, do you think, if they knew?"

Eve directed her attention to a darkly handsome college guy dancing with an attractive blonde. It only took about a second for him to notice her. He danced closer, leaving the blonde to continue her dance alone.

"If they understood . . . truly understood who you are, and what you and your mate stole from them . . ." Jophiel whispered in her ear.

The angel's mere presence sickened her, dredged up within her all of the terror and anguish of her existence. All the regret. All the pain. Ignoring him simply wasn't going to work.

Eve continued dancing, but, masking the motion as part of her gyrations, she shot her elbow back hard, gauging the distance so that she would hit the angel's face. She'd anticipated a satisfying crunch. Fully manifested, angels could be hurt. They healed quickly, but it would still feel good to shatter Jophiel's nose or cheekbone.

The angel wasn't there. Her elbow shot backward, and she danced into its momentum. As she turned, she realized that she had nearly struck a heavyset bald man with glasses, who seemed oblivious to how close he had just come to dying. With her strength, that elbow would have shattered his skull.

Eve had no idea what had made Jophiel so obsessed with her. The angel took it upon himself to track her down every few centuries to remind her of the magnitude of her sins, as though he worried that she might, even for a moment, forget the horror she had caused and have a day or an hour without the weight of the world's guilt on her shoulders.

Really, he was just a whiny little shit.

As if she could ever forget who she was and what she had done. There were nights when the wind was just right and the sky clear and pure that she could close her eyes and still taste the sweetness of the forbidden fruit on her tongue and lips.

The original sin. The original crime. Yes, she was guilty. But she was just a toy, a puppet trapped in a tug-of-war between the Creator and Old Scratch. The Creator should have trusted her. If He'd not made her so ignorant, she would have known better than to fall for the serpent's lies.

Now here Jophiel was to remind her again, and all she wanted to do was scream at the angel and tear out his eyes. Hadn't she suffered enough? Driven out of the Garden, raped and tainted, turned into a monster. When was it enough? She was the mother of men and the mother of all vampires, but she had never wanted to be either. She had been innocent and desired nothing but the feel of her man beside her and the warmth and sunshine of the Garden.

Eve was Forsaken. That much was clear. The Creator would take no responsibility for the soul-destroying evils that had befallen her, turned her into what she had become. For so long afterward—after the demons had used her up and cast her out and she had become this thing—she had been a mad, ravenous thing, spreading the plague of vampirism. Now she did her best to eradicate it from the world, to destroy the monsters who were her children. She wanted—needed—to redeem herself, not in the Creator's eyes, but in her own.

And if that meant the Creator would forgive her, would open His arms and gates and let her in, all the better. That way, she could look into His eyes and ask why He had forsaken her.

Someday, she would know.

The Cherubim stood five feet away beneath a spinning disco ball, his eerily pallid features bathed in reflections of colored light.

"Could their simple little minds even grasp the enormity of what you stole—that you took Paradise from them?" Jophiel asked.

She locked eyes with him, allowing the intensity of the hate she felt for him, and for herself, to travel across the crowded floor.

Jophiel smiled then, and she knew that this time it was indeed an expression of pleasure, for he'd gotten exactly what he'd wanted from her—exactly what he came for.

The angel slowly bowed his head and turned to disappear into the sea of bodies. She considered going after him, plowing through the dancers, fangs bared, but managed to restrain herself. The bastard would've probably enjoyed a tussle, not thinking twice about unleashing his full angelic fury on her among the club's patrons.

Eve seethed, her body trembling from the anger she was keeping bottled inside. No longer dancing, she had faltered at Jophiel's words and now could only stare at the place where the angel had been. Thanks to him, she could not stay here. Eve often took pleasure in losing herself among humanity, reveling in the scents of their blood and sweat, the sounds of their laughter. If she could sweat and bleed and laugh with them, then for a little while, she could feel human.

Jophiel had taken that away.

The music no longer made her feel alive. Eve started to move through the dancers toward the exit, only to feel two hands grab hold of her waist from behind, pulling her back. Her first instinct was to spin around, to use her claws to rip the flesh of whoever dared to touch her, but she pulled back.

Conan Doyle would have been so very proud of her restraint.

The handsome college boy that she'd lured away from his blond dance partner grinned at her lasciviously, hands still clutching her hips, pulling her toward him.

And Eve allowed it.

Lost in her remorse, she let the drunken young guy—she could smell the stink of alcohol seeping from his pores—hold on to her like she was just another party favor. A toy. But she had been treated that way since the dawn of Creation, so why stop it now?

College boy pulled her toward him, his lips mashing against hers in a hungry kiss. And she responded, grinding against him as they kissed, there upon the dance floor.

Desperate to abandon her anger and sorrow, she used the touch and taste of the boy to forge it into lust. Eve found herself inflamed with a nearly overpowering, animal desire. They continued to kiss, their mouths locked hungrily together, and she found it more and more difficult to keep the animal under control. The beast. The monster. She could feel his heartbeat against her chest, the hardness of him through his pants as he rubbed against her leg.

Eve couldn't stand it anymore. Desperate for some kind of release, she allowed the beast in her to surge forward.

The young man yelped, pulling away from her hungry mouth, a crimson trickle running from his lip, down his chin, from where she had nipped him.

His blood in her mouth tasted of lust, and it made her hungry for more. There was a spark of fear in the young man's eyes, which only served to arouse her more. She grabbed his hand in hers, roughly pulling him toward the darkness at the back of the club.

Where they could be alone.

DANNY had returned to the rooftops, the pursuit of his prey easier above the streets, where he could leap from roof to roof.

He was truly amazed and thrilled at the distance he found himself able to cross in a single jump. The horrifying changes in his body had altered him in so many ways, but not all of them were bad. He liked the way his senses were so much stronger, his eyes keener. He liked the strength and speed that came with being whatever he really was. If the track coach back at Newton South could have seen him now, he'd have been amazed.

Once he finished screaming.

The thought made Danny laugh. He threw back his head and howled gleefully as he leaped from one roof to the next, a dark blur in the air above the cars roaring along the street below. Then the laughter was gone, and bitter hatred returned. He snarled as he thought of the coach. Making him scream would be such a pleasure.

Yeah, I'm scholarship material for sure, Danny thought as he ran and then jumped again. He hurtled through the air above Mount Vernon Street, landing with a roll on a rooftop patio, its furniture tied and covered for the cruelty of the coming New England winter.

The farther he moved away from Mr. Doyle's townhouse, the more varied the scents of the city became, but he could still smell her drifting on the cold, night air— could still smell her flow. He had the scent in his nostrils now, and it was like a beacon, flashing in the darkness. All he had to do was follow it.

Danny had calmed a bit in his travels from Louisburg

Square, the intensity of his anger diminishing with activity. He really didn't understand why he was chasing the couple. It just seemed like the thing he had to do at the time. He thought about going home, but decided against it. What was he going to do there? He was too worked up to sleep, and there was nothing but crap on television at this hour, and besides, he was enjoying being out—enjoying the whole adventure of the hunt.

The noise of a door coming open snapped him from his thoughts, and he reacted instinctively. Danny took a step backward, reaching out to take hold of a shadow thrown by a plastic storage shed, drawing it around him like a cloak, and hiding in the darkness. He'd nearly forgotten about this unique talent, but his instincts said otherwise. It wasn't the first time. It seemed as if his brain had somehow been broken down into two parts, the one half that had accepted the gradual transformation into something less than human and all that it entailed, and the other half, which was still kind of in a state of shock—wondering what was waiting for him around the next corner.

A kid no older than Danny came out onto the roof with three of his friends—two girls and a guy. None of them were wearing coats, and he watched as they all pulled the sleeves of their shirts down over their hands trying to keep them warm.

Why don't you just go and get your coats, dumb asses? he thought, watching from his cocoon of shadow.

The girls were cute, but seemed a little young, and it was obvious that the guys were attempting to show off, maybe hoping to get a little something, he guessed. Danny could smell alcohol as they chattered among themselves. He figured whichever one lived in the building, the parents had gone out for the evening, making the liquor cabinet fair game. He listened as they talked about school and some kind of big winter dance, and also how somebody by the name of Darlene Golland was a whore.

One of the guys, the kid Danny figured actually lived in

the building, moved suddenly toward him, dangerously close, and Danny felt a spike of panic. *Had he been seen?*

Danny watched the boy go to the storage shed, open the door, and start to rummage around inside. He emerged with a pack of cigarettes and returned to the friends with his prize. Eagerly they each accepted, the other guy lighting the smokes for them all with a disposable lighter he pulled from the back pocket of his baggy jeans.

He wanted to leave, bored, but at the same time he was fascinated with how ordinary it all was. How long had it been since he had shared a similarly ordinary moment? How long since he'd just been able to relax and be a normal kid?

Jealousy burned in him.

They continued to smoke their cigarettes, talking about nothing really—video games, the new cell phones that they wanted their parents to get for them, what they would be doing then if one of them had a car. It was all so mundane, but it made him hungry for it. He wanted *this*, a chance to be like them again, to be nothing more than a stupid kid who thought he knew everything.

It just wasn't possible for him anymore. And that really pissed him off.

One of the girls—a skinny little thing with pink streaks through her short, black hair—took a camera phone out of a tiny *Lenore* lunchbox she carried and started snapping digital pictures of her friends. They were all acting like goofs, making faces and hanging all over one another.

Danny felt the nearly overpowering urge to rip the concealing cover of shadow away.

But then what? a small voice inside his head asked.

More disturbing images, much too real for his liking, appeared in his mind. He saw himself emerging from the shadows, attacking the boys first, ripping them apart with his bare hands. They would be no match for him, of course, and the girls would be screaming at the top of their lungs, right up until he ripped their throats out. And, damn, what he would do with them afterward . . .

He felt like he was going to throw up, crouched there under the cover of shadow. It took everything he had, but Danny held it together long enough for the teens to finally get too cold and leave the rooftop patio, heading back down to the warmth of an apartment below.

Danny emerged from the shadows a trembling wreck. He didn't like these kinds of thoughts, and the fact that they were happening more and more frequently was freaking him out. It was definitely time for him to go home.

He leaped from the roof out into space, the cold wind rushing past his face as he descended to the next building. *It won't take long to get back to Doyle's,* he thought, preparing to leap again out across the void that separated the structures.

But even as he leaped across the rooftops of Beacon Hill, heading toward the brownstone he now called home, he sensed something. Danny felt less and less comfortable in the human world every day. Now, though, he had the overwhelming feeling that there was someplace else, completely unlike this world, quite close by. It was as though if he just turned down the right alley, or went through the right door and at just the right time, it would be there waiting for him.

Then, as quickly as he'd sensed it, it was gone, leaving him with a painful yearning for a world he did not know, and yet, strangely enough, felt like home.

THE pretty college boy fancied himself a tough guy.

Eve let him have this belief, allowing herself to be thrown roughly up against the metal wall inside the toilet stall in the men's bathroom. It must have been the nip she'd given him, pissing him off. The wound was still bleeding, the taste of blood on his lips arousing her all the more each time they kissed.

The men's bathroom: what a pig, she thought, going with the flow of the situation, even though a bit disgusted. This wasn't about romance and love. This was about being down and dirty, and she couldn't get more down and dirty than this.

College Boy shoved his hand roughly up under her shirt, almost tearing the black, silk blouse that she'd paid five hundred dollars for on Newbury Street late that afternoon. Eve pulled his hand away. The guy was fumbling, and she was more than happy to help him get her undressed.

Then he struck her.

The slap was sudden and vicious, knocking her head to one side. It didn't hurt her, but the shock of the attack . . . her cheek stung with the impression of his hand.

The fucker smiled and for the first time, beneath the drunken college boy demeanor she sensed a predatory thrill coming off of him. This was what he liked—what turned him on. It was all about the control. She had dared to take charge, to pull his hand away. He wanted her to know who was in charge. She almost felt bad about what a rude awakening he was in for.

But not really.

Curious as to where he would take this next, she continued to stare, playing up the fact that she'd been startled by his sudden violence. She could practically see him growing harder as he reached out and grabbed hold of her blouse—*her five hundred dollar blouse*—and tore it open.

The sound of pearl buttons bouncing off the tile floor was the final straw. He threw himself at her, groping for her exposed breasts. The lust in her turned to rage, but no matter the emotion at the moment, Eve was looking for some release.

She pushed him away, slammed him against the locked stall door. Fire erupted in the young man's eyes, the sneer of surprised anger spreading across bloodstained lips. He lashed out at her again within the confined space, but she was ready this time.

Eve caught his wrist.

"So you like to play rough?"

With a twist, she snapped it like a breadstick.

The sound of breaking bone was surprisingly loud, and satisfying. The acoustics in the bathroom were quite good.

The fire left College Boy's eyes, replaced by the glint of intense agony. Eve could see that he was going to scream, but that wouldn't do. She grabbed for the toilet paper holder, ripped what remained of the roll off the spindle with a powerful tug, and crammed it deeply into his mouth.

"Bet I play rougher."

He drove his shoulder into her, attempting to knock her back against the stall, but she refused to move. The poor bastard bounced off of her as if he weighed nothing at all.

"That all you got?" she asked.

Fear mixed with the stink of alcohol wafted from his sweating flesh. He stumbled backward, his good hand going to his mouth, as the other dangled limply by his side, frantically trying to remove the roll of toilet paper blocking his screams.

"You don't want to do that," she purred with a slight shake of her head.

He ignored her suggestion, pulling the wad of spit-soaked two-ply from his mouth and turning toward the door, his good hand fumbling at the lock.

"Help!" he managed to shriek, but nobody was listening. The bathroom was empty, and anybody standing nearby would have been made deaf by the blaring music inside the club.

With taloned hands she gripped his curly brown hair. Eve yanked his head back fiercely and then slammed it hard against the graffiti-marred door.

"Not sure what you're used to, Charlie," she growled in his ear, allowing his head to turn ever so slightly so he could get a good look at her.

The stink of urine, as her potential lover let his bladder void, filled the cramped space of the stall. She knew he was likely to scream again and didn't want to hear it. Eve leaned in close, bringing her razor sharp incisors close to the man's neck, and took a fold of the loose flesh of his throat into her teeth.

"Another sound from you," she whispered close to his ear. "And I'll take the biggest bite I can without thinking twice."

She felt her stomach rumble hungrily as her body started to believe that she was about to feed. And oh, how she would have liked to. Murdering the little shit would feel good, and fresh, hot blood sliding down her throat and coursing through her body would light her whole body up like the longest, greatest orgasm in the world. She remembered it all too well, and longed for it every moment with an ex-junkie's ardor.

But murder and blood wouldn't do anything to assuage her sadness and remorse. Jophiel had stirred it all up in her tonight, and her hatred burned inside her like a tiny sun. Now if it had been *him* pressed up against the stall door, maybe she would've changed her mind.

She hadn't had a meal of angel's blood in a very long time.

But this sadistic fuck wasn't worth her time.

Eve left College Boy lying in a puddle of his own piss on the floor of the bathroom stall, shaking and crying like a baby, praying for God to forgive him and swearing that he wouldn't hurt anyone ever again.

Her blouse was open as she made her way out of the club, the buttons still lying on the floor of the men's room. She gave the dancers an occasional shot of the girls as she strolled toward one of the fire exits. Eve could feel their eyes upon her as she passed, but nobody dared approach her. It was almost as if they could sense her difference now, some primordial mechanism in the brain warning them to keep their distance, which was probably a good thing.

She was no longer in the mood.

Stepping out of the club into a back alley, she reveled in the touch of the cold, night air on her exposed flesh. Eve looked down at her blouse, considering whether or not it was possible to salvage, but noticed some of the delicate material had been torn where the buttons had once been.

"Shit," she muttered under her breath. She'd really liked

this shirt. She was considering going back inside to the men's bathroom to scare the little puke some more, and maybe relieve him of five hundred dollars, when the feeling hit her.

It was as though a wave of unease had just passed over her. The hairs on the back of her neck rose to attention, and goosebumps rippled her cold, undead skin. An awful, high-pitched sound came to her on the wind, and she turned to stare at a dumpster at the far end of the alley, where a commotion had erupted.

Rats—what seemed to be hundreds of them—swarmed and hissed and tore at one another. The fighting vermin resembled a single, writhing entity of grayish-black fur and multiple, hairless tails. They were all screeching as one, tearing and biting at each other, a puddle of expanding red collecting beneath the undulating mass they had become.

"What's this all about?" she whispered to the night, walking from the alley out onto Lansdowne Street. Eve sniffed at the air, searching for the scent of whatever it was that had just passed by. She glanced back down the alley to see that the ground was covered in blood and pieces of dead rat. The swarming had ceased, the survivors scuttling into the shadows.

A hint of something nasty lingered in the air, but before she had a chance to try to identify it, the feeling and the scent were gone.

3

CLAY Smith had been to an eternity of funerals, so many that they had long since lost the ability to touch his heart or bring him to introspection. Wakes were something else entirely; they fascinated him. A great deal could be learned about people—both the deceased and their survivors—just by observing the behavior at a wake. Most often, when the deceased had died of something natural, such as that equal-opportunity killer, time, or something typically stupid, like smoking, wakes were like cocktail parties held in a library, people laughing and reminiscing, but trying to do so with a certain hush to their voices.

The wake of a murder victim was different. No one laughed. There was nothing funny about murder.

Clay stood in the back of the room at Yerardi & Sons where Corey Gillard had been laid out in his casket so that people could say a prayer over his corpse and be quietly grateful that they, themselves, were still alive. As grim as a wake was, for each attendee it was also a quiet celebration of his or her continued existence. Clay could see it in their eyes.

That was the sort of wisdom imparted by immortality.

He wondered how many of them would be so grateful

for life after a few thousand years without the possibility of death.

Don't be so morbid, he thought. *You have a job to do.*

Clay glanced around the room again and studied the mourners one by one. Based on the crime scene, the way the body lay, the lack of a struggle, Boston homicide figured the dead man had known his killer, so it stood to reason that the murderer might well be in this very room.

One way to find out.

He stepped past a little girl in a dark green dress that might have been more appropriate for Christmas, nodded to the girl's mother, and started toward the front of the room, where the casket stood on a low platform. Clay inhaled deeply the aroma of the hundreds of flowers arranged in a display around the dead man. But laced within that smell was the odor of chemical air fresheners used by the funeral home. No matter how fresh the body was when it was embalmed, there was apt to be a stale smell to it. The flowers were usually enough to cover it, but funeral homes always pumped in that overwhelming floral stink, like an overzealous grandmother's perfume.

As he moved past the family of the deceased—Corey Gillard had been twenty-seven and unmarried, so that meant parents, two brothers, a couple of small nieces— Clay didn't bother studying the faces of the grieving any further. The truth wasn't going to be revealed in their eyes. The killer might be struggling with guilt, but in the aftermath of a tragic death, people reacted in all sorts of ways. Emotions overflowed. Too many people in that room were troubled to make any presumptions based on their behavior.

Clay waited while a gray-haired man knelt beside the coffin and said a prayer. When the man stood, sniffling and wiping at his nose, and moved away, Clay slid in to take his place. The kneeler was warm from all of the people who had paused to pay their respects in the half an hour since the wake had begun.

The top third of the casket was open and within lay a waxy figure that had once been a man. That absence of life had always intrigued Clay, for he could not die. Perhaps he might be killed, but many had tried since the dawn of time and no one had succeeded. Death was loss, but to Clay it was not loss of self. It was loss of love and warmth and comfort and fondness, and the acquisition of ache and regret. He thought of human death whenever he saw a squirrel crushed on the road, or seashells littered along a beach.

That was all that remained of Corey Gillard now, a shell.

The dead man's face was slack in some places, taut in others, where the thread used by the mortician had tugged at his flesh. His arms were crossed, hands laid over his heart. Somewhere further south, beneath the heavy maple of the lower two-thirds of the coffin lid, was the wound that had actually ended his life. But it would have been sewn up now and dwarfed by the incisions left by the medical examiner during the autopsy.

What did it matter, though. He was a shell.

The thing that had been within the shell, his soul or spirit or whatever one was inclined to call that spark of life, had vacated the premises. But life left traces behind. No one knew that better than Clay.

And *taking* life . . . that left traces, too.

Behind him, an old woman cleared her throat, impatiently awaiting her turn to pray over the corpse of Corey Gillard. Clay lowered his head as though in prayer, fingers steepled in front of him, eyes closed. He waited a few seconds for appearance's sake, and then reached out to touch the dead man's hand, just a moment of contact, his own good-bye.

At least, that was how it would appear to the people in the room.

When he stood and backed away, allowing the old woman to gingerly replace him at the kneeler, his vision had changed. There was a tint to the air in the room, at least in his eyes, as though a light mist had begun to gather. Clay took a deep breath and ran a hand through his close-

cropped hair, then straightened his tie as he studied
Gillard's corpse more closely.

A ghostly line traced through the room, a thick tether of
ectoplasm that began at the center of the dead man's chest.
It was not his entire soul, but only a fragment, a spiritual
connection that linked every murder victim with his or her
killer.

Clay had been forged by God. He was *the* Clay of God.
There was much about his eternal life he could not recall,
and his earliest memories were cloudy at best. But in addition to the malleable nature of his flesh, the Lord had given
him this gift as well, this curse. In the aftermath of a murder, if he arrived in time, with the touch of his hand he
could see the soul tether that connected killer and victim . . .

And he could trace it back.

The susurrus of low voices in the funeral home surrounded him. There were tears and quiet sobbing and a
great many faces that were simply numb. But as he turned,
his gaze following the soul tether of Corey Gillard, he felt
as though he was somehow beyond the perception of those
in the room, as though they had been frozen in the depths
of their grief and he could wander through, unseen and untouched.

The tether snaked through the room toward the corner
furthest from the door and around a massive arrangement
of flowers complete with a card that read, "In Memory of
Corey, From Your Family at the Arielle Gallery." Clay took
up a position just beside the flowers. People were milling
about, some already leaving, others just arriving, but from
here he could clearly follow the trail of soulstuff that
Gillard's murder had left behind.

At the back wall, near a window, stood a small cluster
of men and women who were the best dressed of the
mourners. The eldest was perhaps fifty, a woman of obvious sophistication, who seemed out of place mainly for the
utter lack of emotion on her face. She spoke quietly to a
man beside her with a goatee and a polished, elegant look,

who was at least ten years her junior. They did not seem like lovers. In fact, Clay judged the relationship to be employer and employee, an observation that quickly spread to include the rest of their small group. There were four other people around them, two men and two women, all in their late twenties to early thirties, of varied races but each with the same sophistication.

All but one.

Even when not speaking to her, the way they stood around her made it clear that the group all deferred to the older woman. From their appearance, and in comparison to the others in the room, he presumed they were neither family nor old friends of the dead man.

Coworkers, then, from the art gallery.

But one of the men with them seemed out of place, a broad-shouldered, square-jawed tough in an ill-fitting suit, who held the hand of a petite, attractive Asian woman. There was a protective quality to the way he held on to her . . . or so Clay thought at first glance. When he studied them again, he corrected himself. Possessive, not protective. They both wore wedding bands, and Clay guessed they were husband and wife.

The Asian woman shook her head and wiped at her eyes. She smiled sadly as she looked at one of her coworkers and gave a self-deprecating shrug, perhaps mocking herself for being unable to stop crying. Her husband's jaw tightened and he cast her a sidelong glance, bitterness unmasked. She seemed to feel his disapproval, and her expression went blank. The woman took a breath and wiped a fresh tear from her left eye.

Clay wondered if she knew that her husband had murdered Corey Gillard.

The tether led right to him, not to the center of his chest, but to his right hand, which must have held the knife that he had stabbed Corey over and over with, twisting it in his gut.

The man leaned over and whispered something to his wife. Regret creased her brow, and she turned to the others, exchanging hugs as she prepared to depart. Reluctantly, she allowed her husband to lead her from the room.

Clay followed the tether, which floated in the air, a serpentine stream of wavering smoke. He pursued them out into the foyer of the funeral home. There were sitting rooms on either side of the front door. In one, two young boys sat on a loveseat, obviously uncomfortable in their suits, attention locked on the screens of their GameBoys. The other sitting room was empty, and the husband held his wife's elbow and escorted her into the room. Clay paused in the foyer, just out of their line of sight, checking his pockets as though he'd forgotten something.

"You said no one knew," the husband rasped.

"No one *does*," the wife replied.

"The way they were comforting you—"

"He was my *friend*. They all knew that much. But no one . . . no one knows—"

"No one knows you're a whore," the husband said, words like hammering nails.

Clay's contact from Boston Homicide was waiting out on the sidewalk. He should have left then, just walked out the door, but he found that he could not. Instead, he glanced into the opposite parlor to make sure the two kids were still absorbed in their GameBoys, and then he rubbed his fingers together, remembering the feeling of Corey Gillard's skin.

A ripple went through Clay's flesh. Bone popped quietly, reknitting. Muscle shifted. Pigment changed. This was what God had made him, a shapeshifter, able to take the form of any creature the Lord ever imagined, and with a touch, to duplicate the appearance of anyone, alive or dead.

When he turned and walked into the sitting room with the murderer and his wife, he wore the face of Corey Gillard.

The husband saw him first. His face went slack, all the color draining from his cheeks. He narrowed his eyes and shook his head in denial, no sound coming from his mouth. When his wife saw his expression, she turned.

Her scream echoed through the building.

"Oh, Corey," she whispered then, holding one hand up to her mouth. "Oh, my God."

Wearing the dead man's face, Clay pointed at the killer. "It was him. He cut me open. He murdered me."

Her hands fluttered, and they both covered her face as she backed away from her husband, gaze shifting quickly back and forth between him and what she thought was her dead lover.

"You . . . you can't be here," the murderer snarled.

Clay smiled with Corey's mouth. "You're right. Corey's not here. He's dead and gone. His soul's in a better place. But guess where *you're* going."

Clay raised his arms, and once again he willed his flesh and bone to shift. Bone spikes thrust up through his scalp, two rows of sharp horns. Skin tore wetly as black, leathery wings sprouted from his back. Of all the shapes he had ever taken, Clay found the form of a demon the most difficult. It left him feeling filthy, his mood dark.

But his mood was dark enough already.

Now it was the killer's turn to scream. The man fell to his knees and began to plead for mercy, from Heaven, from Hell, and from his wife. He reached for her leg, and she recoiled in disgust.

Clay towered over him, appearing as a nine-foot demon, a thing right from the depths of Hell, skin the color of dried blood and thick and hard as stone. Fire spilled from his mouth as he pointed again at the murderer and laughed.

"See you soon," he said.

Then he turned, hooves thumping the carpet, and as he left the room, his flesh changed, and he was himself again. Joe Clay. The human face was not the one he had begun life with, but it was the one he wore most often, the one the world saw.

The two kids in the other parlor were still playing with their GameBoys.

People were running down the corridor now, summoned by the screams. Clay ignored them, turned left, and went out the front door of the funeral parlor.

The sky was gray and drizzling rain. An unmarked police car sat at the curb across the street. When Clay started down the stairs to the sidewalk, the passenger door opened, and detective Adam Hook climbed out.

Detective Hook was forty-four, fit, and handsome in a grizzled, sad, seen-too-much fashion that had probably contributed a great deal to his divorce. His hair was more pepper than salt, and he walked with a brutal confidence that would intimidate most people.

He knew far too much about the things that lurked in the shadows of the world. Clay himself was partially responsible for that. It might have been the reason for the cynicism in Hook's gaze, but it was also the reason they had become friends. Hook wasn't the kind of man who would ever turn away from the truth, no matter how terrifying, no matter how deep the darkness.

"How'd it go?" the detective asked. "Was he in there?"

"Job's done," Clay replied. "Victim was sleeping with the perp's wife. Go on in. You won't be able to miss them. I suspect he may be in the mood to confess right about now, too."

Hook shook his hand. "Much appreciated. I prefer to solve them myself, but this one—"

Clay waved the words away. "Hey, any time. Guy like this, you need him off the street. If I can help, I'm glad to do it."

Hook started up the stairs. "Say hello to Doyle for me," he said over his shoulder. "Haven't heard from him in a while."

"I will. And I'm sure you'll hear from him," Clay said. "The second he needs you."

THE ghost of Leonard Graves had haunted Conan Doyle's house for so long that he was almost immune to the absurdity of having a room there, complete with a bed and bureau, as though he had clothes and needed to sleep. Over time, Dr. Graves had come to appreciate this small space, this place where he could store the memories of his human life, now more than sixty years in the past.

A place where he could rest, and remember.

The room was on the second floor of the old townhouse. Over the years, he had allowed himself to ruminate on his life and accomplishments, so that there were shelves with souvenirs of his adventures, as well as framed newspaper stories. Here, in his room, he often felt the tug of the past. In its way, it was even more powerful than the lure of the afterlife, against which he was constantly struggling, fighting the tide that threatened to sweep him to his final rest.

But Graves had things to do before he left the physical plane, where he could join his beloved Gabriella. He had a murder to solve.

His own.

Times like these, he became lost in contemplation of the past. The bureau drawers were open, and their contents spread across the floor and bed, newspaper clippings from his exploits as an adventurer in the 1930s and 1940s, journals of his experiments and thoughts as one of the preeminent scientists of the day, and yellowed photographs of him as he was when he was alive. There were clippings full of controversy and hate—in those days, no black man could become prominent without drawing the venom of the ignorant and the cruel. Graves traced his spectral fingers over a page without touching it, a story about his capture of a killer the newspapers had called the Butcher of Brooklyn.

It had not been the first time he had captured a killer or thwarted a criminal, but it had been the most public. The New York papers had called him a hero. The mayor had offered the gratitude of the city. Even then Graves had thought it ironic, when so many in the city thought he was trash because of the color of his skin. And when his reputation became national, it had only become worse, particularly because his fiancée was a white woman, an Italian-American, they would call her today.

Things had improved since then, out in the world. The ranks of the ignorant and cruel had thinned, thankfully, but they were not extinct. Not yet. Of late, he'd begun to worry that they were, in fact, coming around again, their numbers growing.

He did not like to think of it.

Most of the clippings were of a different nature. Joyful. Triumphant. And those were bittersweet. The real irony was that the best of his memories were the ones that hurt the most, but he clung to them, savoring the pain.

Better to have lived, to be sure.

And oh, how he had lived.

As a young man, he had been grim and overly earnest, but what else could be expected of a boy who had spent his entire life honing his mind and body to the pinnacle of human capacity? His mother had died when Graves was quite small, and his widower father had determined that through his son he would show the world that race was something ephemeral, that discipline and determination were what made a man.

But as he had matured, Graves had discovered a passion for science that discipline could not instill. While he continued to devour up-to-date theory, and often advance theories of his own, on topics as varied as abnormal psychology, space travel, and vegetable fuels, certain subjects took up more and more of his time. He journeyed across the face of the world as an archaeologist, tropical botanist, and cryptozoologist. Whenever he was back at home in his labs in Washington Heights, New York, he was a part of a social circle that included playwrights, architects, dancers, biologists, and jazz musicians.

The ghost hovered a few inches off of the ground, barely aware that he had given up the pretense of solidity and substance for the moment. His spectral form felt heavy with melancholy as he reached out to brush phantom fingers over a photograph taken nearly seven decades before in the infamous jazz nightspot, Birdland. Graves himself was in the photo, looking smart in a tux, his arm around the trumpet player Henry Watkins. Henry, called "Blat" by his nearest and dearest, was busy lighting a cigarette, too cool to glance at the camera.

The third person in the photo was a woman who stood on the other side of Blat Watkins, hip slightly cocked, an insouciant little smile on her face. Gabriella Gnecco was confident and beautiful, her eyes alight with intelligence. At that time she had been in the United States only four years, and her accent had begun to fade. Graves had thought the petite little Italian girl charming.

That first night, dancing, he had fallen in love.

The newspapers had pounced on the story, serving the romance up to the public. Graves had not cooperated, but the reporters did not rely on cooperation to create a story about a public figure. His love for Gabriella had earned them admiration and scorn in unequal measure, with the emphasis on the latter, but it had also increased the adventurer's celebrity. He had been famous in the city of New York, and then in the northeast United States, but soon his notoriety began to spread around the world. The spotlight brought upon him because of his planned wedding to Gabriella meant a focus on his work as well.

So when Dr. Graves helped the police solve a series of mysterious deaths—leading them to a greenhouse where a curious sociopath had been cultivating poisonous plants—the whole world knew of it. Even now he could close his eyes and drift, touching his own spirit to the soulstream, and practically relive those moments. The triumph. The feeling that came with a job well done, and knowing he had saved lives.

The ghost opened his eyes. A newspaper clipping on the bed caught his eye. *"Nazi Science Spy Busted!"* read the headline, and beneath it, in smaller type, *"Feds Credit Dr. Graves."*

There were many others. Influential individuals at nearly every level began to seek him out. It was thrilling work. Graves had always detested crime, but never imagined that combating it would become such a focus in his life. Slowly, however, he began to realize that pursuing killers, traitors, and madmen had become more than just a public service, a favor to the world. It had become his entire life. His own research had been neglected, and so had his fiancée.

So he tried to withdraw, or at least, limit the amount of time he spent away from his personal pursuits. The effort was doomed. There had been other mysterious figures emerging to share the burden, to take on the cases the police could never handle, but the criminals only grew more dangerous and more ambitious.

By the time he stopped Professor Erasmus Zarin from releasing poison gas into a thunderstorm from the upper decks of the Empire State Building, he had all but surrendered to the reality that had claimed him. His life was no longer his own.

Five years passed as Dr. Graves tried to balance the various passions and obligations of his life. And then it was snuffed out with a bullet in the back.

"Dr. Graves Dead! Famed Adventurer Shot! Identity of Killer Still Unknown!"

He stared now at that headline on the newspaper clipping from October 7, 1943, where it hung on the wall. Conan Doyle—who was unaffected by almost any degree of hideousness—thought it morbid to the point of perversity that he displayed the news of his own murder on the wall. Graves ignored him. He could not live in this room, but he could *abide* here, exist here, and the details of his death were a part of the tale of his existence.

And the mystery of his murder was the reason he had remained so long.

During his life Dr. Graves had been a vehement skeptic of all things supernatural. He was a man of science and debunked charlatanry and fraud wherever he encountered it. His discovery—upon his death—that ghosts did indeed exist, that the souls of the lost dead commonly wandered the physical world in search of some final bit of closure, had been quite a shock.

But, as all good scientists do, Graves adapted. It had taken years before his consciousness had coalesced enough to regain true awareness, something he had never quite understood. But once he had realized what had happened, that he was, in fact, a ghost, he had approached his circumstances with the same intense single-mindedness with which he had lived his life.

As a specter, Graves had learned soon enough how to maneuver in the spirit world, how to navigate the soul-stream, and in death he put to use the skills he had mastered in life, investigating his own murder. Yet it quickly proved a fruitless pursuit. His focus on his task kept him tethered to the fleshly world, but no matter how much effort was devoted to discovering the truth, he could find not a single clue. There was nothing at the scene, nor written in any police report, that would indicate who the killer was.

At first he had suspected Zarin of his assassination, but the ghost quickly discovered that the mad professor was in prison at the time and could not have killed him. Years of pursuing the wrong threads and intimidating Zarin's lackeys had finally led Graves to the conclusion that Zarin had neither killed him nor orchestrated his death.

Finally, at a loss, he had begun approaching the world's mediums and sorcerers, searching for someone who could help him find his murderer. During this journey, his path had crossed that of Arthur Conan Doyle, and the ageless mage had vowed to aid him in his search, to use all of his formidable abilities to solve the mystery.

The ghost of Dr. Graves had been patient . . . and then grown impatient . . . and at last become bitter. He still counted Conan Doyle as a friend and was dedicated to the man's efforts to combat the forces of darkness when they arose, but the time had come when Graves could be patient no longer.

He couldn't wait any longer for Arthur's help.

Spectral, ectoplasmic fingers traced the photograph of himself and Gabriella flanking Blat Watkins. If ghosts had tears, perhaps he would have shed them, then.

A light knock came at the door.

"Come in," the ghost said, turning as the door swung open and Clay entered the room.

"I hear you wanted to talk to me," the shapeshifter said.

The phantom studied him, always amazed at the stillness of Clay's flesh. He was entirely malleable, his substance as fluid as any ghost's, despite that it was solid. And yet he seemed so formidable, as though his brawny form occupied space on more than one level of existence.

"Thank you for coming by," the ghost said.

Clay gestured to the door. "You want it closed?"

"That's all right. I have no secrets."

The shapeshifter nodded, but there was a dark light in his eyes that seemed dubious of the claim. Graves quietly approved. Anyone who said he had no secrets was a liar. He tried to compose his thoughts, staring at Clay.

"You have . . . that is, I've seen you use a remarkable ability," the ghost said. "How does it work, the way you touch the dead and find their killers?"

Clay frowned. "You know that."

"I'm thinking," Graves replied. "Would you care to humor me?"

"All right. Well, it's simple, really. Not the mechanics but the reality of it. I touch a corpse—a recent corpse—and I can see a kind of string of ectoplasm, bits of soul that leads from the victim to the killer. See, in a murder, a trace of the ghost of the victim, or maybe even just some echo of the dead, clings to the killer, leaving a trail that I can follow.

"If I get there in time."

Graves smiled thinly. "And with older remains?"

Clay narrowed his gaze. "The more time that has passed, the less chance that there will be a soul tether to lead me to the killer."

The ghost faltered, lowering his head and nodding. He felt a ripple of despair go through his spectral form.

"What is it, Leonard?" Clay asked. "Whose death are we discussing, here?"

Graves met his gaze. "Mine, of course."

"Of course. I should've realized," Clay replied. "You do realize that I've helped solve a good many murders even when there was no obvious link to the killer?"

"I've been dead more than sixty years."

Clay leaned against the doorframe. "And you've finally decided to stop waiting for Arthur to solve it for you."

Graves nodded.

"Then we should get started," Clay said. "I'll do whatever I can to help."

"Good," Graves said. "You can start by helping me dig up my corpse."

THE next day dawned so gray that it could barely be called morning. What fell from the sky was more mist than rain and the absence of sun cast a pall across the city. Detective Hook drove his immaculate 1985 Cutlass Calais through the crappy weather and tried not to think about potholes. Other guys restored forty-year-old Mustang convertibles. Hook wanted a sedan with burgundy leather bucket seats and enough weight to carry it through a wall instead of just turning into a metal accordion on impact.

It had been his father's car, a couple of decades ago. But his old man was in the ground now, and didn't have any further use for it.

Hook turned down Tremont Street, water hissing around his tires. Up ahead he saw the illuminated circular sign for the T. Three prowl cars were parked at odd angles in front of the subway station and at least a couple of unmarked, all of them with blue lights flashing. A rookie on shit detail strung crime scene tape across the front of the T station.

"It's too early for this shit."

He wasn't the kind of cop who lived on doughnuts. Uniforms tended to embrace the stereotype, hanging out in cafés and doughnut shops when they could manage it. Hook did not smoke or drink, either. His father had drunk himself to death, and his mother had died of lung cancer. Addiction, to his mind, was cowardly.

If his need for coffee in the morning made him a hypocrite, it was not that he did not see the irony. It was just that most days he didn't care.

This morning he hadn't had time for coffee. Not yet.

It soured his mood.

Hook double-parked the silver Cutlass and slid his ID card onto the dashboard, then climbed out.

With a sigh he stared up at the gray shroud of sky. The mist had begun to turn to rain. Hook ran his fingers through his already damp hair, just a contact reminder of the white streaks that had begun to propagate there.

"Geary," he said as he passed a small group of uniformed officers who were keeping the gawkers back. Even the rain would not drive the vultures away.

The officer nodded in his direction. "Morning, detective."

Hook grunted, needing coffee more than ever. He reached into his shirt and pulled out the lanyard that had his badge and ID hanging from it, so that uniforms who didn't know him on sight wouldn't get in his way.

The rookie stringing crime scene tape saw him coming and lifted the tape for him to duck under.

"What's your name, kid?" Hook asked.

"Castillo, Detective."

"Related to Jace?"

"He's my uncle."

Hook nodded in approval. Maybe the kid would turn out to be a decent cop.

He reached for the door to the T station. Through the filthy window in the door he could see Lieutenant Nathanson talking to a CSI photographer. Nate seemed to be giving the guy a rash of shit, and when Hook opened the door, he caught the tail end of it.

". . . anywhere, you got me. Those pictures end up in my hands. Not in the case file, not online, not in some newspaper. From you to me. Anyone else sees those pictures, it's your job. We clear?"

The photographer flinched. He didn't like being bullied, but then, who did?

"Crystal," the CSI guy said.

Lieutenant Nathanson saw Hook out of the corner of his eye and started to turn. Before either of them could say a word, there was a ruckus on the stairs below them. Robbie Stetler, another of the crime-scene unit guys, came running up toward the doors . . . toward the street. He had one hand on his belly and the other over his mouth.

"Oh, Jesus," Stetler whispered. "Oh, fuck."

He didn't make it to the doors. Four steps from the top, he clutched the railing like it was a bit of electric fence, turned, and puked on the concrete steps.

"Nice," Hook observed, wrinkling his nose at the stink.

Lieutenant Nathanson arched an eyebrow and shot him a look. "Wait'll *you* see it, smartass."

"See what?"

The lieutenant smiled. "No. Go on. The joy of discovery is yours."

Hook shrugged and started down into the tunnel of iron bars and concrete columns that was Tremont Street station. A couple of uniformed officers were taking statements from witnesses by the ticket booth. Near the turnstiles he passed several other cops milling around, faces tinted sickly green. All of them looked like the back row of church in the last twenty minutes of Sunday Mass, just itching to get the hell back outside, rain or no rain.

The rest of the CSI crew were still in the process of doing their jobs when he went past the turnstiles and out onto the platform of the closed station. When he approached, the forensics team all turned to give him a grim hello and stood aside a moment so he could have a look.

Something bitter rose in the back of Hook's throat, and he was glad he hadn't had his coffee yet this morning.

"Hell," he muttered.

"Yeah," one of the crime scene cops replied, a fiftyish woman whose dark eyes had seen it all, until now. "What does something like this? What kills like this, without any decent witnesses, with this kind of brute force."

Hook said nothing. He was afraid it would be his turn to throw up. Either that, or he might mention that he'd already given them an answer. *Hell.* He'd had enough experiences with unnatural things—supernatural things—that he had no trouble looking at the human debris on that platform and knowing, without question, that nothing human was responsible.

His meet-up with Clay the day before came back to him now. He'd asked after Conan Doyle, thinking about how long it had been since he'd seen the man. Now he realized that he never wanted to see Doyle. Didn't even really like him. Mainly because every time they crossed paths, it was because of hideous shit like this.

Hook turned and walked back to the turnstiles. Lieutenant Nathanson beckoned to him as he passed.

"Bad news, Adam. We've got two more over on Tremont."

Two more. Hook swore under his breath, then nodded. "All right. Give me just a minute. I've got a call to make."

"Later," the lieutenant replied. "You can call your girlfriend after we've secured the scene. I don't want the unis tracking their boots all over the place."

Hook hesitated, but the lieutenant wasn't giving him any slack. The phone call would just have to wait. He just hoped Conan Doyle hadn't changed his number.

4

SQUIRE loved this time of day.

The hobgoblin, clad only in boxer shorts and a wife-beater T-shirt, squirmed around in the leather recliner, trying to get comfortable.

He called it Squire time, that special time of day when everyone seemed to just leave him alone. He wasn't sure what made these hours between eleven in the morning and one in the afternoon so damn special, but it was almost as if the Dark Gods had set a small pocket of time aside for him alone, a time when he could think only of himself—his wants and desires.

Squire time.

His hearing was ultra sensitive, and he listened to the heartbeat of the brownstone: the gentle hum of the refrigerator in the kitchen below, the ticking of the grandfather clock in the foyer, the exhalation of comforting heat blown up from the ancient furnace in the basement through the many vents that opened into every room.

But not a sound of life. Conan Doyle and Ceridwen had yet to return from England, Danny and his mother had gone out a short time earlier, and Graves and Clay had left the brownstone in the wee hours of the morning, and no one had seen hide nor hair of them since.

Squire was alone.

Well, Eve was in her room. But she was dead to the world and would remain that way until the sun started to creep below the horizon. He could have run a marching band through her room, and she still wouldn't have been able to get that beautiful ass out of bed.

He remembered a time about ten years back when Conan Doyle had suspected the house was under attack by a spell of decimation—a nasty piece of sorcery that was almost like an airborne cancer, though not as pleasant—and had ordered everybody into a circle of protection he'd conjured. It had been up to Squire to pass the news and gather the troops together. He'd saved Eve for last, knowing what it would be like to drag her from her bed.

Squire smiled, raising a hand to his chest, slowly running his nubby fingertips over the front of his shirt, feeling four raised scars through the material. It was probably the fact that he'd pulled back the covers, exposing her naked body that had caused her to practically tear out his heart.

His smile got wider as he continued his stroll down memory lane. He'd almost bled to death from the gashes made by her talons, but what he had seen beneath the covers had made it all worthwhile. *She's one hot tamale,* the hobgoblin thought, scratching at his crotch.

He reached down to retrieve the remote from between him and the cushion and turned on the big-screen television in the large, wooden cabinet across the room. He wasn't sure what he was in the mood for, considering *The Price Is Right* before moving on to one of the multiple movie channels he subscribed to through local cable. He could always find something to hold his interest there. Yesterday while channel surfing, he'd caught an *Ernest* movie he hadn't seen yet, the one where the hilarious son of a bitch saved Christmas. He'd just about pissed himself it was so funny.

He didn't find anything with half of Ernest's entertainment value, so he flipped back to *The Price Is Right*.

"Awesome," he grunted, seeing that they were playing the High/Low game. He was good at that one and would probably kick ass if he had the opportunity to play, but he couldn't see Mr. Doyle agreeing to allow him to appear on the morning game show. Too bad, he would have loved to rub elbows with Bob Barker.

He reached down beside his chair and picked up the can of Pringles he had waiting, just the first of many snacks he would indulge in during Squire time.

"Thatta girl," he squawked through a mouthful of chips, cheering on a housewife that he would've let eat Pringles in his bed any time. She was getting closer to winning herself a pair of Waveriders when the phone started to ring.

"You gotta be kiddin' me," Squire grumbled, spewing crumbs toward the television set. He considered letting the machine pick up, but realized it was probably something relatively important since no one ever called the Doyle residence just to shoot the shit.

The hobgoblin reached down under the leather seat cushion, fishing for the phone, and finally found it behind him, wedged beneath his left buttock. He stared at the caller ID and saw the name Hook. It took him a minute, but then he remembered Hook was the homicide detective that Conan Doyle had assisted with some matters over the last few years.

"Thrill me," Squire said as he picked up, quoting the great thespian Tom Atkins from one of his '80s favorites, *Night of the Creeps*.

There was a long pause, but he knew somebody was there.

"Hello?" He was ready to hang up if nobody started talking.

"Is this the Doyle residence?" the voice on the other end asked tentatively.

"You got it," Squire replied. "What can I do for you?"

He turned the volume down on the television set. His sweet potato of a housewife had won the Waveriders and was jumping around like a duck on a hotplate. Bobby B was practically knocked unconscious by her overflowing excitement.

I'd like to show her some overflowing excitement, the hobgoblin thought, waiting for the detective to spill his reason for calling.

"I'm looking for Joe Clay," the man said. "I saw him last night—but something's come up this morning that I think he—"

"Clay ain't here," Squire interrupted. "Is there something I could do, Detective?"

"You know who I am?" Hook asked, surprise in his voice.

"Mr. Doyle told me all about you," Squire replied. "Said we should give you a hand whenever we could. So what's the scoop?"

"I'm in an alleyway off of Tremont Street," the detective began. "The remains of two bodies were found here this morning by an old lady walking her dogs. And they aren't the first. There's another crime scene just like it in the Tremont Street station."

"Go on," Squire said, helping himself to another handful of Pringles. "What's the angle?" he asked. "You wouldn't be calling here if it was just your average homicide."

"One of the bodies," Hook started. "One of them appears to be partially eaten and the other . . . the other is missing all its skin. The one in the T station was even worse."

Squire swiped the back of his hand across his mouth. "I can see why you called," he said. "Have the remains been removed yet?"

"The T station victim, yeah. But not these two. Not yet," Hook said. "Forensics is finishing up at the scene now and—"

"Don't move anything," Squire told him. "I wanna check out the scene."

"I'm not sure how long I can hold them off," Hook explained. "How quickly can you get down here?"

"Give me a minute to get on a shirt and some pants," he told the detective.

"How will I know you?" Hook asked him.

"Just look for the handsome son of a bitch stepping out of the shadows," the hobgoblin replied, and broke the connection.

So much for Squire time.

DANNY had always loved the New England Aquarium.

He stood to one side, away from the line, as his mother bought their tickets. It was cold today, and the wind was blowing across the harbor. People wearing heavy coats and hats stamped their feet in line, trying to stay warm, but Danny really didn't feel it. He was wearing a heavy hooded sweatshirt, a wool cap on his head to cover his horns, and dark sunglasses to protect his sensitive eyes from the glaring sun and hide their yellow, reptilian look. The clothing wasn't meant to keep him warm, only to hide the changes to his body.

His mother left the head of the line, putting her change away inside her wallet. "Let's go inside," she said. "It's freezing out here."

"Yeah, freezing," Danny answered.

Stepping into the semidark, concrete building, Danny felt a comforting wave of nostalgia. For a brief moment, he was able to tune it all out—the people pushing strollers, the school field trips, the knowledge of how much he had changed over the last few weeks—and he remembered how it felt to be that kid again, that ten-year-old boy who loved the aquarium.

"Hey, are you all right?" his mother asked, grabbing his arm and giving it a gentle squeeze.

Danny didn't want to lose the feeling, the memory, holding on to it with both hands. "Yeah, I'm good." He removed his sunglasses. "Let's go look at some fish."

And that's exactly what they did, starting on the first level, checking out a special exhibit on jellyfish before moving on to the penguin pool. He'd always loved the tuxedoed birds, and he and his mom spent a fair amount of time laughing at their antics within the exhibit that dominated the first floor.

They moved on to the giant ocean tank that rose up in the center of the building. It was one of the world's largest cylindrical saltwater tanks—an elaborate, man-made twenty-four-foot-deep reef. Fifty-two large windows allowed a view of all kinds of ocean life; sharks, sea turtles, moray eels, and tropical fish of all shapes and sizes. Danny slowly climbed the concrete walkway to the second floor, face pressed against the cool glass, losing himself in the underwater world.

There was a diver in the tank, feeding some of the more popular residents. His mesh bag of food trailing behind him, the diver dropped down to an area of caves in the artificial coral reef, and Danny saw a moray eel floating in the darkness there. He loved to watch them feed the morays. The eel gradually emerged from its hiding place, and Danny fixated on its sleek, serpentine form. The animal seemed to be looking right at him, ignoring the aquarium worker who dangled a piece of fish for it to eat. Instead, it slithered through the water, heading for the glass—for him.

The eel swam back and forth in front of the glass, as the diver continued to try to interest it in a piece of fish. It was staring at Danny. Slowly, Danny raised his hand, laying it flat against the glass. The eel attacked, smashing its pointed face repeatedly against the glass, even breaking off a few of its sharp teeth, before swimming off to hide in one of the caves in the artificial reef.

"What the hell was that all about?" Danny heard his mother ask, as she sidled up beside him. The diver was watching him now, swarms of brightly colored tropical fish plucking at the piece of food he'd been attempting to get the moray to eat.

"Guess I pissed it off," he said, looking away from the

tank and the diver's stare. "I'm getting kind of hungry. Want to hit the café for something to eat?"

She thought about it for a moment and then nodded slowly. "I suppose. I only had a muffin about six this morning, I could go for a bite."

The café was on the first level, so they started back down the curving walkway. Danny was wondering what the café would have for him to eat when he heard their whispering voices.

Walking alongside his mother he saw two boys—ten-year-olds, if that. He'd noticed them back at the tank and thought they were with a school group. Now they were alone, walking slightly back and to the side of his mother. They were pointing at him, talking in hushed voices; wrinkling their noses in disgust, touching the tops of their hands as they spoke.

Danny glanced down at his own hands, at the horribly discolored and scaly flesh there. The two kids were laughing now, high-pitched girlish giggles as they reached the bottom of the walkway. They looked over their shoulders at him as they headed off in the opposite direction, hip-checking each other so that they would bump into people as they walked.

The anger rose in him, and there was nothing he could do to hold it back. He started after the boys.

"Danny?" his mother asked, pointing toward the café. "I thought that you—"

"I'll be right back," he grumbled, navigating the crowds like a shark swimming through warm waters in search of prey. His eyes hunted for the two boys who had taken it upon themselves to remind him of his difference, to bring reality crashing down around his ears. He wanted to thank them properly for what they had done.

He saw them hovering around the entrance to the jellyfish exhibit, then one shoved the other through the entrance and took off toward the administrative areas, emitting a high-pitched laugh. The other boy followed his assailant, grabbed him in a headlock, and brought him down to the ground.

Then they were out of the way of the crowd, in a shadowed corner near the administration offices. Danny glanced around to be sure no one was watching him and silently approached the wrestling boys. He exhaled loudly so that they would notice he was standing there. They stopped fighting, staring at him—momentarily defiant. He was sure one of them was about to crack wise, when apparently they realized where they had seen him before.

They were still holding on to each other, watching him cautiously, as he removed the hood of his sweatshirt to give them a good look at his leathery skin, thin lips, and razor teeth. Then he took off his wool hat to reveal the horns beneath. The stink of urine filled the air.

"It's not nice to make fun of people," Danny said, slowly stalking toward them.

They were scared speechless, staring at him with everwidening eyes, frozen in place. He gave them a better view of his teeth, nasty and sharp, as he flicked his pointed tongue over them.

" 'Cuz you never know who you might be offending."

Danny was amazed that they hadn't run away or started to scream. It was almost as if his gaze—something in his eyes—was holding them in place. He'd heard that some kinds of snakes—cobras, maybe—could mesmerize their prey before attacking it.

Cool.

"Do you know who you offended today, boys?"

They stared, mute.

"You've pissed off the Devil." Danny shook his head. "Ain't that the stupidest fucking thing you ever done?"

One of them nodded, a single teardrop running down his face to land on his Patriots sweatshirt.

"So, for being the little fuckers you are, I'm going to drag both your asses back to Hell with me, but first I'm going to rip your bellies open and string your steaming guts across the floor and then . . ." Danny paused, wanting it to be good. "Then I'm gonna eat your eyes."

He could have kept it going, tormenting them some more, but he was hungry, and decided that maybe they'd had enough.

"Naw," he said, picking at his front fangs with the tip of one of his clawed nails. "You'd probably make me puke."

He lunged at them then. "Get the fuck out of here!" he roared, and the kids ran, screaming, running as if the Devil himself was on their tails.

Chuckling, Danny pulled his hat down over his horns and then, throwing the hood of the sweatshirt over his head, he turned around to join his mother at the café.

. . . And saw her standing there, watching him, the look of horror on her face telling him that she'd seen the whole encounter.

"That oughta teach the little shits," he mumbled, walking past her. "Let's get out of here. I'm not hungry anymore."

SQUIRE strolled through the all-encompassing darkness of the shadow paths, chewing on the last of a microwave burrito as his preternatural instincts zeroed in on his destination. This was the gift of being a hobgoblin. Every shadow in the world was connected. Sunshadow, moonshadow, it made no difference. All shadows were a part of the same substance, an entire dimension filled with the stuff, and hobgoblins were one of the few races that could walk the shadow paths. Squire could slip into any shadow, anywhere in the world, and travel the paths until he found his way to the very spot he wanted. All he needed was a shadow to come back through on the other end.

Like this one.

"Here we go," he said, reaching up with both hands and hauling himself out of the surrounding gloom. He emerged from a thick patch of shadow thrown by a heavy, metal dumpster in an alley off Tremont Street.

The goblin pulled the collar up on his short, leather jacket and adjusted the Red Sox cap on top of his strangely shaped head as he emerged from behind the dumpster. He stood there, waiting for somebody to notice him. *Any day now,* he thought, tempted to start whistling.

He looked around as he waited, obviously not too late, judging by the number of uniformed cops and detectives flitting about. *There's definitely something about this alley,* he thought, feeling the thick hair on his arms and at the back of his neck stand at attention. Something happened here once, something bad that left a little piece of itself behind. Whatever transpired here last night was probably attracted to the wickedness inherent in the spot like a fat kid to a box of Twinkies.

"Hey, buddy, what the hell are you doing there?" a cop asked, striding over toward Squire, hand resting on the butt of his gun.

"I'm waiting," the hobgoblin replied.

The cop stopped, giving him the hairy eyeball. "Well you can wait your stumpy ass behind the yellow tape," he barked. "This is a crime scene and—"

"I'm waiting for Detective Hook," Squire interrupted.

The cop looked toward the crowd. "Detective Hook is busy. If you want to leave a name I'm sure he'll—"

"He's expecting me," Squire interrupted again, rocking back and forth on his bright red, high-top sneakers.

"If he doesn't know exactly what I'm talking about, I'm coming back for you," the cop said, then went off, grumbling under his breath as Squire waited.

He watched as the officer reached a guy who had been standing over a sheet-covered body lying on the ground of the alley. The cop nudged the guy, starting to speak and then pointing in his direction. The detective turned to look, and Squire waved.

The man finished up what he was doing then walked toward the hobgoblin.

It's about freakin' time, Squire thought. "Detective," he said aloud, with a slight nod.

"You have me at a disadvantage, Mister . . . ?"

"Squire, short and sweet, just like *moi*." The goblin smiled, showing off his dazzling grin.

"Wait, you're Doyle's driver—right?"

"And so much more," Squire said, shaking his head.

The man looked uncomfortable, looking around, as if this could be some kind of setup.

"I assure you, Mister Doyle will be notified about everything we discuss here. And you do trust Mister Doyle, don't you, Detective?"

The man said nothing, staring down at him.

"Of course you do," Squire said with a smile. "Now why don't we look at those bodies you told me about?"

I T began as a small dot of discoloration in the air, something barely noticeable in the formal living room of Arthur Conan Doyle's Louisburg Square home. But then it started to grow, the faint whistling sound it made intensifying as it increased in size and mass. In seconds what had once been a mark hanging inoffensively in the air above the center of the room became something so much more.

The air was alive, a swirling maelstrom of gray, feeding off the environment. A stray magazine, ash from a recent fire in the fireplace, accumulated dirt and dust, it all added to the growing mass of the unnatural cyclone. From its center, there sounded a rumble of thunder like the stomach of some great beast, anxious to be satisfied. Then there came lightning flashes from within the mass of the whirlwind, and something was revealed at its center. Something more than flotsam and jetsam.

In the belly of the storm, figures grew and shifted. Its mass became more and more substantial, the seething winds shrieking and wailing around it, as if heralding the coming of something great.

Or someone.

"You are home, mistress," the wind moaned in a language as ancient as time itself, the fury of its coming grad-

ually calming. Two shapes sheltered within the womb of
elemental fury emerged. Two travelers, weary from their
journey and grateful to be home.

"Thank you, wind," Ceridwen said in the language of
Faerie, dispersing the last of the traveling wind with a gentle wave of her hand.

Conan Doyle set the bundles and packages that he was
carrying down onto the floor with a heavy sigh. He was
tired, as much mentally as physically. He watched the expression on his lover's face as she looked around the sitting
room, a faint smile tugging at the corners of her regal features.

"It's good to be home," she said, glancing toward him.

"Yes," he replied, stretching his tired joints as he
stepped over and around the bags at his feet. It had been a
busy day. After leaving Cottingley and paying their respects to a number of other locations in the land of his
birth, Ceridwen had decided it would be wise to visit those
few who still worshipped the old ways, those upon the
Blight that had embraced the teachings and attitudes of
Faerie, and thusly had earned her respect and gratitude.
These women and men were kind to her, treated her as
both friend and goddess, and they had laden their visitors
with all sorts of gifts, from handwoven quilts to jarred
peaches.

A long day.

"I wonder where everybody is," Conan Doyle said,
closing his eyes and muttering a spell of connection beneath his breath, communing with his home. "It would
seem that Eve is the only one at home," he said, opening
his eyes.

Ceridwen knelt by the bags, reaching inside one to
slowly withdraw its contents. "Aren't these wonderful?"
she said with awe as she examined her gifts.

"Quite lovely," he replied, but he knew his demeanor
said otherwise. He had to wonder exactly what the elemental sorceress would do with a rooster-shaped teakettle, but

he guessed that was not the point. They were all gifts to the goddess that her devotees loved with all their hearts.

And if there came a time when their goddess asked more of them than rooster-shaped teakettles and embroidered doilies? If a far greater sacrifice was someday needed?

With the threat of the Demogorgon looming in the future, Conan Doyle suspected that even loyal acolytes such as they would be called upon in the world's hour of need.

"What is it, Arthur?" Ceridwen asked, holding a homemade rag doll fashioned to look like the Fey princess.

"I'm just tired," he said, the weight of the future suddenly bearing down upon him now that they were home. "I'm not as young as I used to be, you know." He managed a small smile.

Ceridwen dropped the doll to the floor and moved to stand beside him. "I was going to suggest that we clean up the mess we've made with our return," she said, reaching out to stroke the side of his face with a long, delicate finger. Her breath was warm against his skin and smelled strongly of mint, as she spoke softly into his ear.

"But I guess it can wait—until after you've rested from your travels." Her tongue darted out, snake-like, sensually tracing the inside of his ear.

Conan Doyle pulled her close. "An excellent suggestion, my love." He kissed her fully on the mouth. "I do so appreciate your concern for my well-being."

She chuckled, taking his hand in hers.

So much for rest. There would come a time in the foreseeable future when the opportunity for distractions would be rare. Dark times were on the horizon, and he would need the memories of times such this, when they could surrender to their passions, to give him the strength to deal with the realities of an uncertain future.

A future that was inexorably drawing closer.

5

EVE had awakened restless.

She blamed it mostly on the Cherubim. In her death-like dream state she continued to see his smirking face as he came at her across the writhing dance floor, a floor covered in fighting rats, slick with the blood that oozed from their tattered bodies. It made it hard to dance, but she still tried, slipping and sliding in her Louis Vuitton boots as she danced toward the back doors to escape the angel and get away from the rats.

But she sensed something outside—something that didn't belong there.

Something dangerous.

Now Eve took a sip from her Au Bon Pain latte, trying to push the disturbing dream imagery from her mind as she stared out the front window of the café. Something had caught her eye.

She hoped she was wrong. Anything that might interrupt her shopping spree would be unwelcome. She wanted to replace the silk blouse the college boy had ruined, but as soon as she had entered Copley Place, that simple errand had been fanned into a roaring fire that compelled her to spend. With a satisfied smile, she surveyed the chairs across from her, piled high with shopping bags. Eve had already paid visits to Gucci, Armani Exchange, and Stuart Weitzman, and had even stopped in to Godiva to satisfy a chocolate craving.

It was all about satisfying cravings tonight.

Eve turned her focus back to the front window, predatory eyes scanning the crowds walking about outside. She found the girl again, neo-Goth no more than sixteen, dressed entirely in black, a streak of bright pink running through her straight, shoulder-length hair.

Eve wondered how long it had been since she had been turned.

Goth girl was talking with a little blond chick dressed a little more conservatively in a cutey bunny T-shirt and a cheerleading jacket. *Took the T in from the burbs, did we, sweetie?* Eve thought, breaking off a piece of the croissant she'd bought with her latte and popping it into her mouth.

Girls. Well, at least one of them was a girl.

The neo-Goth was a vampire. The average person wouldn't have the slightest idea, but Eve could pick them out of a crowd of a million. That was just how things were with a mother and her children.

She suppressed the feeling of guilt she always experienced when coming upon one of the poor creatures that had been afflicted with the curse she had begun so very long ago.

The two girls moved toward the escalator that would take them into the main shopping area of Copley Place. Eve popped another bite of croissant into her mouth and took one more swig of her latte as she stood up to leave. Grabbing her bags, she left the store to follow the girls.

At the top of the stairs she quickly zipped into a costume jewelry store and, smiling at the woman behind the counter, asked if she wouldn't mind watching her bags while she went to the ladies' room. The woman obliged, and Eve smiled as she complimented the woman's earrings. Then she walked from the store, her hands now free.

It took her a minute, but she found the girls about to

turn the corner heading toward the water fountain in the center of the mall. They were chatting up a storm, the suburban girl completely captivated by her undead companion.

Eve pretended to study a window display as the pair passed the smoke shop, briefly stepping inside to check out a copy of *US Weekly* before continuing on their way. To anyone else, they were two typical high school girls, but to Eve they had an altogether different story.

Where most saw teenagers shopping, she saw predator and prey.

She couldn't remember exactly when she had taken it upon herself to hunt down the spawn of her curse. *Sometime during the Bronze Age,* she thought. Her memory wasn't all that sharp when it came to matters from the distant past, especially since she'd spent most of it in a bloodthirsty rage. But sometime, long ago, she had decided that it was her mission to clean up the mess she had started. She'd been at it for a very long time, but was nowhere close to completing her quest.

That was the problem with curses; there was always someone new to pass it on.

The two girls ended up on the top level of the parking garage. It was practically deserted. Eve had carefully followed them up the metal stairs, listening to Miss Suburbia whining about not using the elevator. *If she only knew what's about to happen to her, she'd really have something to whine about,* Eve thought.

From the doorway, Eve watched the two walking across the garage. The dark-haired girl had put her hand into the back pocket of the other's jeans and pulled her close. They stopped to share a kiss, and Eve tensed.

The black-clad girl leaned in, clearly happy with the situation. The vampire teen put a hand around her partner's shoulder, as she steered her toward a car parked in the shadows near the wall.

At the driver's side door they started to kiss again. The

vampire roughly pushed her partner back against the car, and the younger girl seemed surprised.

Eve could feel the vampire's excitement and hunger pulsing in the air like the heartbeats they both used to have, and decided it was time to make her move. She darted out from the doorway, sprinting across the garage, just as the vampire revealed her true nature. They all took such pleasure in revealing what they truly were to their prey, it was almost as if they fed on the terror as well as the blood.

Goth girl pulled back her head, holding on to the shoulders of her friend, and with a hiss opened her mouth. Glistening white, razor-sharp teeth flashed, the canines distending as she opened her mouth wider to bite.

"Not tonight, sugar," Eve said. She grabbed a fistful of the girl's hair and yanked her head back before her fangs could break the skin of the other girl's throat.

The vampire went wild, spinning around to face Eve, her hair tearing away from the scalp. "You don't know what you're dealing with, bitch," she snarled.

Eve smiled sadly, nodding ever so slightly. "Sorry to say I do."

A spark of recognition appeared on the young vampire's face as she suddenly understood who had interrupted her feeding. They all knew her; they could feel the connection deep inside themselves. It usually played out the same. First came the shock of recognition, followed by sheer panic as they realized their lives were forfeit.

The vampire started to run, but Eve was faster, suddenly in front of the young creature, clawed hands gripping the sides of her face. She looked down into the vampire's eyes, paralyzing her with a stare.

"Please," the vampire begged, but Eve had made up her mind thousands of years ago. There would be no mercy for the spawn of her curse.

"I'm sorry," she said, leaning close to whisper in the girl's ear. "But go to your final rest knowing that whoever did this to you will meet up with me sooner or later."

The girl struggled momentarily but then went limp as

she realized the futility of her actions. With a surge of terrible strength, Eve twisted the girl's head and tore it from her body. There was an explosion of blood, but within seconds it turned to a spray of ash. Both the wretched thing's head, still in Eve's hands, and the body that slumped to the floor of the garage dissolved away to nothing before her eyes.

Then there was only dust.

Eve brushed the ashen remains of the girl from the front of her cashmere sweater and jeans before turning her gaze toward the vampire's potential victim. The girl just stood there in her cheerleading jacket, her mouth open, trying to scream but emitting only little squeaks.

"You all right?" Eve asked the girl, checking to be certain that she hadn't been bitten.

The girl stood stiffly against the car, continuing to make those annoying sounds. Eve pressed a well-manicured finger against the girl's lips, momentarily silencing her.

"Hush now," she said. "You're going to be fine, but I want you to remember something. I want you always to be careful. Pretty girls can sometimes be just as dangerous as pretty boys."

The girl stared, wide-eyed.

"Will you remember that for me?" Eve asked her.

As the girl slowly nodded, Eve pulled her finger away.

"Good," she said, leaving the girl and walking toward the exit. She glanced at her watch. She still had more than an hour to shop before the mall closed.

THOUGH he would never have admitted it to anyone, Danny missed Dr. Graves. With the violent fantasies and flashes of savage anger he'd been having the past few days, he would have liked to talk with the ghost. He thought he could have told Graves what was going on with him, but there was no one else he felt that comfortable with. No one else he was sure he could trust.

Lying in bed, the image of the two terrified children

from the aquarium flashed before his mind's eye, followed by the painful memory of the look on his mother's face.

He rolled over, punching at the pillow beneath his head. He and his mother had avoided talking about the incident at the aquarium, but he knew it was only a matter of time before she would bring it up. The anger roiled inside him, and he again wished that Graves were here.

Danny couldn't talk about this stuff with his mother; she was already freaked out enough by the changes in her son. He had considered talking with Mr. Doyle, but since he and Ceridwen had returned, they'd been hidden away in Doyle's rooms, and Danny didn't figure they'd take kindly to the interruption. Clay was away with Graves, so that removed him from the mix, and Danny just didn't feel comfortable talking with the others. Squire would probably just laugh at him anyway, and Eve . . . well she was just so damned hot, he would be too embarrassed to share his feelings with her.

He flipped over again, trying to get comfortable and hoping to drift off to sleep, but his body refused to let him. His skin was itching like crazy.

Finally, Danny tossed off his covers and stomped across the room to the bathroom. *Maybe a hot shower'll help,* he thought, turning on the faucet and letting the water run over his hands. Standing by the tub, waiting for the water to heat up, he glanced down casually at the center of his chest, at the small hanging growth he'd noticed there earlier.

Is it bigger? he wondered, squeezing the rubbery sack between his dripping fingers. *Great, something else to worry about,* he thought, before being distracted by a faint sound of screaming from outside.

He turned off the water in the tub and returned to his room, listening. Somebody outside was pretty upset, and by the scent he picked up, he knew exactly who it was. There were too many people in the house for him to go up the stairs unseen, and use the door to the roof. Instead, he opened his window and climbed out onto the stone ledge,

then began to climb. His claws fit easily in the crevices between the stones. Window frames and gutters made easy
handholds.

In seconds, he was on the roof. He wanted to see what
the story was, and then he would go back to his room, take
a long, hot shower, and hopefully get some sleep.

The November air felt good on his tingling flesh, as he
padded barefoot across the rooftop to look out over the
edge at the apartment building on Mount Vernon Street.

The cute girl and her sleazy boyfriend were there again,
and this time they were in the middle of a heated argument;
something to do with the guy talking to another girl at a
club while she sat alone like a big loser, waiting for him to
come back. He, of course, denied the whole thing, telling
her that she was drunk and blowing everything out of proportion.

They're both drunk. He could smell the stink of alcohol
wafting off of them as if they'd doused themselves in it like
perfume.

The argument was becoming more heated, and then the
guy did what even Danny knew you should never do to a
drunk and angry girl.

He laughed at her.

Her response was quick and brutal. She slapped the be-
mused grin right off his face, shrieking every four-letter
word in the book at him and telling him she never wanted
to see him again.

What happened next took Danny totally by surprise. It
looked as though the guy was going to leave, but then he
spun around and punched the girl square in the face. The
vicious blow knocked her off her feet, and she tumbled to
the ground. Her head bounced off the sidewalk, and she
twitched once and then lay still. The smell of blood was in
the air again, and it aroused the fury that lay in Danny's
heart like a prowling beast, ready to pounce.

He tried to step back from the edge of the roof. *It's none
of my business.*

But the girl had hit her head on the sidewalk pretty hard.

And the son of a bitch shouldn't have hit her in the first place. Maybe once he would have been too afraid to step in, but now there wasn't room in him for fear. Only for rage.

Danny vaulted over the edge of the roof and dropped all the way to the ground, the air whistling past his face as he fell. He landed on all fours with nary a sound, right in front of Conan Doyle's brownstone, then bounded across the street. Using the guy's car for cover, he peered around the BMW. The bastard was trying to haul the girl to her feet, half carrying her and half dragging her toward the stairs of her apartment building.

And that was where he dumped her, looking around to see if anyone had seen what he had done.

The prick wiped blood from his lip where she had slapped him and pulled the keys from the pocket of his sport coat.

Danny emerged from the shadows in front of the car. When the guy spotted him, his eyes narrowed for just a second with annoyance, and then widened in confusion and fear. The stink of fear suddenly filled the air.

"What the fuck?" the guy said, as Danny sprang at him.

The rage cheered him on, telling him that what he was doing was right—that people like this deserved everything they got.

"You like to hit girls, huh, asshole?" Danny growled, snatching up a fistful of the guy's jacket.

The guy threw a feeble punch, striking Danny on the chin, but he barely felt it. He rammed his horned head forward in a savage head butt. His horns sliced the asshole's forehead, and Danny shoved him up against the car. The guy was dazed, blood running down his face in streams from a pair of nasty gashes in his forehead.

"Tough guy," Danny spat, running his clawed hands along the side of the gray sports car, digging furrows into the expensive paint job. "You got your car, your looks, your money. You think you can do anything you want."

He grabbed the guy by the throat and hauled him off his feet. Expensive shoes dangled inches above the pavement.

"But you can't," Danny sneered, looking into the guy's bloody face. "And I'm here to remind you of that."

He slammed the guy down atop the roof of the car, and he bounced, rolling down across the windshield to lay moaning on top of the hood.

Danny laughed, a short, nasty barking sound. This was the best he'd felt in weeks.

He grabbed the guy again, dragging him across the hood. One of the guy's eyes was starting to swell, and Danny reached down with a claw and raked the swollen flesh, tearing open the skin. Blood spurted from the wound.

The guy screamed. It was the greatest sound Danny had ever heard. All of the fear he'd had of himself was gone, now. By knocking his girlfriend around—knocking her unconscious—this guy had bought himself a world of hurt. He deserved whatever he got.

Son of a bitch did me a favor.

Danny covered the guy's mouth with a hand.

"Shhhhhh," he hissed, bringing his demonic features closer. "Don't want to wake up the neighborhood, do we?" His tongue flicked out, licking away some of the man's blood.

It tasted like honey.

That was when he realized that his skin didn't itch anymore, his bones didn't ache, and he felt as though he could take on the world single-handedly.

All it took was blood.

He grabbed hold of the guy's neck, beginning to sink his curved, black claws into the soft flesh, eager to get to the blood.

When a voice stopped him.

"Hey, kid," said the gravelly voice. "You really want to be doin' that?"

Danny watched as Squire emerged from a patch of shadow thrown by a window box on the front of one of the other buildings that lined Mount Vernon Street. He was smoking a cigar and stank of booze.

The goblin just stood there, staring at him with red, yellow-flecked eyes, and Danny felt his rage begin to subside.

"He would have deserved it," Danny said, tossing the unconscious guy back atop the hood and stepping away.

"You goin' in?" Squire asked, motioning toward the house with his large, potato-shaped head.

"Yeah," Danny said. "Yeah, I think I should."

"Good answer." Squire took a puff from the foul-smelling cigar, and the two of them walked side by side to the steps leading into Conan Doyle's home.

WHENEVER Clay drove, he had to force himself not to check the rearview mirror incessantly. The eyes drew him. In an ordinary mirror he could see his entire face, and though his appearance often intrigued him, he had grown accustomed over his long life to seeing a different face and shape in the mirror. The human features he most frequently wore—the identity he called Joseph Clay—was familiar, but no less a mask than all of the others. Monsters and dead men, the faces were never consistent, and so nothing he saw in a full-size mirror could surprise or distract him.

But in the car, the rearview mirror only showed his eyes, and over the centuries it had become far too tempting for him to search those eyes for some semblance of sameness. Large or small, blue or brown or hideous red, he stared into his own eyes for a sense of himself. If he could find it there, some commonality that existed in each of the forms he took, he might begin to believe he had a soul.

The rented Jeep Grand Cherokee thrummed as he drove south on the interstate, keeping his eyes on the road. His ipod lay on the console, set on shuffle, playing a truly eclectic selection of music. Eclectic tastes were inevitable for someone who had been alive in a time when the only musical instrument in the world was the human voice.

The ghost of Doctor Graves shimmered beside him in a rough approximation of sitting in the passenger's seat. Of course, Graves could not feel the seat or make any real contact with it, but Clay had long since found that ghosts took comfort in the ability to mimic ordinary activities.

Graves had been careful only to partially manifest. With the morning sun streaming through the windows of the Cherokee, there would be no way for him to appear alive. Passing motorists would take a glance and see a transparent man, the trace of a person riding in the passenger seat, and there would have been staring and shouting and possibly accidents leading to twisted automotive wreckage and loss of life.

Instead, Graves manifested in a state between the ethereal realm and the physical world. The specter would be visible to supernatural beings such as Clay, but the only humans driving by who would be able to see him would be the rare medium or psychic sensitive. That could still lead to a car accident, but Clay figured such people would be less likely to react to seeing a ghost.

"You've been awfully quiet," he said.

At first the ghost did not respond, as though he hadn't heard. Graves stared straight ahead like the road before them was the most fascinating thing he had ever seen. Though handsome, his features had a natural stoicism about them that lent a grimness to his aspect, even when his mood was light. This made him difficult to read.

The ghost wavered in the sunlight, an insubstantial gauze, like heat haze on summer blacktop.

"Leonard—"

"I don't like to go home," Graves interrupted. The ghost glanced at him. Clay kept his hands on the wheel. "Even before my death, I spent little time in Swansea. To be going home now just to disinter my bones . . ."

The smile that crossed the specter's face sent a chill through Clay. He had seen death a million times, but could never know what it felt like from the other side, from the afterlife.

"I'd tell you we could turn around," Clay said, "but the answers might be waiting in your grave."

The ghost of Dr. Graves shook his head. "No turning back. If I gave up trying to solve this mystery, I'd only be haunting myself. I'd be in Hell. I've been wandering long enough. It's time for the truth."

Graves seemed more ephemeral than ever, the sunlight threatening to wash him away completely. He stared out at the road again, and Clay decided perhaps that was best for now.

The minutes passed in silence, and eventually he lost track of the time and the miles. Not too far north of the New York border he got off of Route 95, following a winding road right into the heart of Swansea, Connecticut. What surprised Clay immediately was the aura of money that emanated from every structure, every person, every car. The lawns were perfectly manicured, the school a brand-new sprawling brick monster, the awnings in front of the shops immaculate.

Graves directed him up a wide avenue with a beautifully landscaped island running down its center. The homes began with stunning and moved on to astonishing, mostly Federal Colonials and Victorians built at the tail end of the nineteenth century or the dawning days of the twentieth. Closer to the center of town the houses were right on the edge of the road, and Clay knew some of them had been taverns and the like at one time. These were the oldest. As they moved away from downtown Swansea, the homes became more stately, set back farther from the road. There were sprawling estates with black wrought iron gates and trees older than the nation.

"You grew up here?"

The ghost's ethereal substance rippled with pique. "You're surprised? I would not have expected racial presumptions from a creature as old as you."

Clay smirked. "I have no race, my friend. But if nothing else, I'm a student of history. You were born, when, 1910?"

"Oh-nine."

"Very few black Americans could have lived like this in those days."

The ghost gestured with a spectral hand. "Park at the curb."

Clay pulled over and killed the ignition. He glanced at Graves, who rose up, passing through the car roof as though it were as insubstantial as he. Brow creased in a frown, Clay popped open the door, locked up the Cherokee, and shut the door.

The ghost drifted toward the wrought-iron fence, going through the motions of walking, though it could not precisely have been called that. Graves's spectral form had altered. He had a long coat on now, the sort of greatcoat that had been commonplace in the nineteen forties, the era of his murder. When he passed through the iron bars he turned to glance back, and Clay saw the straps across his chest that indicated he was wearing the holsters for the phantom guns he sometimes carried.

Not carried. Manifested, Clay thought. They're ectoplasm, just like Graves.

"What are the guns for?"

"Just in case," Graves replied. He stood on the other side of the fence, waiting.

Clay glanced around. A black Mercedes went by. The moment it had passed him, he *changed,* his form shifting, bones popping, flesh flowing and diminishing until where he had stood a moment earlier there was now only an ordinary squirrel.

The squirrel darted through the black, wrought-iron bars and started across the grounds of an enormous estate. For long minutes the squirrel followed the ghost up a hill, through a screen of massive oaks and pines, and soon enough they came within sight of a mansion on the hill. It had a circular driveway and columns in the front. There were several smaller buildings to the south of the main house, and a carriage house with a stone driveway and a sign in front.

There were too many cars, and Clay realized this was

not a house. Like many such properties whose upkeep was so expensive, it had been altered into something else. From its appearance and the ambulance in front, he presumed it was an assisted-living residence for senior citizens, and the carriage house some kind of administration building.

The ghost of Dr. Graves swept on across the groomed lawn, beneath the trees, and spared nary a glance for the home where he had been raised.

The squirrel followed, not understanding the nature of their destination until they made their way around behind the main building and he saw, down a hill cut by a winding gravel drive, an old cemetery. It, too, was well kept, though perhaps only for appearances. None of the headstones appeared to be new, or even recent. Some were so old that the elements had eroded all but the suggestion of names and dates.

At the back of the small cemetery were two family crypts. The larger and more ornate of the two, a pristine marble thing worthy of Athens, bore the name WILLIAMS. The other, smaller and set back toward the woods at the rear of the property, had the word *GRAVES* emblazoned above the iron door.

"Morbid, isn't it?" the ghost said. "Or perhaps ironic. Graves. What else would be in a crypt? A child's humor."

Yet he laughed softly and shook his head.

"My mother always thought it amusing. But she had a dark humor." The ghost glanced over at the squirrel. "You're going to be little help in that form."

Clay hesitated a moment, concerned about prying eyes from the retirement home. But there was little to be done about it. With no more effort than standing, he transformed again, flesh flowing in the space between heartbeats, and he wore the skin of a man again. Better to be caught out here with the face of Joseph Clay than with the inhuman features of his natural form.

"You grew up in that house?" he asked.

The ghost of Dr. Graves allowed himself a quick look at the massive mansion, but quickly turned his eyes away.

"Not precisely. My family lived in the carriage house. They were servants to Stewart and Annabel Williams for decades. My father was their butler."

The ghost drifted as though moved by unseen wind. He stared at the crypt where his parents' remains had been put to rest, where his own bones lay even now, and spoke as though in the grip of a dream. Yet it was no dream, only memory.

"You can see the wealth that is here even now. Imagine its opulence in those days. The Williamses were extraordinarily kind and seemed genuinely unaffected by differences of race. Class, certainly. As kind as they were, they were still the wealthy, and my parents their servants. But perhaps that puts an ugly face on something that was simply symptomatic of the age.

"My father liked to say that being rich had stolen their imagination. That they had all of that money but did not know what to do with it. Many times he said if that money was his that he could change the world, that he would make people's lives better. He dreamed about having the money to travel and educate himself.

"The Williamses had one son, Peter, but he died in the battle of the Somme during the Great War. They never had any other children. Annabel and Stewart died in 'twenty-six. He had a heart attack in the fall, and by Christmas, she was dead. By then, with Peter dead, they'd changed their wills. I inherited it all. The property. The architectural firm. Every penny."

Clay watched him, thinking how strange it was that a ghost should be so haunted by the past. It occurred to him that perhaps the spirits of the dead were the most haunted creatures of all.

"Did you build the crypt?" he asked.

Graves turned, sunlight streaming through his translucent form. "No. Again, the Williamses. My mother passed shortly after Peter went to war. When they realized that the public cemetery in Swansea was segregated, they had this crypt built here for my family.

"For servants, you understand. And colored servants, to boot. They were before their time. Sometimes I think my father underestimated them. In fact, I'm sure he did. They left their money to me, after all. I'm quite certain the white society in Connecticut was scandalized."

Clay watched him silently for a moment, then walked over and stood beside him. "Your father must have been very proud of you."

The ghost nodded, his expression wistful. "He was. I took care of him until he passed. He died sitting in a theater watching Charlie Chaplin in *City Lights*. One moment I heard him laughing, and then everyone else laughed and it was too quiet next to me. I looked over and he'd gone. Very peaceful."

Clay could see the picture in his mind of Graves's father, a dead man, still smiling, cast in the silver glow of the movie screen, sitting in a theater filled with laughing people. Graves himself was dead and now, more than three-quarters of a century later, it seemed strange to offer his condolences.

The ghost saved him from having to say anything.

"Open it."

Clay blinked and looked at him. "Just like that?"

With one spectral hand he reached out and traced his fingers along the iron door, though he could not have felt it. The ghost could easily have passed right through on his own, but Clay understood that he did not want to do so alone.

"I've waited long enough," Graves said. "Open it."

Clay didn't need to shift his shape to have inhuman strength. He gripped the handle of the iron door and twisted. Metal shrieked, and something snapped in the lock, and he pulled. The hinges had weakened over the years, and the door scraped the ground as it opened. A sound like the gasp of relieved spirits rushing out to the daylight came from within, and the sunshine flooded the crypt.

The ghost hesitated at the threshold.

Clay walked right through him, stepping into the sepulchre. Three low marble tables had been placed inside the crypt, and upon each of them had been arranged a coffin.

"Which?" he asked.

"The middle," Dr. Graves said from the doorway, his whispered voice just as much a ghost as his flesh.

Clay first walked the inner perimeter of the crypt, examining the corners. He looked over the other two coffins and the platforms upon which they stood, and then at last he stood by the center dais, running one hand over the surface of the coffin.

"Why did you never come here before?"

The ghost of Dr. Graves at last entered the crypt. "I was afraid that I would not be able to leave, that being this close to my body would trap me somehow, or perhaps send me on, forcing me into the afterlife before I had discovered the identity of my killer."

"You're here now."

"My frustration has overcome my fear at last."

Clay nodded. "All right. But stay over there, just in case."

He tore the lid off of the coffin with a splintering of wood. Out of the corner of his eye he saw Graves ripple and fade as though about to disappear. Clay paused, worried, but then he realized it was only the shock of seeing his final rest so abruptly interrupted and not that the spirit world was calling Graves back.

"Tell me about Professor Zarin," Clay said, mostly to distract Graves as he reached in and touched the cool, dry skull inside the coffin. "He was the biggest thorn in your side in those days, right?"

"Zarin was . . . persistent. A madman, but organized. He truly thought the world ought to answer to him, and if they would not, he'd punish them. I came into conflict with him many times."

Clay bent over the coffin, tracing his hands over the bones, searching for any sign of prior disturbance. But no one had been here. No one had ever dared to break into this crypt until they had arrived.

"He must have been your primary suspect."

The ghost drifted around the crypt, brushing up against the coffins of his mother and father. He seemed quite distant, as though he were quietly communing with their long-departed spirits, sharing love and regrets. And perhaps he was.

"Leonard?"

"Hmm? Oh, yes. I haunted Zarin for years, but I came to believe he wasn't responsible. My investigation revealed that Zarin had been in jail at the time of my murder and was furious that someone else had taken my life. He even swore to destroy whomever was responsible for robbing him of the pleasure of killing me."

Clay arched an eyebrow. "Nice. And he must be long dead, anyway, so no answers there."

"On the contrary," Dr. Graves replied.

Clay turned to look at the ghost, troubled to think that while he stared at Leonard Graves he also had his fingers thrust into the ribcage of his skeleton.

"What do you mean?"

The ghost turned up his collar, a thoroughly human gesture and one that lent a strange solidity to him. He shivered as though cold and stared not at Clay but at the coffin. He was too far away to see his bones inside, but the view must be troubling enough.

"Just what I said. Zarin's still alive, though he must be well over a hundred by now. If he'd passed through the spirit world, I would have felt his death. Our fates were always entwined. I just . . . would have known."

Clay nodded, lost in thought now. Like Graves had been in life, Zarin had been a brilliant but otherwise ordinary man. That he could be alive after so many years seemed improbable, though not impossible. Still, they were starting this investigation all over again. That meant he could take nothing for granted, no matter what conclusions Graves had already come to.

He grunted, knitting his brows as he looked down into the coffin. Troubled, he moved around to the other side and peered in, reaching down to run his fingers along each rib. Though little of the sunlight touched the bones, what illumination existed was enough for Clay's inhuman eyes.

"What is it?" Graves asked. "Have you found a . . . what did you call it? A tether?"

Clay finished examining the remains. With a deep breath, he cast aside the cobwebs of his ruminations and shook his head. "No. There's no soul tether. But as I told you, I didn't expect there to be. It's been sixty odd years, far too long for a trace of the spirit to still be left behind."

The ghost slid his hands into his pockets and stepped out of the sunlight streaming through the door into the shadows of a deep corner in the crypt. In the dark, he seemed almost alive. His transparent flesh seemed to have greater texture.

"So, what's troubling you?" Graves asked. "What did you find?"

Clay ran a hand across the stubble on his cheek and looked back at the coffin, at the bones of his friend.

"The newspaper reports of your death say you were shot in the back."

Dr. Graves nodded. "Yes. The bullet came from a rifle. It struck me near the spine, midway between neck and pelvis. I remember that much. But you know that. We've discussed this."

"Yes. We have," Clay said. He stared at Graves. "The thing is, Leonard, if you were shot where you say, or anywhere on the upper body, the odds of the bullet not striking bone are astronomical. Logic dictates that it must have struck bone."

"Of course."

Clay rested his hand on the edge of the coffin. "There's no evidence of a bullet wound on these bones."

"But I remember . . ." Graves whispered, gaze darting around, searching the shadows, lost.

"If this is your body, my friend, what you remember is impossible."

6

WEARING his fine suit of man-skin, Baalphegor-Moabites strolled the early morning streets of Boston, taking in the sights of humanity.

He stopped to watch as a deliveryman carefully wheeled a metal cart loaded with baked goods toward the side entrance of a nearby shop and breathed in the succulent aroma of freshly prepared foodstuffs through the nostrils of his flesh mask.

"Watch it, pal," the human said from behind the cart, as he struggled to maneuver it across the sidewalk.

The demon was amused. *He called me pal.*

It was a wholly satisfying experience to be able to walk among them undetected. The flesh of the large man provided for him by the *listener* was a perfect fit, much better than some of other skin suits he'd worn on previous visits to the realm of humanity.

"It smells delicious," he commented in the human's tongue, perfectly comfortable in his disguise as he stepped out of the deliveryman's way. Baalphegor was surprised at how quickly it all came back to him. He had not spoken this language in quite some time, but there it was, as if he'd used it only yesterday.

The human scowled. "Wish the same could be said for you." His homely features wrinkled in distaste. "You smell like shit."

The suit of flesh did give off a rather pungent aroma, even though Baalphegor had been very careful not to spill any of the bodily fluids on his person as he had prepared it. But then again, he had been ravenous upon his arrival, and had fed upon the human listener who had helped him to complete his journey.

Baalphegor looked down at the clothing that adorned his disguise and saw that he had gotten quite a bit of his meal on himself.

"Not shit," the traveler from the beyond said with a shake of his large head. "Blood." He moved his own facial features around beneath the mask, attempting to form a smile.

The deliveryman quickened his pace, and Baalphegor waved farewell as he continued his own journey up Commonwealth Avenue.

He would have loved to spend what time he had remaining exploring the great city of Boston, remembering how it was the last time he had visited. But alas, that wasn't to be the case, for the demon had risked much to travel here for matters most dire.

Matters of life and death.

Since his arrival from beyond the pale, he had walked, refamiliarizing himself with the world that had come to fascinate him so much in his long lifetime. It was truly a most remarkable place, and if he had the capacity to feel emotion, he would have expressed deep sorrow to know that very shortly, it would exist no more.

The Devourer is coming, the demon mused.

Soon the Demogorgon will be here.

EVE shook away the cobwebs of sleep as she padded down the winding staircase of Conan Doyle's home, drawn to the delicious aroma of something cooking.

Passing the grandfather clock in the hall she saw that it was a little after five, and the sun had almost completely set. She loved this time of year, when the sun went down so much earlier, giving her more hours of freedom. Conan Doyle had a spell he could use to protect her from the sunlight, but its effects wore off within a day or two without the sorcerer's constant attention, and the magic did something unpleasant to her. Under the influence of the spell, Eve's skin crawled as though she was covered in filth. It had other side effects as well, including nausea and migraines, if she tried to keep the magic going long term.

Screw that. She preferred the night.

She entered the kitchen, her bare feet slapping on the cold tile of the floor as she went to the refrigerator and pulled open the door. Squire was at the stove, basting something with melted butter. Whatever it was, it had four legs and the remains of wings.

"What the hell is that?" she asked, finding the Tupperware bottle of blood that she kept for her morning pick-me-up.

Squire scowled as he looked at her. "What's it look like?"

"That's why I'm asking," she said, raising her voice before popping the cover off the container for a swig of the viscous fluid.

"It's a turkey, for Christ's sake," he grumbled, finishing up his basting and sliding the rack back into the oven.

"With four legs?" she said, allowing the refrigerator door to slam closed behind her.

"Didn't say it was from around here," the hobgoblin grumbled, placing the container of butter on the counter and removing the thick oven mitt from his hand. "And good evening to you, sunshine," he said with a snarl. "Wake up on the wrong side of the casket, did we?"

"Fuck off," she spat, walking to one of the stools at the island in the center of the room. She took another gulp from the bottle. "You know I don't sleep in a casket here."

"And you do at your place?" he asked, going to one of

the lower cabinets and removing a pan and a mixing bowl. He placed them on the counter.

"It's not really a casket," she said. "It's more like a sarcophagus. It's really nice."

"I bet," Squire said, pulling out a stool to get at some of the upper cabinets where he retrieved some more baking supplies.

"What's the occasion?" she asked, watching him step down from the stool, arms loaded. "Big, four-legged turkey cooking in the oven, vegetables on top of the stove. Did I oversleep and wake up on Thanksgiving?"

"Mr. Doyle and Ceridwen got back from their travels sometime yesterday, and I thought a little home cooking would be just the thing to welcome them."

"Nothing says welcome home like a four-legged turkey," Eve said with a wink, taking another swig of blood.

"So it's got four fucking legs, what's the big deal?" he asked, pulling a two-tiered step over to the counter and climbing up to work.

"What are you making now?"

"Corn bread." He poured a tablespoon of vegetable oil into the pan, then climbed up onto the counter, turning on the upper oven.

"Jeez, how come I never get a spread like this when I come back?"

"'Cause you're a bitch," Squire said casually, over his shoulder, as he continued preparing the corn bread.

Eve nearly choked. She wiped a crimson dribble from the corner of her mouth. "Have I mentioned how much I hate your guts?"

"Not in the last few minutes," Squire said, pouring ingredients into the large bowl.

"It's nice to see the two of you getting along," an unmistakable voice said, and Eve turned to see Conan Doyle coming into the kitchen. Ceridwen followed, carrying shopping bags from some of her own favorite establishments.

"Hey, bossman," Squire said. "Dinner should be ready

in an hour or so. I'm making some of that Southern-style corn bread you like."

"You spoil me, Squire," Conan Doyle said, and then turned to Eve. "And how are you, my dear?"

"Just fine." She closed the cap on her bottle, sated for the moment. "How are things in England?"

She noticed the scowl appear on Ceridwen's face.

"Things have changed," the mage replied. "But the rest, I believe, has done us good."

Conan Doyle and Ceridwen looked at each other then, and Eve could have sworn she saw something almost spiritual pass between them. *This is good,* she thought. The two of them belonged together. Conan Doyle was a pain in the ass normally, but he'd become an even bigger pain when Ceridwen wasn't in his life. It was good they had found each other again.

"I see you did some shopping," Eve said to Ceridwen.

"Why, yes," the Fey sorceress replied, holding up her multiple bags. "Following your advice. I told Arthur that if I am to remain in this world, I would need to adorn myself in raiment befitting my stature."

Conan Doyle slowly crossed his arms, fixing Eve in his patented icy stare.

"Good girl," she said, reaching out to pat Ceridwen's arm. "You're learning."

The sound of the oven door slamming caused them all to start, and they looked over to see Squire standing on the counter where he had just placed his corn bread in the oven.

"Oh yeah," the hobgoblin said, using the portable step to climb down. "Before I forget, I met with Detective Hook yesterday about a couple'a bodies they found in an alley off Tremont."

Eve saw the change in Conan Doyle's demeanor immediately, and the atmosphere in the kitchen turned serious.

"And your findings?" Conan Doyle asked.

"Not really sure," Squire replied, washing his hands and then drying them with a hand towel. "One of the bodies was skinned, and the other chowed on. Think we might have something demonic walking the streets."

Eve frowned. *Demonic*. The word brought a sudden recollection of her adventure at Sultan's, and the moment in the alley outside the dance club when she had sensed a presence.

"Now that you mention it, I might've sensed something nasty in the air the other night," she said.

"And this is the first you've thought to mention it?" Conan Doyle asked, giving her the haughty, paternal glare that always made her want to punch him in the face. It never seemed to occur to him how ridiculous it was for him to scold her as though she were a child. Her, of all people.

Eve shrugged. "Dark things are passing through this city all the time. I didn't think of it again until now."

"Until the part with the partially eaten and skinned bodies," Squire suggested.

"Exactly," Eve said with a nod, wanting to jump over the island and smash the cheeky little bugger's potato head against the marble counter.

Conan Doyle stroked his chin, deep in thought.

"Aren't there rules about the demonic walking the earthly plane?" Ceridwen asked.

"Quite right, my dear," the mage said. "But with the way things have been of late, it's hardly surprising that a creature from one hell or another might try to test the rules."

Squire leaned back against the counter, folding his stubby arms across his chest. "So, what do you think?"

"I think a hunting expedition may be in order." Conan Doyle looked at Eve. "May I call upon your services?"

She slid from the stool and slid it back under the island.

"You may, and I think I have just the outfit."

LAUGHTER and gaiety fill the night, as illuminating as the lanterns placed all about the perimeter of the stone amphitheater. At the far side of the Boboli Gardens, away from the Pitti Palace, the Florence Symphony plays beautiful music that seems to pull fairy magic from the evening sky, drawing down the sparkle of the stars themselves.

Or perhaps Dr. Graves has simply had too much champagne.

This place does seem magical tonight, though, an oasis of wealth and laissez-faire amid the desperation of the European war theater. To think that an American could be so welcome in Italy . . . Dr. Graves has been surprised by the reception he has received. Yet Florence has ever and always been a city of light and of art and music, not of war.

Champagne glasses clink. Women in elegant gowns and dapper men walk arm in arm along the paths farther away from the symphony. Chairs have been set up on the garden lawn near the musicians, and those rows are filled, but far more guests seem to prefer to mingle in the gardens, beneath the stars, with the musical accompaniment.

He spots his fiancée, Gabriella, chatting with a young Florentine woman of her acquaintance . . . old friends, reunited. The two wave to him and then smile at one another like schoolgirls. Graves had tried to convince Gabriella to stay behind, but she would not hear of it. If there was danger, she trusted him to deal with it, to keep her safe. He cannot quite bring himself to wish she had stayed back in New York—not when he sees her in this gown, dark ringlets of hair falling around her shoulders, a Roman goddess come to Earth. She leaves him breathless.

And it is good for her to be out of New York for a while. In the States, the newspapers never let her be anything but the fiancée of Dr. Graves, with all that entails. Gabriella is a white woman planning to marry a black man. New York society burns with fascination at the fame Dr. Graves has achieved, and with every aspect of his life, including his engagement. But beneath their fascination, there lurks disdain. No matter how much of a novelty he might become to them, he will never be more than that. Regardless of how many times he might prevent some horrid crime, even saving their lives, he is still a black man.

Professor Zarin would have poisoned their skies, their water, and perhaps even brought the glorious Empire State Building crashing down, if not for him. The society ladies smile and call him a hero. Wealthy men pat him on the back and congratulate him, even thank him for his efforts. But between them always is the distance created by the unspoken acknowledgment of race.

Italy is better. The country is not free from prejudice. Yet here, in this war-torn country, he feels more welcome, more at home. They love him in Europe, and while some might hate him for the color of his skin, there are far more people here who only want to meet him, to know him. Stories of his adventures around the world reach Florence in the newspapers, but by the time they are translated in Italian, his feats have been blown all out of proportion.

Graves has been to dozens of events like this one, but this is one of those rare moments when he does not feel the reluctance and resentment that often accompanies his presence. It is a welcome relief, a chance to exhale from so much time spent holding his breath, holding his tongue.

And the music is sublime.

The symphony transports him with a melody that seems to speak to the heart of him, to the little boy he had once been. He feels sure he knows the tune, as though he's heard it a thousand times in his mind. But perhaps that is the hallmark of true genius in music, that it speaks to the soul with such passion that it seems to be something one has always known.

A waiter passes, and Dr. Graves snatches a fluted champagne glass from his tray. He smooths the front of his jacket and begins to navigate the maze of Florentine society that mingles around him. Many people greet him in Italian as he passes. They smile, and some even clap a friendly hand upon his shoulder or arm. Dr. Graves nods and smiles and moves on.

A perfect night. The only way it could be more perfect is if he and Gabriella could dance beneath the stars with the symphony playing. But there will be no dancing for Dr.

Graves tonight. He needs to maintain his focus if all of these people are to survive until morning.

The presence of a bomb mars his enjoyment of the evening.

Graves scans the crowd, lifting his champagne flute and hiding behind it as he studies the people around him, looking for anything out of place. He takes a sip. As he lowers the glass he sees a thin, blond man with grim, craggy features look nervously away. The man sets off through the crowd, headed toward the symphony.

Holding his breath, Graves watches as the nervous man looks back once, then continues away skittishly. He is headed directly for the symphony.

Champagne glass in hand, Graves smiles at two silverhaired gentlemen and nods amiably even as he starts after the nervous man.

"Dr. Graves?" one of the silver-haired men says.

He turns to study the man more closely. The gentleman has a professorial air about him and appraises Graves through glasses that sit on the bridge of his nose. His hair is a bit wild and unkempt. He and his companion stand out from the other men in attendance at the celebration. If they are wealthy, they are also eccentric.

"Indeed, sir," he says. "I don't think I've had the pleasure?"

"No, we haven't met, sir," the silver-haired man replies. "I am Doctor Giovanni Arno. This is my associate, Vincenzo Mellace. I must tell you that we are great admirers of yours. We follow your achievements with much enthusiasm."

Graves tries to be polite, but his gaze darts past the men, trying to follow the skittish man as he makes his way through the crowd toward the symphony. He glances at Gabriella, just to be certain she is far, far away from the nervous gentleman.

"I appreciate that," Dr. Graves says. "But many of those stories are greatly exaggerated."

Arno laughs and strokes his beard. "I hope so. I would

be deeply troubled if everything I had read was true. Nevertheless we are more interested in your scientific and medical achievements than your leap from a burning zeppelin last month."

Though he needs to extricate himself from these men, to get after the blond man, he cannot help being charmed by Dr. Arno. But they are all in peril, and the danger grows with every moment these men delay him. Several of his agents who travel in the criminal underworld have indicated that Zarin will set off a bomb here in some bizarre attempt to strike at the Axis forces. A number of Italian officials are in attendance this evening, but only a lunatic like Zarin could possibly think killing men and women here would have any influence over the war effort.

Yet from past experience, Graves knows it is just the sort of thing Zarin would do.

He glances toward the symphony, sees the horns gleaming in the starlight. The violinists stand as one and begin to eke out a hauntingly beautiful melody, that same one that seems so familiar to him.

The skittish man is nowhere to be seen.

"Gentlemen, please forgive me," he says, as diplomatically as he is able. *"I do appreciate your kind words, but there's a matter of some urgency to which I must attend. If I might seek you out shortly, I'll be only to happy to discuss my experiments and research."*

"Oh, yes, of course," Mellace says.

But a frown creases Dr. Arno's forehead. *"If you must."*

"I must. With apologies."

As he turns and rushes off, weaving through couples who are arm in arm and clusters of men talking business and women talking war, he hears Arno mutter something to his companion.

"Another rude American. I'd hoped otherwise. Perhaps what they say about the Whisper is true, after all."

Then the two men blend with the crowd behind him, their voices gone. The words stay with him, even as he slips past a waiter, moving toward the rows of seated guests and *the symphony beyond them. That haunting melody still plays.*

And he thinks of the Whisper.

It had been a perfect opportunity for the newspapers in New York and elsewhere to reveal the resentment society felt toward him. When he plays the hero, the world loves him. His achievements in science and his explorations around the globe have made him the pride of New York, a darling of the press. But like tigers, they had lain in wait for the moment when they could turn on him.

The Whisper had provided that moment.

Shortly after Dr. Graves had begun to use his extraordinary mind and the body he has honed to near physical perfection to combat crime and espionage, the Whisper had appeared upon the scene. Graves had seen him as a kindred spirit, another man with extraordinary abilities, dedicated to the betterment of mankind and the defense of the helpless. According to the newspapers, the Whisper was able to hypnotize criminals into changing their ways, using only the power of suggestion. His voice alone could compel them. He was said to have rehabilitated dozens of hardened men in the New York area.

Graves had been hopeful, looking forward to his first encounter with the Whisper. Yet when they finally met, he discovered the truth about the Whisper—whose real name was Simon Broderick. The people deserved to know the truth, the deception that Broderick had perpetrated upon them, the cruelty and evil that lurked within a man they thought of as a hero. Dr. Graves had exposed the Whisper as a fraud.

Simon Broderick had taken his own life.

In New York society, the font from which Broderick had sprung, new bitterness developed toward Graves. Many now hate him for what they perceived as his humiliation of the Whisper, claiming that was what had prompted the man's suicide.

As if they needed another reason to be wary of Dr. Leonard Graves.

And now he has encountered that bitter wariness here in Italy. Perhaps there is nowhere in the world where he could escape it.

Frustrated and angry with himself for the disappointment and resentment that lingers in his heart, Graves moves up to the rear of the seats that have been arranged in the gardens.

The violins have given way to a lilting chorus of horns. He glances at the symphony and starts toward the musicians along the central aisle. Several people notice him, but no one attempts to stop him. Graves peers at each row of guests, searching one side and then the other for the suspicious, stealthy man who darted away upon seeing him.

Only guilt makes a man flee like that.

Whoever the rabbit is, he must be working for Professor Zarin. Which means that the madman truly is up to something here this evening. Perhaps the rumors of a bomb are true.

If so, Graves has to move fast. If he cannot find that man, he realizes, he will have to warn the guests, tell them to evacuate the gardens. He has to get Gabriella out of here. The violins come back in to join the horns and the music rises toward a crescendo that any other night would have lifted his heart.

Frantic, now, he spins around as he moves toward the head of the aisle, right in front of the symphony. The musicians have begun to notice him now. The conductor will not turn, will not allow himself to be distracted, and the music goes on. But a woman in a shimmering bone-white gown points at him, and a round-bellied, balding man stands and begins to bluster at him.

Graves cannot hear him, so near to the music.

He spins again, searching for the skittish man.

How could he have just disappeared?

The melody sways, a haunting air. Then comes a jarring, discordant cello note. Graves frowns and turns to see the cellist pointing past him, toward the Pitti Palace.

The bullet strikes Dr. Graves in the back, scraping spine and ricocheting inside him, punching through his heart.

Death and darkness claim him, the echo of that discordant cello still in his ears.

ON the drive south from Connecticut the weather had taken a turn for the worse. In New York the sky had begun to cloud over and by the time they were passing through Jersey it had begun to rain lightly. A cold, November rain.

Clay kept his eyes on the road and his hands on the wheel. The Cherokee's wipers shushed out a gentle rhythm. The ghost of Dr. Graves seemed to have weight and substance in the gloom, and when Clay chanced a look over at him, he saw that the spirit had turned to peer out the rain-slicked window into the gray nothing beyond.

Graves had just finished relating the tale of his own murder. Clay had been aware of the basics, but had never known the details. Hearing it from the man who'd lost his life that day made it all the more tragic. The world had lost a great man, but Graves had lost his life and his love.

"It's just like death," the ghost whispered.

A glance at the speedometer told Clay he was going too damned fast. He eased up on the accelerator and edged slightly away from the tractor trailer that careened along in the next lane, water hissing up from under its tires.

"What is?" he asked.

"This. The storm," Graves replied, still staring out the window. "Gray nothing. Only shapes in the mist."

A stranger to death, Clay did not know how to reply to that. They traveled for several minutes with only the shush of the wipers and the patter of the rain for company. Clay thought about turning on the radio but did not want to seem as though he was attempting to prevent further conversation. The highway thrummed beneath them.

"You haven't told me how you know these people in Washington," the ghost said, his voice sounding far away, as though in a dream.

Clay glanced at him. The ghost watched him intently, eyes crystal clear, as though they were the only part of him truly in this world.

"I'm surprised Conan Doyle hasn't shared that part of my background with you."

"Arthur shares only what he wants to share," Graves said.

With a barely amused grunt, Clay nodded. "You've noticed that, have you? That's Doyle, all right."

The ghost shifted, floating slightly forward and sideways. He still appeared to be sitting on the passenger's seat, but didn't seem to notice that his knees were partially lost in the glove compartment of the Cherokee.

"Are you purposely avoiding my question, Joe?"

Clay smiled and reached up to scratch an ear. "You might say that. Not for long, though. It's just that it's not my finest moment."

Dr. Graves did not push, only waited for him to continue. Clay stared out through the Cherokee's windshield at the traffic and the rain, and flexed his fingers on the wheel.

"All right, the simple version. During a period of my life, I lost track of who I really was. Let's say I was confused for a few decades and leave it at that. The point is, some unsavory people in the American government decided my abilities could be put to unpleasant use. That went on far longer than I like to think about, them manipulating me. When it was over, I dealt with those responsible, but there were others . . . they weren't the ones who did it to me, but they could have intervened and chose not to. That's government, for you. The period I refer to as my 'memory lapse' covers the years when you were active, including your death. Given what they were using me for, it's even possible I pulled the trigger myself."

If ghosts could flinch, Graves did. Otherwise it was merely an ectoplasmic shudder, a flicker of the ethereal substance of his spirit.

"You're saying you might have killed me?"

Clay frowned, knuckles tightening on the wheel. "I was joking, but I guess it isn't funny. It's not impossible, but not likely, either. We'll find out in D.C. The point of all of this is that there are people I knew in those days, people who were still alive when it was all over, who owe me for what they did or what they didn't do . . . or just because I let them live."

A grim silence fell between them, then. Neither of them approved of outright killing, but Clay would bend the rules if there was no other choice. Especially in the aftermath of his memory lapse.

"I'm going to call in a marker," the shapeshifter went on. "Professor Zarin was public enemy number one for the better part of a decade back then. I want to see what I can find out about him and about his current whereabouts. Maybe we'll learn something you haven't been able to discover on your own."

This time, when Clay glanced at him, Graves seemed less substantial, as though he had merged with the storm outside, his form made up of mist and rain and gray skies.

"I appreciate your help with this, Clay. I'd be lying if I said I was confident in the investigation I conducted on my own. After that night—after my murder at the symphony— it took me quite a while to accept the truth. Years passed in the tangible world. I had never believed in the afterlife, so getting used to being spectral was very difficult.

"When at last I stopped being so stubborn, I did my best to investigate, but I did nothing but chase threads that led nowhere. At the time I had difficulty manifesting properly and tended to terrify anyone I wished to speak with. All those tabloid reports of people seeing my ghost . . . obviously, those stories are true. That was my investigation, and it's how I encountered Arthur for the first time. Once he had vowed to help me solve my murder, I gladly left it with him."

Clay heard in his tone how much Graves regretted leaving it to Conan Doyle for so many years, but he said nothing. Pointing out the obvious would help nothing.

A soft smile touched the corners of the ghost's mouth, and his eyes lit up.

"What?" Clay asked.

Graves waved a phantom hand as though to brush the question away, but the smile did not go away. He shook his head.

"Sometimes," the ghost said, "especially when I'm in the spirit world, I still hear that one song, the melody that the symphony was playing in the moment the bullet struck me.

"I like to think it's Gabriella, calling me home."

7

CONAN Doyle's house loomed above Louisburg
Square that afternoon. The day had dawned beautifully, but
by mid-afternoon the sky had darkened and now seemed to
threaten rain.

Julia Ferrick stood on the sidewalk in front of the old
brownstone and stared up at the imposing facade of the
house. Most days it seemed unassuming in spite of the obvious wealth of the neighborhood. That was the way its
owner wanted it. The last thing Arthur Conan Doyle
wanted to do was draw attention to himself.

Yet today the place exuded a strange air of desolation,
like an abandoned house or a mausoleum. Nothing stirred
behind the windows. Just looking at it, Julia got a sense of
emptiness from the brownstone. As she walked up the
steps and took out her keys, her certainty that no one was
at home only grew.

As did her worry for her son. If no one was here, not
even Squire or Dr. Graves, they were likely off doing
something dangerous. No matter how adept Danny had become in taking care of himself, no matter how tough he
was or thought he was, she remained his mother.

The key turned smoothly in the lock and the door, perhaps slightly off center, swung inward. Julia pocketed the keys.

In her entire life, she'd never imagined owning a key to the house of a man she wasn't sleeping with. But, then, how could she ever have conceived of the relationship she had developed with Mr. Doyle and his friends? Her son lived here, now, with others who could understand what he was going through.

As she entered and closed the door behind her, she felt like an intruder. No matter how welcome they claimed she was, Julia was an ordinary woman, and that made her an outsider in the house where her son now lived.

"Hello?" she ventured, stepping into the house.

The plastic bag in her hand crinkled as she shifted it from one hand to the other. It contained a copy of *Killbillies*, a new video game Danny had been talking about. She did not really approve of him playing such things, especially when he had seen enough horror with his own eyes to last an eternity. But her son had seemed tense and distant of late, and she wanted to surprise him with something that would put a smile on his face, even if just holding the hideous thing made her want to shudder.

Julia set her pocketbook on a small table beneath the mirror in the foyer and moved deeper into the house.

"Hello?" she called. "Anyone home?"

The house swallowed her voice without echo. Julia shivered and glanced around, wary of the shadows. She tried to tell herself how foolish she was being, like some little girl afraid of the thing in the closet or the monster under the bed. But in this house, there was no telling what lurked in the shadows. Being frightened wasn't childish, it was smart.

Still, she'd come to bring the game to Danny, and she would feel ridiculous if she left without giving it to him.

The stairs creaked underfoot, and the house shifted and popped with the usual noises of a structure as old as Conan Doyle's brownstone. Julia made her way up to the top floor and down the hall to Danny's room. She rapped on the closed door, not expecting an answer.

None came.

The plastic bag crackled in her hand as she tightened her grip. She turned the knob and pushed the door open, stepping inside.

The room stank of teenaged boy sweat and sulfur and another smell, equally unpleasant, that made her think of coffee grounds and meat just beginning to go bad. To call it a mess would have been far too complimentary. Julia winced as she crossed the threshold, forcing herself not to give in to the temptation to pick the place up.

Danny lived here, now. It wasn't her house, or her room. If this squalor was the way he wanted to live—pizza boxes on the floor, filthy clothes, pyramids of soda cans, towels that looked so dirty they might well stand up on their own—that was between her son and Mr. Doyle.

A noise escaped her with a shudder of disgust. No longer afraid, but wanting more than ever to leave the house, she went to Danny's bed and dropped the plastic bag with the video game onto the twisted sheets and spread.

Something caught her eye, and her mouth pursed in revulsion and concern. Dark stains dotted the sheet; blood and something else that she knew seeped from her son's flesh whenever his molting skin drove him to scratch too hard, pulling off the dry, scaly stuff before it would have fallen off on its own.

Julia tried very hard to focus on Danny as her son and not on the thing he was becoming. When she saw things like this, she could not escape the terrible thoughts that crossed her mind or the dread that touched her heart.

A sound came from outside the window. Julia flinched, pulse quickening, and turned to see a dark figure crouched like a gargoyle outside the glass, silhouetted by the stormy skies. The rain had begun to fall, and it spattered the glass.

She stared in horror at the thing, thinking that Doyle's house was under attack by monsters yet again. Only as she opened her mouth to scream did she realize that the creature that had frightened her so was her son.

Danny slid the window open and came inside, dropping to the floor in a crouch. Slick from the rain, his skin took on a cinnamon hue. He might have frowned as he looked up at her, but in the gloom, and him with no eyebrows, it was hard to tell. All she could see was the pinpoint red gleam in his eyes and the sharpness of his horns. She could not be certain, but it seemed to her that the horns had grown slightly, just in the past few days.

"Mom," he said, his tone curt. "What are you doing here?"

Julia could have simply told him about the game, tried to make small talk, been the mother she always tried to be with Danny. But the edge in his voice, in the way he held himself, troubled her.

"My son lives here. Do I need another reason?"

Danny rested a hand on the windowsill and looked out at the storm. His body was rigid, muscles taut, as though he were about to spring back through the open window, or scream . . . or as though he wanted nothing more than to run away, and keep running.

"What is it, Danny? What's happened?"

She expected him to snap at her, to cut her with the typical thoughtlessness of teenaged boys. Instead he took a deep breath and turned slowly to look at her again, and she saw that this was not the belligerence and sullenness natural to boys his age. Of course it wasn't. Julia made that mistake constantly, but only because she wished so desperately that her son were ordinary, that he was anything at all like other kids.

He wasn't being a wise guy. He was just shut down, distant, and hard, as though something had gotten under his skin and made him afraid, and he didn't want her to see his fear.

"Danny, what's—"

"Nothing," he said, more firmly this time. The red gleam in his eyes grew wider, and he glared at her. "Nothing is wrong, Mom. In fact, the last few days have been pretty fantastic. Look, it's . . . I'm glad you came by, but I can't stick around. Mister Doyle's got something he wants us all to help with."

Julia nodded. "I figured as much. The house is empty."

"Not really. Everyone's just busy. Gathering things to hunt the . . ."

His eyes flashed darkly, as if she'd caught him at something. Julia wasn't sure what it was.

"To hunt what?"

He sighed. "I know you worry, Mom. I'm fine. I will be fine."

"You don't seem—"

Her son snarled at her and leaped across the room. He grabbed her arm hard enough to hurt, and Julia cried out in shock and pain as he pulled her close to him. The brimstone stink of him was in her nose, and she stared into his eyes and for the first time she was not afraid *for* her son, but *of* him.

"I told you, it's nothing!" he snapped, and he released her.

Julia withdrew, rubbing her arm where he'd clutched her. Where he'd bruised her.

"I've got to go. The others will be waiting. We've got a demon to kill."

From the open door came the sound of a man clearing his throat. Danny and Julia both turned, and she felt a wave of relief wash over her as she saw Mr. Doyle standing in the hall outside the door. His expression was stern and unrelenting.

"Julia, are you all right?"

She stopped rubbing her arm, though it throbbed painfully. "Yes, of course. I'm . . . we're fine."

The irony of the hollow sound of her lying voice was not lost on her.

"Perhaps you are," Mr. Doyle said, studying Danny gravely. "And perhaps not. Regardless, it's clear to me that something is indeed troubling young Daniel. That makes my decision much simpler. I need someone to remain behind and keep watch over the house in case someone should use our absence to try to attack—"

"Oh, bullshit!" Danny snapped. "Don't you start, too!"

"Hey," Julia said. "You don't talk to—"

"I'll talk to anyone any way I want. You don't have a fucking clue what I'm going through, neither one of you. So why not stop trying to make out like you're all concerned and sympathetic? Just stop! This is bullshit. I'm fine. The rest of you are going out to hunt that thing down, and I should be there, too!"

"Danny, you know that in the past my enemies have drawn me away from this house as a prelude to attacking it. You've seen it with your own eyes. I assure you, this is hardly 'bullshit.' In fact, I'd hoped that you and your mother could stay together and keep an eye on things."

The way Danny glared at Mr. Doyle and took a menacing step toward him made even Julia back farther away.

"I'm not house-sitting. Can't you get Squire to do it?"

Mr. Doyle did not waver. Instead he lifted his chin, staring down at Danny over his long nose and mustache. When he spoke, his voice seemed to fill the entire room, though he did not shout, and his English accent, usually subdued because of the time he had spent living in the States, grew strong.

"Boy, if you're going to come at me, you'd better bring a friend, because I eat two for breakfast."

Danny faltered, blinking as though coming out of some trance and realizing what he had been doing.

"I'm sorry," he said, reaching up to drag his hand over the rough skin of his scalp, touching the tips of his horns as though to remind himself they were there. "It's been . . . not the best of weeks."

Julia crossed her arms and stared at him. Danny avoided her gaze.

"Apology accepted," Mr. Doyle said. "But you will stay here, Daniel. As for your suggestion that Squire remain behind, there is a great deal to be done, and I need operatives whom I can trust to do what they're told without question. For all of his grumbling, Squire is loyal. He has earned my trust over many, many years."

"So I'm not trustworthy, now?"

Mr. Doyle stared at him. "Watch over my home, Daniel. I am entrusting it to you."

Without waiting for a reply, the man nodded to Julia and turned on his heel. He strode away and mother and son stood together listening to the sound of his retreating footsteps.

When the house had fallen completely silent again save for the creaks of age, Julia took a step toward her son.

"I wish you'd talk to me, Danny. Normally I'd say if you didn't want to confide in me, you should talk to Dr. Graves. I know you two have gotten close. Is it . . . are you upset because he's gone off for a while?"

"Oh, please," Danny sighed, rolling his devil's eyes. "Don't project onto me. I'm not the one who misses him. You're the one in love with a fucking ghost. You're so wet for a dead guy it's disgusting."

Julia couldn't catch her breath. She stared at her son in horror, searching his eyes, trying to make some sense of his behavior.

She slapped him as hard as she could across the face. His skin felt tough as leather, and he barely flinched.

Danny snickered and walked past her.

"Where are you going?" Julia demanded. "Mister Doyle told you not to leave."

"You house-sit," he sneered without a backward glance. "I've got better things to do."

Then her son was gone, and Julia Ferrick was alone.

She sat on the edge of his bed, tugging at the sleeves of her blouse as though she might withdraw down inside of it and hide. Her face felt hot, and her eyes began to burn with tears. She did not bother trying to wipe them away.

My boy, she thought. *What's wrong with my boy?*

•   •   •

BAALPHEGOR stood in front of the Beacon Street townhouse, staring at the dark, brick building, awash in the preternatural emanations that drew him there.

Something wasn't right, and the demon held back, watching the building for signs of danger. This world could be a dangerous place for the likes of his kind, and he did not want to chance an encounter with one of the realm's protectors if it wasn't really necessary.

Finally deciding that there was no actual threat to him, Baalphegor approached the front entrance, taking the door-knob in his flesh-covered hand. The door was locked, but it was nothing to break the fragile mechanism that sought to prevent his entrance, and he pulled open the heavy, wooden door and stepped into the warmth of the foyer.

The demon closed his eyes, feeling out where he needed to go. What he sought was located somewhere in the upper levels of the structure, and he moved toward the stairs.

Baalphegor stopped short at the sound of a jangling chain. A canine came down the steps at a very quick clip, growling menacingly as it reached the bottom of the stairs.

"Daisy, no!" a human voice ordered from somewhere on the level above the lobby, as the dog's owner began his descent.

Baalphegor watched the animal slowly stalking toward him, its fleshy jowls pulled back to reveal sharp, pointed fangs. The beast was far more intuitive than the dominant species of the planet, knowing at once that he was not what he pretended to be.

That he was a danger.

The demon bared its own fangs, pulling back its mask of human skin so that the animal could see what exactly it was challenging. The dog was certainly intuitive, but far from intelligent, and sprang at him, its open maw aimed to tear out his throat.

Baalphegor caught the beast in his arms, just as its owner reached the bottom of the stairs. The rotund male with the receding hairline had arrived in time to see the demise of his beloved pet.

The dog had done what it had intended to do, ripping at his throat, but its bite had torn away only the fleshy costume that he wore, the demon's own skin beneath untouched. The animal thrashed in his grasp, a flapping swath of skin hanging from its bloody muzzle. Baalphegor lowered his mouth toward the struggling beast. The flesh mask on his face began to rip as his jaws unhinged, and he shoved the animal down his gullet.

The human let out the most pathetic of whimpers, falling back onto the staircase, clutching at his flabby chest.

Baalphegor continued to feed, drawing more and more of the animal inside him, its bones snapping and popping as they were crushed, until at last the dog ceased its useless struggle. The long, fluffy tail was the last thing to be consumed, disappearing down his throat as he stood in the hallway, feeling the fullness of the animal in his belly.

The demon turned his attention to the human lying prone on the stairs. The man was dying. Baalphegor had no doubt of that. The stink of a human body on the verge of death tickled his nostrils as he loomed over the man. He considered killing the thing, ending its suffering, but then thought better of it. He had far more important things to do with his time than performing acts of mercy on the local wildlife. Instead, he stepped over the man's body and began climbing the stairs.

At the top of the third flight, he felt it. For a moment he listened to the sound, inaudible to the human ear, and then moved down the corridor to an apartment door on the left. He knocked, noticing that the skin covering his hands had torn, revealing his own, scaled flesh beneath. This particular suit was proving to be far less durable than others he had worn in the past.

"Yes?" said a woman's voice from the other side of the door.

He could feel her watching him through the small hole

in the center of the door. Baalphegor placed his own eye
against the hole, attempting to look at her.

"I need you to open the door," he said.

"No, I'm not going to do that," the woman said, her
voice frantic. "I suggest you go away, or I'll call the police."

The demon stepped back, raised his foot, and kicked the
door open. It struck the woman, and she cried out as she
fell backward.

"No, I don't think so," he said as he entered the human
dwelling.

The woman screamed in terror and scrambled backward, rising to her feet and holding up her hands to defend
herself.

Baalphegor fixed her in his dark gaze.

"Silence," he commanded, and she did exactly as she
was told. "Close it," he ordered, pointing at the open door,
and she scuttled to the door, pushing it closed against the
broken frame.

She was terrified, staring at him with huge, fear-filled
eyes.

"Take anything you want," she told him, playing with a
golden chain that hung from her neck. "Please, just don't
hurt me—or my son."

Baalphegor strode closer, and the woman stumbled
back against the wall. He could feel her eyes upon him,
gawking at the areas of flesh on his disguise that had been
torn away.

"Your son," he said, still listening to the psychic emanations coming from somewhere within the domicile. "Take
me to him."

The woman shook her head frantically. "No, please,"
she begged. "He's suffered enough—please."

He was about to pluck out one of her eyes, when he was
interrupted by another woman entering the short hallway.

"Mrs. Hoskins, is everything all . . ."

The woman, dressed in white, locked eyes with him and
then immediately ran toward the phone on a nearby wall.
Baalphegor reacted instinctually, springing across the

room to land in front of her. She ran directly into his arms—the stink of her fear arousing his hunger again. He unhinged his jaws, engulfing her head and biting it away at the neck.

The headless body dropped to its knees, a geyser of blood erupting from the stump of the neck with such force that it covered the ceiling in a spray of red.

The older woman had started to scream again, he had to silence her once more with a steely look and a threatening wag of his finger. She then lost consciousness, sliding down the wall in a broken heap. For a moment he believed she had expired, but then he heard the sound of her breathing and knew that she had only fainted.

Softer than before, he heard the psychic cries from somewhere at the back of the dwelling and went in search of the source. In a room awash with sunlight, the demon found what he had been searching for. He stood in the doorway, staring at the large bed in the center of the room, and the small, curled figure lying upon it, hidden beneath a blanket.

"What is this?" he asked, stepping into the room, the sharp, antiseptic aroma permeating the space causing his senses to recoil. Equipment used for the care of the sick was positioned around the bed, and Baalphegor realized the unthinkable. He reached down and pulled the blanket away, wanting to see, yet dreading the revelation.

"What have they done to you?" he hissed, gazing down at the sight of a boy, his body pale, withered, and thin, curled into the fetal position. His eyes were open, staring off into nothingness, a thin trail of saliva leaking from his mouth down to the pillow beneath his head.

"He did it to himself," said a voice from behind him, and the demon spun around to see the woman standing in the doorway, her eyes fixed upon the figure lying on the bed. "An overdose—three years ago. He's been like this since."

"How . . . unfortunate," Baalphegor growled, and as the words left his mouth, the child slowly began to move, writhing upon the bed, as if aroused by the sound of his voice.

"He was always such a sad child," she said. "Different. But he never wanted for anything, my husband saw to that, God rest his soul."

The woman stumbled into the room, her movements stiff, erratic, there was the spark of madness in her eyes. His arrival, the revelation of his existence and what it meant for the world, often had that effect on humans.

"I know you, don't I?" she said blearily, pointing to him. "You don't look the same . . . but you were there, at the hospital, the night Charlie was born."

"Yes," Baalphegor answered. "But this is not your child." The demon reached down to the figure writhing upon the bed.

"What do you mean? Of course he's mine. His name is Charlie, I named him after my father." She stood at the foot of the bed and reached out to lovingly touch the boy's leg, swaying, eyes roving like a lunatic. The skin wetly sloughed from the leg, and she pulled back her hand in horror.

Baalphegor chuckled, amused by her fear.

"No," he said with a shake of his head. "He's mine."

The demon allowed the claws hidden away beneath the man-flesh to extend, protruding from the ends of his fingers. He reached down and ran the sharp nails over the boy's skin, ripping it, and peeling it away to reveal another skin beneath. "Most definitely mine."

The newly exposed skin was tough, leathery, like that of this world's great reptiles. It glistened wetly in the sunlight streaming in through the windows.

The woman screamed again and hugged herself. Her body seemed to fold in on itself, recoiling in disgust and terror from the thing she'd thought was her child.

"Your human babe was stolen away, replaced with this changeling modeled to look like your very own."

"You did this?" the woman asked, mesmerized by the

sight of the young man's new flesh. Again she began to sway, and to whimper.

"I did," Baalphegor replied. "And on many more occasions than just this." He took handfuls of the shedding flesh and threw it down upon the floor. "They were my children—receptacles for a power found only upon this misbegotten world."

The woman was crying now, standing powerless at the foot of the bed. "How is this possible? How could I not know?"

"Come now, woman," the demon berated. "Don't tell me that you didn't sense the child was different."

She nodded, tears streaming down her pathetic face. "Yes, but nothing like this, how could I possibly imagine something like this?"

Baalphegor growled, rolling the demon spawn onto its back. He reached down to his child's chest, the tip of his finger playing with a loosely hanging sack of flesh. It resembled an underdeveloped piece of fruit, withered upon the vine.

"It should be so much larger," Baalphegor said. "Swollen with the juices of humanity." He pinched his claws at the skin where the sack connected to the body, ripping it away.

"What . . . what is it?" the woman asked with a mixture of curiosity and revulsion.

"It is power," the demon said, dangling the small sack from his fingers by its stem of skin. And then he opened his mouth, dropped the growth into his maw, and began to chew.

The experience was immediate, a flow of memories rushing through the demon's body. Baalphegor saw it all, and from what he witnessed he acquired a strength totally foreign to one of his kind. Through the boy's collected humanity, the demon now knew the ways of the human animal as if he'd been born to it, and from this knowledge, came power.

Baalphegor knew his child's life as if he had lived it

himself, but he was suddenly enraged by what he knew. As the euphoric sense of strength passed, the demon turned his attention and rage upon the woman.

"You knew that he was different—that his body was changing," he snarled, advancing toward her.

She backed away, shaking her head from side to side.

"And you were just as afraid as he—you encouraged him to take matters into his own hands."

The woman spun around, running toward the door to escape his wrath.

Baalphegor extended his hand. Power coursed through his veins, and the door slammed, refusing to open as the woman frantically tugged on it.

"You knew he would attempt to kill himself."

The woman leaned back against the door, terror etched upon her aged features. "He was as afraid as I was," she screamed in defense. "He was afraid that he was turning into something horrible—something evil."

"He was becoming something beautiful," the demon growled, again wielding his newfound power, lifting the woman up from the floor to hang in the air. Baalphegor watched as she struggled in his grip.

"He . . . he decided to do it on his own," she screamed.

"You provided him with the pills," Baalphegor spat, sickened by the sight of this foul creature. And before he was tortured by the sound of her voice again, he manipulated the magics that held her fast, sending her body rocketing across the room and through the large, plate-glass window, to plummet to the street below.

He heard the sounds of a wet impact and screeching brakes as the woman's body landed in the middle of Beacon Street.

It was a death too good for her, the demon thought, standing over the atrophied body of one of his children. The child continued to twitch and writhe, as if knowing that his sire had returned for him. But this was no longer his spawn; it was nothing more than a shell of what could have been.

Ballphegor reached down, taking the child's face in his hands, wrenching the head savagely to one side. Bone snapped.

A small mercy for us both.

The demon then raised his hand, passing it over the dead body, calling forth a cleansing fire to consume the changeling's remains.

A horde of fat black insects, big as cockroaches, scuttled along the alley behind the Charles Playhouse. Conan Doyle watched expectantly as others crawled down the rear wall of the theater and emerged from the dumpster there. An urge centered in the middle of his chest tugged him forward, and he took a step after the ticks.

"Arthur," Ceridwen said, reaching out for him.

They linked hands, and instantly a dark, summoning magic crackled around their fingers, the residue of the spell they had cast. It would remain until the ticks had been banished back to the pocket, shadow world from which they'd been summoned, or until they'd been destroyed. The hair on his arms stood up as a frisson of static electricity passed over both him and Ceridwen. At night, the magic that pulsed around their hands and created a dark aura around them both appeared black, but Conan Doyle knew it was the same dark cherry as the ticks themselves.

He had summoned the Malachi ticks once before. That time, many years past, he had found the monster he'd sought, but paid the price.

Eve and Squire followed a few feet behind, the vampiress completely silent. The hobgoblin might have been if not for the crinkling of the open bag of potato chips he carried with him. Conan Doyle sighed at the sound, but said nothing. The noise was annoying, but it would not keep them from accomplishing their task.

"Tell me how this is supposed to work again?" Eve asked tartly. Patience had never been her strong suit.

Ironic, really. He would have thought an immortal would learn that, if nothing else.

"The Malachi ticks—"

"They're getting fatter," Squire said, around a crunching mouthful of chips. "That's pretty gross."

Eve laughed. "Listen to you. What a candy ass. I'm going to call you Little Mary Sunshine from now on. Oooh, that's gross!"

"Ah, screw."

"Mary."

"Twat."

Conan Doyle winced. "Would you two please stop?"

Eve and Squire both snickered.

"Yes, Dad," the vampire said.

"Seriously, boss," Squire went on, "what is up with those things? They really are disgusting. I know you sort of explained this already, but I confess I wasn't exactly paying attention."

At Conan Doyle's side, he heard Ceridwen laugh softly. He glanced sidelong at her. The cherry red aura that pulsed around them both gave a scarlet cast to her eyes, but amusement danced within them.

"Very funny," he whispered.

"He's charming," said the faerie sorceress.

What frightened Conan Doyle was that he thought Ceridwen was serious. As grave as her demeanor could be at times, Squire's coarse humor provided her with a welcome diversion.

"Let me try to put it as simply as I can," Conan Doyle began.

"That's wise," Eve muttered.

"We summoned the Malachi ticks at the subway station, where the demon murdered those two men," Conan Doyle said quickly, before Squire could muster a retort. "Like bloodhounds, they can follow its scent. More than that, they track the magical residue it leaves behind, absorbing it along the way."

Ceridwen glanced back at Eve and Squire, her pale,

blue-tinged features almost luminous in the dark. She was far too elegant and ethereal for these surroundings . . . for this world. But she'd chosen to be here with him, and he was grateful.

"That is why, Squire, the ticks are growing fat, as you so deftly phrased it."

"Hear that, Countess Chocula?" Squire muttered to Eve. "I've got a way with words."

"Mary."

Squire punched her arm. "Quit it."

Eve shoved him with such preternatural force that Squire crashed into the wall behind the theater, fell over some trash cans, and sprawled on the ground in a clatter of metal and garbage.

"Lovely." Conan Doyle sighed.

Ceridwen held his hand more tightly to calm him. No one else could have managed it, but her mere presence was enough to soothe him. They followed the Malachi ticks out of the alley and across a parking lot. What a strange sight they must have been. Yet Conan Doyle did not worry about drawing attention in the theater district. There was never any shortage of odd sights in this part of the city. And ordinary humans could not see the ticks, so there was no danger of people running off, screaming in terror at the sight of them.

The hundreds of scuttling black things had begun their existence looking much like scarabs or roaches. Now their backs had swollen to several times their normal size, filling with the stink of magic, like leeches filled with blood.

The trail led across the street and down a narrow side road, only wide enough for a single car. Raucous laughter came from an Irish bar. They received stares from the attendant at another parking lot, a tiny patch of pavement whose owner must have made a lot of money from the theater crowd. The parade of ticks turned down another alley between two apartment buildings. Rats screeched and rustled in the garbage along the alley but did not show themselves.

They feared the ticks.

"Do you smell that?" Eve asked.

Conan Doyle frowned and sniffed at the air. He turned and cast her an inquisitive glance.

"You don't? How can you not? The stink of blood and brimstone. Arthur, you must smell it. It's . . . disgusting."

Eve wrinkled her nose.

"Now who's a girl?" Squire murmured.

"I am a girl, dumb ass." She hissed, baring her fangs.

"It's been all of creation since you were a girl."

Conan Doyle sniffed the air again. He paused to glance at Ceridwen. She only shrugged. Then Conan Doyle felt once more the magical tug of the summoning spell they'd used to call up the Malachi ticks. He and Ceridwen started forward again. They had to follow the ticks, no matter where they went.

Then one of them popped.

The tick burst with a wet noise and sprayed something pink and pasty across the paved alley.

"Ah, hell, *now* I smell it!" Squire said, pinching his nose and backing away as though a skunk had sprayed him. He tossed aside his bag of chips, abandoning them in his quest to keep from vomiting.

"What is that stench?" Eve asked, joining Squire against the alley wall.

Before Conan Doyle could reply a second tick burst, and then another and another in quick succession. The ticks were rupturing and popping. He stared at them in disgust, until Ceridwen yanked him backward, away from them.

"Don't get too close," she said. "There is no telling how you would be affected by demonic energy that's been concentrated like that."

"Oh, this is just so nasty," Squire said, his voice a nasal whine because he continued to pinch his nose. "Bad enough we've got ticks, but ticks exploding with demon spunk . . . that's just wrong."

Conan Doyle bristled and would have shouted at Squire

or at least admonished him, except that the hobgoblin was right. The stench of the accumulated demon residue when the ticks exploded made his stomach roil and bile burn up the back of his throat. It took all of his self-control not to bend over and vomit there in the alley.

"Come, Arthur," Ceridwen said.

Quickly, she led him back the way they had come. He felt the tugging of their summoning spell pulling him toward the ticks but forced himself to go away from them. Squire and Eve hurried along ahead of them. They reached the small parking lot across from the Irish bar. The attendant stared at them harder than ever. Eve glared at him, and for a moment Conan Doyle thought she might do something rash.

Then Ceridwen stood up to her full height, and a blue-white light seeped from her eyes, pluming into the air like smoke. The attendant gaped.

"Do you want to keep those eyes?" the Fey princess asked. She spoke softly, but her voice carried like the breeze across to the man.

The attendant went to hide inside his tiny booth, back to them. He did not so much as glance in their direction again.

"So much for the exploding ticks, huh?" Squire asked.

Eve slid her hands into the pockets of her long, leather coat. "Are they all destroyed, do you think?"

Conan Doyle studied her. Of the four of them, she might have been the most out of place here. Squire and Ceridwen and Conan Doyle himself were eccentric in appearance, but with her long, lush hair and her makeup so perfect, and dressed in clothes that cost a small fortune, she might have been a model who had just stepped out of a fashion shoot.

The vampiress was a study in contrasts. But he supposed eternal life could do that to a person.

"Yes," he said. "Or they will be momentarily. Even if we attempted to find those that are still following the demon's trail, they'll burst before we ever reach him."

"Guess we need a new plan, huh?" Squire said. Dejected, he sat on the curb and put his chin in his hands. "Wish I hadn't left those chips back there. I'm sure they're totally skunked."

Ceridwen linked arms with Conan Doyle. They seemed always to be touching now, and he relished it. It was as though he could not survive without the little touches, the constant contact.

"I'm not sure it's a total loss," the sorceress said. "Eve, you've got the scent now, correct?"

"Yeah," she said, and Conan Doyle noticed her attention had wandered. Eve turned and glanced back the direction they'd come. "I might be able to follow it. Worth a try, anyway." She turned toward them again. "But, listen, did any of you think the scent was—"

"Familiar?" Squire asked, looking up intently from the curb.

Eve nodded.

"Yeah," Squire agreed.

"Familiar in what way?" Conan Doyle asked.

"I'm not sure. Just . . . familiar," Eve replied. She glanced at Squire.

"Can't quite place it," the hobgoblin added. "Let me chew on it a bit."

Conan Doyle felt a chill race up his back and his skin prickled. At the edge of his awareness, he sensed something. He started to turn toward Ceridwen to see if she had felt it, too, but then he noticed her attention had already been diverted upward.

"Doyle, what is it?" Eve asked.

Up on the roof of the building beside them, a figure crouched, staring down at them. Eve and Squire began to react as though prepared for a fight, but Ceridwen shot them a withering glance and held up a hand to forestall any rash action.

A chill, unnatural breeze swept along the street and up the side of the building, rasping against the brick. The figure there rose and let the breeze snatch her from the edge of the roof, and she glided gently down to the street sixty feet below.

She alighted only feet from Ceridwen, a young woman of astonishing, delicate beauty, ruined by the filth of this world. Dark circles limned her eyes, and her black hair was wild and unkempt, and streaked with spun gold. Streaks of mascara ran down from the corners of her eyes as though she'd been crying, but Conan Doyle felt certain it had been painted on that way for effect.

Clad in baggy black pants with too many pockets and a belly-baring pink camisole frayed around the edges, she sported multiple piercings in each ear, her nose, her lip and brow, and her navel. Conan Doyle imagined there were others but tried not to think too much about them.

By any measure, she was the filthiest, rattiest fairy girl he'd ever seen. She looked more like an underage junky whore than one of the Fey. And she met them each, eye to eye, one at a time, with such an insouciant pout that he thought she needed a year with a stern governess even more than she needed a coat.

"Evening," the city fairy said, and she glanced playfully at Squire, then turned to examine Eve with a lustful glimmer in her eye. "My, aren't you yummy?"

Squire laughed and shook his head.

"Sorry, sweetie. You're not my type."

"Your loss," the filthy Fey girl replied, still the coquette.

Ceridwen stared at her in fury. She raised a hand, black fire crackling around her fingers.

Conan Doyle blinked. "Wait! Ceri, no!"

She stared at him. They all did. He hesitated. The fairy girl had not attacked them. Did none of them realize—Ceridwen, at least—that the girl must have some purpose for approaching them?

He turned on the filthy thing. When she moved, shifting her weight suggestively from one hip to the other, a low musical trill accompanied her, and the air around her seemed to shimmer. Filthy she might be, as urban as fairies ever became, but she still had the magic of the otherworld in her.

"Kneel!" Conan Doyle snapped, pointing at her.

The girl glanced at Eve. "See, babe. He knows how to treat a girl."

Eve smiled, and it seemed perhaps she was not immune to the fairy's questionable charms. "Maybe I could learn. But not tonight."

The city fairy shrugged. She turned to Conan Doyle. "Fuck off, old man. I don't kneel. Not for anyone. And if you unzip, I'll just bite it off."

Conan Doyle's nostrils flared in disgust. He took a step toward her. "You stand before Ceridwen, princess of the Fey, niece of King Finvarra. You will kneel if you wish to address her."

The fairy girl shook back her hair, the gold streaks glittering like stardust, and from seemingly nowhere she produced a package of cigarettes and a lighter. Slowly, she tapped out a butt and put it between her lips, then lit it, drawing smoke in. The tip burned to embers in the night. The pack and lighter were gone as mysteriously as they had appeared, and only the burning cigarette remained.

She took a deep drag, then let the smoke plume from her nostrils. At last, she looked at Ceridwen. Slowly, with obvious ceremony, she closed her eyes and bowed her head.

"I have no allegiance, Princess. But there's weird shit going down in all the realms, these days. I don't fuckin' . . . I don't kneel."

She raised her head and stared at Ceridwen with purple eyes.

"This is a hard world the humans have made. You learn never to turn your back, never to give anyone the upper hand. You have my respect. That will have to be enough."

Conan Doyle held his breath. He glanced at Eve and Squire, amazed that for once they knew when to keep their mouths shut. He could see the vampire tensing, ready to lunge, to tear the fairy girl apart if the need arose.

"Your name?" Ceridwen said, her tone clipped.

"Tess. That's what I'm called, at least."

Slowly, Ceridwen nodded. "All right, Tess. We are well met, for now. Should the time arise that you are forced to proclaim allegiance, we may remember this night, the two of us. Now, then, what business do you have with us."

"A favor."

Squire grunted. "Right," he muttered. "She's gonna do you a favor after all that?"

Tess laughed, a light, musical sound, and winked at Eve as though the rest of them didn't exist.

"Actually, I'm here to do all of you a favor. Conan Doyle and his Menagerie. Yes, I know who you are. All the seelie and unseelie in the city know. How could we not?

"There's trouble on Beacon Street, this very moment. You've wasted long minutes being pompous and difficult. Something from another realm, not Faerie and not this world, something of dark magicks, something *demon* . . . has taken lives there just in these last few minutes. Whispers travel the street. I'd heard you were hunting. Thought you might like to know."

"Where on Beacon Street?" Conan Doyle asked.

Tess shrugged. "Just follow the screams."

Another breeze blew up, and she lifted her arms as it carried her away, along the street and up over the roof of the Irish bar. If the parking lot attendant noticed, he didn't say a word.

8

WITH a wave of his hand, Conan Doyle wished them all unseen.

Beacon Street remained tied in a knot, the traffic backup affecting all of downtown Boston. *I would surely detest being a commuter this evening,* Conan Doyle thought, walking with his entourage toward the scene of the crime.

"Stay in my general vicinity," he instructed, "the spell loses its potency the farther you wander away from me."

They approached the building, observing a sports utility vehicle, its rooftop obviously crushed by something falling on it, being hoisted up onto the back of a tow truck.

"I bet whatever did that," Squire said pointing to the vehicle, "came from there." He craned his neck to look up at the shattered third story window.

"Man, can't pull the wool over your eyes, can they?" Eve said, walking away from them toward a coroner's van parked on the other side of the street.

"You need to stay with . . ." Conan Doyle began, but realized his pleas were falling upon deaf ears. Instead, they all followed the vampiress.

"Do you smell it?" she asked, hopping up into the back

of the vehicle, crouching slightly as she unzipped the body bag to take a look at the contents. "I'd say this was our sky-diver."

Ceridwen brought a delicate hand to her face. "The remains stink of demonic magicks," she said.

"Bingo." Eve wrinkled her nose in distaste.

Conan Doyle climbed into the back of the van with Eve, examining the body. "It was certainly the fall that resulted in this unfortunate woman's death," he observed. "But it was dark magic that took her there."

"I say we check out the dead broad's digs, before any evidence is removed," the hobgoblin said, hiking up his pants and adjusting the rim of his baseball cap.

"An excellent idea, Squire," Conan Doyle said, stepping from the van.

"And they said watching reruns of *CSI* was a waste of time," Squire muttered as they returned to the apartment building across the street.

Detectives and uniformed police officers were still milling about as they entered the building, went up the stairs, and into the apartment. A crime scene photographer was taking pictures of a headless corpse lying upon the kitchen floor.

"Wonder where the head is?" Squire mused aloud, bending down to look under the kitchen table and chairs as Doyle studied the spray of blood on the ceiling above them.

Ceridwen stood by a withered houseplant in the corner of the living room, her hands gently caressing the yellowed leaves back to full vigor. "There was a demon here," she said. "The proximity to the foul beast nearly killed her."

Conan Doyle squatted down on his haunches, examining an identification tag hanging from the belt loop of the corpse's trousers. "LeeAnne Fogg," he read. "She was a registered nurse." He rose, his knees popping uncomfortably. The wear and tear of the passing years was sneaking up on him yet again, and he made a mental note to partake of some of Faerie's recuperative elixirs once things had calmed a bit.

"Hey!" Eve called, motioning for them to follow her.

The police officers in the room moved from their path, gently pushed aside by the Conan Doyle's sorcery, still unaware of their presence. He, Squire, and Ceridwen followed Eve down a short corridor and into a room now frigid with cold from the broken window. Conan Doyle noticed that a blanket had been placed over the open window, likely to protect any physical evidence from being blown away. Two lab techs finished up whatever it was they were doing, the sudden desire to leave incited by Conan Doyle's spell.

"Here's the point of departure," Eve said standing in front of the billowing blanket, but Conan Doyle's gaze was fixed upon the large bed positioned in the center of the room. Piles of ash lay on the sheets in the shape of a human body, the bedclothes untouched, though it had taken incredible heat to immolate the victim.

"So what do you think?" Squire asked, eating from a bag of corn chips. "Spontaneous human combustion, or what?"

Conan Doyle shook his head as he reached out, allowing his fingertips to sink into the ashen remains. Closing his eyes, he concentrated, reading the traces of dark magicks left behind.

"I'd like a sample of this," he said, turning to Ceridwen.

"Wait," Squire said, shaking out the last of the corn chips from the bag and dropping them into his mouth. "You can put them in here," he explained, wiping his greasy fingers on the front of his clothes.

"Where'd you get those?" Eve asked.

"I found 'em in the kitchen—got a problem with that?" he asked defensively.

"Scavenger," she snarled.

Squire brandished his stubby middle finger then turned to offer Conan Doyle the corn chip bag.

He politely refused, again turning to Ceridwen. "If you would be so kind, my dear."

The elemental sorceress waved her hand, her movements like the first gestures of a graceful dance. A bubble of air solidified in the path of her hand, and she directed it down to the burned remains where it engulfed a few ounces of the ash, lifting it into the air to float before his face.

"Thank you, love," he said, taking the solidified bubble and placing it in his jacket pocket.

"So what's your handle on this, boss?" Squire asked. "From what I seen here, this ain't your run-of-the-mill demonic manifestation. This prick's got balls—big ones."

Eve strolled around the room, her predator's eye looking for anything that could be of use. "We were talking before about rules. There are rules against demons this powerful being able to cross over."

"You're correct," Conan Doyle said. "The dimensions are not meant to be porous."

Ceridwen wrapped her arms about herself as if cold, but Conan Doyle understood it was much more than that.

"The fabric of things seems to be unraveling since the Nimble Man and the release of Sanguedolce," the Fey sorceress said. "Perhaps the demons have begun to think that the human world doesn't have its protectors any longer."

"A disturbing thought," Conan Doyle said as he moved toward the door. "If you're correct, then we will have to remind the denizens of the dark realms that protectors still exist. And I suggest we use our current demonic invader as an example."

"I like the way you think, boss," Squire said. "Time to open up a big ol' can of whupass. 'Course, I'll mostly just be opening the can. I prefer to let the rest of you do the whupassing . . . ass-whupping. Whatever."

"Candy ass," Eve said. "What a coward."

Squire grinned. "I'm a delicate flower."

Ceridwen furrowed her brow, her perfect, cold beauty almost alien in the shadowed hallway. "Squire, I will never claim to understand you. I have seen you in combat. You can be quite formidable when you choose."

The hobgoblin shrugged. "What can I say? I'm a lover, not a fighter. I'd much rather watch Eve getting all dirty and bloody, fighting in clingy outfits, than do it myself. If I could do that, and have beer and pizza at the same time . . . that'd be Heaven."

Conan Doyle sighed and tuned them out, unable to listen even a moment longer. He knew that when circumstances turned dire, there were no better allies in the world, no greater hope for humanity than his Menagerie. But sometimes that idea frightened him.

They descended the stairs to the lobby, exiting the building in the November cold.

"What now?" Eve asked, pulling the collar of her stylish cranberry colored leather jacket up against her neck.

Conan Doyle removed his gloves from his coat pocket and slipped them over his hands. "Ceridwen and I will return home to further analyze this sample of remains. Something tells me there is more to be learned here."

"And us?" Squire asked, his eyes shifting toward Eve standing beside him.

"You two will find its scent," he said, placing his arm around Ceridwen's waist and directing her toward Charles Street. "And hunt it down."

"Is that all?" Squire asked sarcastically.

Conan Doyle thought for a moment. "Teach it a lesson," he said, walking away. "Show it that humanity is far from being unprotected."

WHERE the hell are they going now? Danny wondered. He was perched on the rooftop, watching his friends go their separate ways. They were supposedly checking out some scene of potential demonic activity, and if that wasn't something that could take his mind off his troubles, nothing would.

He considered leaping across to the building, checking

out things on his own, but thought better of it. All he'd need is some cop to see him, and then the shit would really hit the fan. All he needed was to give Conan Doyle another reason to be pissed at him.

He slumped down to the roof, closing his eyes, letting the cold night air wash over him. He was thinking about his mom, the look on her face after he'd grabbed her.

Did I really want to hurt her? he wondered, a twinge of fear causing the strange growth on his chest to tingle. He scratched at himself. He'd just been angry. He could never really hurt his mother.

Or could he?

For a brief instant, he imagined his teeth sinking into the flesh of her throat, her warm, salty blood exploding into his eagerly waiting mouth.

"Shit!" Danny said aloud, scrambling to his feet. He wanted to scrub his brain of the imagery. *What the fuck is wrong with me?*

He decided to return to Louisburg Square and take whatever penance Mr. Doyle could dish out. Then he would tell the man what had been happening, and how much it scared him.

But another image flashed through his mind. He saw himself chained in the basement of the Beacon Hill home, a dirty mattress on the floor, a metal pan of water nearby.

That irrational rage surged up inside him.

Nobody's going to lock me up like a dog, he thought, baring his fangs in a snarl. *I'd just like to see them try.*

"Such anger," said a voice from the shadows, and Danny spun toward it, ready for anything. He hoped for a fight—he was itching to spill some blood.

The guy who emerged from the shadows was big, and he stank of rancid meat, but he wasn't the kind of threat Danny was hoping for. He immediately pulled back on his rage.

"Don't do that on my account," the man said extending his hand. His fingertips were bloody, squared off, missing. "I was nearly two blocks away when I sensed you."

The guy was smiling now, and Danny noticed the rips in the flesh of his jowly face. For a moment, he could have sworn he saw another kind of skin beneath it. Maybe he'd been wrong; maybe this was exactly the kind of situation he was looking for.

"So you sensed me, huh?" Danny said.

The guy moved strangely, as if he weren't comfortable in his own skin, and his eyes were crazy, too, a milky yellow that reminded Danny of pus.

They look kind of like mine.

"I can't believe how fortuitous this is," the big man said. "It saves me from having to find you."

Danny chuckled, a throaty growl coming from somewhere in the vicinity of his toes. "Well, you've found me. Now what are you going to do?"

The man tilted his round head to one side, studying him. "Arrogance as well as anger," he observed. He smiled again, and this time Danny could see that the skin around his mouth was torn, as if he'd opened his mouth too wide.

"You are indeed your father's son."

Danny was taken aback. "What do you mean by—"

The man moved faster than a guy that size had any right to move. He lunged and slapped him across the face with such force that Danny went down hard, the taste of his own blood filling his mouth. He liked the taste; it made him angry. Springing to his feet, he bared his fangs.

"Come," the stranger said, motioning to him with his squared off fingers. "Show me your potential."

Danny charged, swinging his fist as hard as he could. He relished the feel of his hand connecting, the texture of flesh tearing on the roughness of his knuckles. He punched the man again, and then a third time.

The man stumbled back, but didn't go down. He was bent over, covering his face, and Danny could see tatters of flesh hanging from between his fingers.

"So, do I have potential, or what?" he asked, running his rough, pointed tongue over his stained knuckles. Feeling like the badass he knew he was.

"Oh yes," the man replied. "There's potential indeed. It appears that this world agrees with you."

The man righted himself, and Danny gasped.

His face was practically gone, torn away to reveal a reptilian visage behind the mask of human flesh. Dropping down on all fours, his limbs bending in ways impossible to the human anatomy, the man—the thing—came at him across the rooftop. Danny stepped back as the creature sprang to its feet in front of him, bones popping obscenely as they reconfigured to reflect the armature of a biped.

The beast attacked, pummeling him again and again.

Danny wanted to fight back, to release the bestial anger and frustration that had been building inside him for weeks, but shock stayed his hand, and all he could do was take the beating—blow after savage blow that drove him back across the rooftop. Finally he felt the backs of his legs hit the ledge, and then he was falling backward.

Panic spiked through him, but then he felt a vicelike grip lock onto the front of his sweatshirt, and the relentless beast hauled him up and tossed him back onto the roof. Danny struggled to shake off the weird numbness he was feeling throughout his body, tried to ignore the trickling blood that ran freely from his injured face to stain the ground before him.

"You show me respect by not striking back," the monster said, the suit of flesh he wore hanging from his hands and face in tatters.

"Believe me, I would if I could," Danny said, spitting the taste of blood from his mouth.

The monster smiled. "Deep down, you know," it growled, "your true self knows my identity."

Danny scowled. "Let me guess," he scoffed, "you're my father."

And the monster nodded. "Yes," it hissed, reaching up with its clawed hands to pull away the flesh that hid its true visage.

"No fucking way," Danny shrieked watching as the monstrosity revealed itself. "It was a fucking joke!

Y'know, the whole Darth Vader thing . . . Jesus is this fucking bad!"

"Your heritage is no joking matter," the demon said, sloughing off its skin and standing there in all its horrific glory. It was much taller than it had appeared within the man-flesh.

Danny felt it deep inside. He didn't want to believe that something this awful could have anything to do with him, but he knew it was true—he felt it in every fiber of his changing being. This *thing* was somehow part of him.

This demon.

The words left his mouth before he even had chance to stop them. "What . . . what do you want?"

The demon glided toward him. He'd never seen any living thing move in such a way. Freaky as it was, it was also strangely cool.

"I've come for you," it said, reaching out one of its long, skeletal hands to touch his chest. "To take you away from here."

Danny felt the fleshy growth beneath his clothing begin to throb painfully.

"Your true nature is screaming to emerge," it said. "Eager to escape the restricting confines of humanity." The demon looked around, peering out over the city of Boston. "And it is good that you leave here while you still can, for soon this will be nothing more than rubble and death."

"What are you talking about?" Danny said, shaking his head in confusion.

"The reverberations are felt across the world . . . across all dimensions. The Demogorgon approaches. I came back to the human world because I knew if I did not come now, soon there might have been no world left for me to visit. I came back . . . for you."

The demon held out his hand. "Will you come with me?"

The monster that he was becoming chattered inside with glee, anxious to be part of something bigger, but Danny shook his head. He'd heard about this thing before, the Demogorgon. Conan Doyle and the others were practically obsessed with it. This thing—the demon—talking about it made him understand for the first time what it really meant.

This wasn't just another monster for them to thrash. The whole world really was in jeopardy. His mother would die. The world . . . He shook his head again. Julia Ferrick had raised him as her son. No matter what he looked like, no matter what instincts he might have, under the skin he was still Danny Ferrick. She'd given him humanity, and it was still strong inside of him.

"I'm not like you," he said, knowing there was only partial truth to his words.

The demon smiled again, a Cheshire cat grin that chilled him to the very bone. "But you will be," it said, reaching out to lovingly stroke his face.

"You will be."

" YOU getting anything?" Squire asked.

Eve scowled at the hobgoblin, as the two of them walked down Newbury Street, on the hunt. "You just asked me that a minute ago."

"And?"

She tilted her head back slightly, sniffing the cold, prewinter air. The November night was crisp. The glow of headlights washed over them, but she ignored them, searching for that scent. "When I get something you'll be the first to know."

Squire grumbled, shoving his hands deep into the pockets of his leather jacket. "It ain't right," he said, waiting for her to respond.

Eve sighed. "What isn't right, Squire?"

"Funny you should ask," he responded. "Don't you feel it? Something ain't right—it's all out of whack."

She hated to admit it, but the little prick was right. There was definitely something not quite right of late. The air was filled with smells that didn't belong—aromas that weren't there before the nasty business with Sanguedolce, and the Nimble Man. Nasty things carried on the winds of change.

"I think the son of a bitch has figured out how to mask his scent or something." Squire stopped to buy a pretzel from a vendor near Newbury Comics.

He offered Eve a bite.

She shook her head. "No thanks," she said, looking around, feeling a certain sense of futility to being out there tonight. "Y'know, I'll hate myself for saying this, but I think you're right."

The goblin feigned surprise, pretending to choke on his pretzel. "What was that I heard?"

"Oh knock it off, you asshole. You heard me."

"Yeah, and it was music to my ears," he said, enjoying the moment immensely.

They moved off of Newbury onto Massachusetts Avenue, walking across a section of sidewalk that passed over the turnpike.

"It's no good," she said. "The signals I'm getting are all wrong."

"I told ya, it's fucked up," Squire said, finished with his snack, and licking his fingers clean of salt. "I bet it's got something to do with that skinned body I saw," he said, stroking his chin.

"Go on," she said, turning onto Boylston Street.

"Well," he started. "One of the bodies was partially eaten, but the other one was skinned. Why would he chew on one, but not the other, unless he didn't want to damage it? The skin's missing. What if it's not a trophy?"

Eve paused and regarded him. "You think he's wearing it?"

Squire tapped a finger to his temple. "That's the thought that I have. I'll bet he's using it to mask his nasty demon funk."

"I've heard weirder theories," she said, waiting for traffic to thin before she started across the street toward the Hynes Convention Center.

A car beeped at them, and the two turned in unison to flip off the driver. They got to the other side and headed up the side street toward the Sheraton Hotel.

"What we need, no offense, is something with a more discerning sniffer," the hobgoblin said, tapping the side of his bulbous nose.

"Who do you have in mind?"

He smiled the nasty grin that always made her want to slap him, then abruptly shot across the street toward a parking garage that had once been attached to one of the city's better movie theaters, now turned barroom.

"Y'know, I've kind of had my fill of parking garages lately," Eve called after him.

"I need some shadow," Squire hollered over his shoulder.

As she caught up to him, the hobgoblin cast a sidelong glance at her, smiling broadly. "You ever get one of those ideas where it just hits you over the fuckin' head, and you realize you're a genius?"

"Every day," she drawled. "Why don't you tell me what your bright idea is and let me be the judge of your genius."

A bright spotlight inside the parking garage created a deep patch of shadow next to a trash barrel with a bright orange top. "Give me a few," he said, disappearing into the darkness just like he'd dive into a deep pool of water.

No matter how many times she'd seen him do it, she was still impressed with what an amazing talent it was. Near invulnerability, superhuman strength, and animal-like reflexes were one thing, but the ability to travel using shadows? That was just too cool for words. Of course, she'd never share that with him, the miserable piece of crap that he was. That would be the day when she ever admitted to being envious of Squire.

Leaning back against a nearby wall she turned her attention to the pool of shadow, attempting to peer inside its seemingly impenetrable depths, searching for any sign of the hobgoblin. She glanced at her watch, becoming antsy. She hated to stand around doing nothing. Conan Doyle was depending on them to come up with something, and even if they didn't she at least wanted to be able to explain to the arch mage that they'd tried everything that they could.

"C'mon asshole," she muttered, pushing off the wall and moving closer to hobgoblin's entrance to the shadow path. She focused on the darkness. "Hey," she yelled at it, hoping that wherever he was, he could hear her. "We don't have all night, let's go."

Nothing.

She was seriously considering heading next door to the bar, when she heard something. Eve turned back to the shadow beside the trash barrel.

"Is that you?" she asked, leaning toward the pool of inky black. "If it's not, I'm taking off to get a drink, and you can just—"

The beast exploded out of the darkness, pinning her to the ground with its mass. Its skin was as black as the shadows from which it sprang, powerful muscles rippling beneath. She hurled its growling bulk off her, springing to her feet as the nails on her hands morphed to talons.

"Let's go, fucker," she said, studying the creature, not sure she'd ever seen anything quite like it before.

It eyed her from where it had landed, its beady, red eyes shining from within deep pools of shadows that made up its large, blocky head. It whined pathetically, tilting its head to one side; then sniffing the air in her general direction.

"That's it, Fido," she sneered. "Get a good whiff of the bitch that's gonna hand you your balls."

It emitted a strange, garbled sound like it was barking under water. But it did not advance. Instead, it backed up and barked at her again.

Eve hissed, flexing the claws on her elongated hands, preparing to strike.

"What are you doing?" Squire asked, his head and body emerging from the shadows. He was holding a chain and spiked collar in his hand.

Eve stared at him, gaze shifting from the hobgoblin to the slavering shadow beast and back. "This is what we're going to use to track our demon?"

Squire patted the front of his leg, and the large beast galloped over to him, its curled tail tucked between its legs, its strangely shaped ears hanging lower on its large head.

"What did ya do to him?" Squire asked, patting the beast.

"He attacked me," Eve tried to explain.

"Shuck just got a little excited when I told him he was goin' for a walk," Squire explained. "Got away from me before I could put his leash on."

"Shuck?"

"It's his name, and his species." The hobgoblin made baby noises toward the animal, allowing it to lick his face with a tongue that resembled a giant leech engorged with blood. "He's a Black Shuck. A friend let me borrow him."

"That's just disgusting," Eve said, watching as the beast continued to lick Squire's face as he slipped the collar over its enormous head.

"Naw," Squire said affectionately. "He's a good boy, ain't ya Shucky?"

Eve brushed the front of her leather jacket. "It got schmutz all over me," she said, checking out the legs of her jeans.

"It'll be worth a little schmutz once you see what this bad boy can do," the hobgoblin said, patting the side of the big beast. It sounded like he was beating on a drum.

"I take it shuck are good trackers?"

"The best when you're talkin' about demons," Squire explained. "These guys hate the fuckers. It's a natural instinct they got."

Eve crossed her arms, waiting to be impressed. "Well?"

Squire smiled, holding on to Shuck's leash. He leaned forward and whispered in the animal's ear. "Do ya smell it, boy?" he asked. "Where is it—can ya find the demon for us?"

Shuck suddenly became very alert, its nose raised,

sniffing eagerly. Then it began to growl, quickly padding toward the exit.

"See?" Squire said proudly, as he was dragged along behind the beast.

Eve walked quickly behind the pair, curious as to how this would play out. They were heading back toward Beacon Street.

"He's just taking us back to where we started," Eve yelled, scrambling to keep up.

"I don't think so," Squire said.

The looks they were getting were something. People actually tried to stop Squire to ask what kind of dog Shuck was. The animal didn't give him a chance to answer, pulling him along at a good clip. The hobgoblin was practically running, his stubby little legs having a hard time keeping up with the nearly galloping shadow beast.

The scene of the crime had been cleaned up pretty well. Only the crime scene tape would have given away what had happened there, if they hadn't known. Shuck sniffed around a building across from the where the demon had struck and perked up abruptly. With a growl, he leaped over a black, wrought-iron fence that separated two buildings.

"Ah shit!" Eve heard Squire yelp.

"What's the matter, Mary?" she said, coming to stand beside him. "Did you lose your doggy?"

Squire stood at the gate, peering through the bars into the darkness. "Nope, there he goes."

Eve looked in the direction of Squire's stubby, pointing finger and saw the black beast climbing, spiderlike, up the side of the building.

"He's not really a dog, is he?" Eve said.

"Never said he was." Squire looked around to make sure nobody was watching as he climbed the fence. "I'll meet you up there," he said and dove into a pool of shadow, disappearing from sight.

"Great," she said, stepping back, gazing up toward the roof of the apartment building. Then she leaped over the wrought-iron fence and, following Shuck's lead, began to climb up the side of the building.

Eve threw her leg over the top of the roof, arriving just as Squire emerged from a puddle of darkness across from her. "Where is he?" she asked, searching for the animal.

Its flesh was so black it practically blended with the darkness of the night, but they spotted the beast lying down, chewing eagerly on something it had found.

"Whatcha got there, boy?" Squire asked, walking over to the animal.

It growled at him, baring razor sharp teeth.

"Don't you growl at me, you ungrateful mutt!" Squire snapped.

As Eve approached, it glared at her as well, but the animal's growling ceased at once, its long, pointed tail wagging furiously. As if presenting her with a gift, Shuck picked up what it had been gnawing on and brought it to her, dropping it at her feet.

Eve looked down, the smell of death wafting up from the large, bloody pile. "That's skin, isn't it?" She poked the flesh and strips of torn clothing with the pointed toe of her boot.

"It certainly is," Squire said.

"Thought so." Eve looked back at the shuck. It was now sitting down, looking at her adoringly, tail wagging.

It gave her the creeps.

9

THE headquarters of the Federal Bureau of Investigation was located in a nondescript, monolithic concrete structure named after J. Edgar Hoover, its former director. The Washington, D.C., office block's only distinguishing characteristic was the row of American flags—one of each version the nation had ever used—flying from its face. Without the flags, there would have been no way to tell which side was the front.

It was early morning, the sun only beginning to disperse the night's chill, when the ghost of Dr. Graves approached the J. Edgar Hoover Building. He walked invisibly beside Clay, unnoticed by anyone outside and by the agents providing security just inside the front doors.

In a charcoal suit with a stylish blue and red tie, Clay looked dapper as hell. Graves had never seen him in a suit before. Then again, that was Clay's magic, wasn't it? As a shapeshifter, he knew instinctively how to blend into any situation. Dr. Graves had never learned that ability. In his era, it would have been impossible for a man of his race to blend in.

Now, though . . . well, it was a simple thing for a ghost to blend. He simply went unseen.

Under the name Joseph Boudreau, Clay found that he was expected. Special Agent Al Kovalik had put him on a list, but entry into the FBI headquarters obviously required identification. The shapeshifter had a great many identities and documents to prove he was all of those people. During his lifetime, Graves had only ever been himself, so it was somewhat disconcerting for him to be party to all of this deception.

But they were in.

The ghost shadowed Clay all through the building. Security had given "Joseph Boudreau" a plastic pass that he clipped to his lapel. Whatever information Kovalik had given about his visitor, Clay was allowed to continue on his own.

They rode the elevator with a collection of the most sober individuals Graves had ever encountered and two young agents, apparently partners, who were apparently sharing a private joke, given that they kept glancing at one another and snickering. The ghost enjoyed the moment with them. Whatever life existed in a wandering spirit always felt enhanced when in the presence of the pleasure of the living.

Clay caught him smiling and raised an eyebrow in surprise.

Then they were off the elevator and moving through the building again. People in severe suits strode the immaculate halls, but it surprised Graves to find that in large part it seemed an ordinary office environment. People laughed. A secretary had birthday balloons tied to her desk.

Graves paused to study the balloons. When he had first regained awareness after death, even before he truly understood that he had become a specter, certain things had the ability to fascinate him, to lull him into a strange blissful state. Orchestral music. Sleeping humans. Bunches of brightly colored balloons.

Clay coughed into his hand.

The ghost blinked and turned, remembering their purpose. Dr. Graves felt disoriented as he fell in once again behind Clay, moving in a pantomime of walking, though his feet never touched the ground. It disturbed him to learn that he could still drift in that way.

The occurrence remained on his mind as Clay chatted amiably with an attractive woman of Middle Eastern descent—Graves thought perhaps Pakistani—whose desk marked the entrance into Al Kovalik's particular kingdom.

"Yes, Mister Boudreau," the woman said. "Special Agent Kovalik has been expecting you. Just give me a moment."

She excused herself and slipped into Kovalik's office. Half a minute later she emerged, but left the door standing open.

"Go ahead in, sir. Can I get you anything? Coffee? A cold drink?"

"I'm all set, thanks."

The moment Clay went into her boss's office, he was forgotten. The ghost lingered and watched her a moment as she returned to her computer terminal and to her work. The phone rang, and she picked it up, nonsense business chatter, dates, and times followed.

The ghost of Dr. Graves strode past her desk. Clay had closed the door behind himself but Graves passed right through it.

"—fantastic surprise to hear from you," a gray-haired man said as he embraced the man he knew as Joe Boudreau.

Clay stood back and held him at arm's length. "You're looking good, Al," he said, and he patted the man on the shoulder before taking a seat in front of the agent's desk.

Kovalik had thin, narrow features and reminded Graves of Jimmy Stewart. He had to be in his early seventies at the least, though only the lines in his face showed his age. His eyes were alight with sprightly intelligence, and he moved like a much younger man.

"And you, as always, look the same, Joe," Kovalik said. A ripple of uneasiness passed across his face. "I'll never get used to that."

Clay shrugged. "It's a gift."

With a laugh, Kovalik slid into his chair and splayed his hands on the desk in front of him. "How've you been keeping, Joe?"

"No complaints. You enjoying the new position?"

A shadow passed over Kovalik's face. He picked up a pen from his desk and idly tapped it against the wood. The smile that came as he shook his head was loaded with regret and cynicism.

"You know, if someone had told me fifty years ago that I would still be in the Bureau at this age, and that I'd be liaison with the CIA and NSA, doing due diligence on synergy to make Homeland Security watchdogs happy, I'd have told them they were nuts."

"No, you wouldn't have," Clay said.

Kovalik raised an eyebrow. "No?"

"You would have said, 'What the hell's synergy? Or due diligence? Who's Homeland Security?'"

The laugh that came out of Kovalik was half a cough and half a snort. "It's good to see you. I mean that. Whatever the hell you really are, Joe, it's good to see you."

Clay smiled. The ghost of Dr. Graves was surprised to find that he seemed to be genuinely fond of this old man. Once upon a time, Kovalik had been tangentially involved with a program that had brainwashed Clay and used him as an assassin, doing government dirty work. But it was obvious he didn't blame Kovalik.

Everyone deserved a second chance in life, or so Graves had always thought. Now he knew that sometimes the second chance came after life was over.

Again, Kovalik tapped his pen. "All right. So much for the mushy reunion. Why are you in D.C., Joe? What can I do for you?"

Clay sat forward in the chair, gazing intently at him. "You can tell me about Erasmus Zarin and the murder of Doctor Graves."

Hearing the words aloud, in a conversation that did not involve him, made the ghost shudder. Graves haunted the office, standing just beside the chair Clay sat in. Kovalik could not see him, but Clay glanced at him from time to time.

Graves watched closely, barely aware that the ectoplasm that comprised his spectral form had been altered. Unconsciously, he had manifested the phantom guns that he often wore. They hung now in holsters beneath his arms.

Kovalik tapped his pen, then dropped it onto the desk. "When you said you had some odd questions for me, I believed you. But that is an exceedingly odd request. May I ask why?"

"Talk to me first, if you don't mind. Then I'll tell you why."

The aging FBI man, who must have had serious pull at the Bureau in order to still be active, but who must also have pissed off a great many people in his career to avoid being made at least deputy director by now, nodded curtly.

"All right." He slid deeper into his chair, hands on the armrests. "But there isn't much to tell, I'm afraid. For the first few years after I joined the Bureau, Zarin remained an enemy of the state. He was one of the most wanted men in America, a total anarchist. Today, we'd call him a terrorist, though he didn't have much of an ideology. At least not that I was aware of.

"This was about a decade after the murder of Leonard Graves, but even then there was a lot of talk about it. The agents I worked with . . . a lot of the older guys had either known Graves or at least known *of* him. The guy was a hero. A legend, really. The pulps had Doc Savage and the Shadow, but we had Leonard Graves. The fact he was black meant you were always going to have some asshole making racist comments. Racism was just the way things were back then. But I don't have to tell you that. You lived it. You know."

Graves narrowed his eyes. He moved around behind Kovalik, reached out a ghostly hand, and laid it upon the back of the man's neck.

Kovalik shivered.

When the ghost glanced up, he saw Clay staring at him.

"You'd have been surprised to hear, back in those days, the way they raved about Graves. Most of those guys, skin color didn't matter to them. Not when it came to Doctor Graves. I'd go so far as to say that his cases, his exploits, probably made a big difference in their attitudes."

The aging FBI man nodded as though in remembrance. "They certainly did for me."

"And Zarin?" Clay prodded.

"Like I said, not much to say. Graves was the first one to capture Zarin. After that, the lunatic went to prison for a while. He got out just after Graves was murdered. Eventually they arrested him again, but this time it stuck. The evidence against him was extraordinary.

"An incident occurred in prison. Zarin attempted to escape, according to the files. He was crippled—"

For the first time that day, Clay's aura of calm was disrupted. He sat forward, narrowing his eyes as though unsure what he was seeing. "What? Are you sure?"

Kovalik shrugged. "Of course I'm sure. It's all in the file."

"The first I've heard of it, that's all. Sorry, go on."

Dr. Graves was barely listening. His mind raced, and the spectral stuff of his essence shuddered. Ghosts could not feel changes in temperature, but he shivered. This was the first he'd known of Zarin's injury. He caught Clay glancing at him and shook his head to indicate that this was news to him.

"I'm unclear on the details. I can pull the file and get back to you on it. Anyway, once he realized he was going to be in prison for the rest of his life and that even if he got out, he'd never walk again, Zarin gave a detailed account of his crimes to the Bureau. Everything. The details were sometimes hideous, as I recall."

"But he didn't confess to murdering Doctor Graves," Clay said.

The gray-haired, stork of a man tilted his head. "That's

right. There were two crimes that the Bureau had figured Zarin for that he absolutely refused to admit any culpability in. The way he almost embraced the rest of his sins created the consensus that he might have been telling the truth."

The ghost moved up beside Clay and leaned in.

"Ask what the other crime was, the other thing Zarin wouldn't admit to," he whispered.

Kovalik narrowed his eyes as though he had heard, and perhaps he had. Not the words, but something. Older people found it more difficult to hear the living, but some of them developed a greater ability to sense the dead as they neared their own final years.

Clay asked.

"Another assassination. The murder of Roger Alton Bennett, who was the mayor of New York at the same time Graves was killed."

"I remember," Clay said. "He fell from the Empire State Building. That was a murder? I thought a suicide."

Kovalik smiled. "The Bureau. That's what you were supposed to think."

"That was only a few weeks after I was killed," the specter whispered to Clay.

Again, Kovalik frowned. "Did you hear something?"

"You never solved Bennett's murder, either?" Clay asked, ignoring the question.

"Neither case was ever solved. The Bureau worked on both of them for years and came up with absolutely nothing. Zarin had tried some anarchy at the Empire State Building once before, the way I remember it, and Doctor Graves stopped him. They spent a lot of time on that connection, and you can see why. There's some logic there. But Zarin denied it, and no one could ever prove a thing.

"In the end, they gave up. They already had Zarin, so there seemed little point. If you want to know more, I can get you the file on Zarin, but it won't tell you anything more about the Graves murder."

The ghost moved nearer to the desk. Kovalik shivered,

and for just a moment his gaze shifted from Clay to the place where Doctor Graves's ectoplasmic form shimmered in the air. Graves had not manifested. For all purposes he was still invisible. But Kovalik had noticed something, some disruption.

"What happened to Zarin?" Clay asked. "Where is he now?"

Troubled, Kovalik forcibly returned his gaze to Clay.

"I can't tell you that, Joe."

Clay stiffened in his chair. All the friendliness went out of his face. He stared at Kovalik, and the old man met his intimidating gaze with steely resolve.

"I can't."

Clay sniffed dismissively. "You can do whatever you want, and you know that, Al. It's always a choice. You've kept your mouth shut about terrible things in the past, ugly things. I thought you promised yourself you'd never make that mistake again."

"Joe—"

A look of utter remorse and grief passed across Kovalik's features. Graves had to turn to see what had caused this reaction, and he saw that Clay had altered his features. Where the dapper man with the salt-and-pepper hair and the well-tailored suit had been now sat a small blond girl with blue eyes and a red ribbon in her hair.

The girl—or Clay, wearing the form of the girl—spoke in Russian.

Graves was fluent.

"You could have saved me, just by speaking up," the little Russian girl said. "The bullet hit me in the throat, so I couldn't scream. The assassin wanted my daddy, but he had to make sure I didn't scream. When Daddy was dead, I didn't matter anymore. He left me there to bleed to death. And you could have stopped it."

Dead these many years, Graves still flinched. In horror, he propelled himself away from Kovalik and the little girl. He closed his eyes, and when he opened them again, the girl was gone, and there was only Clay.

Clay, who had had so many lifetimes, trying to figure out what God had intended by leaving him here in this world, and who had been so badly used by so many.

"Jesus, Joe, you didn't have to—"

"Silence is not an option, Al."

Kovalik nodded. "All right. All right. Zarin's still alive, but he's not in prison anymore."

"He's . . . what?"

The FBI man waved the protest away. It was obvious he just wanted to get through the truth. "He's in his old hide-away in upstate New York. The guy's a cripple. He can't go anywhere. And he's more than a little crazy. He's sur-rounded by helpers he believes are his, I don't know, min-ions or lackeys, call them what you want. They're Bureau agents."

"Oh, for God's sake," Clay sighed, shaking his head. "Can't you people ever just leave well enough alone?"

The ghost listened in growing horror.

"He's dangerous as hell," Kovalik went on. "But his in-ventions have proven invaluable to this country. He thinks he's creating them for an international terrorist cell, to fur-ther his anarchist agenda, and his supposed assistants give him reports telling him all about his success, the effect he's having, but it's all bullshit. Like *The Truman Show*."

"I don't even know what that is," Clay said, his tone quiet and a bit sad.

Kovalik sighed. "You're going to rock the boat, aren't you, Joe? You're going to fuck that whole setup."

Clay nodded.

The FBI man closed his eyes and took a deep breath. After a moment, he chuckled softly and opened them again.

"I'd like to at least know why you care. Why try to solve Graves's murder now? The guy's been dead for more than sixty years."

A flash of anger went through Dr. Graves.

With an instant's focus, barely a thought, he manifested

fully, there in the room, standing beside the chair where Clay sat.

"Because *I* need to know!" he said through gritted teeth.

"Jesus!" the old man said, pushing away from his desk, legs pistoning to drive his chair backward until it struck a bookshelf. A framed photo of Kovalik with his wife tipped and fell, glass cracking on impact.

Graves crossed his arms, glaring at the FBI man. The sunlight streaming through the window passed right through him, and he knew precisely the effect his appearance would have. One look at him, one look *through* him, and there was no denying what he was.

"I can't rest until I have an answer, Agent Kovalik. It haunts *me*, you understand? If the FBI can't solve my murder, then it's up to me, isn't it?"

"Jesus," Kovalik said, whispering now.

His hands shook as he pointed at Graves, and his face had paled so much that the man himself looked almost like a phantom.

"You . . . you can't be . . ." Kovalik said, then glanced at Clay. "He can't be . . ."

Clay stood, brushing lint off of the sleeve of his suit jacket and straightening his stylish tie. "Al Kovalik, meet Doctor Leonard Graves. You should be honored, Al. Most people need a medium for this kind of introduction."

The FBI man just shook his head back and forth, staring first at Graves and then at Clay.

"Yes," the ghost said, gliding toward the man and passing right through his desk. "We'd like the file on Zarin, and whatever you have on my murder. And yes, sir, we will be paying Professor Zarin a visit. And while we're gone, there is one final favor we require of you."

Shaking, Kovalik glanced at Clay. "Joe?" he asked, expression as pleading as his tone.

"Listen to the vengeful ghost, Al, or he'll haunt you the rest of your life. Almost as much as the things you let them get away with all those years ago, the things you let them make me do."

Anguished, gaze heavy with shame, Kovalik turned toward the ghost again.

"Yes?"

"Go to Connecticut, to my childhood home. Joe will give you the information you need. You're going to exhume my remains. As I understand it, technology has provided a great many new tools for autopsy since my time in the world."

Clay rapped on the desk to draw Kovalik's attention.

"We need a cause of death, Al."

The gray-haired man took a long breath, steadying himself, grasping at these words as the one solid thing he could hold on to.

"But, Joe, everyone knows the cause of death. He was . . ." he glanced nervously at the ghost. "Doctor Graves was shot in the back."

"No," Clay said. "No, I don't think so."

FROM the corner of his eye, Conan Doyle watched as Eve played with the fire on one of his Bunsen burners. The vampiress yawned lazily as she leaned on one of the workstations in his laboratory, turning the knob on the burner, making the blue flame larger. The morning sun was kept out of the lab by heavy shades. She ought to have been in bed, but she was too wired from the night to sleep just yet.

Instead, she was fidgeting.

Conan Doyle shot her an impatient look. "Don't play with that, please."

"Sorry," she said, shutting down the flame and turning her back to the table.

The Black Shuck lying at her feet began to growl. "Shut up," she snarled at it. "Why don't you go bother Squire or something?"

She stepped over it and headed toward Conan Doyle. Shuck rose to its feet and followed.

"It appears that you have yourself a new friend," Conan Doyle said, tapping some of the ashen remains found upon

the bed at the Beacon Street apartment into a bubbling con-
coction in a container over another Bunsen burner.

"It won't leave me alone," she complained. "I tried to
get some shut-eye but it cried outside my door the whole
time, and when Squire tried to take it downstairs, it practically bit his arm off."

Conan Doyle chuckled. "It likes you," he said, leafing
through an ancient text to be certain he hadn't forgotten
any of the ingredients.

"Yeah, and I love it like a garlic cocktail," she spat,
looking down at the beast sitting by her side. "Don't I, you
ugly son of a bitch?"

It yelped in response, whining pitifully, as if understanding the hurtful things she had said.

"So the ashes were definitely demonic in nature, now
what?" Eve asked.

"From our informants within the police department,
we've learned that the woman who was murdered—Mrs.
Barbara Hoskins—lived in the Beacon Street apartment
with her teenage son, Charlie, who had suffered extensive
brain damage after a suicide attempt a little over three
years ago."

"So her son was a demon?" she asked.

Conan Doyle nodded. "Yes—a changeling, I imagine."

"Like Danny," Eve said, and he could see that her
thoughts were taking her into territory that he'd already
visited a number of times since learning the origin of the
burned remains. "You do realize that the kid's missing?"

"I'm aware," Conan Doyle said, satisfied with his
preparations.

"You don't think there's any kind of connection, do
you?" Eve asked.

He walked to the door of his lab and opened it. "Ceridwen?" he called into the solarium across the way. "If you
would be so kind as to come here."

"I cannot be certain," he replied at last, then turned to
kiss Ceridwen gently on the cheek as she came up behind
him.

Taking Ceridwen's hand, he led her back to his bubbling preparation. "All I need is one drop," he told her, still holding on to her hand. Conan Doyle picked up a scalpel from the table, running the blade through the Bunsen burner flame to sterilize it before bringing it toward one of the Fey princess's fingers.

"I hope you realize how honored you should feel that I'm allowing you a sample of my blood," Ceridwen said, as Conan Doyle skillfully pricked her index finger with the scalpel's tip.

"I am honored every moment you allow me to remain in your presence," he said, giving her finger a squeeze to help form the bead of crimson that was crucial to his spell.

"All right, I'll bite," Eve said. "What is the Faerie blood needed for?"

Conan Doyle held Ceridwen's finger over the bubbling liquid, waiting for the bead of blood to drop. "This conjuration will allow me to see an image of the demon changeling's sire."

The drop of Ceridwen's blood finally fell into the roiling, brackish fluid.

"Thank you, my dear," he said, handing her an alcohol wipe to cleanse the wound.

A thick, swirling smoke started to form above the potion.

"So, you think the demon who killed those people and went around wearing that skin Squire and I found last night is this Charlie's sire? You think the kid's father is responsible for offing him?" Eve asked. "Why would he do that?"

"Please, Eve," Conan Doyle scolded. "I can't concentrate with you prattling on."

She threw up her hands in frustration as he intensified his focus on the swirling, gray fumes, willing them to reveal the answer.

Conan Doyle raised his hands, moving them toward the now much-larger cloud hanging over the boiling contents of the glass container. He prodded the amorphous mist with the tips of his fingers, crackling bolts of preternatural power leaping from him into the billowing mass, urging it to take shape.

The shuck began to bark as the mist seemed to come alive, moving in the air, morphing into a three-dimensional shape.

"Shut up!" Eve spat, her attentions also focused on what was forming in the air above Conan Doyle's workstation.

The smoke writhed, a face gradually taking the shape of a demon most foul. Conan Doyle studied the cruel eyes and horrible, jagged grin that looked as though it could still rip and tear the flesh from bones even though composed of smoke. He knew this face, confirming the most disturbing of suspicions.

"Damn it all," the mage cursed as the details on the smoke image became increasingly more precise.

"Is it as you feared?" Ceridwen asked him. "Is it Danny's sire?"

Eve flinched. "Danny's sire? I thought we were talking about the dead kid from Beacon Street."

Conan Doyle sighed, eyes affixed to the frightening visage of Baalphegor-Moabites floating in the air. "I'm afraid they are one and the same."

"You knew who Danny's dad was?" Eve asked, her voice raised in surprise, and perhaps a little annoyance. Shuck leapt to its feet, aroused by her excitement. Its tail of solid black wagged eagerly.

"It used to be a far simpler task to keep track of the comings and goings of demonic entities," Conan Doyle explained calmly.

"Why haven't you told him?" she asked. "Is this one of the little secrets you've kept for a rainy day? Something to use as leverage just in case?"

Conan Doyle felt a spark of anger toward the woman, but it went no further. He and Eve had been associates for many years, and in that time he'd done things that he was not proud of, but knew were completely necessary to achieve his goals, and thusly benefit all of humanity.

Arthur Conan Doyle was no angel, but he liked to think that he fought on their side.

"His father is a monster most foul," he said, keeping his voice calm. "And what exactly would the boy take from that?"

Eve said nothing, crossing her arms, temporarily speechless, but it wouldn't last for long.

Conan Doyle was alerted to a sound outside the door.

It was Squire, arguing with somebody, telling whoever it was that he wasn't to be disturbed.

The door to his laboratory was forced open, and Julia Ferrick barged into the room, a befuddled Squire behind her.

"Sorry, boss," he apologized. "I tried to get her to leave but—"

"No worry, Squire," Conan Doyle said and then turned his attentions to Danny's mother. "What can I do for you, Julia?" he asked, waving his hands through the smoke, dispersing the demon's head. "You seem rather upset."

"You bet your ass I'm upset!" the woman yelled. "Where is he?" she demanded. "Where's Danny?"

Conan Doyle smiled calmly, walking over to stand beside her. "Danny is an adolescent, Julia," he explained. "Never mind the fact that he has certain preternatural abilities awakening as well. I'm sure there's nothing to worry about."

He glanced toward Eve, wondering if she would decide to hold her tongue.

"Yeah," Eve said. "I'm sure he's fine. Probably just got fed up with all the grown-up bullshit going on around here and decided to get some air."

Julia shook her head slowly. "He hasn't been right," she said sadly. "It's almost as if he's fighting something—on the inside." She touched the center of her chest. "And I think he might be losing the fight."

There were tears in the woman's eyes, and Conan Doyle put his arm around her shoulders. "We won't allow anything to happen to your son."

Ceridwen took Julia's hand. "Come, we'll go to the kitchen and brew ourselves a pot of tea."

Julia pulled a Kleenex from her pocket and noisily blew her nose. "I'd rather a drink of something a little stronger if you've got it."

"Fine then," Ceridwen said, leading her from the room. "A strong drink it is."

"Hey, Julia," Eve called to her, and Conan Doyle tensed.

The woman stopped, wiping at her nose with the tissue.

"Don't you worry about a thing," Eve assured her. "Squire and I are taking Shuck here out tonight—we'll find Danny and bring him home."

Conan Doyle breathed a sigh of relief.

The shuck moved to stand alongside Eve, and from the look on Julia's face it seemed to be the first time she had noticed the unusual beast.

"What the hell *is* that?" she asked, her face wrinkling up in disgust.

"This?" Eve said, looking down at the animal.

It looked up at her lovingly, tail wagging furiously.

"This is the ugly son of a bitch that's gonna help us find your son."

CLAY did not need to sleep.

And Graves, of course, was dead.

They'd driven all day to reach Rochester, in upstate New York. The dismal Rochester weather seemed entrenched, the skies a kind of gray that Clay thought only existed in shadow dimensions and in old black-and-white movies set in London.

Kovalik had given them the address of the compound where Zarin lived, surrounded by FBI agents he thought were his loyal servants and suckups. The place was in the northern part of town, in sight of a massive factory, but set atop a hill among trees whose branches seemed almost bare enough for winter. The massive, sprawling house had a Victorian air, but its size was such that Clay felt certain it had once been a hospital, or perhaps a mental asylum.

"Are you sure you wouldn't rather try to sneak in?" Dr. Graves asked.

The ghost had taken up his familiar position in the passenger seat of the Cherokee.

"Trust me, Doc. This is what I do," Clay said as he drove up to the guard station at the gates of the old estate.

But as he pulled to a stop by the guardhouse and rolled down the window, it was not Joseph Clay who glanced out amiably at the guard who strode toward the Cherokee. It was Special Agent Al Kovalik, complete with silver hair and circles under his eyes. His suit was even rumpled and ill-fitting, the way that such clothes often fit on men in their seventies whose bodies had begun to diminish.

"Can I help you, sir?" the guard said.

Clay smiled. "Good. The politeness, I mean. It helps to keep up the appearance of a private residence. Wealthy people pay their employees to be polite. The government pays its employees to be wary and brusque."

The guard faltered. Clay studied him. Perhaps twenty-five years old, this was likely his first assignment with the FBI and he figured it was a shit detail. Stuck up here in Rochester, this handsome, dark-skinned kid with intense, intelligent eyes must have been bored out of his mind.

Until today.

He put his right hand on the butt of the pistol that rested on his hip.

"Sir, I'm afraid I'm going to have to ask you to drive on. The center is not expecting any visitors."

Wearing Kovalik's face, Clay smiled. He glanced at the ghost of Dr. Graves—whom the guard, of course, could not see—and then looked back at the anxious young man.

"Kid, I'm reaching into my jacket pocket now for some I.D. Don't spook and shoot me in the head, okay? That would completely ruin my thus far positive impression of your job performance."

The guard narrowed his gaze suspiciously. Clay saw

two impulses warring in him. He was not supposed to acknowledge that there was anything government-related
going on at "the center," but the temptation to react to
Clay's words was great.

"Sir, I have no idea what you're talking about. If you
need directions—"

Clay nodded, but reached inside his jacket pocket.

The guard tensed, grabbing a small radio clipped to his
jacket with his left hand and unsnapping the guard over his
pistol with his right.

"Careful," the ghost said, the voice practically in Clay's
ear.

With Kovalik's lips, Clay smiled. He drew out a wallet
and slowly let it fall open in his fingers, extending it out the
window.

"Special Agent Albert Kovalik. Check my clearance,
kid. And then your pulse."

The guard kept his right hand where it was and snatched
the ID wallet with his left. He retreated to the guard shack,
watching them carefully the whole way.

"You did well, by the way," Clay/Kovalik called to him.

Less than three minutes later they were driving through
the open iron gates. The guard had been even more polite
once he'd realized who Kovalik was, and beamed under
the man's praise and promises to put in a good word. Similarly, as Clay followed the winding drive up to the enormous house with its sprawling wings, they spotted agents
on the grounds who watched the Cherokee intently but did
not move to stop them.

The ghost shimmered in the gloom of the afternoon. Inside the Cherokee, Graves stared at Clay. "How did you get
Kovalik's ID? You can't . . . that isn't part of your
shapeshifting?"

Clay laughed. "Not hardly. Clothes I can do. Something
like this requires more finesse. I lifted it from his pocket
before we left."

"Is he going to be angry?"

All the humor went out of Clay, then. "Probably more

frustrated than angry. But angry would be fine with me. He could stand a little inconvenience now and then."

Graves did not ask him to elaborate, and Clay was glad. Now wasn't the time for talking about the things that haunted him. They were here about Graves, and *his* ghosts.

A pair of agents met Clay at the front door. Graves remained invisible to the mortal eye. They all politely pretended not to notice the snipers on the roof of the rambling Victorian asylum as they walked inside, the agents just as polite as the guard at the gate, now that they knew who they were dealing with. Or who they thought they were dealing with.

Kovalik might be old, but he was powerful and influential and had been involved in creating Zarin's fictional environment here in the first place. Yet if Clay understood the situation correctly, he had never visited. Until now, of course.

An icy blonde woman with hard, angular features met them in the foyer, a vast room with high ceilings and a grand staircase at the back. There was a long counter at the front that might have been an admissions desk when the place still served its earlier function—whatever that had been. Now it was a kind of command center with rows of small monitors showing the video feed from dozens of security cameras. Two agents stood behind the counter, one of them paying attention to the cameras and the other quite obviously intrigued with the new arrivals.

The blonde was flanked by two younger agents, men who seemed eager to impress their visitor. The fortyish woman did not seem nearly so interested in sucking up.

"I'm Special Agent Munson. I'd like to say we're prepared for your visit, but since I received no notification that you would be coming—"

"As you know, Agent Munson, our business lends itself to things happening quickly and quietly. Had I been at leisure to call ahead and make an appointment, I would have done so."

"Well, let me give you the five-cent tour," she said, still

obviously ticked off. "The west wing is used for sleeping quarters and common areas for the agents attending to this project. This main section is security, of course. And the east wing remains the province of our special guest and all of the work he does for us."

While Clay spoke to Agent Munson, the ghost of Dr. Graves floated around the foyer, inspecting the security command station, studying Munson and the other agents, and finally passing through the steel door that led into the east wing.

Clay wondered what he was up to, but could not speak to him, given that no one else could see him.

"I haven't come for the tour," he said, putting an edge on Kovalik's voice. "I need to see Zarin."

All five of the agents in the foyer stared at him. One of the men with Munson actually flinched. Munson narrowed her eyes and shook her head.

"I'm sorry, Special Agent Kovalik, but you know that's impossible. You helped set up the protocol for this project yourself. What kind of cover could we give you? What explanation could we provide to Professor Zarin to explain your presence here? And even if we were clever enough to do that, whatever you might want to learn from him might endanger the careful fiction we've created for him."

Clay crossed his arms, attempting to make Kovalik's thin, old-man body as imposing as possible. "Just the same, I've come to see Zarin. There are questions that must be answered. You'll have to trust me to be as circumspect as possible."

Now Munson grew angry. Her fair skin flushed deeply. "I can't allow that. His phone calls are created by us. The newspapers he sees are all fiction. He doesn't even know the Internet exists. Do you have any idea how much work has gone into this?"

Clay walked over to the security desk and peered at the various monitors. In one of them he thought he saw a metal apparatus of some kind with a man's head thrust out of the top, but then the image went dark. The security guard had shut off the monitor.

He spun to stare at Munson. "You're actually asking me that question? Have you ever thought about how much this operation costs the United States government? It's all about value, Agent Munson. The benefits of having Zarin around, the things he's created for us, have outweighed the costs up until now.

"But understand what I'm saying to you. The conversation I'm about to have with the professor has benefits that far outweigh the costs of fucking up your op. If that wasn't true, I wouldn't be here. The powers that be have decided that we've squeezed most of the value out of Zarin anyway, and now we need him for something else. Maybe the last thing we'll ever need him for. And maybe that means all of you will get assignments where you're not sitting on your asses in this gray factory town all year.

"On the other hand, none of that matters. I say that all as a courtesy to you, Agent Munson. Or do I need to give you a lecture about command structure?"

Munson and her two silent lackeys looked confused. Then the woman scowled and shook her head. She reached up a hand and brushed her hair from her face.

"No, sir. You don't."

"Good," Clay said. Making Kovalik's face as stern as he could, he turned toward the two agents behind the security desk. "Now buzz me in."

"Sir, you shouldn't go in alone," Munson said.

"He's paralyzed, isn't he?"

"Yes. But you'll want to be careful. Past that door, he's living a life he's spent decades creating for himself. He's got his own security."

"Booby traps?" Clay asked, amused.

"More or less. I mean, they don't work. We put them in ourselves, and nobody was going to risk that. But don't forget who he was, fifty years ago. That's Professor Zarin in there, no matter how insane he is."

Clay strode over to the door to the east wing, the door Graves had ghosted through several minutes earlier.

"I haven't forgotten," he said as he grabbed the door handle. "Now, buzz me in."

The five agents stared at him. Munson gave a nod, and one of the men behind the counter touched a button. The door buzzed and clicked, unlocking. Clay pulled it open and stepped inside, pulling it tightly shut behind him. He heard the lock click.

Tempting as it was to shift back to his true appearance, or at least to the comfortable face of Joe Clay, he had to keep wearing Kovalik's face for the benefit of the security cameras. He didn't want Munson and her crew interfering before he and Graves got the information they needed.

The corridor had the antiseptic odor of a hospital, but there was something else there as well; something animal. The fluorescent lights cast a grim, morguelike gloom along the hall, and the whole feel of the place reminded Clay of another era—an era he spent doing terrible things for terrible men and walking corridors much like this one. It was as though time, in this place, had stopped.

There were windows in the corridor, but he noticed that none of them provided a view of the front gates or the drive. If Zarin could make it this far, he'd never be able to see what was on the outside. But, of course, he couldn't make it this far. Clay frowned. Why bother, then, keeping this corridor looking so antiquated, and keeping the view limited?

A glance around gave him the answer.

Cameras.

Just as the security team in the foyer had cameras everywhere, Zarin must have his own surveillance cameras. Only they would only pick up what his federal babysitters allowed them to pick up. The video feed of the foyer and the front gate would show Professor Zarin only what Munson and her associates wanted him to see.

This corridor was little more than a movie set.

And here he was, a new addition to the cast.

10

CLAY wondered how far ahead Graves had gone but did not want to talk to the ghost as long as he could avoid it. Not when Zarin and Munson were both likely monitoring his progress. Calling out for someone who wasn't there might cause interference he didn't want. Best to hold off a confrontation as long as possible.

Still, the ghost must be far ahead, and he wondered what Graves had encountered.

The corridor forked to the right, and there was another steel door. From the other side, muffled by the door, came the distant sound of music. He could barely make out the tune.

Clay reached for the knob.

A series of clicks sounded to his right, and he turned just in time to see metal plates in the walls sliding aside. Behind them, set into shadowy recesses in the wall, were the mouths of long gun barrels.

"Oh, shi—" he began.

The guns barked, rapid fire, a staccato burst of bullets that exploded from the wall and struck him, one after another. Clay staggered back as the bullets struck him, driving him into a window whose glass cracked but did not shatter on impact.

He dropped to his knees, breath coming in gasps. The mouths of those guns plumed smoke like a dragon at rest, and then the metal plates slid back into place, hiding the weapons away.

"Son of a bitch," Clay snarled.

He clutched at his stomach, forcing himself to keep the guise of Al Kovalik intact. A strange frisson filled the air, but he recognized it immediately. It had become familiar to him of late. The hairs on his arms and the back of his neck stood up, and he raised his eyes to see the ghost of Dr. Graves standing in front of him, one eyebrow arched quizzically.

"That looked like it hurt," the ghost observed.

Clay laughed. He stood and stretched, ran his hands through Kovalik's gray hair, then used his shoe to brush aside the rubber bullets that were spread across the floor.

Rubber bullets. Of course. No way would Munson risk sending FBI agents in here pretending to be Zarin's lackeys if there were real bullets in those guns. If the professor started to distrust one of his lackeys, or wanted to set an example, he'd use a stupid trap on them, like some early James Bond villain. Clay wanted to laugh. What did the FBI agents do? They must have fallen down and had to just wait until someone came and dragged their "corpse" away. *Course, they're probably thrilled when it happens to them,* he thought. *It means they can get off of this shit detail and into something else. Some of them probably piss the old lunatic off on purpose, just so they can get terminated.*

"Sorry, professor," Clay called, assuming there was audio monitoring in the hall as well. "You're going to have to do better than that."

The ghost of Dr. Graves stepped up beside him. "What are you going to do? It's a steel door. If you just break it down—"

Clay glanced at him, keenly aware that he was being observed, and that the cameras would not see the ghost. He thought about it. He could play along, explain that he'd been augmented by the government and sent after Zarin, something that might sound somewhat true to both the professor and Munson, to cover up for how strong he was.

But what would he buy? A couple of minutes?

"I wanted to do this quietly, but this is taking too long," the shapeshifter said, to everyone who was listening. "So no more screwing around."

He kept wearing Al Kovalik's face, just in case Munson was stupid enough not to realize right away that something was very wrong here. But he hauled back and kicked out at the steel door. It crumpled in the middle and tore off of its hinges with a shriek of metal.

On the second kick, it caved in completely and clanged to the ground in the corridor beyond.

"This is going to get messy," Graves said as he moved past Clay into Professor Zarin's inner sanctum.

"It's been messy for sixty years," Clay said, not caring who was listening now. "We're just trying to clean it up."

The question was, how long would Munson allow this to go on? Clay knew the answer, too. Right up until the moment that stopping him became more important than keeping up the ruse of Zarin's captivity, or the moment Clay himself revealed the truth to the old nut job.

Clay strode across the bent metal door. It shifted underfoot, clanking against the ground. The ghost walked beside him, soundless as ever. Now that they were inside, the music he'd heard earlier was louder, and he could make out the tune. Cole Porter's "Night and Day." The melody drifted along the plain, industrial hallway almost eerily, as though it were haunting the place far more than Dr. Graves ever could.

"What the hell is that music?" Clay asked.

The ghost kept pace with him. There were many rooms along the corridor, or at least many doors, all of them closed. A stairwell on the right had been blocked off, though Clay was sure he could get up that way if necessary.

"I don't know," Graves replied. "I could hear it as I

made my way through the place, but it kept moving, as though the source of the music was mobile."

Clay pondered that a moment.

Then he heard two clicks from the ceiling just ahead. Panels slid aside, and a trio of silver tubes lowered on robot arms, their tips glowing with red light like the burning embers on the end of a lit cigarette.

"Oh, hell, what now?"

Bursts of red light erupted from the weapons, laser beams that strafed the corridor, passing through the spectral form of Dr. Graves and dancing harmlessly across the chest of Al Kovalik. Clay stared down at the lights that crisscrossed his body.

He sighed. "Come on, this is ridiculous."

In his mind, he pictured FBI agents falling down and acting as though they'd been burned horribly by the lasers, all for the benefit of a paralyzed mad scientist, watching on his little closed circuit TV.

He could barely contain the urge to laugh.

"Let's go," he told Graves.

The ghost swept along beside him. They could still hear the music, the final strains of "Night and Day" reaching them as they strode down the corridor and came to an elevator. Clay stared dubiously at the elevator before finally pressing the button.

"This should be fun."

Another tune started playing eerily in the distance. Now it sounded as though it came from above them. This was another Cole Porter tune. "I've Got You Under My Skin."

The elevator doors slid open almost soundlessly. They stepped inside, the ghost standing so that only half of his body was within the elevator. It looked like he had been cut in two by the doors when they closed. He stuck his head out and then pulled back into the elevator.

"Nothing out there. No one is following," he said.

"They're waiting to see what happens," Clay replied. "They're going to have a lot of explaining to do, but they're not sure to whom, just yet."

The old elevator rattled as it ascended. Clay stared at the numbers atop the door. The options had been limited. Basement. First floor, which they'd started on. Second floor. Third floor. At random, he'd chosen the second, but the elevator didn't stop there.

Clay had to suppress a small chuckle.

A hiss filled the elevator, and he glanced around curiously. For a moment he'd thought there might be snakes slithering into the contraption, but instead he saw several vents at foot level, all of them pumping a fine greenish mist into the elevator.

He sniffed the air, then glanced at the ghost. Graves seemed only slightly more substantial than the mist, his spiritual form merging with the coalescing mists.

"What do you suppose it is?" he asked Graves. "Dry ice?"

"With a chemical compound," Graves replied. "I'm not sure if it's meant to be poison, or just to knock you unconscious. You might want to consider feigning unconsciousness to see what happens next."

Clay shrugged. "I don't think so. I'm impatient."

"It's your show," the ghost said.

"For the moment."

The elevator stopped on the third floor, but the doors did not open immediately. For several long minutes Clay stood with his arms crossed, whistling along to the Cole Porter melody, letting whoever might be watching through whatever cameras were in the elevator get a good look at Special Agent Al Kovalik being bored by the poison gas.

A vacuum turned on, and in seconds it sucked most of the green mist out of the elevator.

The doors opened. The sight that greeted them struck him mute. Just outside the elevator on the third floor stood a fat, ugly orangutan in a butler's jacket, with a small speaker-box around its neck like gaudy jewelry. The music came from the speaker.

The orangutan carried a machine gun, and it was aimed right at Clay.

"Good Lord. Solomon?" Graves whispered.

"No, come on," Clay said, shaking his head. "You know the monkey?"

"It can't be the same one," the ghost said quickly. "But perhaps a descendant of the creature that once served Zarin."

The orangutan bared its teeth and hissed at Clay—it could not see the ghost—and it stomped its foot, apparently frustrated that he wasn't paying closer attention to it.

The music of Cole Porter ceased abruptly, the song cut off mid-note. The speaker crackled, and they heard labored breathing.

"Welcome, sir," buzzed the voice on the crackling speaker. The orangutan studied Clay suspiciously, baring its teeth again.

"Zarin," Graves whispered, as though up until this very moment, the ghost had been unable to believe his old nemesis still lived.

"You are both formidable and persistent. How you—" a hacking cough interrupted, and then Zarin had to take a moment to catch its breath. "How you managed to survive my defense systems, I shall be very curious to learn. After that, I suspect one of us will soon die."

Clay raised his hands, staring at the orangutan a moment before turning in a slow circle, letting any cameras get a good look at him. Or, rather, at Al Kovalik.

"I didn't come here to die, Professor Zarin," he said, mustering as much sincerity as he could manage. "And I haven't come here to kill you, either. I only want to ask you a few questions."

There was a pause. The orangutan grunted and shook his machine gun as though in frustration that he hadn't been ordered to perforate Clay yet.

"Who are you?" Zarin's rasping voice asked. He coughed again.

Lying would do him no good at this point. And with luck, Agent Munson and any other observers would be so confused wondering what the hell Al Kovalik was up to that it would take a while before it occurred to them that he wasn't Al Kovalik after all.

"My name is Clay," he said. "And I wanted to ask you a few questions about the murder of Doctor Leonard Graves."

"God damn it!" Zarin screamed, voice shrill and speaker box crackling. "For the last time, I did not kill Graves. I wish I had. If I knew who did, I'd have killed the killer, tortured him for weeks, stripped his skin, murdered his family in front of his eyes. I wanted him . . ."

Zarin broke down in a fit of coughing that made the orangutan falter, eyes clouding with concern. When it saw Clay watching it, the ape flinched and snarled, raising the machine gun's barrel and training it on him, finger on the trigger.

". . . for myself," Zarin finished, when he was through with the thick, ragged coughing jag.

Clay waited a few seconds until it sounded like Zarin had caught his breath. Then, carefully and clearly, he spoke.

"I believe you, Professor. I don't think you killed Doctor Graves. But I'm trying to find out who did."

Silence reigned in that impossibly surreal insane stretch of hallway. The elevator doors slid closed suddenly behind him. The ghost of Dr. Graves drifted over toward the orangutan and then started to investigate the rest of that corridor, obviously trying to figure out where Zarin was hiding.

"If you discover the identity of Graves's killer, you'll share the information with me?"

Clay nodded without hesitation. "Absolutely."

"Then come in. But know this. If you make any sudden moves, Solomon will pull the trigger. And if you manage to survive being shot a second time, know that he has the strength to tear your head from your shoulders."

"Nice to know," Clay replied.

"Solomon, bring him to me."

The orangutan hesitated, then swayed a moment, obviously disappointed that he had not been able to pull the trigger. He gestured with the gun for Clay to walk to the right, and they started off in that direction.

"Bizarre, isn't it?" the ghost of Dr. Graves said, falling into step beside him, the orangutan following, gun trained at his back.

"Oh, yes," Clay said, voice low.

"He's a madman," Graves said, grim and serious. "The FBI have created this situation that makes him seem a buffoon to you. Don't allow yourself to forget for a moment that, no matter how insane he is, no matter how ridiculous they have made him, Professor Zarin murdered hundreds of people with his schemes. Once upon a time he was both cunning and vicious. Insane and vicious may be just as deadly a combination."

"I'll keep that in mind," Clay whispered.

The orangutan poked him in the back with the barrel of the machine gun. Though he knew the gun probably had only rubber bullets or blanks in it, still it was troubling, and annoying. Even real bullets would not kill Clay, but this animal had been badly used. He faulted both Zarin and the FBI. He did not want to have to kill Solomon.

"Turn left," Zarin's rasp came from the speaker box behind them.

Clay did as he was told. The ghost of Dr. Graves remained silent beside him, perhaps ruminating over the strange reunion that was about to take place.

"At the end of the corridor you will find a carved cherrywood door. When you reach it, knock."

With Solomon following behind them, Clay and Graves followed Zarin's instructions. The corridor was just as featureless and industrial as the rest of the professor's lair. The cherrywood door—intricately carved with scenes from Victorian times, men driving coaches drawn by many horses, a fox hunt, ladies in beautiful dresses strolling a promenade—was the first elegant thing they had encountered. It was one of the finest pieces Clay had ever seen.

He knocked.

Behind him, Solomon grunted eagerly, and Clay heard the orangutan shuffling from side to side.

With a click, the door swung open to reveal a beautifully appointed room hung with priceless European tapestries and lined with ornately carved bookshelves, upon which sat leather-bound volumes of great age. The high, vaulted ceiling had windows set into it so that there was a turret made almost exclusively of glass to let in the light of the day. Clay thought it ironic, here in Rochester, where the sky was so often gray, as it was today.

A light rain had begun to fall, and it trickled down the turret windows in weeping streaks.

On the far side of the room was a strange chamber, a kind of electronic womb only two-thirds complete. Computer screens showed readouts that would never have shown up on a modern computer. Monitors revealed images picked up from the cameras spread throughout the complex, both those that were real and those that were being fed by Munson and the rest of her team. Some of the screens showed what appeared to be other rooms in the building, laboratories and steam-driven steel construction. Clay was intrigued. If there'd been time, he would love to have known what sorts of things Zarin had designed for the government in the fifty years of his bizarre captivity.

But even a creature who had lived nearly forever did not always have the time he desired.

In the midst of that strange electronic cocoon stood a kind of metal crèche, and as they entered, rotors whirred and it began to turn in place. The machine reminded Clay of the iron lung of another era, or a strangely fashioned diving bell. It twisted in place, and he continued to cross the room with the ghost at his side and Solomon behind him.

Then he was face-to-face with Professor Erasmus Zarin.

"He lives," Graves said beside him.

Clay did not respond. He could not be sure what he now witnessed could truly be considered living. The only part of Zarin that remained visible was his head. His eyes were sunken, and his flesh pulled taut over his skull like some dried, leathery nut. When he spoke, he had few teeth, and those that did remain were yellowed and rotted.

"Professor Zarin," Clay said, nodding in greeting.

"Mister Clay. Whoever you are," Zarin said, and he grinned. It was among the most hideous sights Clay had ever witnessed. "I must say, now that I've got you here in person, you look somewhat familiar. Have we met?"

"Perhaps once, a long time ago," Clay replied, unsure if Kovalik and Zarin had ever encountered one another in person.

"Before you ask your questions, I have one of my own."

"Shoot."

The orangutan grunted something and shuffled around beside him, long arms raising and lowering the machine gun eagerly.

"No, Solomon. He did not mean that you should shoot," Zarin said patiently. "It's only an expression."

The ugly, orange-furred ape managed to look dejected and sighed.

"What's become of my operatives?" The question had an edge of expectation.

Clay was about to answer when Graves interrupted.

"Careful," the ghost said. "He'll have trained them well, or thinks he has. Don't say you used gas to incapacitate them or that you beat them all yourself. He's too proud to believe it. He's angry, but he's also curious."

Hesitating a moment, Clay looked at Graves. The ghost stood with his arms crossed, glaring at Zarin in a right-eously heroic pose. Clay had never known Graves in life, but he had read of his exploits in the newspapers of the era. Even then, he had been impressed. The man had brought himself through sheer force of will to the pinnacle of humanity's ability, both physically and mentally. When he was just a wandering specter, brooding as he haunted Conan Doyle's house, it was easy to forget how significant Graves had been in life.

In that moment it seemed he had never died, only gone away for a while.

Clay had few choices. He could tell the truth, blowing the FBI's operation. He could claim to have shapeshifted into a mouse and snuck in, but that might also bring Agent Munson running.

"I've developed a process through which I can bend light around me, making me effectively invisible when I wish to be. They didn't see me until it was too late. Most are unconscious. Three of them are dead."

"Which explains why they did not come when you tripped the silent alarms," Zarin said. "Yes, there are many . . ." He had another fit of coughing. A bit of spittle ended up on his chin, but he could not wipe it away, so it remained there.

"There are many strange things about you," he went on. "More technological trickery. You'll have to tell me how you survived the machine guns at the door. The gas I can imagine, and the lasers—well, if you can bend light—"

"Exactly," Clay agreed.

He glanced nervously at the banks of monitors behind Zarin, then at the orangutan, and finally at Graves.

"What's that you keep looking at?" Zarin asked.

"The ghost of Doctor Graves."

Zarin blinked, brows knitting as he processed this response. Then he smiled and uttered a small laugh that became a barking cough. When he had caught his breath he nodded.

"All right. I can see you are impatient. I remind you that Solomon would love dearly to shoot you many times. Hopefully, our discussion remains amiable. It sounds as if we desire the same thing, after all."

"The man who killed Doctor Graves."

"Precisely," Zarin said. He glanced at the orangutan and with a whir of rotors the massive iron sarcophagus that contained his body twisted with him. "Solomon, behave. Do not shoot unless I give you the word. Do you understand?"

The orangutan grunted and sighed, taking a step back. But he kept the machine gun trained on Clay.

"Now, then, Mister Clay, as much as I would enjoy a longer discourse, I don't think this is going to take very long. You're going to ask a simple question or two, and I'm going to give you two regrettably simple answers. Did I have anything to do with the murder of Doctor Graves? As I said, the answer is, no. Do I know anything about his murder or who might have perpetrated it? Again, no. If I did know who killed him, I would have exterminated the usurper decades ago."

Zarin's withered head, thrust up from that iron contraption, smiled that hideous grin again.

"What else would you like to know?"

Clay ignored the question. The time had come to stop playacting for Agent Munson's sake. He glanced at the orangutan, then turned to the ghost of Doctor Graves. Sometimes his clothes appeared to be more modern, but not today. The phantom had crafted his ectoplasmic substance to look precisely the way he had at the height of his notoriety. He wore a long coat, a white shirt, open at the collar, and dark trousers, all tailor-made to accommodate his extraordinary physique. The coat hung open, and Clay could see Graves's phantom guns in their holsters under his arms.

"Do you believe him?" he asked.

Graves nodded. "Unfortunately, I do."

"Maybe you should take it from here, then," Clay said.

"What are you doing?" Zarin rasped, then coughed to clear his throat. "Who . . . who are you talking to?"

Clay smiled. "I told you. The ghost of Leonard Graves."

"Are you mocking me? You come into my house and you mock me?" Zarin demanded, his voice tightening.

"I wouldn't dream of it."

Even as he spoke, Clay noticed the specter resolving more fully. The ghost had a greater density when Graves manifested so that humans could see him. Haunting required focus. The strange misty ether that made up the substance of the ghost churned as he moved more fully out of the spirit realm and into the world of flesh and blood.

Zarin cried out in surprise and fear.

"Solomon! Kill them!"

Clay braced himself. The orangutan fired. The rubber bullets staggered him, but he managed to remain standing. They passed right through Graves and thunked harmlessly off the walls and tapestries. One of them struck the binding of a particularly old book, the force of the impact destroying it.

The orangutan screamed angrily, chattering, and began to stomp one foot in protest. He glanced at Clay and Graves, then at his master, and back again, waiting for a new order.

Body useless and withered and trapped in a metal box, Zarin could only stare at the ghost. His breathing was ragged and drawn out, and he shook his head in denial.

"Can it be?" he whispered.

"It is, Erasmus," Graves said. "It is."

"But, then . . . all I have done . . . all I have believed . . ." the paralyzed old madman said, turning to stare in horror at Clay. "There is an afterlife?"

"Ask the ghost."

Zarin flinched and started another fit of coughing. He stared at Graves and shook his head again. "The soul exists?"

"It does," Graves replied.

"And I . . . am damned?"

The ghost of Dr. Graves stared at his old nemesis, a lunatic anarchist who had poisoned entire communities, taken hundreds of lives, murdered the children of political figures for his own brand of terror and influence. He crossed his arms.

"Can you imagine any other result of your actions?"

Zarin seemed to muse on this a moment. Then he nodded, taking the news in stride. "There is no other way around it, then. I must find a way to live forever."

Clay stared at him. The man really was insane. All too familiar with Zarin, Graves was unphased.

"Erasmus," the ghost said, "what do you know about the murder of Roger Alton Bennett?"

Zarin glared at him with such venom that Clay was sure the man wished Graves alive again so that he could kill him.

"Two things, only. First, I know that I did not kill him. Second, that Mayor Bennett's murder was the perfect crime. The killer slipped past security, both at the Empire State Building and the mayor's personal bodyguards, without anyone the wiser. He left not a single clue, not a trace of his passing. And he lifted that enormously fat, slobbering fool off of his feet and hurled him bodily over the side of the observation platform.

"The only man I ever met with the cunning and the stealth and the strength to have committed that murder, sir, was Doctor Leonard Graves. But you, sir, were already dead by then."

Clay frowned. He'd made the connection as well when Kovalik talked about the fact that the only two crimes Zarin had denied committing were the murders of Graves and Mayor Bennett. But what was Graves getting at?

Solomon the orangutan brandished his gun but did not fire again. He danced from one foot to the other, chattering and growing more and more agitated. His eyes were full of confusion and anger.

"Wait a moment," the ghost said, moving forward, his long coat swaying as though moved by some unseen wind. "How did you discover those details of the case? I read all of the accounts of Bennett's murder, and—"

"The police were made to look like buffoons," Zarin said. "Do you honestly think such details would have been made public?" The withered head turned to look at Clay. "You won't forget your promise. If you find the killer, you'll return and tell me his name?"

Before Clay could respond, the room filled with a strange, eerie bit of orchestral music. It was a beautiful melody, a kind of lilting thing that might have been written for a wedding or a funeral.

"Clay," Graves whispered. "Do you . . . please tell me you hear that."

The music came from the speaker-box that hung around Solomon's neck. The orangutan stood completely still, no longer chattering or agitated. The confusion was gone from his eyes, replaced by a cold intelligence.

"Zarin," Clay began, turning to look at the madman.

"How do you know that music?" Graves demanded furiously. "If you know nothing of my murder, how do you know—"

"It isn't me!" Zarin protested, staring wide-eyed at his faithful pet. "I'm not doing—"

He broke off into a jag of coughing that sent yellow spittle flying from his mouth.

Solomon bolted toward Zarin, silent save for the slap of his feet on the floor. Unaccompanied by the usual screech of his species, instead carried along by the music playing from that speaker-box.

He leaped into the air.

"No!" Graves shouted, crossing his arms to reach under each arm and pull his phantom guns.

Clay changed shape even as he started after Solomon, turning from Al Kovalik to the towering giant whose cracked, dry, claylike flesh was his true form. But he was too late. They were both too late.

The orangutan wrapped one impossibly powerful, incredibly long arm around Zarin's throat and twisted. Bones cracked, muscle and skin tore. Had he another moment, he would have torn the lunatic's head completely off.

But Graves fired. Ghost guns barked. Phantom bullets streaked across that room and punched through Solomon's torso. The orangutan was blown back off of the massive iron contraption that held Zarin's body and struck the bank of monitors.

When he hit the ground, Solomon was dead.

Clay ran over to the orangutan, trying not to look at the ruined mess that was Zarin's head.

"What the hell was that?" he said. "Why would the thing go wild like that?"

But even as he asked those questions, he knew there was more to it. He had seen the change in the beast, the cold intelligence there. Either Solomon had not been the simple ape they'd thought, or there had been some other influence here.

"I've got a better question," Graves said. The ghost floated toward the orangutan's broken corpse. "What was this thing? These guns are just as much ghosts as I am, Joe. They shouldn't have hurt an ordinary animal. They only affect the supernatural."

Clay stared at the shattered body. "The impact and the fall did all of the visible damage."

"I agree," Graves said. "But you saw the bullets strike. They shouldn't have touched Solomon's flesh, but they hit *something*."

Clay might have said something more, but claxon alarms began to sound, filling every room. There was banging somewhere nearby, doors being flung open. Any second, Agent Munson and her people would arrive, none too pleased and with a great many questions that Clay and Graves would not feel like answering.

"We're going to need to rent another car," Clay said.

As the ghost shimmered and vanished from the room, Clay ran toward the massive metal apparatus that had become Zarin's coffin. He leaped onto it, crouched, and leaped again, shooting upward.

The ancient shapeshifter crashed through the glass turret, fragments scattering all around him. He came down hard on the roof, but even as he landed his flesh shifted and transformed, and a moment later, a tiny sparrow darted away from the sprawling Victorian manse on that hilltop and flew off across the gray skies of Rochester.

11

BEHIND Conan Doyle's brownstone home there lay a small garden courtyard hemmed in on three sides by the house. The brick rear wall of the structure behind the Louisburg Square house made up the fourth side of the courtyard, but it was well hidden in the wild tangle of the garden. Some of the trees were thick and long-limbed, others tall but slender as saplings, exotic things that would have been unfamiliar to local botanists. Indeed, some would have been unfamiliar to human botanists, and the flowers were rarer still, and more varied. The garden thrived with color. Scents of vanilla and orange and lilac hung in the air, mixing with a hundred others.

For this was Ceridwen's garden.

Once the Fey sorceress had decided to remain in the human world, to remain with Arthur, he had insisted she take the suite of rooms on the first floor, at the rear of the house. There were half a dozen tall windows and elegant French doors, all of which looked out into the courtyard. It had been a meager garden, then, but Ceridwen had made it come alive with color and scent.

In the center of the garden she had built a fountain. The stones had been drawn up through the ground and put into place with her elemental magic, and then she had summoned water from deep in the earth. When Ceridwen was not in residence, the fountain was a mere trickle, only enough to give the birds and squirrels and chipmunks something to drink, for this was their paradise as well as hers. Paradise in the midst of urban filth. Yet when Ceridwen entered the garden, the fountain would leap and spray, casting a sheen of moisture across the air and making a million tiny rainbows.

Though the other residents of the house visited from time to time, for the most part the garden afforded her utter privacy. Arthur was her only frequent visitor, and he enjoyed the tranquility it provided as much as Ceridwen. With so much uncertainty in their lives, so much dread as they sensed the darkness encroaching on all sides, this place was the perfect sanctuary. A haven.

Ceridwen sat on the edge of the fountain, water spraying her back, causing her turquoise gown to cling to her skin. She hung her head back and let the spray play across her face. It soothed her, and she let out a long breath.

A pair of sparrows began to sing to one another in the rowan tree that grew beside the fountain. She laughed softly and stood up, swaying with the music of the birdsong. Ceridwen twirled around several times and then paused by a wild lilac bush that had grown taller and thicker than any in this world. Lilacs were out of season, but in her garden such trifles never mattered. Of all of the flowers that grew in the human world, lilacs were her favorite. The scent intoxicated her.

She held a branch and inhaled the aroma of the blossoms. A pleasant feeling passed through her, a contentment difficult to achieve of late. Much as she loved Arthur and enjoyed sharing this with him, there were times when solitude was her only salve.

Her mouth craved something sweet. She ran her tongue out over her lips and glanced about for a bare patch of soil. On the far side of the fountain she saw a perfect spot and she strode to it, letting her fingers touch branches and leaves and flowers in greeting as she passed.

Ceridwen dropped to her knees and plunged her fingers into the soil, the rough earth giving way to her, thirsting for contact. The years had tainted the soil of this world with chemicals, yet she had found that even in the most poisonous of places in the realm of mankind, the soil remembered a purer time, when the connections between it and Faerie were many and strong.

The ground trembled a bit, and then a sprig of wood burst from the soil. Ceridwen shuddered with pleasure as the sprig grew to a sapling and then to a tree, bursting with blossoms. The blossoms darkened and grew heavy, and a cascade of seconds passed before they had become fat, ripe cherries.

She rose and plucked a bunch of cherries from a branch, then popped one into her mouth. With her tongue and teeth she stripped its sweet meat from around the pit, and then she swallowed even that hard seed. Like water and fire, earth and air, the garden was a part of her.

"It's beautiful," a voice came from behind her.

She knew at once it did not belong to anyone human. The tranquility of her garden had been shattered by the arrival of an intruder, and the dread that had infected all of the realms in every dimension shuddered through her once more.

"What is your name?" she asked without turning.

"I did not think beauty was possible in the Blight," the voice replied.

Ceridwen ate another cherry, but its sweetness was lost on her. She dropped the rest and spun on one heel, standing in the shadow of the cherry tree. The sorceress raised her chin and glared imperiously at the intruder.

"I am a princess of Faerie, gnat. You'd do well to take care how you address me."

The emissary from her uncle's court was clad in the colors of stream and leaf, but over those clothes he wore a cloak of purest black that was like a velvet slash across the beauty of the garden. At his side hung a silver sword, its scabbard gleaming against the cloak. His thin features were the same pale hue as her own, tinted with a hint of blue.

Her words caused him to flinch.

His bright green eyes widened and then he lowered his gaze. The emissary drew back his hood to reveal rich brown hair.

"In harsh times, we are wont to become harsh ourselves," the emissary said. "Forgive me, majesty. It is unlike me to be so brusque and unseemly for a messenger from your uncle's court."

"I asked your name," she said curtly.

The emissary raised his eyes. "I am called Abhean."

Ceridwen narrowed her eyes. "I have heard the name. You are the Harper?"

Abhean nodded. "In happier times, that's true. When times grow dark, there's little call for my music."

"I'd think more call than ever."

"I am master of the harp, but also of the sword, and one can serve the king better than the other."

Ceridwen strode toward him. "You may rise, Harper, and tell me your purpose here. The Fey so rarely enter the Blight."

Abhean stood and rested his hand on the pommel of his sword, slightly at attention, a formal air about him. "I beg your forgiveness, Princess Ceridwen, for my rudeness upon my arrival. Entering the Blight has me on edge, and I have behaved inexcusably."

"The humans live in this world, the Blight as our people call it, every day, and only some of them behave inexcusably. Nevertheless, you are excused, but only if you will arrive at the purpose of your intrusion immediately."

The Harper executed a small bow. "Of course, Princess—"

"Merely Ceridwen, please."

"If you wish."

"So I do."

"Ceridwen, then. Your uncle, King Finvarra, has sent me to ask you to return immediately to his court. He bade me tell you that he fears for your safety because of the way the Blight trembles. The seers spy a shadow that covers all of the worlds. All of the signs indicate that something terrible has awoken and threatens this world."

Ceridwen nodded. "Yes. I know well the peril the human world faces. Yet it is that very danger that forces me to stay. The terror that the seers have predicted threatens all realms, not only this one. But here is where it will come first and where we have the best chance of stopping it."

Abhean arched an eyebrow and took a deep breath. He let it out slowly and shifted awkwardly on his feet.

"You have something else to say, Harper?"

"I'm sorry, Ceridwen, but I am ill prepared for your refusal. The king gave me only a message to deliver. I had not imagined you would deny him."

"Yet I must."

The handsome Fey warrior regarded her with those eyes, so bright green they were mesmerizing. "If I may be so bold—"

"I doubt that I could prevent it."

"—there is trouble at home as well. Trouble of a different sort. The ill feeling that the seers have perceived has unsettled all of Faerie. Those who supported Morrigan or who refuse to believe the extent of her surrender to darkness resent the king. There is a great deal of political turmoil. I fear the outcome, Ceridwen. I fear we may see a return to the Twilight Wars."

Horrorstruck, she stared at him. Images of shadow spreading across the land, of all of Faerie torn by civil war, of blood and savagery and monsters ravaging the land, played across her mind. Her mother's screams echoed inside her skull.

"Surely it cannot have grown that dire so quickly."

Abhean lowered his gaze. "I fear it will come to that before long."

For long moments, Ceridwen stared at him. She glanced

around the garden and back at the house, the French doors that led into her bedroom standing open and inviting. She thought about Arthur, and the love that had reignited. More than anything, however, she thought of the Demogorgon, the unimaginable evil that even now made its way across the universe toward this world.

The humans could not stand alone.

She would not let Arthur face the Demogorgon without her at his side. Ceridwen felt sure he would die, and if so, she had to perish at his side. In her heart, she knew this. Fate weighed heavily upon her.

"You know how to find me, should the worst come to pass. Should the trouble here be averted, I will come to my uncle's side immediately. Carry that message to him, with my love."

"As you wish," Abhean replied.

The Harper reached within his cloak and removed his harp. He plucked at its strings and bade her farewell even as he began to fade away, as though he had never been there at all. Warrior and poet, he had ever been a great ally to Finvarra, for with his harp he was a Walker Between Worlds.

With him gone and some of the lightness returned to the garden, Ceridwen went to the fountain. Droplets of water fell around her and upon her, fresh and cool upon her skin.

She reached into the water, and the fountain ceased, leaving only a rippling pool.

Ceridwen brushed her hand across the surface of the water once, twice, a third time. "Kate," she whispered. "Moya. Emmy. Kiera."

Faces appeared on the water, images that wavered with the brush of her hand on the scrying pool. With a touch, she turned the scrying pool to ice as clear as a mirror, and the images settled. Each of the women glanced up, one by one, as she called their names. They would not be able to see her, but they would hear her voice, these lovers of the natural world who had made offerings to her, who had been her eyes in the human world during the years when she refused to return here.

One by one, they answered her, softly, reverently.

"There is trouble in Faerie, my friends," she told them, and immediately sensed their anxiety, their fear. "No, no. I am in no danger at the moment. It is the realm I fear for, not my own safety. You must spread the word to all of those who believe, who would serve me. If there is any sign of further discord in Faerie, if any of you sense anything, or if any of the sprites and such with whom you communicate bring unwelcome news, you must inform me immediately."

"Yes, Mistress," they replied, one by one, these faithful few who had given themselves, heart and soul, to the ideals that Ceridwen believed in, to nature and the elements.

"Blessings upon you," Ceridwen said, for it was what they wished to hear.

She slid her hand over the ice, and their faces disappeared. The scrying pool was empty for a moment, and then she whispered ancient words and ran her hands over it again, attempting to use it as a window to see into Faerie.

She scried nothing but darkness.

There would be no seeing through to other worlds now. The magic that held the worlds together was trembling. The Demogorgon was coming. Ceridwen knew she ought to warn Arthur immediately, tell him of the conversation with the Harper and all that had transpired. But of course he was well aware of the Demogorgon's approach.

Arthur believed it was still very far away. Perhaps years. They would prepare for its arrival as best they could. Meanwhile, they had to combat the horrors that arose in this world.

Yet if the realms were so unstable now, with the Demogorgon still far off, how much worse would it get before the most ancient of evils arrived?

The question alone made her tremble.

•   •   •

SHUCK lifted his muscular, black leg, and let loose a stream of steaming urine that scoured the brick wall and stank of vomit.

"Jesus," Eve said. "I'm not even breathing, and I can smell it."

"Yeah, their piss is pretty potent," Squire said, holding on to the beast's chain and waiting for it to finish. He gave the chain a sharp tug. "C'mon pal, we ain't got all night."

Eve scanned the city streets; her acute senses extended outward. "Let him sniff," she said with annoyance. "It's not like we've got anything to follow."

People coming down the street gave them a wide berth as they saw the large animal, one guy muttering beneath his breath that he didn't know it was legal to keep circus animals as pets.

"Now I'm just getting annoyed," Eve announced as they continued down Washington Street, Shuck's face practically pressed to the ground as it attempted to find a demonic trail.

"More so than usual?" Squire asked. "Dare I ask?"

"It's Conan Doyle," she said, glancing in the window of a store at a display of winter jackets and boots. When she found herself in a mood like this, she had the compulsion to buy. "I can't believe he's known who Danny's real father was all along."

Shuck stopped at a wrought-iron trash receptacle, its sensitive nose taking in the various aromas that were left there, probably since the barrel had been installed. The way it planted its large paws, it was clearly not going anywhere until it was finished.

"Look, Evie . . ."

She quickly shot him the look.

"Eve," the hobgoblin corrected. "How long have you known Mr. Doyle? Probably longer than I have, and I know that the guy has his own way of dealing with things. Does he often withhold pertinent information? Fuck, yes, but as my good friend Billy S., used to say, *Though this be madness, yet there is method in't.'"*

"You didn't know freakin' Shakespeare," she scoffed.

"Who said anything about Shakespeare? I was quoting Billy Scuzzarella. Ran a gelato stand in Brooklyn. Fuckin' awesome gelato. But what I'm trying to say is that Doyle's got his own way of doing things, and he doesn't really give two shits about whether we like it or not."

A gaggle of teenage street kids, their clothes at least three sizes too big, started across the street toward them.

"Hey, what kind of dog is that?" one of them asked. "Is dat a Pit? Big motherfuckin' Pit if it is," he finished, his posse cracking up.

"We should probably get out here," Eve said. "We're starting to attract attention."

Squire gave the chain a tug, and the shuck growled menacingly. "You're the one that wanted to let him sniff," he said. "C'mon boy, let's get going, there'll be plenty of other things that stink."

The kid's friends stayed back, standing in the middle of the street, but it didn't stop the leader from heading over. "Hey, you hear me aks a question?" he asked, toothpick moving around from one side of his mouth to the other. "I aksed you about your dog."

Eve stood between the kid and the still sniffing beast.

"No, it's not a Pit. Satisfied?"

He gave her what he probably believed was his charming smile, trying to look past her at the animal. "It a mix?" he asked. "Looks like he part bear or somethin'." He turned around to see if his friends had heard his latest gem.

"Yeah, he's a mixed breed, who doesn't like strangers," Eve explained. She was getting cranky.

The kid smiled again, and she wanted to tear the smirk right off his face.

"Is it only the dog that don't like strangers?" he asked. "Cause if it ain't, my name is Tyrell, and we ain't strangers anymore." He held out his hand for her to shake, and that was pretty much the straw that broke the camel's back.

Eve shook her head with disgust, stepping out of the way to allow the kid access to Shuck.

"Be my guest, Tyrell," she said.

The kid moved closer to the black-skinned beast, his friends egging him on.

"This is a bad idea, kid," Squire said, having given up trying to move Shuck along.

"Don't worry, Squire," Eve told him. "Tyrell just wants to make friends, isn't that right, Tyrell?"

The kid smiled again, squatting down to Shuck's level and extending his hand for it to smell. "Yo, big dog," he made a strange sound with his mouth trying to get Shuck's attention. "I'm talkin' to you."

Shuck was a blur. He knocked Tyrell down and sprang onto the punk's chest, nearly pulling Squire off his feet. The shuck had the kid's arm buried in its mouth up to his elbow, and the kid was screaming.

"Ah, shit!" Squire said, pulling back on the leash, trying to get the animal off of the kid. Shuck wouldn't budge, his growl sounding like the engine of a heavy piece of machinery.

Eve stifled a laugh as she watched Tyrell's terrified friends take off down the street, leaving their buddy to his fate. He was crying now, his eyes squeezed shut, refusing to look at the nightmarish visage that was perched over him, with his arm buried in its mouth.

She could just imagine how nasty *that* must have felt.

Eve approached the beast, bending over to whisper in its black velvet ear. "Let go."

Shuck growled louder, looking at her from the corner of its eye.

Tyrell was shrieking now, thrashing beneath the beast's weight, but getting absolutely nowhere.

"Maybe if we smash him over the head with something really heavy he'll only take the arm," Squire suggested.

Eve ignored the hobgoblin, reaching out to take Shuck's ear in her hand and twisting it. "Did you hear me?" she scolded. "Let go!"

Its growl intensified, but still she held on to the ear, bringing her own face closer to its own. "Let. Go."

Shuck pulled back its head, dropping Tyrell's arm from its mouth. From what she could see, the arm was still intact, although the jacket was a lost cause.

"Good boy," she said happily, letting go of its ear. "Now, let's get out of here."

They left the kid moaning in the street.

"So what now?" Squire asked, tugging on the leash to make the beast keep pace with them. "We're getting absolutely nowhere with this. Who knows if he's still even in the area."

"No, they're around here somewhere," Eve said, hands shoved into the pockets of her coat as they walked toward the Common. "Our demon daddy seems to have a thing for Bean Town, enough to have left two of his kids behind. Nope, I think he's still here somewhere, and I'd bet dollars to doughnuts that Danny's with him."

"Dollars to doughnuts?" Squire asked. "How old *are* you?"

She gave him a glance from the corner of her eye.

"Never mind," he said. "Where are we going anyway? We've pretty much handled Tremont Street and—"

"Boylston," she said.

Squire stopped, tugging back on Shuck's leash to make him stop as well. Eve continued on through the Common on her way toward the Public Garden.

"Why are we going to Boylston?" the goblin asked. "And it better not be for the reason I think it is."

Eve turned around, walking backward as she spoke. "It's the only place I can think of to pick up a trail."

"No, Eve," Squire said, shaking his large head. "We can't go there—it's forbidden. Mr. Doyle had to call in a lot of favors to fix stuff the last time you paid them a visit. We have a truce now. We stay out of Peking Tommy's, and they don't organize a hunting party to take you out."

"I needed information that I knew they had," she said, smiling as she remembered her last visit to the Chinese restaurant that was kind of a neutral zone to the various supernatural beings that called the city of Boston their home.

Most of them didn't care for Conan Doyle and his Menagerie. They didn't think the mage had a right to interfere with the various breeds of monsters and magical creatures that had filtered in from other dimensions over the ages and made their lives in the midst of human cities, with people none the wiser. They were all for letting the current dominant species tumble to the back of the line to make way for another—preferably one of their own.

"I admit things got a little out of hand," Eve said. "But I got what I went in for."

"You trashed the place—never mind the netherfolk you fucked up in the process."

"They shouldn't have lied to me."

"We can't go there, Eve," Squire said. "It could make a bad situation a hell of a lot worse."

She walked over to him, feeling her ire on the rise. "Look," she said, staring him down. Even Shuck backed up with a frightened whine. "I'm getting tired of the bullshit. This is the second night we've been out here with nothing to show for it. This demon's clever, I'll give him that, but he needs to be found. So does Danny. And your fucking bloodhound here isn't doing shit."

Shuck tilted his head to one side and whined.

"I just don't think it's a good idea, Eve," Squire said.

"We told Julia we'd find Danny and bring him home," she said. "Do you want to listen to her sob when we come home empty-handed?"

Squire said nothing.

"Come on," she said, putting on her nicest smile. "I promise to be good."

SINCE Danny Ferrick had come to live in his home, Conan Doyle had done his best to treat the boy with respect. The most vital element of this had been to provide the boy with a sense of privacy. Danny already believed—

and rightly so—that the primary reason he'd been invited to reside here was so that Conan Doyle and the others could keep watch over him. Yes, it was true he would be more comfortable around individuals who would not be troubled by his nature and that he would not suffer the slings and arrows of those who would be cruel to him—or be terrified of him—because of his appearance.

But the young man had been afraid of his demonic nature. Conan Doyle knew that for all of his bluster, Danny wanted to become a part of the Menagerie and help to combat the forces of darkness because he wished to combat that darkness in himself.

And Conan Doyle had all but convinced himself that the boy was succeeding. The arrival of the young man's demon-father had complicated matters, but it had been easy for Conan Doyle to ascribe Danny's behavior to the shadowy influence of his sire.

Now he felt like a fool.

He felt sure there was more at work here than the return of Danny's demon-father. Thus, any privacy he had afforded the boy in his home must now be sacrificed for his well-being. A demon was at large—perhaps two—and they had to be stopped, no matter what it cost in blood or broken trust.

The door was locked. Conan Doyle shook his head. To think that any room in his own house could be locked against him. He waved a hand, and a tiny, nearly invisible spark of magic jumped from his index finger and touched the knob. The lock clicked, and the door swung open several inches.

Gently, he pushed it farther, opening it wide, and he stood on the threshold surveying the room, trying to see what Danny would see when he entered his own room. The last time Conan Doyle had stood here, all he had been able to see was the mess. It was difficult to see such squalor in his own home and not attend to it, but he had not wanted to coddle or interfere with the boy.

Now, he had to see past that mess, for surely Danny

would not notice it. Several things stood out to him immediately. Without asking, the boy had nailed a hat rack up on the wall. Half a dozen different hats hung there, from a Boston Red Sox cap to an old-fashioned Stetson.

Anything to cover the horns that had humiliated him so much.

The hat rack was the only spot of neatness in the entire room. Danny favored hooded sweatshirts to cover his small prongs, but the hats appeared almost to be waiting, held in abeyance, for a time when a sweatshirt hood would not be sufficient to hide the horns.

Danny knew they were growing. Of course he did. And he knew they would continue to grow.

There were books and old compact discs strewn around the room among the filthy clothes. But the books were buried, while most of the CDs were on top, and some were spread upon the bed. His MP3 player and the small computer his mother had bought him sat on the desk against the far wall. CDs had been stacked all around, music he had borrowed from Squire and Eve.

The music he had continued to pursue, but he had not read anything in quite some time, this young man who had once loved to read sports biographies and mystery novels.

Conan Doyle also noticed a conspicuous absence in the room. Once, Danny had kept a great many photographs of his mother and of himself as a child, some featuring friends he surely no longer had. There were no more photographs in the room.

He entered.

Something caught his eye, and he turned to peer through the open bathroom door to see that shards of mirror glass littered the floor and the sink. Conan Doyle stepped into the bathroom and turned on the light. The switch felt rough, and he glanced at it to see that a dark streak of blood had dried there.

He frowned and went to look at the mirror. Shattered, presumably by Danny's fist.

On the rim of the sink there were more streaks of blood

and a print that clearly showed one of the demon-boy's fingers. In his mind, Conan Doyle could almost picture the boy examining his growing horns in the mirror and cutting his fingers on the razor sharpness of their points.

The mirror allowed him no denials. Daniel Ferrick could wish all he wanted and hide from the rest of the world. But he could not hide from the mirror, or from himself.

Conan Doyle nodded and stepped back from the sink. He turned and went back out into Danny's bedroom. Now he began a more methodical search, pacing the room, studying the debris of a teenager's life.

At the foot of the bed a black smear marred the floor. Conan Doyle knelt and touched a finger to it and found the stuff hard and tacky. He sniffed it, and frowned deeply. He glanced up at the windows and went over to them. On one windowsill he found the same substance.

Roof tar.

He opened the window and thrust his head out, looking left and right. Some of the stones were scored and chipped, and in the grooves between them were gouges that might have been left by a mountain climber's pitons. Or a demon's claws.

Conan Doyle craned his neck to look up toward the roof. Then he withdrew, slid the window closed, and left the boy's room. He took the back stairs up to the door carved with wards and banes and opened it, stepping out onto the roof.

He stood a moment and pondered what Danny had been doing up here. Had he simply sat and looked at the stars at night?

No. He had wandered. The boy was long past simple rumination, Conan Doyle felt certain.

He went to the edge of the roof above Danny's window, then followed the short wall that bordered the roof along its perimeter until he came to a spot where the stone had been partially worn away. Scuffs and claw marks showed that Danny had spent a great deal of time in this one spot.

He might have traveled over rooftops, gone anywhere in the city, but much of the time he'd spent out the window had been spent right here.

Now all Conan Doyle had to determine was why.

He glanced up. Immediately across from his vantage point and one story down was a window. Through it, he could see a girl in a black bra and underwear brushing her long hair in front of a mirror. Her mouth moved, no doubt singing along to music Conan Doyle could not hear through the closed window and from this distance.

How much time, he wondered, had Danny Ferrick spent crouched here, watching this girl? Had it been only natural curiosity, human voyeurism, or had darker thoughts taken root in the young man's mind?

No, not young man, Conan Doyle reminded himself. *Young demon.*

It appeared that Danny had become far more deeply troubled than any of them had realized. He cursed himself for not being more attentive. Yet he also knew it was too late for recriminations. What he required now was a solution.

No matter what it cost in blood and broken trust.

SQUIRE didn't like it, he didn't like it one little fucking fragment.

Eve approached the tiny, red-painted restaurant with the burned out neon dragon above the door as if she owned the place. Peking Tommy's was practically invisible to the Joes moving along busy Boylston Street. The magical wards and sigils scrawled in the doorframe and around the windows acted as a deterrent to the normal folk, preventing them from having any interest whatsoever in going inside. Peking Tommy's appeared to humanity to be nothing more than a bad case of food poisoning waiting to happen, and that was exactly how the owner, Tommy Chow, wanted it.

Now if those wards had been designed to keep out the

mother of all vampires and her really shitty attitude, everything would have been peachy. But no such luck.

An old-fashioned bell over the door tinkled merrily as Eve swept into the foyer. It wasn't bad enough that they were entering a forbidden zone, but they were going in with a shuck in tow.

What part of this plan did I think would work? Squire pondered.

Oh yeah, none of it.

The old woman at the reception stand looked up from where she had been snoozing, her small, almond-colored eyes immediately registering and recognizing just who had walked through the door. She barked something in the ancient Hakka dialect, and the foyer went strangely dark, as if the light had been suddenly sucked from the room.

Here we go.

There was a flurry of movement, and where the old woman had been standing there now stood a nine-foot-tall crow with fiery eyes. Shuck began to tug on his leash, eager to play with the giant bird, but Squire held him back. This was Eve's game. She said she could handle it, and Squire was more than happy to oblige.

There were mints on a nearby table, and Squire helped himself to a handful, popping a few into the curious Shuck's mouth as well.

The crow's voice boomed, a powerful wind whipping up as it slowly began to flap its huge wings.

"English," Eve yelled over the pounding wind, her hand covering her eyes from the dust and dirt that was being tossed around. "I'm a little rusty on my ancient Chinese dialects."

A handsome guy dressed in a black T-shirt and chinos appeared out of the darkness beside the giant bird.

"How about this, then," he said with no trace of an accent. "Get the hell out."

"Is that any way to talk to a lady, Tommy?" Eve asked.

The green, gold, and red dragon tattoo that ran along the right side of Tommy Chow's face seemed to writhe upon his flesh as if agitated—like it wanted to leap from its perch and devour the woman who had aggravated it so.

"There is a truce, Eve," he said, restraining his obvious anger. "You know better than this—as do you, hobgoblin." Tommy peered around Eve to look directly at Squire.

"I told her this was a bad idea," Squire explained, reaching for another handful of mints. "But when has she ever listened to me?"

The giant crow spread its wings, liquid fire dripping menacingly from its eyes, as it shared a quick exchange with Tommy. Squire's Hakka was rusty, but he thought that the two were probably discussing the quickest way of dispatching them. Then again, for all he knew it could have been about an overflowing urinal in the head.

"I didn't come here for trouble, Tommy," Eve said with a gentle shake of her head.

"But you are well aware of the turmoil your presence here will cause."

She nodded. "Yep, and I came anyway."

The dragon tattoo on the proprietor's face was definitely moving, the dragon having shifted its gaze to glare at Eve with hungry eyes.

"Leave now, and I'll forget this ever happened," he said. "The truce will remain intact."

"Sorry, Tommy," she said apologetically. "But I can't do that. I need to go inside—to talk to some folks."

The crow spread its wings, supernatural energies leaking from the tips of its feathers. Tommy held up his hand, stopping it from doing whatever it was about to do.

"You realize I would be within my rights to destroy you now."

"Yes," Eve agreed. "You would be within your rights to try."

The two glowered at each other. Shuck began to whine, and Squire knew exactly how the beast was feeling. The tension was so thick in the foyer that a piece of it could have been cut from the air and used like a club to beat the living crap out of something.

Somewhere within the restaurant a glass shattered, breaking the unbearable tension just a tad.

"I'm willing to give you something," Eve said to Tommy. "An object of great value to show how serious I am about keeping my word."

Tommy folded his arms across his chest, tilting his head curiously to one side. "What will you offer me?"

She'd hooked him for sure. Tommy Chow was a purveyor of ancient and bizarre antiquities, from this world, and the worlds beyond. Conan Doyle had had some problems with the man and his questionable methods for obtaining these items, but they'd worked out their differences when Tommy had acquired a certain object of power that Conan Doyle had been jonesing for.

From her pocket Eve produced a short, silver dagger. Tommy tensed, obviously wondering if he was going to have to defend himself. But instead of using the blade on him, she used her free hand to tug on a lock of her hair, and then passed the dagger's edge across it. When she'd returned the blade to its place inside her jacket, she held out her hand, offering Tommy the lock of her hair.

"For you," she said.

Tommy's eyes widened in surprise and appreciation. The value of this gift on the black market, or merely for his personal collection, was extraordinary. But if he was going to accept he had to act quickly, for once it left Eve's body, the lock of her hair would decay rapidly. If he was to accept her deal, he would have to find a way to preserve it at once.

"And what will I be allowing you to do if I accept?" Tommy asked, his eyes glued to the small piece of raven black hair resting in the palm of Eve's hand.

"I just want to talk," she explained. "There's a demon in town, crossed over from one hell or another. We've got three corpses already, and a friend of ours is in trouble. Conan Doyle's asked me and my ugly little friend to send our wayward traveler back to the Inferno."

Tommy narrowed his eyes. "A lot of strange things happening lately. Signs and portents. Broken rules. I'm not sure how much difference one demon's going to make."

Eve held the lock of hair in her open palm. She stared at him. "Don't fuck around, Tommy. You like the world the way it is. Me, Conan Doyle, and the rest of us, we're doing you a favor every time we stop this world from crumbling into the abyss."

Bored with the whole thing, Shuck plopped down onto the lobby floor and began to eagerly lick at his crotch. Squire considered doing the same.

Tommy stared at Eve a moment longer and then said something in Hakka to the giant crow. The bird gradually returned to the shape of the old Chinese woman. She darted toward Eve, reaching out with a liver-spotted hand to take the proffered prize, but Eve closed her fingers over the precious piece of herself.

"Do we have a deal, Tommy?" she asked. "Old sins forgiven?"

Squire admired the fact that Eve could add that kind of irony to conversation without sounding bitter.

The old woman looked to the man as well, waiting for his reply.

Slowly Tommy nodded. "Yes, but I must accompany you inside."

"Sounds fine," Eve said, opening her hand again.

The old woman carefully took the lock of hair from Eve's open palm and scurried off in search of some way to preserve it. Squire was certain that Tommy had something that could do the trick in one of his back rooms. You could find Hitler's toilet paper back there, and probably Robert Johnson's guitar and Daniel Webster's mummified testicles as well.

There was awkward silence in the foyer until Eve spoke again. "Now I wouldn't expect that hair to wind up in the possession of somebody who would wish me harm."

Tommy smiled, the tail of the dragon tattoo tickling the right-hand corner of his mouth. "Of course not, although I could think of at least fifty individuals who would pay me a king's ransom for a piece of you. It would be very profitable for a poor businessman like myself."

"Poor? If you say so. But you're not a fool," Eve replied.

"Exactly," he answered with a slight nod. "The repercussions of said business transaction would be most unpleasant." Tommy turned, walking toward a pair of closed wooden doors adorned with the silhouettes of two roaring dragons.

"Not to be rude," he said, hand upon the wooden door handle. "But you're bad for business, and if you could make this quick it would be greatly appreciated."

"We'll see what we can do."

Squire tugged upon Shuck's chain, and the great, black beast grunted as it climbed to its feet.

"Does that . . . thing have to go in as well?" Tommy asked, peering around Eve.

Shuck growled menacingly.

"He's part of the package," Eve said. "Might be instrumental in us finding the right person to talk to."

Tommy made a face to show that he was displeased, but would have tolerated just about any indignity to get his hands on that lock of hair.

"Just talk," he said, turning to Eve as he pulled open one of the heavy wooden double doors.

"Just talk," she reassured.

The smells of all kinds of Chinese food, including some dishes that had not been prepared properly elsewhere in centuries, wafted over to greet them. Squire's belly immediately began to grumble.

The dining room was about half full, not bad for a weeknight, and all of the patrons looked up from their meals to stare at the newcomers.

"Excuse me, ladies and gentlemen," Tommy said, looking around the restaurant.

Eating utensils clattered against plates, and the drone of hushed whispers began to grow in the air. As far as Squire was concerned, there wasn't a lady or gentlemen in the bunch.

"A matter of grave importance has caused me to allow this interruption," he explained. "A terrible threat has come to the city, one that concerns us all." His eyes hit upon every table, every customer. "I am certain that we all wish to cooperate as best we can with efforts to rid our city of such a threat, just as I am certain you will all recognize our visitors. I have allowed them the opportunity to speak briefly with any of you that may have pertinent information you might wish to share."

Tommy paused. No one looked happy, but Squire was relieved when none of them immediately tried to tear out Eve's throat.

"I thank you for your understanding in this matter. An appetizer of your choice will be provided free of charge for any inconvenience this might have caused." With a slight bow, he presented Eve to the crowd.

If looks could kill, Eve would be nothing more than a quivering puddle, Squire observed. A waiter passed by, and he reached out, grabbing hold of the tall guy's arm. The man looked down at him with disdain, but he didn't give a rat's ass.

"Get me an order of dumplings to go," he told the man, keeping an eye on the crowd. "Get 'em to me before the place goes shithouse, and there'll be a little something extra in it for ya."

Eve walked farther into the dining room, Tommy Chow watching her every move. She was eyeing the tables, every goblin, troll, street fairy, lycanthrope, and two-bit sorcerer getting a moment of her undivided attention. Squire could tell that she wanted them to know that she was well aware of who was present.

For future reference.

"You know who I am, and who I represent," she said, reaching down to one of the tables nearby and helping herself to a glass of water. She took a sip.

Squire chuckled; *the bitch certainly knows how to work a room.*

Smacking her lips, she continued. "A demon has crossed over and is somewhere in the vicinity." She pointed to herself and then to Squire and Shuck. "We need to find it."

The black beast's head was sniffing the air, the aroma of various spicy dishes arousing its senses. Shuck tried to pull him toward one of the tables, but Squire planted his feet, continuing to listen Eve.

"Normally there'd be no problems with tracking something like this," she said, looking around the room again. "But I'm sure you're all aware that things have been a little different lately."

The myriad creatures at the tables around the room seemed to respond to her observation, looking down at their plates, or at their companions, many with knowing smiles.

"So I was hoping for some volunteers," Eve continued. "Any hints of the whereabouts of this thing would be greatly appreciated, and remembered in the future."

Some of the creatures hung their heads, not making eye contact, while others glared at her defiantly, as if wishing to start something.

The restaurant remained quiet, nobody giving up a thing.

"So, it's either you guys don't know anything," she said, finishing her water, and setting the glass down on the corner of a table. "Or you just don't want to share—which would really hurt my feelings."

Squire watched, certain that she was filing their faces away in some little dark corner of her mind.

"All right, then," she said. "Thank you all for your time. I'm sure I'll see you all again soon. One by one. Somewhere dark."

As Eve went back toward the foyer, she smiled at Tommy. "Sorry for the trouble."

Squire gave Shuck's chain a snap, and the two of them

followed Eve through the door. The waiter was in the lobby with his dumplings, and he pulled his wallet from his back pocket to pay.

"No charge," said a voice, and Squire looked up to see Tommy standing behind him. The owner said something to the waiter in Hakka, and the man handed Squire his take-out. The smell wafting from the bag was absolutely delicious, and Squire couldn't wait to dig in.

"Much obliged," Squire said, Shuck tugging him toward the door. Eve had already gone outside.

Tommy bowed. "Give your master my regards," he said. "It has been some time since we last conversed."

"I'll tell him you were askin' for him," Squire said, as the anxious Shuck pulled him out the door.

He found Eve in front of the building leaning against a busted parking meter. "Well that was a waste of fucking time," she growled.

"Not completely. We got dumplings," Squire said, tearing open the bag and reaching into the container to sample one of the Chinese delicacies.

"Pssssst!"

Squire turned in the direction of the sound, dumpling midway to his lips. "What now?" he asked, popping the doughy, meat and vegetable treat into his mouth.

A small, pale hand waved them over from around the next corner.

Eve shot Squire a cautionary glance and headed toward the whisperer. Reluctantly, Squire followed at her heels, Shuck trotting happily along beside him, glancing back and forth between Eve and the bag of dumplings.

She rounded the corner, stopping at the mouth of the garbage-strewn alley that ran behind Peking Tommy's. Squire would have thought some of the rubbish would have made it into one of the two dumpsters back there, but apparently that was wishful thinking.

Something fluttered up from a patch of darkness in front of them. Eve stumbled back, stepping on Squire's foot with the pointed heel of her boot, causing the goblin to yelp in pain. He reached down to his injured foot, accidentally letting go of Shuck's chain. The creature reacted instinctively, going after the potential threat that hovered in the air before them.

An ear-piercing scream filled the night as the shuck leaped at the fluttering object. He snatched it out of the air in his jaws and brought it down to the alley floor.

"Help!" a tiny, panicked voice cried. "Don't let the black devil eat me!" The bloodcurdling screams continued.

"What've you got, Shuck?" Squire asked, limping toward the beast.

The thin, almost emaciated figure had pale skin, tinted blue and marbled with darker veins.

The hobgoblin glanced at Eve. "Street fairy."

"They're busy, lately. Sticking their noses in," she replied, staring at the creature.

Squire reached down to grab Shuck's chain. "Let go, boy," he commanded, but the beast wasn't listening.

"Help me! Help me, please!" the filthy little winged creature shrieked, doing its best to fend off the snarling shuck. It wasn't the same breed as Ceridwen and Tess, the street fairy they'd run into the other night in the theater district. This little fellow stood perhaps eighteen inches high. Small, but not so small that it might be confused for a sprite.

"Shuck!" Squire snapped, tugging on the leash.

Eve stepped in and kicked him, her booted foot connecting with the animal's side. "Leave him alone," she said with a snarl.

Shuck dropped its prey, spinning around to face Eve, preparing to attack her.

"Come on," she said slowly, lowering to a crouch even as she spoke the challenge. Her fangs had elongated and her fingers lengthened into eight-inch talons like curved blades. "Attack me, and it'll probably be the last thing you ever do."

Squire hoped she didn't hurt the mutt, but he wasn't getting between them. While the two faced off, he went to the fairy, helping the creature to stand.

"It bent one of my wings," the street fairy complained, fluttering the mothlike appendages.

Definitely not a sprite, Squire thought. They were beautiful, their wings like a butterfly's or a dragonfly's.

"You're lucky he didn't eat you," he said, pulling the fairy over to the alley wall.

Eve and Shuck glared at each other, a low rumbling growl filling the night, and Squire really wasn't sure which one was responsible. Then, when things looked as though they were about to break, Shuck suddenly dropped onto its back, exposing its belly in a sign of submission.

"All right, then," Eve said, bending down to rub the animal's solid, black flesh. "Next time I tell you to do something, you do it."

The animal whined, as if agreeing with her.

"Now," she said, turning her attention to the filthy little creature next to Squire. "What do you want?"

The tiny fairy sneered at them, gingerly touching his wings to see if they were badly damaged.

"My people . . . we've heard about this demon. We've already tried to help you—"

Squire studied him closely. "You're talking about Tess. The fairy chick we met the other night?"

The little winged creature rolled his eyes and sighed. "You're quick on the uptake, handsome. Yes, Tess. And a bunch of others as well. Things have been getting ugly back home, or so we've heard. Word comes now and then, though we're outcasts. None of the Fey back home would even acknowledge us if we tried to return to Faerie. Still, we have family there. It's ugly. We tell ourselves it doesn't matter. This is our home now. But all of a sudden, things are getting pretty ugly here, too."

Squire snorted. "All of a sudden?"

The fairy sniffed arrogantly. "You know what I mean."

Eve crouched down, trying to get as close to his level as possible. "We do, yes. And we appreciate your help. Yours, and Tess's, and all of the street fairies. It's nice to know we're not the only ones who want to keep the darkness at bay."

Squire almost called her on what she'd said. Eve had no real interest in keeping the darkness at bay. She loved the dark. But for once he decided not to bust her chops. He knew very well that there was darkness, and then there was *darkness*.

The fairy looked up at her, a smile on his homely face. The stink of alcohol came off his tiny form in waves. "I was in the bar having myself a little refreshment," he told her. "I heard some things that might help you."

"Why didn't you tell me inside?" she asked.

The fairy shook his head. "Fraternizing with the enemy is frowned upon," he said, looking around conspiratorially. "But what they don't know, won't hurt them—or get me and mine hurt."

"What do you have?" she asked.

"You're looking for the demons," the fairy said. His voice had dropped to a tiny whisper. "I know where they went."

"Demons?" Eve questioned. "More than one?"

The fairy nodded. "At first there was only one, but now there are two." He held up two fingers for them to see.

Squire looked at Eve, not liking the direction this was taking.

"Danny," she said, and all he could do was nod.

Her assumption had been right. The boy was with his father.

12

THE new rental was a silver Lexus. Clay had charged it to an account set up by Conan Doyle. Dr. Graves knew that the mage had spent decades amassing wealth and wished to put it to good use, financing his war against he darkness. Clay had been alive far longer, but the immortal shapeshifter had apparently not exercised as much fore-thought, for he seemed more than happy to use Conan Doyle's money.

Graves realized it would be a mistake to make too many assumptions about Clay, however. If he truly was what he claimed to be, what Arthur believed him to be, there was no telling how many lives he'd led and forgotten by now.

Hours passed in comfortable silence. Graves could have slipped into the spirit world and been in Manhattan in no time at all, or simply passed the time there in quiet peace. But Clay was taking the time to help him, devoting more attention to the mystery of his murder than anyone had in decades, despite Conan Doyle's assertions otherwise. The least Graves could do was keep him company.

They spoke in brief spurts of conversation, of music and art, war and history, medicine and science. Though Clay had never been human, Graves found him the most humane of companions, a being who truly believed in the capacity for greatness inherent in the human race, and a creature of rare wisdom.

They drove across the Tappan Zee Bridge into Westchester County, the late afternoon sunlight glaring on the windshield and washing out Graves's spectral form so that when he glanced down he found that he was nearly invisible even to his own eyes.

"Do you mind if I ask you a personal question?" Clay asked.

Graves arched an eyebrow and studied the strong, handsome profile of his companion. The shapeshifter's preferred form was neither young nor old, yet the features were distinct, and the ghost wondered if once upon a time Clay had known a man with this face, if perhaps this chosen appearance was some memorial to a lost friend.

He made a mental note to ask, even as he nodded.

"Of course."

"When we solve this thing . . . when you finally know who took your life, and how, and why, are you really going to move on? Forever? You've spent all this time wandering the world as a spirit, but it isn't like you've been haunting the wreckage of the past. Strange as it sounds, you've made a new life, after death. You have purpose. Is the pull of whatever remains for you afterward so strong?"

The ghost cocked his head and gazed at Clay. For all that he wore the face of a man, for all the ordinariness with which he held the steering wheel and drove the car and blinked and breathed and spoke and laughed, Graves felt he was among the very few who never forgot that Clay was not human. Not in the least. He had been alive upon the Earth since the world began, and it was possible he could never die. From anyone else, the question might have been too personal, too prying. But he understood that Clay truly wished to understand something that was beyond his experience, or his imagining.

"I've always said as much, haven't I? My Gabriella and I never married—I waited too long, and then it was too late for me, for us—but I love her still. All I've ever wanted is to be with her again. The current of the soulstream is strong, my friend. Any time I must delve deeply into the ether, going farther into the spirit world, its pull is almost inescapable. I hold on. But when the mystery of my murder is solved, there will be nothing to keep my spirit from departing at last for whatever awaits me."

Clay glanced over at him curiously, once and then again. "Nothing at all?"

A chill passed through the specter. Graves felt a queasy discomfort he had never felt in all the time since his death.

"What do you mean?"

"Nothing, it's just . . ." Clay shrugged. "I guess I had the idea that something was brewing between you and Danny's mother. You've been looking out for the kid, but it seemed like more than that."

The ghost was taken aback. The words fell like dominos, and even as Clay spoke them, he recognized the truth. How he had managed to avoid noticing it, to hide it from himself, he wasn't sure. But now that the words had been spoken it felt so painfully obvious, and the fact that it had been so obvious to Clay embarrassed him.

"I . . . I'm very fond of Julia. She's endured a great deal, and yet her love for Danny remains untainted by it. I admire that."

"I'm sorry," Clay said, flexing his fingers on the wheel, staring at the road ahead. "I didn't mean to make you uncomfortable."

"No, it's all right," the ghost replied. "I simply haven't dwelt much upon the situation. I'm . . . well, it's absurd, really. I'm dead, Joe. Fond of Julia or not, there's nothing there to pursue."

Clay focused on the road. "Maybe not. But I get the impression she's pretty fond of you, too."

"You're reading it wrong," Graves said, wishing now that the subject had never come up. "Where could that lead? Should I haunt her life? I worry for her and for Danny. I try to look out for the boy. I'm afraid for him. But whatever I might feel for Julia, Gabriella will always be the one I love. I'll do everything I can to see that Julia and Danny are looked after when my spirit moves on, but the soulstream pulls at me. Somewhere on the other side, Gabriella waits for me."

Clay nodded, and said nothing more.

The Lexus rolled on in silence.

GABRIELLA'S skin is the olive hue common to her native Italy, dark compared to some, but not nearly dark enough to avoid the stares of white people as she rides the IRT train out to Flushing Meadows with Leonard. One of the things Dr. Graves admires most about her is that she does not merely ignore the stares and whispers of bigots who are disgusted or angered by the sight of a white woman with a black man. No, Gabriella just does not care.

God, how he loves her.

All of his life has been devoted to science, the pursuit of knowledge, and the improvement of the human condition. In all that time he had given little thought to love. It is an unquantifiable variable, and so, to him, it is as much a bit of superstition and fancy as ghosts and magic. When it struck him, he was far from ready for it, and for the first time he has been forced to accept the existence of love.

The train rattles and sways. Gabriella and Dr. Graves hold on to the same metal pole on the standing-room-only train, but their hands do not touch. He gazes at her wide brown eyes and the gentle curve of her neck, and he knows what it must be to believe in sorcery. Surely, this must be it.

It is warm, today, a late spring preview of what the summer of 1940 will hold for New Yorkers. Dr. Graves ought to have taken a car out to Queens, but Gabriella insisted on riding the train. All that she has heard and read about the Fair has given her the impression that the experience is meant to be a universal one, that throngs of peo-

ple are almost required to fully understand the impact of the exposition.

And so they ride the train and suffer the dark looks of those who disapprove of a white woman escorted by a black man, no matter that he is better dressed than perhaps anyone else on the IRT that day. It isn't the clothes that make the man, he has found. For far too many people, it is the skin. So they smile at one another, and they talk when the rumble of the train is not too loud, but their hands do not touch, and there are words absent from their conversation. To be too obvious with their love would be to invite calamity.

This has been the case ever since Gabriella came to live in America to be with Dr. Graves. Along with the other adventurers and crime fighters who have cropped up in recent years, such as the Whisper and the daredevil pilot known as Joe Falcon, he has achieved a certain notoriety. This celebrity has meant that for every righteous bigot ready to punish him for his audacity, there are two or three who will pull the fool aside and mutter in his ear that the man he is about to taunt or chastise or attack is Dr. Graves. Some are drawn away from conflict reluctantly, and others are sheepish and apologetic.

As if their behavior would somehow have been excusable had he been some other man.

Taking the train was, perhaps, not the best idea.

But it was Gabriella's wish, and so he says nothing.

"We're almost there," she says.

Dr. Graves—Leonard—smiles. The train pulls into World's Fair Station and shudders to a stop. All in all, the ride is worth the nickel apiece they had paid. The passengers are disgorged upon the platform, and Leonard and Gabriella join the hordes walking along the broad boardwalk. The sun shines brightly, and as one they look up and see the two towering symbols of the World's Fair straight ahead. The triangular spire of the Trylon rises perhaps one hundred and fifty feet into the air, and beside it rests the massive globe of the Perisphere. The structures gleaming white in the sun, Leonard is astonished to find that the photo-

graphs he has seen in the papers did not do the architectural centerpieces of the Fair any justice at all. These symbols, so proudly male and female, are breathtaking to behold.

"It's beautiful," Gabriella says, and she reaches out to take his hand.

Leonard flinches and almost pulls away, concerned about the crowd around them. But her smile chides him, and he twists his fingers more tightly in hers. If there is anywhere in America where they might be together without fear of reprisal, shouldn't this be the place, this monument to Progress, this World of Tomorrow?

Once within the fairgrounds, they find themselves carried away with the beauty and marvel of the place. Leonard cannot believe he has waited this long to visit the World's Fair, for it is everything he hoped it would be. In his heart he has always believed in the forward momentum of the human race, in Progress, and the whole atmosphere of the Fair reeks with faith in that very philosophy. Strolling through the Court of Peace and past the Lagoon of Nations, examining displays in the Medicine and Public Health Building and the complexes erected by Ford and Firestone and AT&T, and enjoying the individual identities of the presentations made in the Court of States, it is impossible not to absorb the hope and confidence of the whole proceeding.

After long hours of exploring—just the beginning of their adventure at the Fair—they stand in front of the Italian Pavilion and stare up at the white marble steps and the waterfall that cascades down them into a pool at the base. A statue of the goddess Roma caps the steps. A warm breeze blows up, and spray from the waterfall dampens their faces.

Gabriella laughs and turns to him, eyes sparkling. This place is a touchstone for her, a gift that he hopes will make her feel she is not so far from home after all.

"It's amazing here."

"What is?" he asks.

"All of it. But I meant, well, the feeling. You must sense it, too. Hitler and the Soviets and their war, it all seems so *far away, standing here. This is the world to come, once their foolishness is done with."*

Leonard nods. He does sense it. Gabriella has put words to what he's been feeling since their arrival. Yet Hitler's lust for power is not going to simply go away. Of that he is certain. He will not stop in Poland.

And though on this perfect day the war in Europe seems so far away, it has already marred the World's Fair. The Soviet Pavilion is gone; dismantled and taken away. The pavilions representing Poland and several Baltic States are closed, shuttered up tight.

Yet he sees the faith in the future in her eyes, and he agrees.

"It is spectacular," he says. "I only wish I had brought you here sooner."

Gabriella reaches up and traces the contours of his face with the tips of her fingers. "We have forever, love. There's no need to rush."

And so they do not rush. It is the middle of the afternoon before they ride the curving, moving stairway called the Helicline, that carries them inside the Perisphere. The sight of so many people all moving together, smiling and full of life, erases the last lingering shadow of Leonard's earlier thoughts. He is with Gabriella in the World of Tomorrow. Nothing else matters.

As they have strolled through the Fair, several times they have caught a glimpse of the Parachute Jump, a prominent feature in many newspaper articles about the amusements offered to visitors. Now, hand in hand, they find their way almost instinctively to the area of the Fair that has come to be known as the Great White Way. The change in atmosphere is palpable. The laughter here is more boisterous and the music more raucous. There is no theme to the Amusement Zone, no grand philosophy or intent. It exists solely for pleasure. Once upon a time, Leonard would have looked askance at such endeavors, considering them pointless. Love has changed his mind.

The Parachute Jump awaits them as they meander

*through the Amusement Zone. A banjo player winks at
Leonard and, feeling oddly lighthearted, Leonard winks
back. Gabriella sees this and giggles, coyly covering her
mouth to hide her laughter. Acrobats tumble past them, and
they stop to watch the show.*

*The Great White Way, an afterthought when they were
making their plans for the Fair, absorbs them completely. At
the Indian village, Gabriella watches, mesmerized by the
beat of drums, as Seminoles dance. When an Indian smoking a cigarette tosses his Lucky Strike aside to wrestle an alligator, Leonard can only shake his head in wonder at the
strangeness of it all.*

*Yet the strangeness is only beginning. They visit the Mon-
key Island at Jungleland Village, Admiral Byrd's Penguin Island, the replica Elizabethan township, and Tiny Town, a
village inhabited by midgets and built to scale. They cross
Empire Bridge to visit the Aquacade, where they watch the
beautiful Eleanor Holm perform elegant water ballet, and
witness high dives that make even the famous Dr. Graves
catch his breath.*

And so much more.

*Exhausted, they stroll back along the Great White Way
long after night has fallen. Fireworks explode overhead,
painting the sky with a rainbow of falling stars. Their fingers
are still entwined, having rarely parted, and they walk ever
more closely together, something they would not dare to do
elsewhere. But in the World of Tomorrow, all things are possible.*

*The Trylon and Perisphere are bathed in multicolored
spotlights, surreal in their Utopian perfection. Yet Leonard
is happy amid the dancers and singers and clowns—and the
scents of exotic foreign foods—that fill the Amusement Zone.
Carefree, in a way he has never been before.*

*At last, as they leave the Great White Way, they come
upon the Parachute Jump again. The line is short enough to
be inviting. The entire structure of the two-hundred-and-
fifty-foot attraction is festooned with decorations from the*

Life Savers Company, promoting their candy. The sponsorship is amusingly apropos.

When their turn arrives, Leonard pays eighty cents so that the two of them can share one of the eleven wooden benches that hang below brightly colored cloth parachutes. At the first jerk of the cables suspending them, Gabriella turns to look at him. Her smile is wide and giddy with fear and excitement, but she does not speak. The look is enough to express all that she is feeling.

Leonard holds her hand, and they ascend.

The wind blows. They rise higher and higher and laugh together in delight at the view of the Fair at night that spreads out below them.

"Gabriella," Leonard says, not looking at her. Not yet.

"Yes?"

He turns and gazes at her. "I never want to spend a day without you. Marry me, Gabriella, so that that day will never come."

Her smile is shy and electrically intimate, all at the same time.

The parachute reaches the top of the tower. There is a clank above them.

"Will you?" Leonard asks, searching her eyes.

"You know I will."

With a loud clack, the mechanism releases. They plummet downward, ten feet, twenty feet, and Gabriella screams with wild, terrified laughter.

The parachute opens, halting them in midair, and then they float gently downward.

Leonard slips one hand behind her head, feeling the silk of her hair between his fingers, and he draws her to him. He kisses her, long and slow. And if the other parachutists cast unpleasant looks at them as they disembark from the ride, he chooses not to notice.

His heart is full of the unquantifiable variable, that magic that is love.

The future awaits.

•   •   •

DANNY knew he ought to be terrified, but somehow he was not.

He kept pace with the demon as it moved through the vast labyrinth of subway tunnels beneath the streets of Boston. They had been traveling for what seemed like hours, and he wanted to ask it, ask his father, where they were going. But they were moving much too quickly. In amazement, he watched the demon move, scrabbling along the ground, clinging to the sides of the tunnel walls so as not to come in contact with the electrified third rail. What amazed Danny even more was that he was able to do it as well.

He had only been with his sire for a matter of a few hours, and already he was learning more about himself and his capabilities than he had during his entire stay with Conan Doyle.

Danny was even getting used to the rats.

Upon entering the first tunnel through the Symphony Hall station, he had heard them squeaking and thought nothing of it. But it had grown louder and louder, and he'd realized that his father's presence seemed to have an odd effect on the rodents. Even now, as the two demons crawled along the side of a Red Line tunnel, the rats were scrambling in pursuit, a moving blanket of gray and black bodies on the floor of the tunnel.

They were coming up to another station, and Danny wondered if they would pass this one by as well. Baalphegor had said they were going somewhere away from prying eyes so they could have privacy. Danny was growing more curious as to where exactly that place was.

Up ahead, his father sprang from one side of the tunnel to the other, the station closer now. Clinging to the wall, he turned to peer down at the growing swarm of rats below him. The rats raced by, streaming into the T station. Late night commuters shrieked and jumped and ran around the platform and bolted for the stairs. The rats skittered around their feet, nipping at their ankles.

Danny grinned.

When the station was in utter chaos, Baalphegor climbed up the wall and onto the ceiling of the subway tunnel, then crawled into Andrews station above the heads of the panicked people. His father beckoned to him, and Danny followed, careful not to lose his grip as he crawled above the mayhem.

His father waited for him, nearly invisible in a deep pool of shadow upon the ceiling. Danny joined him, the screams of the Red Line passengers bringing a smile to his lips.

"Where are we going now?" he asked, stifling a giggle.

Baalphegor's deep, yellow eyes studied his expression, and he immediately became self-conscious.

"What's wrong?" Danny asked, glancing away from the intensity of his sire's gaze.

"Nothing," the demon replied. "It's just that you're so much more human than others of my seed."

"This is human?" Danny mumbled, looking at the skin of his hands, and the razor-sharp claws that adorned his fingers. "I'd hate to see my brothers and sisters."

Baalphegor looked away. "Yes, you would, for they are all dead."

Danny was startled by the statement, for the first time seriously considering the existence of others like him—actual siblings.

"All of them?"

But the demon was already on the move again, crawling buglike across the ceiling, making his way toward the exit. Danny followed.

Blending with the darkness of the night, the two emerged from the subway station, concealing themselves in shadows thrown by the buildings around them. They were in South Boston now, and his curiosity continued to pique.

Where the hell could we be going in Southie? he wondered, trying to keep up with his father as the demon darted from one patch of shadow to the next.

Baalphegor came to a sudden stop and pointed a long, crooked finger at the burned-out remains of a building surrounded by a hastily erected chain-link fence. The smell of fire still hung in the air.

Studying the wreckage of the old building, Danny came to realize that it was the shell of a Catholic church. He reached down into the ash and rubble, retrieving a piece of stained glass. There was part of a face on the fragment, some saint or another. Not really knowing why, he put it inside the pocket of his jeans.

The demon motioned him through the jagged frame of a tall window, and Danny went through the archway. His father followed.

"A church," Danny said aloud, looking about. "Why here?"

Baalphegor loped toward the shattered, scorched altar and stopped just in front of it.

"Once this was a place of goodness and light," he whispered, his head darting around, taking in the destruction. "Now that light has fled, leaving behind an empty, beaten corpse. This is a good place for us to be."

The demon continued up onto the altar. Part of the ceiling had come down atop it, covering it with rubble and blackened, charred wooden beams. Baalphegor perched atop the rubble.

"Come closer," he hissed, motioning with both his hands. "There is much for you to know of your true heritage."

Danny felt the urge to bolt from the burned-out shell of the church, run out into the night and never stop until he got back to Louisburg Square. A part of him wanted to see his mother right then, and he had to wonder if that was the humanity she'd instilled in him, afraid to face the truth of what he was becoming.

No. Not becoming. It's what you've always been.

"Come," Baalphegor urged.

Danny climbed up onto the damp and blackened beams, the stench of fire permeating the very air. He stopped before the demon, admiring the shape of the creature and everything it seemed to represent. His father had been created to kill. With his sleek body, his speed, the severity of his claws, and that mouth filled with rows of razor-sharp teeth, he could serve no other purpose.

Will I look like this someday? he wondered briefly, that little human part of him crying out in fear.

"They say I'm a changeling," he said, overwhelmed with the desire to know the whole truth at last. "That I was switched with a . . . with a human child."

He was surprised how difficult it was for him to say it—to admit that he wasn't human. That he never had been.

The demon stretched languidly upon his perch. He appeared strangely comfortable in the burned-out surroundings.

"*Changeling* is their word, not mine," Baalphegor said. "The fairies have done such things since time began, and the humans coined the word for them. But our kind have always done the same, though for different reasons. It is not that we covet human children. We place our offspring among the humans to ensure our own survival, changed to appear human, at least for a time."

Danny didn't understand. "Why?" he asked. "What do I have to do with you surviving?"

Eyes flashing with anger, his father lashed out at him, talons renting the air in a blur. Danny stumbled back across the rain-soaked plaster and charred wood, nearly tumbling to the floor, but he caught his balance. He looked down to see that his shirt had been torn open, his bare chest revealed.

"What the hell was that for?" Danny snarled.

Baalphegor pointed, and Danny glanced down, following his gaze to the strange, sacklike growth on his chest. It had become even larger and more engorged. Danny could feel it throb, an internal pressure intensifying within the dangling cyst.

"That is how we survive," Baalphegor said, reaching out to gently cup the object.

Danny attempted to swat his hand away but missed. "Don't touch me," he ordered with a snarl.

The demon grumbled, and Danny wasn't sure if it was a sound of anger, or one of amusement.

"The contents of that sack of flesh," Baalphegor said, "are the entire reason you were changed. Dark magic transforms the flesh of one of our offspring. The child is then exchanged for a human babe, its unwitting parents completely fooled. The humans raise the demon child as one of their own. Only when the child approaches adulthood does the flesh begin to reverse its transformation, and its true nature reveals itself."

The sack of flesh throbbed painfully, rousing Danny's anger all the more. "See, now again I'm asking you why. What do you get out of demon babies being raised in a human family?"

Baalphegor shifted upon his throne of rubble and leaned closer. "Though despised throughout the myriad realities, the human species retains something of immeasurable power and potency, absent from almost all other species."

The demon craned his neck, looking about the remains of the church. "Some would say it originated from Him, the one whose house we now despoil with our presence, that there is in humans some divine spark given willingly to those creations He most admired."

Danny's thoughts raced as he attempted to understand.

"Are . . . are you talking about the soul?" he asked.

The demon flinched as he turned to glare at his son. "The soul, the self, one's humanity, it's all the same to me and mine. It is a source of unimaginable power, and humans possess and squander it."

Danny narrowed his eyes, brows knitted, and stared at his father.

"I have a soul?"

"In a manner of speaking," Baalphegor nodded. "When transformed as infants, our children *grow* a soul, absorbing humanity from their fragile human parents and others around them. Conscience and experience come over time.

"But do not fool yourself, child. You are far from human. You were bred to be a collector. From the moment that I snatched the mewling human babe from its cradle and put you in its place, you have been collecting memories and experiences, sentiment and emotion. You've been absorbing humanity."

Danny looked down at the swollen sack of flesh hanging heavily from his chest. Suddenly it felt much heavier. "This?" he asked, his hand reaching up to touch it, but falling away. "This is my soul?"

The demon grinned, the horrific nature of the expression exemplified by the rows upon rows of long, shark teeth.

"You could call it that," Baalphegor replied. "That sack—your soul—is the reason that you and so many others were left here."

Danny couldn't take his eyes from the dangling polyp. "This is all that . . . that separates me from being like you?"

Baalphegor extended his neck toward the sack. Danny swore that he could feel the demon's eyes on it.

"Yessssssss," he hissed like a snake. "Without it, your metamorphosis will be complete, and your human nature will be sloughed off like an old skin."

Taking a deep breath, Danny mustered the courage to reach up and touch it, to hold the sack of life—of his humanity—in his hand. It felt warm, a sort of vibration passing through it different from that of his heartbeat.

"What will you do with it?" he asked, imagining what it would mean to be like the creature squatting before him.

"I will use it for magic," Baalphegor explained. "Powerful magic to tear aside the curtains of reality, to take us far away from this dimension before its untimely end."

His father's words concerned him. *What does he mean by untimely end? Is he talking about the Demogorgon?* But he was distracted from the fate of the world by something far more personal and immediate.

His own existence.

Danny glanced cautiously at Baalphegor. "What if I don't want to give it to you?" he asked the demon as he gripped the hanging sack of flesh, protecting it from harm.

Baalphegor drew back, folding his long spidery hands across his chest. "That is your decision, as it was the decision of my other offspring to make. I will not take it—it must be given up willingly."

Danny stepped backward, sliding down the pile of rubble to the edge of the altar below. "I'm not sure if I can do that," he said. His brain felt as though it was on fire, and he would have given anything to erase what he had learned this night. "It's all I've ever known—being human."

The demon stood, stretching its long, sinuous body, powerfully defined muscles evident beneath the dark, leathery flesh.

"Instinct will show what you truly are," Baalphegor said. Then the demon went rigid, tilting back its head and sniffing the air.

Danny couldn't smell anything except the smoky stench of fire, but it appeared that his father did.

"I'm hungry," Baalphegor stated, springing from the altar wreckage with a powerful leap that cleared nearly half the church. He landed in a silent crouch by the door. "And I imagine you are as well."

Danny didn't want to admit it, but there was an aching pain in the pit of his belly. It had been awhile since he'd last eaten.

Baalphegor beckoned him to follow, and he did, moving as silently across the rubble as his father did. And soon he smelled it as well, an odd, pungent aroma that he was sure he had experienced before, but never like this. It was almost as if his olfactory senses had changed again, growing stronger, processing the scents floating in the air differently than before.

The demon reached out, taking him by the shoulder and drawing him closer.

"There," the demon whispered, his breath vile, but strangely comforting.

He pointed toward the fence surrounding the church. An old woman stood there dressed in a heavy winter coat, her hat pulled down practically over her eyes. On the ground to either side of her were dirty shopping bags filled with empty soda and beer cans. She worked her fingers over a string of beads, muttering beneath her breath. Danny could see a silver crucifix dangling from the end of the black beads.

"What's she doing?" he asked.

"She's speaking to a power that doesn't live here anymore."

There were tears on the old lady's face, and Danny felt a sudden pang of sympathy for the stranger. In return, he felt the flesh dangling from the center of his chest swell just a tiny bit more.

Baalphegor tensed, a kind of crackling energy leaking from his body as he prepared to pounce. Danny knew what he was about to do and stopped it.

"No," Danny said, reaching out to grab hold of his father's arm. "Let her go. Find something else to eat. Rats or something."

The demon turned to him.

"Still held by the shackles of humanity," Baalphegor growled.

"Yeah," Danny responded, attempting to pull his father back into the church. "Come on, let's go back inside."

The demon smiled horribly. "But I'm hungry."

"We'll find you something else."

Baalphegor was gone in a flash, his movement an even darker blur on the night. Within seconds, he was back, the frightened old woman clutched in his arms, breath coming in ragged, terrified gasps.

She was still alive, teary eyes wide with sheer terror, too frightened even to scream.

"Why look for something else when the food is right here for the taking?" the demon asked.

The old woman's eyes met Danny's, her plaintive gaze searching his, pleading for him to save her.

"Help me," she squeaked, and for the briefest of moments he found her terror and helplessness delicious. The ache inside his belly grew almost painful as it begged to be satisfied.

The woman started to struggle, and that was all that Baalphegor required. He dipped his mouth to her throat, sank his teeth into the flimsy flesh there, and ripped it away like cotton candy.

Danny was stunned at how silent it all was. Baalphegor lifted his face, blood and strings of flesh dripping from his bear-trap mouth.

"Will you join me?"

Repulsed, Danny stepped away from him. Baalphegor reached down, digging his claws through the heavy winter coat and into the soft body beneath. With a display of utmost savagery, the demon tore the innards from the body, spattering Danny with warm gore as organs ripped loose. Baalphegor tossed this pile of viscera to the floor before him.

Danny gazed down at the blood that now splashed his clothes. He could feel it on his face, smell it in his nostrils. Before he even knew what he was doing, he felt his tongue sneak from his mouth to lick away the flecks that dappled his face.

"What are you doing, Danny?" asked a familiar voice from somewhere in the church.

He whipped around, lifting the sleeve of his shirt to wipe away the blood that stained his face, and saw Eve jump from a hole in what remained of the east wall of the church to land among the tumbled pews. Her eyes glinted menacingly in the darkness as she slowly stalked toward him.

"It's not what you think," he said.

But he saw the look of revulsion in her eyes. Who knew better than she did precisely what he had been doing?

A horrible roar filled the ruined church, and a massive, dark, shadow thing leaped through the same hole, landing in a predatory crouch. The thing might have been a really big dog, but Danny sensed it was something else entirely. The shadow beast bounded down the aisle, dragging a cursing, snarling something behind it.

The something was Squire.

Danny froze, watching as the black-skinned animal bore down upon him, and he braced for the inevitable impact. Eve was on the move as well, and when he glanced into her eyes and saw the cold judgment there, he felt certain he was about to die.

As he tasted the blood of the old lady still on his tongue, he realized that might be for the best.

"Get down," roared a voice from behind him, and Danny did as he was told.

Baalphegor hurled the woman's body like a child's broken toy, right into the path of the raving beast. The animal went wild, attacking the corpse in its fury, while Squire screamed for it to stop.

Danny turned to face his father. The demon was muttering something, a sound very much like the angry drone of insects, and his hands moved around in the air, trailing darkness as they seemed to weave the fabric of night into a hole hanging in the air.

"Quickly," the demon croaked, directing Danny toward the pulsing circle of darkness.

He started toward the conjured escape, but then found himself turning to look at his friends. Squire was beating the slavering beast with a piece of blackened wood, but Eve was looking directly at him—her eyes beckoning to him. She shook her head no, and reached toward him as though she could pull him back. Danny looked away. The taste of the old woman's coppery blood was still on his tongue.

It was too late.

He dove into the icy embrace of the dark portal and left hope behind.

13

GHOSTS haunted the present, but were forever haunted by the past. Only when they at last abandoned the flesh and blood world and allowed their spirits to move on were the spirits of the dead, the lost souls, free of this shadow. Dr. Graves had learned the truth of this over the years since his death, every time he visited a familiar place or saw a familiar face. Each fond memory existed as an unsettling ghost to him and troubled him far more than his lingering spirit had ever troubled the vibrant world of the living. His history was his personal ghost.

The Empire State Building was a part of that history.

It still towered above New York City, a monument to another age, a time when men had dreamed big and had had faith in Progress. Now it was taken for granted, just another office building, despite its landmark status. People streamed in and out of its doors on their way to and from meetings, without any inkling of the awe its construction had inspired among those who had watched it rise steadily toward the heavens in those precious days of 1930, when America had desperately needed the hope it symbolized.

Clay strode through the three-story lobby, glancing around in wonder, putting on the air of a fascinated tourist.

A camera would have completed the illusion but wasn't necessary. To security guards he would look like any ordinary man, neat and well groomed, his blue jeans new and his leather jacket fashionably weathered. He joined a dozen other tourists in front of the elevators that would carry them up to the observation deck on the eighty-sixth floor.

The ghost stayed with him. With so many people it was impossible to avoid sharing the same physical space with someone, and those tourists whom Graves passed through shivered at the touch of his spectral substance. One elderly woman he touched rubbed at the back of her neck and glanced around nervously, her eyes alight with confusion and fear. He wondered if she sensed his presence as the nearness of death and worried that her time had come.

At half past eleven o'clock on the evening of the tenth of May 1944, the mayor of New York City had ridden one of these very same elevators up to the observation deck. The time was well after the hour when the public was allowed to visit the observation deck, but Roger Alton Bennett had become mayor because he was a persuasive and powerful man, used to getting his way. The doorman and elevator operator who gave Bennett his way that night, and the two employees of a radio station on the eighty-fifth floor who happened to ride up with the mayor, reported that he was alone. No other unauthorized visitors entered the building that night. Access to the observation deck after hours was restricted. The elevators still in operation that late at night did not stop on the eighty-sixth floor without the override key the elevator operators had, and the doors from the stairwell were locked to prevent employees of the building's tenants from entering.

Roger Alton Bennett did not ride the elevator back down. He took a faster route to the street, off of the observation deck. City officials called it an accident. Rumors emerged from the police department and in the papers, claiming Bennett had taken his own life. The rumors became so rampant that at last the commissioner had held a press conference during which he had revealed that there were signs of a struggle on the observation deck, including traces of blood, indications that the mayor had not taken his own life but had instead been murdered. The inability of the New York Police Department to uncover any further details or to provide any suspects or theories about who might have been responsible for Bennett's murder had raised a furor in the city that lingered for more than a year.

All of this had taken place months after Graves's own murder. A wandering spirit, lost and searching for answers to the mystery of his death, it had been years since he had learned of the controversy surrounding Bennett's murder. The mayor had not precisely been his friend, but they had been allies. Still, he had been a ghost, obsessed with his own death, and had never been drawn to inquire further into Bennett's terrible, violent end.

Until now. Kovalik and Zarin had both implied a connection between his murder and Bennett's. It would be impossible to do an effective physical investigation of a murder well over sixty years in the past. Blood traces, broken glass, signs of struggle . . . such things did not last forever.

But a building this old and historic had a great many ghosts, and they lingered, echoes of the past.

The elevator doors opened, and Clay stepped out onto the eighty-sixth floor. There were fewer people on the observation deck than Graves would have expected. The ghost moved among them, glancing at Clay from time to time. His friend watched him, but kept silent. New York had more than its share of lunatics and seers, but it wouldn't do for him to appear to be talking to himself up here, where security guards were on edge, expecting attempted suicides or terrorist attacks.

The ghost slipped between two little girls, beautiful twins with caramel skin who might have been the daughters he and Gabriella would have had if fate had been kind. He tore his gaze away from the smiling, excited girls and looked out through the protective glass that had been erected many years ago to prevent people from throwing things off of the observation deck—and from jumping.

The view of New York City that spread out before him was sheer magic. Had he still been a creature of flesh and blood he would have caught his breath, and gooseflesh would have risen on his arms. As focused as he had been in his life, he had never been immune to such wonders. New York had remained a truly remarkable city.

And yet beneath the reality of that teeming metropolis, he could still see the ghost of a simpler era, when the buildings were smaller and more elegant, and the view from the top of the Empire State Building was like looking down from Heaven.

Clay stepped up beside him and splayed his fingers on the glass. He peered out at the city.

"Anything?" he whispered.

"I haven't begun," Graves replied. "A bit lost in the past, I'm afraid."

"That's why we're here," Clay reminded him. He glanced at the two little girls who were watching him curiously, obviously wondering to whom he was speaking.

The ghost of Dr. Graves closed his eyes and slipped into the spirit realm.

A city of ghosts lays out before him. Each block and tower is a gray silhouette in a churning mist of phantoms. New York, seen from the other side.

Graves feels the familiar pull of the soulstream but only vaguely. He is far from the ivory gate, here, still only a whisper of a thought away from the flesh-and-blood world. He drifts outward, floating above the city, and turns to face the dark streak that is all he can see of the Empire State Building from this side.

The ghosts, as he suspected, are everywhere. They float in lazy circles around the antenna at the top of the building and flow across the observation deck. Dead, desperate, lonely eyes stare out of windows. Some are instantly recog-

nizable, men and women in business suits that speak of many different decades. Others are little more than wisps, lingering spirits tied to the anchor of this building for some reason. He spies the lost souls of several men in the rough clothing of construction workers and understood immediately that these ghosts had lost their lives putting this building together, beam by beam.

Graves walks across the sky above the ghost city, stubborn in his insistence upon behaving as though he still has substance. He passes into the building—the spirit world's reflection of the building—and the ghosts on the observation deck slow, moving warily, like birds cocking their heads and waiting, worried that a predator is near. Even the nothings, the wisps, the vague unfocused spirits of the lost, seem to pause.

The specter whose form is most distinct belongs to a middle-aged woman with a sour, pinched mouth and grim eyes. She wears the sort of pantsuit favored by some professional women in the 1970s. She cannot help him directly—he needs an older ghost, a phantom who has haunted this place far longer—but perhaps she can provide information.

"Who are you?" he asks.

"Laura. I was Laura," she says.

The other ghosts have begun to move again, though still slowly. They give Graves and Laura a wide berth. He reaches out, and the ectoplasmic fabric of his spirit encounters hers, hands passing through one another.

"Can you tell me, what shade is the oldest, here? I must speak to the old ghosts of this place."

Laura tilts her head and regards him closely. Some of her solidity wavers and begins to drift apart.

"Why? We don't know you. This isn't your place. It's our place. We're tethered here, moored like ships. Like zeppelins. Do you know they used to moor zeppelins to the top?"

Graves smiles. The soulstream flows around them both, around them all, and the entirety of the ghost city. It blows through the spirit world like a wind, growing stronger nearer to the gate. Here, it is just a gentle breeze, but still it is tempting. He likes the image of zeppelins moored to the world of flesh and blood.

"I did know that," he says. "I saw them do it, in my life."

"You're not moored here," Laura says, suspiciously.

"No," Graves agrees. He glances around. *It might be his imagination, but it seems to him that there are fewer ghosts here now.* "And you won't be forever. Only until you figure out what's holding you back."

"I'm afraid," she says. "I watch children with balloons on parade day, and there are always some who can't hold on to the strings. They cry while the balloon rises up and up and disappears, and I wonder where they go. I'm afraid to go where the balloons go."

Graves stares at her. Again he tries to touch her hands, forgetting for a moment, despite so many years of death, that they are only phantoms.

"So am I," he says.

Laura smiles.

"Can you help me?" Graves asks. "I need to find the old ghosts in this place."

"Why?"

"A man was murdered here, a long time ago. Sometimes the ghosts are the only witnesses."

She blinks warily and draws back her hand.

"What man?"

"The mayor of New York."

"Who are you?" she says, and she wavers again, and her lower body seems to drift, becoming a wisp.

"In life I was called Leonard Graves. Doctor Graves."

"Oh, no," Laura says, her blue ghost-eyes widening, and then she is all wisp, slipping away through gray mist walls.

"Wait!" Graves calls, but even as he does he turns and sees the last few spirits there vanishing. *They dart out into the air around the blur of a building, disappear into the city of ghosts or deeper into the building itself.*

"What the devil is this?" he asks.

There are no ghosts to answer.

He slips out of the building again and sees the phantoms staring at him from a hundred windows. They withdraw, disappearing instantly, after only a fleeting glimpse.

Graves pursues, gliding now through the ether, to a ledge where the trio of high-steel workers stand in their gloves and boots and rolled up sleeves.

"Go away," one of the ghosts says, and there is danger in his gaze.

"My name is—"

"We know who you are. The dead travel fast, as do whispers."

Now Graves grows angry. His hands ball into fists. The workers stand shoulder to shoulder, their spirits resolving, solidifying. "Go away, Doctor Graves. You're not welcome."

"I only want to know who killed Mayor Bennett. You men would have been here. You must have seen what happened that night."

The worker on the left, his pug nose flaring in disdain, turns and spits a jet of soulstuff through the ether.

"You should know better than anyone."

One by one they drift, turn to wisps, and slip deeper into the spirit world.

Graves curses and follows. He focuses his spirit and lets the soulstream carry him. Phantoms blur around him. The city of ghosts is gone, the silhouettes of buildings disappear, and then he is standing in a place of nothing. Outlines of faces whisk by in the air, though here as well some of the specters are just coalescing clouds of mist.

The turbulent river of soulstuff that flows around his legs drags at him, and with each moment he is deeper and deeper within the spirit world—the otherworld. Soon he will see the twin spires, the ivory gate to the After, beyond which Gabriella awaits.

The workers are nowhere to be found. None of the Empire State Building's ghosts are here. They have all fled.
From him.

Graves stops where he is and fights against the pull of the soulstream. He turns to wade against the current. He must return to the world of flesh and blood and discuss all of this with Clay, but already he knows where that conversation will lead. In the back of his mind, he has known all along. The mystery only grows deeper and deeper. In their search they have found no answers, only more questions. There is only one place that their investigation can lead them now.

To Florence, Italy.
The scene of the crime.

CONAN Doyle leaned his head back in the leather chair, puffing upon his bent Briar pipe and letting the rich, slightly sweet smoke of the fine English tobacco fill his lungs. He had to think, and smoking a bowl allowed him the special focus he needed.

As he expected, Julia Ferrick was the first to break his concentration. She shifted in her seat, sighing with exasperation, hoping that one of the others in the sitting room would meet her eye and thus be inspired to action as well. But the others remained silent, knowing what Conan Doyle required.

"Are we just going to sit here?" she finally blurted out, uncrossing her legs and then crossing them again. She folded her arms defiantly across her chest and waited for a response to her challenge.

The others said nothing, choosing to let Conan Doyle answer the woman's inquiry. He let the smoke escape from his lungs, forming a grayish cloud around his head.

"We're not just sitting, Julia," he began, nibbling on the end of his pipe. "I'm thinking, and there is an enormous difference between the two."

She started to wiggle her foot, like an angry cat swish-

ing its tail. Conan Doyle knew she was upset, and right-
fully so. The situation had progressed from bad to worse.

At sunup, Eve, Squire, and the shuck had returned from
their hunt with the most disturbing news. His worst fears
had become a reality when they explained that Danny had
indeed been with Baalphegor, and that the boy had been in
the presence of the demon traveler when the murder of an
innocent had occurred.

"There's something you're not telling me," Julia blurted
out, her foot moving so quickly that it was nearly a blur.
"You know something, all of you."

Squire sighed, slipping down onto the sofa, but he said
nothing. It wasn't his place.

Conan Doyle was not sure if Eve would have held her
tongue, and was glad that she and the shuck had retired for
the daylight hours. There was a way in which he wanted
the information to be revealed to Julia, and he was not at
all sure Eve was capable of the delicacy required.

He could feel Ceridwen's eyes upon him and glanced in
her direction, falling deeply into the depths of her gaze.
Everything that she wished to communicate at that moment was there in her look. The Princess of Faerie didn't
have to speak a word.

They could hide it no longer. Julia had to know what
was happening.

"You're correct," Conan Doyle said, turning his gaze to
the upset woman. "We do know more, but have kept it
from you not out of malice, but as a way to shield you from
the severity of the situation."

She leaned forward in her chair, planting both feet on
the floor. "Tell me," she commanded. "What's happening
with my son?"

"Try to remain calm, Julia," Conan Doyle cautioned.

"Don't patronize me!" she shouted, jumping to her feet.
"Tell me what you know about my son this instant, or . . .
or I'm going to the police."

Squire placed a hand over his face and leaned his head

back on the sofa. "That'd be good," he muttered. "They deal with the demonic every day."

Ceridwen left her chair to calm the woman. The gentle, soothing aroma of lavender filled the room.

"Please, Julia," she said. "Your anger is misdirected. We want nothing more than to help Danny survive."

The woman leaned upon Ceridwen, distraught. "Tell me," she said quietly.

Conan Doyle refilled his pipe. "You know what Danny is . . . what his true origins are."

The woman listened intently, Ceridwen's arm still around her for support. Putting a wooden match to the fresh bowl, Conan Doyle puffed to ignite the tobacco.

"His father—his demon sire—has managed to cross into this plane of existence, it chills me to say." He shook out the match and placed it in a bronze ashtray. "He has made contact with his . . . with Daniel. I believe Danny has something the demon wants."

Julia raised a weak hand to cover her mouth as though to stop herself from screaming. Her eyes were wide with anguish, and the strength went out of her. She stumbled backward, fumbling for her chair. Ceridwen helped her to sit, remaining by her, just in case she was needed.

"What? What could Danny possibly have that this . . . *thing* might want?"

Conan Doyle leaned forward, steepling his fingers, gazing into her eyes and trying to lend her strength. There was no easy way to tell her what came next. "There were three murders on Beacon Street yesterday. A woman, her son, and her son's nurse. After examining the boy's remains, I've determined that he was a changeling as well, and that he and Danny shared the same sire."

Julia's face paled. "He killed his other son?"

The pipe stem scraped gently against Doyle's front teeth. "The boy had been incapacitated in some way, hence the need for a nurse. The demon took what it needed, and then disposed of him. In fire."

"And this demon," she said softly, reaching into her

pocket for a Kleenex. She wiped at her eyes, taking a deep breath before returning her attention to Doyle. "This demon has taken my son?"

"Possibly. But you must understand that there is another possibility. Danny may have gone with the demon willingly."

She seemed taken aback. "Willingly? Why would he do that?"

Conan Doyle hesitated. He wished there were a way to save Julia Ferrick from the truth, or to keep at least the worst of it from her. But if she was to help them save her son, she needed and deserved to know everything.

"Despite your feelings for him, Danny is not your true son. You know this, Julia. What you do not know is that the demon changeling child that you raised was put in this dimension to collect the precious life energies of the human experience. There are many different breeds of demons. Hundreds, at the least. This breed are known as collectors."

Julia frowned. "What the hell does that mean?"

Reluctantly, he explained it all to her, the process by which the demon changelings were altered and exchanged for a human child, and the way they absorbed human experience and emotion. He told her about the growth that would be on Danny's chest, now, and what the demon would want him for.

The tears flowed freely down Julia's face. She wiped at them and her running nose. "So the demon . . . he wants to, to *eat* this thing?"

Conan Doyle nodded. "More or less. The energies stored within this growth are quite potent. In the hands of an experienced magic user, it could prove remarkably powerful."

Julia got up from her chair and went to the window, looking out onto the tranquil, fenced-in park in the center of Louisburg Square.

"Why hasn't he tried to escape?" she asked, turning around slowly to face Doyle. "If he came to you—could you help him?"

Conan Doyle looked at Squire, who reclined on the couch, his hand still covering his face.

"I don't think he wants our help," the hobgoblin said, taking his hand away and sitting up. "When Eve and I found them, it looked like they may have just killed an old woman." He paused a moment and then let go with the awful truth. "And we had interrupted their meal."

Julia Ferrick paled. In moments, she seemed to age a decade. Conan Doyle felt for the woman. To be involved in matters such as these when not fully indoctrinated in the ways of the weird, and to love so completely a creature already damned . . . he could only imagine the gamut of emotions she was likely experiencing. If anything could salvage Danny's burgeoning humanity, it would be his mother's love.

She seemed to steel herself, standing taller, taking a deep breath as she wiped at her nose and eyes.

"So that's it then," she said.

"What is, Julia?"

"You'll hunt him down, Danny and his . . . father, or whatever the hell you want to call him. You'll hunt him down and kill them both, right? It's what you do—track down threats to the world and destroy them?"

She was trying to be brave, so matter-of-fact, as if she had known this was coming all along.

"There is still a chance that he might be saved," Conan Doyle explained.

A glimmer of hope ignited in her eyes. He was amazed by the bond that existed between this woman and the demon she had raised as her child. He wondered how often she thought about her real son, the human baby taken by the demon, and how often she felt a bit of hatred toward the unwitting monster left behind in his place. Conan Doyle shivered inwardly, not wanting to dwell upon that child's probable fate. He had a great deal of respect for the way Julia had dedicated herself to Danny, had loved him, regardless of what he was.

"The growth," Conan Doyle said, pointing to the center

of his chest with the stem of his pipe. "If removed, will cost Danny any chance of retaining his humanity. The metamorphosis into a full-blooded demon will begin almost immediately."

As if in a trance, Julia crossed the room, a sliver of hope urging her on. "But if the demon doesn't take it . . ."

"Eventually the energies, his humanity, will be reabsorbed into his system, halting his swing to the demonic. But you have to remember, that is likely why Baalphegor has come, to reclaim what he believes rightly belongs to him."

"Baalphegor?" she asked. "You know its name?"

"Let's just say that I've encountered his evil before, and I am frightfully aware what he is capable of," Conan Doyle said, images of the years he fought in the Twilight Wars and the unspeakable evil he encountered flooding his memories.

Evil as virulent as the most contagious of viruses.

"You must know that there's a chance Danny has already chosen his fate, that the demonic nature that is his legacy has asserted itself, and any hint of the boy you raised as your own is gone."

She nodded slowly, and he returned the gesture.

"Very good then," Conan Doyle said, setting his pipe down. He quickly glanced at his watch. "It'll be dusk soon, Eve and Shuck will be rising." He leaned toward Squire. "I want you to go out into the city again," he told the hobgoblin. "But this time I want Ceridwen to accompany you."

Conan Doyle looked over to his lover. He removed a glass vial filled with gray ash from his shirt pocket. "I'll give you this sample of the murdered boy's remains, a collector's remains. I suspect it could provide the edge we've been searching for in tracking Baalphegor and Danny."

Ceridwen rose gracefully from her seat. "And you, my love?" she asked, taking the vial from him. "How will you be spending your time?"

"The fact that Baalphegor was able to cross over to this plane with little difficulty concerns me," Conan Doyle said. "I believe a conversation with the Sentinel is in order."

Squire headed for the door. "I take it you'll be using Ochoa to try and make the connection?"

"He is the current liaison."

"Yeah," Squire said. "Good luck with that. Might want to think about stoppin' at a Dunkin' Donuts for some coffee. I don't think that guy's been sober since they tossed his ass out of the Vatican."

Ceridwen kissed Doyle lightly, her long lashes like the touch of a butterfly's wings on his cheek, before she followed Squire from the room.

Conan Doyle picked up his pipe, intending to return it to his study. Julia still stood by her chair, looking lost.

"I want to help," she said. "I can't go home—I need to do something."

"I'm sorry I wasn't clear," he replied. "I need you to accompany me, Julia. There's no telling when we will catch up with Danny, but I have no doubt that we could not save him without you. Without your love for your son."

BENJAMIN Ochoa lived in Roslindale, a rough greater Boston neighborhood at least a twenty-five-minute ride from downtown during rush hour.

They took Julia's car.

"Who is this guy?" Julia asked, dropping her car keys into the small leather bag she carried over her shoulder. It had taken six rides around the block to find a parking space, and they still had nearly a block to walk to the man's house. "Squire said something about the Vatican?"

Conan Doyle turned up his collar against the wind and smoothed his graying mustache. "Benjamin Ochoa was a Catholic priest before he was excommunicated for his dealings in the paranormal. In fact, he was the Vatican's top researcher on the supernatural, revealing to them things that they would rather not know."

"What kinds of things?" she asked, as they walked through the quiet, blue-collar neighborhood.

"Ochoa discovered that this plane of existence is but one in a multitude of others, and that these other realms are populated by all manner of creatures, many of whom do not recognize the power of the Vatican's god."

"And let me guess," Julia chimed in. "The Pope and his boys didn't care for the idea of other worlds and branded Ochoa a heretic, tossing him out on his ass."

Conan Doyle stopped before an ordinary looking Dutch Colonial and double-checked the number—357. It was painted a deep shade of cranberry, with white trim. There was even a Thanksgiving decoration—a turkey in a Pilgrims' hat—attached to the door.

"Not too far from the truth," he replied as he started up the short walkway to the front door. "Father Ochoa was touched by the worlds he was attempting to communicate with, and it changed him—tainted him. He became a sort of mouthpiece for the denizens of these places, an ambassador, if you will, and the Vatican did not care for what they had to say. They quietly excommunicated him, bought him this house, and keep a close eye on his activities."

Standing on the stoop, Conan Doyle rang the illuminated doorbell, faint electronic chimes sounding within the house.

"What did they say?" Julia asked as they waited.

"Pardon?"

"The other places . . . the other worlds, what did they say that the Vatican didn't like?"

"What one would expect from the infernal realms," Conan Doyle explained. "That the Catholic god was but one of many, that its power was waning, and there would come a day in the not-too-distant future that their faith would be forgotten."

"I can see how they'd be uneasy with that," Julia said, looking a tad uncomfortable. "Is it . . . is it true?"

"What is truth?" Conan Doyle asked, hearing a sharp click as the door was unlocked from within. "All things were created, and logic dictates there must be a Creator. The Roman interpretation of that Creator is one among many. The truth is always difficult to hear."

The door slowly opened, and a grandfatherly old gentleman peered out curiously through the glass of the storm door.

"Benjamin," Conan Doyle said, raising his voice slightly to be heard through the glass. "This is Julia Ferrick. There's been a breach. Her son is involved, and we need your help."

Ochoa continued to stare, and for a moment Conan Doyle thought that he was going to close the door in their faces, but then he reached out, unlocking the storm door. A draft of warm air flowed from inside as he pushed open the door.

"Come in, come in" he said, his voice a soft rasp. "The phone lines to the Vatican will certainly be on fire tonight." He paused to gaze up and down the street at they passed into the foyer.

"It's been awhile, Benjamin," Conan Doyle said, as the old man closed the door and locked it.

He shuffled past them, his slippered feet sliding across the threadbare hallway carpet. "I was just putting on a pot of coffee," he said. "Would you care to join me?"

"Certainly," Conan Doyle replied, and he and Julia followed Ochoa into a room off the front hall.

Newspapers covered just about every surface, and beneath them were stacks of ancient texts and scrolls.

"Please excuse the mess," he fretted, moving the things from the surface of a loveseat to the floor. "I have the most difficult time keeping a cleaning service. A few visits and they no longer want to come. It's quite perplexing."

Conan Doyle and Julia sat upon the loveseat as Ochoa continued to fuss about. The mage sensed an aura emanating from the room—from the very house—and could understand why the cleaning crews feared it. Glancing toward Danny's mother, he could see that it was having an effect on her as well. The unnatural, the sick evil, had permeated the walls, floor, and the very furniture upon which they sat.

"There," Ochoa said, straightening up with a grunt and wiping dust from his hands. In the corner of the room was an antique liquor cabinet, and he went to it, opening the creaking wooden doors and removing a bottle of Wild Turkey and a glass.

"I was about to have a cocktail," he explained, abandoning the pretense of coffee. "But if *you two* would like coffee, I'd be more than—"

"That's fine," Conan Doyle interrupted him. "No need to bother, I'd like to get right down to business if you don't mind."

Ochoa chuckled, unscrewing the cap from the bottle and filling half the glass. "Something tells me I'll need a stiff one after this. Better start early and fortify myself."

He screwed the cap back onto the bottle, picked up his glass, and returned to his seat. "What can I do for you, Arthur?" he asked as he lowered himself into the embrace of an overstuffed chair.

Conan Doyle felt as though the loveseat beneath him was squirming with life, but he knew that it was only the residue of visitations past. He would have much preferred to stand, but did not wish to insult his host. He forced himself to concentrate on the matter at hand.

"A demon of the highest order recently stepped through to the city. So far it's responsible for at least seven deaths that we are aware of."

Ochoa downed the drink as if it were water, already squirming from the recliner to return to the cabinet. "A demon of the highest order," he repeated as he retrieved the bottle and refilled his glass.

"A collector," Conan Doyle specified.

The old man's drink stopped midway to his mouth. "Really?" He turned his watery gaze to Julia.

The woman sat quietly, looking as though she were ready to jump from her skin—*small wonder with this level of preternatural residue,* Doyle thought.

"It is actually Julia's son that is our reason for being here. The boy is a changeling, and the demon that has crossed over threatens his humanity."

"Boy?" Ochoa scoffed. He returned to his chair, this time sitting on the edge of the navy blue recliner, just in case he needed to get back to the cabinet quicker, Doyle imagined. "This isn't a boy we're talking about here."

The woman's ire was immediately rankled. "No, it isn't *a boy*, he's my son."

Conan Doyle reached out and placed a calming hand upon her arm, willing her his support. "We've come . . ." he began, but Ochoa interrupted.

"Have you told her the truth, Doyle?" He gulped at his refreshment, as if dying of thirst. "Have you told her that her child isn't human, that he is only the most clever of predators?"

The woman's agitation was growing, intensified by the evil miasma that radiated from their surroundings.

"Her child . . . Danny, is a special case. I've been assisting with his training, and—"

"Training," Ochoa spat, resting his empty glass on his knee. He started to shake his head from side to side. "You can't train evil, Doyle," he said, his voice beginning to slur. "You might think you can—teaching it to do tricks as it walks among you, pretending to be what you all so desperately want it to be."

Conan Doyle stood. "I believe that's enough, Benjamin," he said, fixing the man in his icy blue stare.

"I'm surprised at you," the former priest said. He rose slowly and lurched toward the liquor cabinet.

"Don't you think you've had enough?" Julia snapped.

The old man turned his full gaze upon them, his deep brown eyes pulsing with intensity. "It's never enough. Once you open that door, and see what's on the other side . . . waiting . . ."

He couldn't get the cabinet open fast enough, grabbing hold of the bottle in trembling hands. He filled the glass to the brim, spilling its contents as he brought it to his mouth, the golden brown liquid dribbling down the front of his running suit jacket. Ochoa drank more than half of the glass, then leaned against the bar, gasping for breath.

"I suppose you want to speak to a Sentinel?"

"Yes," Conan Doyle answered sharply.

The old man seemed to resign himself, gulping down the remainder of his drink. "We'll do it in the cellar." And he lurched from the room.

"The cellar it is then," Conan Doyle said, turning toward Julia, who still sat upon the loveseat.

He wondered if she wished she had stayed at home.

14

THEY stood in the center of an elaborate pentagram drawn in salt. Whatever was happening around them sucked the air from Julia's lungs.

Ochoa had brought them down the wooden staircase into the basement. Her mind was already on fire as she tried to make sense of what the two men had said about her son.

She was so worried that she wanted to scream, but was beginning to suspect that her troubles may have just begun. She was tempted to leave the house and wait in the car until Mr. Doyle was finished, but an insane curiosity had kept her here.

She'd kept her mouth shut, biting her tongue as they'd stepped into the basement room. It looked as though it might have once been a playroom, but now it was empty and dark, the one window painted black, and a single bare bulb providing the only illumination.

Ochoa hadn't wasted any time getting started. He'd taken two jars of salt from a wooden box in the corner and set to work drawing an elaborate star in the center of the room. When he was finished, he'd commanded Julia and

Doyle to stand within it, while he connected each of the star's points with a line drawn in thick, white chalk.

Then he'd joined them in the center of the circle and shed his sweat suit. Julia had gasped aloud at the sight of his pale, naked body covered with a multitude of scars, and he had turned around, being sure to give her a full view of his withered genitalia.

Still leering, Ochoa had held out a dagger to her. The knife was very old, its metal almost black from the passage of time. He had turned it ever so gently as to make sure that she could see the dried, crusting blood on the blade. Then, seemingly satisfied, the old man had dropped to his boney knees and brought the knife to his chest. She found herself moving closer to Doyle, tempted to hide her face behind his shoulder. Instead, she had watched as Ochoa cut himself with the dagger, the dirty blade digging into the pale, hairy flesh just below his left nipple. He'd cut himself again and again, blood dripping from each new wound, and she'd understood the scars that adorned his body.

Ochoa had spread his arms, turning his face up to the ceiling and begun to sing a strange song that sounded more like somebody choking on a piece of food than any tune Julia had ever heard.

At first she had blamed the dimming lights on her own eyes, but the light was indeed receding. Then she'd noticed the blood, lifting from Ochoa's pale flesh, snaking in the air like the tendrils on some strange underwater life-form. The tendrils of blood entwined together to form a single, snakelike mass that left the confines of the star to swim within the increasing darkness outside.

"Whatever you see, whatever you hear, whatever you do," Doyle had calmly instructed her. "Do not leave the center of the star."

Soon there was nothing but the darkness and Ochoa's insane chanting, and Julia thought that she just might suffocate. It was as if the gloom, having fed on the light, had moved on to the air inside her lungs.

She brought a hand to her chest, gasping aloud, feeling

Mr. Doyle's hand upon her back, silently coaxing her lungs to function again. And just as she thought she might lose consciousness, tiny explosions of color appearing before her eyes, they did indeed start to work again, and huge draughts of oxygen filled her lungs. By then the stench that permeated the air made her wish that she had indeed passed out.

Something moved in the darkness.

Instinctively she grabbed Doyle's arm. "What's happening?" she gasped, watching as her breath billowed from her mouth. The temperature had dropped precipitously. It was freezing cold down there.

Ochoa continued his song as the terror built within her.

"He's established our connection," Doyle explained, softly. "Think of him and his blood as a kind of key. That key has been inserted in the lock and—"

"It's been opened," Julia finished, her eyes riveted to a particular section of darkness where something seemed to be moving, ready to emerge.

A child bounded from the shadows, a high-pitched scream upon his lips, and Julia recoiled, almost falling out of the pentagram.

"Careful," Doyle said, firmly gripping her elbow and helping her to regain her balance.

Her eyes were riveted to the filthy child. He looked to be about ten years of age, naked and covered in a thick layer of filth. He was gnawing on the body of a dove, its white feathers stained red with its own blood. There was a thick, leather collar around the child's scrawny neck, and the chain attached to it led back into the ocean of darkness behind him.

"Come forward, Hellion," Doyle commanded, his voice booming in the room. "Matters of importance limit my time."

Julia heard a wet, dragging sound, like a heavy bag of laundry being pulled over loose stone, and she watched the boy's chain grow slack. A voice came from the darkness, so thick and rasping with mucous that she nearly retched, even as it made her want to run and hide.

"Is that Conan Doyle, I hear?" it asked.

Doyle must have sensed her urge to flee, and he turned to her again. "Do not leave the star," he said, forcefully.

"Who is with you, Arthur?" the horrible voice asked, closer now, just about to peek from the all-encompassing shadow. "Someone new—someone not familiar with the ways of parley?"

The speaker emerged then, and the small child threw back his bloody face and howled like a dog. *Thing* was the only way her brain could describe it. It was like nothing she had ever seen before. It had no real shape, its massive bulk composed of limbs and other parts of what appeared to be living things. Looped around its neck was a thick muscular tentacle, its undersurface covered in hundreds of red suckers, each filled with tiny, razor-sharp teeth. Below that it wore a delicate gold chain, and at the end of the chain dangled a little girl's head.

The thing spoke again, and Julia was repulsed to see that the voice came from the head of the girl-child, its dead eyes opening, the tiny mouth moving.

"She looks as though she just might run," it gurgled. "Wouldn't that be fun?"

The thing seemed to grow taller, as if showing off its body composed of all things dead. Julia wanted to be sick, but held it together, believing that all this would help get her son back.

The little boy had finished consuming the white bird, feathers sticking to the drying blood that smeared his feral features. The child saw that she was looking at him, and he lunged with a growl. The chain snapped tight, held in the grip of a hand and arm that had been stripped of all flesh by hundreds of maggots writhing upon the deep red surface.

"With whom am I speaking?" Conan Doyle's voice boomed again.

The demonic entity undulated. "You wound me, Arthur,"

the little girl's head said. "Have I changed so much since last we spoke?"

"Yidhara-Thoth," Doyle said, and the creature bowed, or at least, that's what Julia believed it did.

"You do recognize me," it said excitedly.

The beastly boy strained upon his leash, trying to pull himself to the star, but the monster, this Yidhara-Thoth, kept it back.

"Not at first," Doyle responded. "Pit-spawn tend to blend together in my mind."

The entity laughed wetly. "Oh, we are each unique in our way. Perhaps when you meet my brothers and sisters you will realize that."

"When I meet your brothers and sisters, Yidhara?" Doyle asked. "Why would I meet them at all, unless a breach of trust has occurred."

The demon was silent, its body writhing as if something were attempting to escape from within.

"Just as I suspected," Doyle said indignantly. "An oath forged upon the field of battle has been broken."

"Pfaah!" the monstrosity spat, a thick wad of phlegm flying through the air to land upon the child's back. "What does it matter, Arthur?"

The little boy started to screech in pain as the substance boiled his flesh. It thrashed upon the ground, and Julia felt her motherly instincts kick in as her feet began to take her forward.

Doyle reached out quickly and clutched her arm roughly, pulling her back beside him.

"You dare much, Hellion!" he snarled.

"Come now, Arthur," Yidhara said softly. "Pit spawn, as you call us, have always crossed over from time to time, even after the treaty was signed. It's never bothered you before."

Julia could sense Doyle's growing anger, and then could see it, as his fingertips crackled with a blue electrical energy.

"There is something hidden in your tone, thing-from-the-pit," Doyle said. He lifted his hand, the energy forming a crackling sphere, and the hell-beast recoiled farther into the darkness. "Do not force my hand."

"You know as much as I that it is unraveling, that soon this plane of existence will be no more."

"Blasphemy!" Doyle roared, the ball of blue light growing all the brighter in his grasp.

"The Devourer is coming, and it will satiate its all-encompassing hunger on the sons and daughters of Adam."

With those words from its master, the beast child squatted and defecated, chattering wildly, eyes rolled back in its filthy head.

Julia thought she was going to be sick.

"You think this world already dead?" Doyle roared. "That your filthy kind can come and go as they please . . . that humanity's guardians will stand for it? That *I* will stand for it?"

Everything in the basement room was suddenly deathly quiet, and Julia focused her gaze upon the swirling ball of magic.

"In the amount of time it would take for me to send you hurling back to the bowels of Hell that spat you out, I have the ability to marshal the forces of a dozen dimensions: from Faerie to Paradise, to the most ancient, primeval chaos, I will call upon them to punish you and your kind for their assumption."

Yidhara yanked violently back on the chain it held, pulling its pet closer to its side. "I did not come to hear a declaration of war," the creature grumbled. "You have asked a question of me, and I have answered it. We of the hellish planes know of the Demogorgon's inexorable approach and seek to enjoy what will soon be no more."

Doyle seemed to calm slightly, closing his hand on the glowing orb of power. "Go back to your place in the darkness, Hellion. Go back and tell them that we shall be dealing with this Devourer, that the earthly plane will not fall victim to its insatiable hunger. And until that time, and beyond, this world is off-limits to their kind."

Yidhara chuckled, reaching out with a rotting tentacle to stroke the head of the filthy child squatting by its side.

"Such confidence," the demon said. "I will tell them, and hopefully, it will deter any future visitations, but you know how difficult they can be. Now, as is the right of ritual, I require payment for my time."

"The indignities that your kind have perpetrated upon this world of late, and you require payment?" Doyle seemed annoyed although the crackling energies had dissipated.

"You command us to obey the rules of tradition, and yet refuse to do so yourself?"

Doyle sighed. "Take your payment, then. A single memory. One moment only."

"Not from you," Yidhara said. "From her." The demon pointed another maggot covered hand at Julia.

Julia shuddered in horror and looked to Doyle in desperation.

"She has nothing to do with this, take one of my memories or none at all," Doyle insisted.

"She participated in the parlay. She stands within the star. She is most certainly a part of this."

The child had begun to play with himself, yanking at his penis, and Julia looked away. She knew nothing of this world into which she had been catapulted. But the demon was right, she had participated, she did listen. And who would benefit more than she would?

Now it demanded its payment.

"Let him take it," she said, her voice barely a whisper.

"I'm not sure you understand," Doyle said, eyes narrowing with fear for her. "To have something like that even momentarily a part of your thoughts, in your mind, could prove quite devastating."

"I promise to be gentle," the demon whispered, laughing throatily. "Just a single human memory to take back to the pit. It is cold there, and this will be just the thing to keep me warm."

Doyle looked at her hard. "Are you sure about this?"

Julia nodded, even though she wasn't.

"One memory," Doyle instructed, holding up a single finger.

"Do you grant me permission to enter the pentagram?" it asked politely.

"I grant permission for you to enter and to remove a single memory from her, without causing her any harm and without touching me or the priest," Doyle said. "And I promise you pain unimaginable if you should attempt to take anything more."

A thin, dripping tentacle emerged from a brown, stained orifice, crossing the distance between them. It paused at the edge of a star's point, and passed within the confines.

"Are you sure?" Doyle asked again, and this time Julia knew that there would be no turning back.

She did not answer him, stepping from his side to approach the appendage that writhed in the air, waiting for her.

"One memory," she said to Yidhara-Thoth, and the child's head around its neck responded in kind.

"One memory."

The tentacle darted forward, its tip entering one nostril and slithering up into her nasal cavity. She could feel it go higher, up into her skull, and was surprised at how little the violation hurt her. Nausea churned in her gut.

The pain didn't begin until it stroked her brain.

Julia gasped as she felt the probe stimulate her memories. It was like being beneath an avalanche, the remembrances of her life tumbling from the storage closets within her mind. And the tentacle touched each and every one, sorting through them, careful to find the special moment it could claim as its own.

Before she knew, it found what it was searching for. She had been enjoying the recollection, the memory of holding her son in her arms for the very first time. Tears welled in her eyes as she recalled the weight of him, his very special baby smell.

"Oh, Danny," she whispered, all her love transferred to him as a bond between mother and son was forged.

Then it was gone, as if it had never happened. The tentacle withdrew from her skull, sliding the precious memory out of her mind.

A memory of love lost to her.

On its way to Hell.

THE investigation into the murder of Dr. Graves had been an exercise in frustration. Clay felt more confused than he was willing to admit to the ghost, but he could see Graves felt the same. Each inquiry seemed to open up entirely new avenues of mystery. But his frustration had made him all the more determined. If they had to travel to Italy for answers, then that was precisely what they would do.

The flight from New York to Florence had a layover in London. Clay sat on a bench in Heathrow Airport, reading the newspaper and enjoying the whole feel of the place. He enjoyed the United Kingdom and its people. Every region of the world had its own texture, and the pleasant atmosphere of London had always made him comfortable. In the late twentieth century and into the twenty-first, the British had managed to combine a certain cultural propriety with a calm that defied the stuffy stereotype.

It was a phenomenon Clay had seen before.

This is what happens when an Empire falls to entropy instead of conquest. The people of Great Britain had, over time, grown content to let someone else worry about holding the reins of the world.

He sat at his gate with the newspaper and a heavy paperback he'd bought at Waterstone's. A young mother played with her toddler a few feet away, tickling her so the girl giggled wildly. It was a beautiful sound. The television that hung above the waiting room showed a news report, but the sound was turned down and words scrolled across the bottom of the screen.

And the ghost of Dr. Graves hovered nearby.

Traveling with him had become maddening. Clay got along quite well with Graves and was pleased to be helping him. But the hours they had spent on the plane and now in the airport were torture. The ghost wandered the plane, and now the terminal, and whenever the whim took him he would come back and speak to Clay, even attempt to begin a conversation, though he knew quite well that Clay could not respond without seeming like a lunatic, talking to someone nobody else could see.

Driving around the northeastern United States had been no trouble. Graves had been an ideal companion. But traveling in public presented a challenge that set Clay to grinding his teeth and sighing.

Fortunately, it seemed the ghost had at last realized how difficult his attempts at discussion had been for Clay. For the past half hour he had stood by the broad windows that looked out at the tarmac and watched planes taking off, his spectral form like a strange, transparent human veil draped upon the glass.

"Ooops," the young mother said.

Clay lowered his paper to find that the todder—a little girl no more than three—had fallen just inches from his feet. She looked up at him, face filled with the shock of her fall, and he smiled at her.

"You all right, princess?" the mother asked, hoisting the little one into the air.

Reminded of her tumble, the girl began to cry. The mother held her, whispering assurances in her ear and rocking her. The woman glanced past her daughter's head and saw Clay watching her. She smiled sweetly, acknowledging her motherly indulgence. Clay returned the smile and watched as the two walked around together.

Moments later, they were running around together again.

Clay lifted his paper and tried to find his place in the article he'd been reading. Even as he did so, the cell phone in his jacket pocket issued a familiar trill.

He plucked it out and glanced at the screen to find that the incoming call came from a blocked number. Clay frowned as he thumbed the TALK button.

"Hello?"

"Joe, it's Kovalik."

"Al. I'm usually a good judge of tone, but I can't read yours. You've got information for me, but is it good news or bad?"

"It's information, Joe. Good or bad, that's up to you. I can tell you it's odd."

Clay gave a soft, humorless laugh. "Yeah. There's a lot of that going around. You retrieved the remains of Doctor Graves, I take it?"

"We did, yes," Kovalik replied.

"And?"

The line went quiet, and for a moment Clay thought he might have lost the connection.

"Examination shows no evidence of a gunshot wound to the back. 'Course, it's possible the bullet didn't hit bone, so—"

"It did. At least, the way he remembers it."

Again, Kovalik went silent. Clay figured he didn't like to be reminded of his visit from the ghost of Dr. Graves.

"What else?" Clay prodded.

"DNA comparisons are a match. These are the bones of Leonard Graves, but as I said, no evidence that he died the way all of the reports indicated."

Kovalik cleared his throat. Clay heard the scratch of a match being lit and then the old man taking a drag on a cigarette and exhaling.

"You shouldn't smoke," Clay told him.

"I quit twenty-seven years ago. I took it up again this week. Indulge an old man."

"So, how did he die?"

"Fractures at the top of his spine lead my gravediggers to believe the cause of death was strangulation."

The toddler raced past him. Clay pulled his feet out of the way so the kid wouldn't take another tumble, and the mother gave him a coquettish glance in thanks as she pursued her little tornado.

Clay stood, phone against his ear, and glanced around for Graves. The ghost had wandered away from the window. Apparently he'd lost interest in the planes taking off and landing. Clay spotted him crouched beside an old couple who sat together, lost in their ruminations and yet still with their hands intertwined. They were so ancient by human standards that they were nearly mummified, but Clay understood why Graves was drawn to them. There was an air of satisfaction and contentment that surrounded them.

"I find that hard to believe," Clay said as he approached the ghost. "He was a formidable man."

"I'm just giving you the report," Kovalik said, a bit testy.

The ghost seemed to be studying the lines on the old couple's faces and did not notice his approach. Clay was forced to speak.

"Len," he said.

The old couple looked up. The wife seemed a bit put off and nervous, but the husband only raised an eyebrow.

"I know you, son?" he asked, Scottish accent thick.

"No, sir. My mistake."

Graves had glanced up at the sound of his voice. Now that Clay had his attention he started back toward his seat.

"You're sure about this?" he asked Kovalik.

The cell signal flickered. ". . . as I can be. It's impossible to confirm."

"What is it?" the ghost asked. Even as nothing more than a wandering spirit, a faded, transparent outline hanging in the air, Graves still had an air of power and command.

"Strangulation," he said.

The ghost shook his head. "I have no recollection of that. I told you how I died."

"Hold on, Al," Clay said into the phone, then he stared

at Graves's ghost. "You told me how you remember it. But it's pretty obvious now that isn't how it happened."

Graves opened his mouth, spectral form wavering as though a ghostly breeze had blown through the spirit world. But he said nothing.

"There's more," Kovalik said.

"Go on."

He listened as the FBI agent gave him the rest of the details his forensics specialists had discovered. Clay put a hand to his head and massaged his temples. Twice he told Kovalik to repeat himself. Finally, he thanked the man and said he would get back to him. The last thing he wanted to do was have a conversation with Graves while Kovalik was still on the line.

"What?" the ghost said, shifting anxiously through the air.

A crackling voice came over the intercom announcing final boarding for a flight to Athens. The little girl who had been so entertaining to Clay raced by, passing right through the ghost of Dr. Graves. The child stopped running, glanced around a bit frightfully, and went to sit down.

"Katherine?" her mother said, the worry plain in her voice. She went to sit beside her daughter and also passed through Dr. Graves. She shivered, and the flirtatious smile she'd begun to turn toward Clay vanished from her lips.

The presence of ghosts could be disconcerting. To Clay, they were most disconcerting when they were staring at him from inches away.

"Joe, what did he say?" Graves asked.

Clay had closed his phone. Now, even as the ghost prodded him urgently, he flipped the phone open again and pretended to dial. Then he held the phone against his ear so that anyone watching would think he was talking to someone on the other end of the line instead of to himself.

"According to Kovalik's people, your . . ." he glanced around and lowered his voice. "The skull shows signs of surgery. It was opened up at some point prior to death."

The ghost flickered like a candle flame and faded

quickly, so that even Clay could not see him. Slowly the specter manifested again, and the expression on Graves's face said it all.

"That's impossible. How could that have happened, and I be unaware?" the ghost said, barely looking at Clay. "It can't be. They must have the wrong body."

Clay shook his head, still pretending to talk into his cell phone. "DNA comparison is a match."

Graves shook his head in confusion, eyes searching for something, though Clay could not tell if he was looking now into the shadows of the solid world, or the mists of the spirit realm.

"What else?"

"Something very odd," Clay went on. "There's discoloration on the inside of the skull consistent with exposure to certain chemicals, and residue of mercury . . ."

He let his words trail off. The sudden dawning awareness in the ghost's eyes told him all he needed to know. Graves stared at him, then began to shake his head again.

"No," he said. "That never happened. Not to me. He never—"

"What, Leonard? What aren't you telling me? This is all familiar to you, isn't it?"

Slowly, Graves nodded. The ghost drifted away, not bothering to mimic the walk of the living. Clay watched him, there amid a throng of people moving to and from their destinations, going about their lives in this beehive of activity, all of them full of life and excitement and purpose.

And then there was Graves, alone and isolated and invisible to them all, just a trace. A memory.

"The Whisper," Graves said, turning back toward Clay.

"What are you—"

The ghost slid his hands into his pockets and leaned as though against a wall or post. "The Whisper."

•   •   •

VOTIVE *candles burn and flicker in the darkness of St. Patrick's Cathedral. Dr. Graves stands in the shadows of the transept near the entrance from Fifty-first Street, watching the nave. An enormous man moves through the pews, raising the kneelers and picking missals up from the seats, slipping them into the holders on the back of each pew.*

The sheer size of the man is unsettling. Hank Reinhardt stands a hair below seven feet tall and has shoulders so broad that he must turn sideways to pass through certain doorways. He spent years as a bone-breaker for a loan shark in Hell's Kitchen before he learned that there was more money in being the shark himself. When Hank became his own boss, and people didn't pay on time, he turned to murder.

He never killed his clients. Then he would have never gotten his money. Instead he murdered their wives or mothers, girlfriends or little brothers.

And now he cleans up after Mass at St. Pat's.

Graves watches as Reinhardt goes to the mop and metal, wheeled bucket he'd rolled out moments earlier. Once the man had been cruel and cunning, and now he is a slow-witted giant, going through the motions he has been taught. He crosses himself and kneels before the altar, then begins to mop the floor in long, powerful swipes.

For several years, the Whisper has operated in New York as a vigilante, tracking and capturing criminals the police cannot seem to locate, or to hold. Yet when the Whisper turns them over to the police, these killers and thieves are docile, even helpful, wishing to make amends. The Whisper has sent many letters to the New York Times *explaining that these men could now be useful members of society, that he had mesmerized them and they will never hurt another soul. Upon much research and testing, his claims had been confirmed. Prominent attorneys argued that these men should not serve prison time, but rather be allowed to pay society back in other ways, since they could no longer harm anyone else.*

At least two dozen hardened criminals were irrevocably altered by the Whisper before Dr. Graves discovered the truth and revealed it to the world.

Reinhardt is the last of them. The only survivor among the Whisper's triumphs. All of the others have been murdered.

So when a shape rises in the vestibule, a silhouette in the wan golden illumination of the candles and the few lights still burning in the cathedral, Graves is not at all surprised. This is what he has been waiting for. He does not even shift, hidden deep in his own pocket of shadows, for he dares not give his presence away yet.

The figure moves silently along the central aisle, ominous in the heavy black coat that hangs on his thin, powerful frame like a cloak. A wide-brimmed hat and black scarf hide his features, but his eyes gleam in the candlelight as he seems to glide toward Reinhardt.

The massive killer, now a simple servant of the church, senses his presence and turns. A smile blossoms on the ugly, brutal face as he recognizes his benefactor.

"Hullo, Mister Whisper," Reinhardt says in his guttural, accented voice.

Perhaps the Whisper replies, but all Graves can hear is a low murmur, like the wind in the eaves.

He steps out from the shadows of the transept, drawing his two pistols from the holsters under his arms. Graves cocks both weapons, and the sound freezes the Whisper in place. Soft laughter fills the cathedral as though it comes from everywhere and nowhere at once.

"Well, Doctor Graves," the Whisper says, without turning, "it appears you will hound me 'till death."

"You have brought it upon yourself, Broderick."

"I was a hero, and now the city thinks of me as no better than the criminals I removed from the streets."

Graves takes several steps toward the Whisper. Beneath his wide-brimmed hat, the man does not so much as twitch.

"You are no better than they are, Broderick. In fact, you're far worse. You held yourself up to a higher standard, let the people think you were decent and noble, when you were nothing but another lunatic. You made them think you were a hero, and instead you were the worst kind of fraud."

The giant, Reinhardt, frowns and glares at Graves. "This fella bothering you, Mister Whisper?"

"I served society, Graves!" the Whisper says, and now, slowly, he turns.

"You cut into their brains," Dr. Graves says through gritted teeth. "You soaked their minds in chemicals, burned their brain cells, performed surgery."

"For the betterment of those men and for the world," the Whisper says, but his voice is dull and emotionless. He sounds tired.

"Mister Whisper?" Reinhardt asks, and comes to stand beside the dark figure whose features are hidden beneath the brim of his hat, even from the candlelight.

"You're a barbarian and a lunatic, sir. I thought exposing you would end with you in a prison cell. Instead, it's made you a murderer."

The Whisper laughs. "There's just no pleasing you, is there? You humiliated me in front of the world, Graves. Mayor Bennett excoriated me in every newspaper in the city, holding you up as a hero, and me as a fraud. I've been forced to admit that you and Bennett are right. Men like Reinhardt can't be helped."

Graves aims his pistols at the Whisper, trying to focus on the man's chest, though his eyes gleam in the shadow of his hat brim.

"So you killed them all. Strangled every last one of them."

"Merely correcting my error," the Whisper says, the words dry and cold, as though they come not from his lips but from the shadows of the cathedral itself.

"You're coming with me, Broderick," Dr. Graves says, pausing in the aisle now, careful not to get too close.

"So you can humiliate me further? I'd rather not."

"*Mister Whisper?*" *Reinhardt asks, glancing quizzically from one man to the other.* "*What should I do?*"

The Whisper tilts his head slightly back to glance up at the giant. In the candlelight, his features are grizzled, gray stubble grows on his chin, and there are dark circles under his mad eyes.

"*Protect me, Reinhardt. The black man wants to hurt me.*"

"*Don't listen, Hank—*" *Graves begins.*

But he sees it is already too late. Hate lights up Reinhardt's eyes as the giant starts toward him.

He lumbers in between Graves and the Whisper. The very moment he blocks Graves's aim, Reinhardt cries out in pain and confusion and staggers forward. He drops to his knees and tumbles toward Dr. Graves, who is forced to catch him.

"*No!*" *Graves shouts.*

Reinhardt is so huge that he cannot hold the man up. Twitching, gape-mouthed and wide-eyed with shock, he slips to the ground. The black handle of a hunting knife juts from his back. The copper stink of blood fills St. Patrick's cathedral from door to altar.

Graves extricates himself from the dying man and looks up, both guns ready. A shadow disappears behind the altar, into that intimate place meant only for priests and other servants of God. But, of course, Leonard Graves has not believed in God for many years. He believes in science, and he believes in justice. The world needs nothing more.

Pistols gripped firmly in his hands, he races past the altar and slips through an open door beside a heavy tapestry. It is all darkness in the rear of the church, shadow upon shadow. He pauses, listening to the dark for any sign of footsteps. Up ahead he can hear the Whisper moving, hear him breathing. For all of his vaunted stealth, he is making no attempt to disguise his exit route.

Gunshots echo through the cathedral, and Graves drops into a crouch, peering into the corridor ahead for the flash of a muzzle. But the shots come from around a corner. It

*makes no sense. What is the Whisper firing at if not at him?
There comes the cracking of wood and the slam of a door
crashing open.*

*Again, Graves pursues the savage, hating the twist that
things have taken. For several years it seemed a kind of
golden age of heroism was growing in New York, and in
America. The courage of the soldiers going off to war, the
valiant efforts of the United States to stop the march of
Hitler's killers across Europe, and in Manhattan, Graves
had fought injustice with the grudging approval of the au-
thorities and the blessing of the people. The Whisper had
joined the fight, and then Joe Falcon. Only recently, several new adventurers have appeared, including a mysterious masked woman the papers were calling the Siren.*

*But if there ever had been a golden age, to Dr. Graves,
it is over now. The Whisper has tainted it forever.*

*Windows along the corridor allow just enough light
from the street and the moon so that he can see the door
hanging open as he rounds the corner. Graves throws himself against the wall and slides quickly along, guns at the
ready. He expects some attack. In his black coat, hat, and
scarf, the Whisper could hide well enough in those shadows, but there is no sign of him.*

*Graves lunges through the door, pistols out ahead of
him, fingers twitching on the triggers.*

*The only thing behind the door is a staircase leading
upward. He hears only the faintest footfall above, but that
is enough. The Whisper is running for the roof. It makes no
sense. There is no escape up there. But Graves reminds
himself that the Whisper is no ordinary man. He might well
have rigged up some way to glide down.*

He follows.

*Stairs lead to a metal-runged ladder, and the ladder
leads to a hatch, which yawns open above, moonlight
streaming in. No silhouette appears above, ready to put a
bullet through him while he climbs, but still he holsters one
pistol and points the other upward, climbing one-handed.*

His heart hammers as he emerges onto the steeply

canted roof. Small spires rise all along each side, and at the front, above the vestibule, two enormous towers stab at the night sky. The lights of the city surround him, but it is the glow of the moon that makes the roof of the cathedral seem to glow a ghostly gray.

The Whisper is there. He walks swiftly but carefully along the peak of the roof toward the front of the church on Fifth Avenue. The wind blows his coat back behind him and for a moment it seems he will be blown right off the roof, and perhaps this is how he will glide away to make his escape across the night sky.

But that is pure fancy, and unlike Graves. Not even the Whisper can fly.

Graves sights along the top of his pistol, but he is too far away. It would be hard to make the shot from here. Instead he crouches low and scrambles up the slanted roof to the peak. For a moment he stands exposed and vulnerable atop this Gothic masterpiece, catching his breath, surrounded by the echo of the medieval and the lights of Manhattan.

Then he runs.

Leonard Graves has honed his body over a lifetime. He is no ordinary man. Balance, even with the wind, is second nature to him, and he races along the rooftop without hesitation, trusting to his training and his instincts. In a flash of insight, he recognizes for the first time that the entire Gothic cathedral is a single enormous crucifix, the whole building formed in the shape of the cross. The entire design is a symbol of sacrifice.

The Whisper is slower, more cautious. Graves is catching up to him.

"Broderick, you're not going to get away!" he calls over the wind. "I won't rest until justice is done."

Laughter erupts from the night sky and carries to him on the night wind. The Whisper reaches the edge of the roof and steps up onto a low stone ledge there, steadying himself on a stone cross that crowns the apex. Below, on Fifth Avenue, cars rumble by.

"Justice, is it?" the Whisper calls, and the way he hangs back and cries the words to the sky, Graves thinks perhaps the question is not meant for him, but for some higher power. "I had faith! I only wanted to save them, redeem them!"

"You destroyed their minds, and then you took their lives!" Graves shouts.

Balanced upon the roof he draws his other pistol again and points both muzzles at the madman.

The wind snatches the wide-brimmed hat from the Whisper's head and carries it away into the night, flipping end over end as it gusts across Fifth Avenue. Emotion ravages the man's face. There is fear there, and regret, confusion and madness.

In his right hand he holds a custom-made black pistol with a long, thin barrel.

"Throw the gun down!"

With a sickly laugh, mouth twisted into a grin of comic absurdity, the Whisper tosses the gun off the roof. It disappears into the abyss of Fifth Avenue that yawns just behind him. Now he clutches the cross on the roof's peak with both hands, and his expression turns to one of anguish.

"You win, Graves," the Whisper says. "There is no redemption, after all. Not for killers like Reinhardt. Or like me."

He throws his arms wide, head tilted, mouth twisted into a sardonic grin. Then he turns and, coat fluttering behind him in the wind, plummets from the edge of the roof.

"No!" Dr. Graves shouts, but the word is stolen away by the wind.

He races to the edge of the roof, holstering his weapons. He grips the same cross that the Whisper had held on to moments before. Quick as he is, Graves makes it to the edge just in time to see the man hit the street far below. The impact is silent at this height. A car swerves down on Fifth Avenue to avoid running over the twisted, shattered corpse of the broken hero. The fallen idol.

For long minutes, Dr. Graves stands there staring down

at the small, pitiful figure of that dead man, and he reminds himself of his own beliefs. Whether there is a God or not, Leonard Graves believes in redemption. He must believe in it, or he could not believe in justice.

But for the Whisper, both justice and redemption are now forever out of reach.

"SIR, can I get you anything to drink?"

Clay had been staring out the window of the plane, watching the clouds sweep by as the flight from London made its way toward Florence. The flight attendant was a fortysomething British woman who looked every bit her age yet looked the type who might get more beautiful with each passing year. Clay appreciated the wisdom in a woman's eyes, and the elegance with which some of them grew older.

He smiled at her.

"A glass of red wine would put me forever in your debt."

The flight attendant laughed, more than used to being flirted with by passengers. "That's all right, love. Just the cash will do."

As she served him, Clay glanced up and down the aisle. He found the ghost of Dr. Graves hovering behind a pair of pretty teenaged girls who were curled together in their seats, wrapped in one another's arms like lovers. And perhaps they were. Clay had spent enough time watching Graves watch people that by now he knew it was their peacefulness that fascinated the ghost. Their contentment.

"Thank you," he told the flight attendant.

She winked at him playfully and then moved on to the next row.

After the call from Kovalik, Clay had spent the rest of the layover listening to Graves talk about the New York of his era. He had painted a picture with his words of what he called a golden age of heroism, and the notoriety achieved by certain men and women who had risked their lives to fight crime in ways and with methods beyond the capacity of the police.

The story of the Whisper was one of tragedy, and it had left Clay feeling melancholy and cynical. The man had been brilliant and courageous, according to Graves, but also, quite obviously, demented. Barbaric, the ghost had said, and Clay could not agree more.

Clay sipped his wine and glanced back at the ghost again. The connection between Kovalik's new information, the autopsy on Graves's remains, and the murder of Mayor Bennett, was obvious to both of them now. The chemical stains, mercury residue, and evidence of brain surgery on Graves's skull made it clear someone had performed the same operation on him that the Whisper had performed on the criminals he'd "rehabilitated." It had to have been a more complicated procedure for Graves not to have become as docile as the others. None of the Whisper's victims had remembered their surgery, so that was not a surprise, but then why did Graves have memories of the events leading to his own death that were obviously wrong?

All of these questions niggled at the back of Clay's mind as the plane flew toward Florence. But as he took another sip of wine, two questions bothered him more than any of the others.

If the Whisper had killed himself that night on the roof of St. Patrick's, then who had performed the surgery on Graves? And who, if not the Whisper, had murdered Graves and Roger Alton Bennett?

The plane's engines hummed.

Clay took another sip of bloodred wine and glanced out the window at the clouds, but he found no answers there.

15

IT'S nothing like Ceridwen's traveling winds, Danny thought.

Leaping into his father's conjured dimensional doorway was like having himself turned inside out and his guts scraped onto the floor with a rusty butcher knife.

Danny wasn't sure how long he'd been lying in the warm, dry darkness, but he appreciated the coolness of the concrete floor against his aching face. Everything hurt, even what little hair he had left on his body.

Images of Eve, Squire, and the monstrous animal they'd brought with them kept playing in his mind, and he squeezed himself tighter into a ball, trying to protect himself from the painful recollection.

You screwed your friends, Ferrick. Face it, he thought, and he would see it all play out again—how he had chosen his demon sire over the closest thing to a family, other than his mother, he'd ever had. They had seen him licking the dead woman's blood off his face. The look of horror and disdain on Eve's face was etched in his mind, now. And all he could think about was how it would break his mother's heart if they told her what they'd seen.

Danny wasn't sure he could live with that.

She's not your real mother, a voice whispered way in the back of his head, and a cold detachment flowed over and through him. Suddenly it was easier to deal with the idea of betrayal. Danny tried to push the troubling thoughts from his head, to rest and recover from his journey through his father's interdimensional escape route, but his senses were awake now—the smells and sounds of his surroundings urging him to rouse himself.

There was, after all, something very familiar about this place.

For the first time since being spat out of the swirling rip in time and space, Danny was able to open his eyes. His eyelids burned, and his eyes ached. He wondered if this was going to be something he'd have to get used to if he was going to stay with the demon—*with my father.*

Sensory stimuli bombarded him as he pushed himself up into a sitting position. The slight smell of mustiness mixed with the perfume stink of fabric softener, and beneath it all the thick aroma of home heating oil. He was in the cellar of a home, that was obvious, but the surprising thing, as he climbed to his feet, was that he knew exactly whose cellar he was in.

By scent alone, Danny knew he was in the basement of his Newton home. His vision cleared, and he glanced around the room, saw the plastic storage bins of tax information and the boxes of Christmas decorations recently moved closer to the stairs because of the quickly approaching holiday season. His old ten-speed bike stood gathering dust in the far corner.

He smiled momentarily, and then realized that he was alone.

Where was his father?

More importantly, where was his mother? The image of Baalphegor murdering and eating that old woman flashed across his mind, and he could not stop himself from picturing the same barbaric fate befalling his mother.

"Shit," he hissed.

Danny bolted across the room, navigating the obstacles

of the basement with ease, and bounded up the cellar steps two at a time. His pulse raced as he saw that the door up into the kitchen was already open.

When he reached the top of the steps, he barged into the kitchen, heart clenched, holding his breath. He glanced around, and for a moment his hideous imagination showed him a glimpse of precisely what he expected to find. Then he blinked and saw that there was no blood splashed across the countertops or the tile floor, no dismembered limbs strewn across the kitchen. A wave of relief began to sweep over him, but he shook it off. The absence of carnage meant nothing. He still had no idea where his father had gone.

He could be tearing her apart in another room right now, dumb ass, yelled the pleasant little voice in the back of his head.

Frantic, he darted into the living room, and then the dining room, finding them both empty. He hoped that his mother was out shopping or visiting one of her girlfriends.

Starting to calm a bit, Danny headed down the hallway to the foyer, where he noticed the first sign of something amiss. The front door was open wide, and a package— likely a result of his mother's addiction to online shopping—was lying on the floor. He noticed a brown, UPS truck parked by the curb in front of the house.

He picked up the package and placed it on the hallway table. Then he shut the door and glanced up the stairs to the second floor. That was when he smelled it. He knew what it was right away.

The scent of blood. As horrifying as it was to acknowledge what it might mean, it was far worse to realize how much he had grown to like it.

The scent drew him up the stairs. It came from his bedroom at the end of the hall. He paused momentarily, preparing himself. Taking three deep breaths, the stink of blood almost overwhelming him with its intoxicating stench, he strode down the hall, placed his hand against the wood of the door, and pushed it open.

"Holy shit," Danny exclaimed, staring in horror at his room. His posters had been torn down, the walls covered in strange, geometric symbols, written in blood.

Baalphegor was still working, using his claws to paint the sigils upon the egg-white walls and ceiling.

"What are you doing?" Danny asked, transfixed by the bloody shapes.

His father looked at him and smiled. The demon squatted behind Danny's bed, which had been pushed haphazardly into the center of the room. As Danny approached he saw the body of the UPS man, torn open and lying on the floor. The demon dipped his claws into a gaping hole torn in the corpse's belly, using the blood as ink.

"This is really fucked up," Danny muttered, a part of him happy that his mother's body was nowhere in the room.

"That's your humanity talking," Baalphegor replied, scrawling a shape that looked like an upside down, capital *A* upon the lower section of bare wall. "There will shortly come a time when something like this will barely register with you."

A war erupted inside of him, in both his heart and his mind. If ever he had witnessed an act of pure evil, this was it. He knew that—understood how completely wrong it was. And yet it thrilled him as well. And that part of him that loved the scent of the dead man's blood reminded him that this was no different from a lion attacking prey on the veldt or hawks snatching mice up from the fields. He and his father, they weren't human.

Danny's hand self-consciously went to the sack of skin hanging from his chest. It throbbed as he touched it, as if aroused by his attentions. Maybe he wasn't human, but he had been given a gift of humanity . . . a gift, and a curse.

"You're saying that murder, and seeing shit painted on walls with blood, and corpses with their bellies torn open will be like, been there, done that?"

Baalphegor looked away from his work, head turning completely around on his shoulders as he nodded. "It will all be . . . what's the expression I'm looking for?" The demon thought for a moment and then snapped his blood-stained fingers. "*Old hat*. Things like this will all be old hat."

At the moment, Danny really didn't see the appeal.

Baalphegor stood erect, admiring his handiwork.

"What's all this for?" Danny asked.

The demon rubbed his hands together. "This will aid you in the next step toward your evolution."

Danny moved closer to his sire, but was distracted by something that protruded from beneath his bed. The hairy paw of a stuffed animal. He bent down and yanked the stuffed monkey out from beneath the bed, brushing clumps of dust from its fake brown fur. He'd forgotten all about it.

His father had given it to him—his human father. It was right before his parents had separated, right before the skin problems that would eventually lead to the discovery much worse than a case of severe psoriasis.

"What is that?" Baalphegor asked.

Danny chuckled, looking at the stuffed animal's stupid face. "It's a stuffed monkey," he said, holding it up for the demon to see.

"A stuffed monkey," Baalphegor repeated. "Was it once alive?"

"No. It's fake. It's just a stupid stuffed animal."

The demon moved with its inhuman quickness, snatching the monkey from his hands. Baalphegor stared at the toy, his black lips peeling back to reveal rows of razor-sharp teeth.

"My father gave it to me," Danny explained, and then was forced to correct himself. "My . . . y'know, my human father . . . gave it to me before he split from my mom."

"This . . . splitting, it still pains you?" Baalphegor asked.

Danny shook his head. "Naw," he said. "Been over that for years."

"You're lying," the demon hissed. "But it doesn't matter, for soon it will be true. All of this." The creature spread its thin, muscular arms presenting the bedroom. "All that it represents in your life will have no meaning. The hurt will no longer matter."

Danny found himself backing up, away from the demon sire, his eyes for some strange reason riveted on the stuffed monkey. The thought of giving up something so simple . . . it disturbed him.

"I sense your apprehension," Baalphegor said, moving toward him. "And I can understand, for it's all you've ever known." He dropped the stuffed monkey to the floor, his taloned foot stamping down on it, tearing open its belly to reveal the white stuffing within.

"If it makes it any better, remember that this and everything around it will be no more, once the Devourer feeds."

"Mr. Doyle and the others, they'll come up with a way to stop it . . . to stop the Devourer," Danny said, wanting to believe it. He imagined the world destroyed, everyone that he ever loved or cared about dead or worse. *Maybe there is something to this whole evolving thing,* he thought, his hand again going to the swollen growth attached to the center of his chest.

Baalphegor slowly shook his head. "Doyle is a mage, nothing more. Not even the most powerful of this world's mages. Merely one among them. The demise of this world is inevitable. No matter how they fight—no matter the level of sacrifice—it will all be for naught."

Danny stared at the writings in blood where his Slipknot, Insane Clown Posse, and Green Day posters used to hang. The markings looked different now, darker, thicker.

"What do they do?" he asked, pointing them out. "How do they help with the . . . the transition?"

"The severing of a Collector from his accumulated humanity is a painful and emotional experience," the demon explained. "These sigils aid in the process of acceptance."

The demon came closer.

"Do you feel their calming effects on you?" he asked. "Helping you to accept your destiny?"

Danny held the sack in his hand, eyes squinting down at the opaque flesh, attempting to see what was stored within.

What exactly does humanity look like? A soul? Even a
makeshift one like his.

At first he thought the sound was thunder, but then he
realized that it was the middle of November, and there
weren't many November thunderstorms in New England.

Baalphegor looked about, a snarl upon his hideous features. "Now is the time," the demon demanded, extending
his hands toward the growth.

Danny wrapped his hand around it, protecting it. Behind his demon sire he could see the strange, blood symbols expanding, running into one another. The dark
crimson of the blood turned black, and that dark void fell
away into nothing. It was as though the symbols were written in acid that burned away a section of wall, leaving a
sucking hole into space, a vast chamber of darkness beyond.

"What the hell?" Danny whispered. He craned his neck,
trying to see, even as the demon moved to block his view.

Baalphegor sighed, shaking his head. "You're early," he
muttered, turning slightly to address the dark void in the
wall behind him.

"Do you have what was promised?" asked a voice from
the void, and Danny saw something move in the black, a
flicker of a tail, like some kind of leviathan swimming in a
sea of shadow.

"I told you, you're early," Baalphegor replied. "He has
not yet given it to me."

The demon looked at Danny and extended his clawed
hand. "Enough of this dalliance, my son. The time is now.
Remove the sack and place it in my hand."

Danny shied away, turning his body to protect the sack.
In the abyss beyond the wall of his bedroom—maybe beyond the wall of the world—the face of something truly
horrific peered in at him, circular red eyes watching him,
and then it was gone, swimming off with a flourish of a
powerful tail.

"Who the fuck is that?" Danny demanded.

"We haven't the time for this, Baalphegor," the thing in

the darkness hissed. "Complete your part of the bargain. Take the sack and be done with it."

Danny shook his head in fear and confusion. "Bargain? What's he talking about?" He tried to move past his father, to get a closer look at the substantial ocean of darkness that had filled half of his room. "The writing, those sigils you painted on the wall, those weren't for me, were they?"

Baalphegor sighed, a thick, steaming trickle of saliva dribbling from the corner of his mouth to the floor. "Do not make this difficult."

Danny looked back to the darkness, his hand falling away from the sack. And the nightmare that swam in the shadows was there at once, drawn to the sack of humanity like a shark to blood. Danny stumbled backward, startled by the sight of the thing. It reminded him of the piranhas he'd seen at the aquarium—but huge and . . . different.

Horribly different.

Baalphegor sprang at him then, knocking him backward to the floor.

"A bargain has been struck," the demon growled, leering over him. "A bargain that will save my life and start you on the path to fulfilling your destiny."

"What kind of bargain?" Danny asked, glaring up at his father defiantly. "I didn't agree to anything."

"Has he been told?" the thing from beyond asked.

Danny thrashed beneath his father, fear and hopelessness warring in him. He'd already betrayed his mother and his friends, betrayed his humanity. If his demon sire had lied to him, he had nothing left. It wasn't a choice anymore of embracing his soul or his demonic nature . . . it was a choice of nothing or nothing.

"Have I been told what? What the fuck is going on?"

Baalphegor climbed off of him, allowing him to stand. The demon stood at the brink of darkness, the thing that swam in the shadows peering out at them eagerly.

"All he knows is that his evolution is at hand," his sire explained.

"Tell me," Danny demanded as he rose to his feet. "What haven't I been told?"

"There is a special purpose waiting for you, child," the piranha said, its hideous mouth filled with far too many teeth. "Give up the burden of your humanity and achieve this promise all the sooner."

Danny's brain felt as though it just might explode. This was too much for him to handle. How could he hold it all in his head, in his heart? All his life he'd thought he was an ordinary kid, and then his body had started to change, twisting into something horrible and grotesque. When he'd learned from Mr. Doyle what he really was, part of him had been relieved. All the harassment he'd taken, all of the looks, not to mention all of the instincts and urges he didn't understand . . . it was all for a reason.

He wasn't a freak. He wasn't human at all, so he no longer had to live up to the expectations human society put on a typical teenager.

But his metamorphosis had continued, leeching away more and more of his humanity. His reflection was more monstrous, more demonic, every time he looked in the mirror, and his instincts had followed suit. The flashes of violence, the hunger for carnage . . . his true nature explained it all. Mr. Doyle, Eve, Graves . . . all of them had urged him to fight it, had told him he could choose to be good and noble despite his bloodline.

God, how he had wanted to believe them.

If only Dr. Graves was here, right now, he thought. *He would know what to do, what to say.* Everything always seemed so much clearer seen through Graves's eyes. Right and wrong. Danny guessed that was why Graves had been a hero during his life.

But I'm no hero, he thought. *I'm just a kid.*

And not even that. I'm a demon.

Now he was being asked to give up all that he had ever known to become a full-fledged monster. This whole special purpose thing, it was more than he could stand.

A demon, yeah. He caressed the fleshy sack on his

chest. *But as human as I choose to be, as long as I have this.*

"I can't handle this," he said, his hands going to his head, as if to keep it from breaking apart. "This is all too much to deal with."

He heard Baalphegor chuckle, a low, rumbling laugh that sounded like the engine of an idling truck. "It is your humanity that plagues you, changeling. Give it up, and your pain disappears."

Can it be that easy? Danny wondered. *Tear this thing from my body and everything will be all right?*

He looked down at the growth. It was even larger now, storing up his life experiences even to the last moment.

"And then you'll give this to him?" Danny asked, motioning to the creature floating in the darkness.

"That was our covenant," Baalphegor answered. "In exchange they will provide me with escape. This plane of existence, and so many others will be gone soon. I do not wish to share their fate."

Escape. It sounded good to him at the moment, too. To give this up . . . he held the throbbing sack of flesh in his hand again.

"Will . . . will you take me with you?" Danny asked.

Baalphegor chuckled again, shaking his strangely shaped head from side to side. "That would be impossible."

"Your destiny is here," the piranha gurgled excitedly from the darkness.

Danny's thoughts were a whirlwind, the demons watching him—waiting for him to make up his mind—making his fevered brain swirl all the faster. He took hold of the growth with the intention of ripping it from his chest and had started to tug on it, when he felt the most unbelievable pain. It was as if he were taking hold of his guts and pulling them from his body.

Gasping aloud, he fell to his knees.

"It does not want to leave you," Baalphegor stated, squatting down on his haunches, watching him with ex-

cited, golden eyes. "Cut it from your body—free yourself
from its constraints."

"Free yourself," the piranha whispered, over and over, a
chant urging him to action.

He wasn't sure why he did it, but Danny reached into
his pocket, searching for the penknife that he sometimes
carried. Instead he withdrew the piece of stained glass that
he'd found at the church in Southie. He stared at it, rubbing
away the grime to reveal a single eye peering up at him.

Daring him to act.

Danny brought the edge of the glass up to his chest,
ready to press the sharp edge against the thick tendril of
flesh that connected the sack to his body.

*Free yourself. Free yourself. Free yourself. Free your-
self.* The thing that swam in the ocean of darkness chanted.

"You sure you want to do that, kid?" asked a voice from
somewhere close by, and Danny turned to see his closet
doors swing open and Squire emerge. "Just think of the
risk of infection."

Before Danny could respond, there was a roar like a
lion, and something exploded from inside the darkness of
the closet, black and huge and lightning fast, massive jaws
open wide in fury.

Squire had not come alone.

SHUCK landed in a coiled crouch in front of Baalphegor, driving him back toward the pulsing void in the wall.
Squire caught a quick glimpse of the other demonic entity
within the sea of darkness and shuddered at its ugliness,
even as he turned to Danny.

"We gotta get you out of here," the hobgoblin said, taking him by the arm and hustling him toward the bedroom
door.

Danny tore his arm away and twisted around to stare at
the demon that was about to square off against Shuck. At
his father. Squire couldn't tell if what he saw in the boy's
eyes was longing or anger or both.

"It ain't for you, kid," Squire told him. "Come with us, we can help you get over this bad stretch."

The kid looked down into his eyes, and for a minute, Squire believed he had gotten through to him.

Then Danny's eyes flashed, and his lips parted in a nasty snarl as he hurled Squire across the room. The hobgoblin bounced off the wall and landed on the floor in a heap. He shook his head, trying to clear away the cobwebs, and watched through bleary eyes as Danny leaped across the room, tackling Shuck just as the shadow beast prepared to pounce on Baalphegor.

"Son of a bitch," Squire grumbled, climbing to his feet, just as Eve and Ceridwen appeared in the doorway.

"Oh, this is good," Eve sniped, eyeing the dimensional rift that had been opened in the kid's bedroom.

"Yep," Squire agreed, watching as Baalphegor turned his attention toward them, and then four shapes emerged from the pulsing void. They were powerful looking beasties, their bodies covered in thick, spiny shells, like crabs gone horribly, horribly wrong.

"Can't imagine things getting any better than this."

THE world turned red.

Danny saw everything through a crimson haze, as though a red filter covered his eyes. The rage had claimed him. He wrestled the thrashing, black-skinned animal to the floor of his bedroom. With incredible strength, the beast twisted in his grasp, stretching, trying to snap its jaws down on him, to tear a chunk of flesh from him.

"Gonna bite me?" he snarled. "I don't think so."

His demonic nature ascendant, he reveled in the thrashing violence. He brought his jaws down, biting into the thick, black skin, reveling in the rank taste of the animal's blood as it gushed into his mouth.

The beast roared in pain, bucking wildly in Danny's grasp. He had his arms around the animal's neck, strad-

dling its muscular back as he attempted to force the animal
to the ground.

From the corner of his eye he saw Baalphegor and a
quartet of demons he had never seen before—crablike
monstrosities that had emerged from the oil-black darkness of the abyss beyond the world. The demons stalked
toward Squire and Eve.

Danny faltered. His rage was inflamed, but his allegiance was torn between his friends and his father. In frustration, he took his anguish out on the closest thing to him.
Danny grabbed hold of the still-struggling animal's snapping jaws, exerting all his might as he pulled them apart,
wanting so desperately to hear the sound of snapping
sinew and bone.

"Want to bite me?" he growled with exertion, feeling
the musculature of the animal's jaw start to give. "I'll show
you what fucking happens when things try to bite me."

He smelled it before it struck, a strange metallic smell
hanging heavily in the air. It reminded him of the way the
night smelled after a heavy summer thundershower.

The bolt of lightning sliced down between him and the
beast, severing their connection with the proficiency of a
surgeon's scalpel.

Danny staggered backward and crashed into his bureau.
Pictures fell, glass shattered. He clutched the edge of a
half-open drawer and turned, baring his fangs in a hiss.
Pain and rage twisted into hatred, and he longed to eviscer-
ate whoever had dared to attack him, whoever had hurt
him.

Then he saw Ceridwen, floating in the air in the middle
of his bedroom, robes whipping around her in an unseen
wind she had summoned. Her beauty was unearthly and
heartbreaking. She was kindness and grace and the purity
of the sky and the ocean . . .

And she glared at him as though he were her enemy.

"Leave the beast alone, Daniel," Ceridwen said, held
aloft by a swirling funnel of wind. She held her staff out

before her, its frozen, icy headpiece crackling with fire and mystical energies.

The shadow beast had received the brunt of her assault. It lay on its side, shivering as its ebony flesh smoldered. Danny could barely control his anger. Instinct made him crouch, ready to surge up into the air and bring her down, but he knew she could destroy him.

And that just made him all the madder.

"You love it so much," he snarled, grabbing hold of the doglike animal and lifting its prone form up from the floor. "Why don't you fucking marry it," he screamed, tossing it away into the sea of darkness that composed the back wall of his room.

He looked at Ceridwen, a nasty sneer of defiance on his face.

"Not nice," the elemental sorceress said, the frozen sphere at the head of her staff flaring to life. It burned like the heart of the sun.

"Not nice at all."

EVE stood in a corner of the room, a curtain of dark hair falling in front of her face. She didn't like any of this. Not at all. Tensed for battle, she held her talons out in front of her and watched them elongate to wicked dagger tips. She bared her fangs and stared in dismay at Danny and Ceridwen squaring off over the body of Shuck.

This wasn't the way things were supposed to go. They were here to save the kid . . . to redeem him.

Not a person had ever walked the earth who knew more about redemption than Eve. And she knew very well that some could never be redeemed. But Danny . . . he was one of them. She cared for the little fucker, and now he was embracing the darkness.

Eve was going to have to rip out his throat, and then his heart. She was going to have to *end* him to save him.

It wouldn't be the first time she'd lost someone this way. But it never got easier.

And Shuck . . . she'd come to care for the stinking, slobbering beast. It hurt her to see it injured, just lying there on its side. She had to restrain herself from going to it. But as much as it pained her, there were bigger problems that required her attentions.

Before she got to Danny, there were grown-up demons to slaughter.

The first of the crab-things attacked with a chittering hiss, its razor-sharp claws snapping in her face. The demon Baalphegor held back, almost as if he were waiting to see how the crabs would do before deciding to join the fray.

All he had to do was ask. The crabs weren't going to do shit.

She lunged forward as the lead crustacean reached for her again, grabbing hold of its arm and twisting. The creature squealed in pain as she tore the arm away with a crack of carapace and an explosion of foul-smelling fluids. She held the limb, using it as a weapon to drive the other demons back.

"Pretty good, eh?" she said, licking the spatter of ichor from around her mouth.

"Not bad," Squire said, leaving her side, returning to the closet behind them.

"Where do you think you're going?" she demanded, still holding the crustaceans at bay.

"Give me a sec," the hobgoblin said, diving into a pool of shadow at the back of the closet.

"You little shit," she hissed, just as another of the creatures attacked. She stabbed with the limb, its point puncturing the carapace that covered its belly. This beast squealed as well, falling back to join its brethren. Beyond them, the back wall of the room pulsed with living darkness, some hell dimension or other on the other side. Baalphegor had ripped a hole between the planes.

Conan Doyle was going to be pissed.

Eve braced herself for another attack, then heard a clatter behind her as Squire returned, tromping out of the closet.

"You better have come back with a really big axe," she snapped.

"I've got something better than that," he said. And then she heard the unmistakable sound of a clip of bullets being loaded into a weapon.

Eve chanced a quick look behind her and saw that the hobgoblin had returned with one of the largest, semiautomatic rifles she had ever seen. It was huge in Squire's grasp, but he held it like a pro, flipping the safety to the "off" position.

"If you would be so kind as to get out of the way," he said, absurdly formal.

She barely had enough time to dive to one side before the little shit opened fire.

THE weapon was a modified 50-caliber, semiautomatic rifle that Squire had picked up from the manufacturer down in Tennessee. Guns normally weren't his thing. He preferred the simpler killing tools like swords, knives, and battle-axes—preferably enchanted. But every once in a while a firearm came along that captured his fancy. The last one had been back in 1920, when he'd first laid eyes on the Thompson Machine Gun. It had been love at first sight, and he hadn't been smitten like that again until he saw the 50-caliber in action.

The hobgoblin planted his feet, screaming for Eve to get out of his way. As she moved, he pulled the trigger, spraying the demonic crustaceans with a shower of bullets modified to deal with the infernal. John Paul himself had blessed the steel-jacketed babies that were ripping through the creatures' shells like they were papier-mâché, a favor that Squire had called in just before the Pontiff joined the heavenly choir in 'oh-five.

The crustaceans squealed in agony, as parts of their bodies were turned to paste and dark shards of carapace. They started to retreat, the survivors hurling themselves back into the ocean of darkness at the back of the room.

Squire continued to fire the weapon into the throbbing void, hoping for a few more lucky hits.

In his excitement, he'd lost sight of Baalphegor, and it wasn't until he heard Eve screaming above the noise to watch his ass that he realized the demon was crawling across the ceiling above him. He raised the heavy weapon, preparing to shoot the son of a bitch down, but just as he pulled the trigger, Eve leaped to his aid.

Squire screamed at her, but it was too late. Blessed bullets erupted from the gun and strafed both Eve and Baalphegor.

The hobgoblin cursed and jumped out of the way as they both dropped from the ceiling in a bloody heap. He tossed the weapon aside and hurried to kneel by Eve.

"Come on, speak to me, darlin'," he said, reaching out and rolling her over, gasping at the number of holes the bullets had punched in her clothes and in her flesh. Blood soaked her blouse and jacket.

Her eyes snapped open, bright red with her curse, and she hissed at him, baring her fangs.

Squire gave her his biggest smile. "Would it help if I said I was sorry?"

Eve shot up a hand and clutched his throat in an iron grip.

"Do you *see* this outfit? Do you have any idea what this cost? I'm gonna make you hurt as much as I hurt now," she hissed, blood still leaking from her wounds.

Explosions of color danced around the outskirts of his vision as he tried to breathe, but Squire caught sight of Baalphegor, the demon's body leaking precious fluids as he pushed himself up from the floor. He tried to get Eve's attention but she was too caught her up in her petty nonsense to notice.

She looked as though she was just about to do something awful to his eyes, when he managed to squeak a single word.

"Demon."

Baalphegor had propped himself halfway up, and his

claws were sketching the air, halfway through the process
of casting a spell.

Eve saw that Squire was focused not on her, but behind
her. She twisted around, tossing him aside, but it was too
late. Tendrils of black magic erupted from the demon's
hands, pulsed once, and then simply exploded, the sheer
force of the magic summoned obliterating the structure
around them.

Reducing it to nothing but rubble and the stench of
brimstone.

I T was as if Danny had been removed from the passage
of time.

The energy from Ceridwen's staff had expanded outward, engulfing him in a light that seemed to permeate
straight to his soul. He was frozen, hanging in the air, powerless.

She floated like a goddess before him, her robes flowing around her, moved by a wind that he could not feel.
Lightning sparked from her eyes, and a cold, blue mist
churned around her hands like tiny, twin storms.

"This is not you, Daniel," she said, her voice booming
in his ears.

He wanted to scream that she was wrong, but the pain
was too great for him to speak. The ice-cold blazing fire
generated from her staff engulfed him, attempting to burn
away the darkness within him.

How could she understand what it was like to know, to
finally understand, that he was evil to his core? That he had
been born a demon, a creature of darkness, and that he still
was this thing? Whatever chance he'd had to be human, he
had surrendered it when he stood by and let his father
slaughter that old woman, when he had tasted her blood,
when he had not balked at the murder of the delivery man.

Ceridwen might blame it on his sire, but she did not realize that his bestial nature had been festering inside him
for months now, becoming harder and harder to control

with every passing day. The sorceress saw what she wanted to see. She was trying to convince him that the monster that existed inside him could be caged—controlled.

But what if he didn't want it to be? What if he wanted to set it free, to allow it to mature? To allow it—*him*, to achieve his special destiny, whatever the hell that was? He had loved the humanity his mother had given to him, cherished all of the memories and experiences and emotions that even now existed inside the tough, fleshy growth on his chest.

His soul. His humanity. And oh, God, it hurt so much. To have those feelings, that humanness, be a part of him and to have done the things he'd done and seen the things he'd seen . . . to know what he was . . . the guilt and horror and anguish was just too much for him to withstand.

Better to surrender to evil than have to feel the sorrow and regret.

The darkness welled up inside him, pushing back the light. Danny opened his eyes to see the shocked expression on Ceridwen's face as she sensed the change in him, and he used it as his opportunity. He attacked her; slashing with his claws, raking a bloody furrow across her shoulder.

He was free of her power.

And then the world exploded around them.

RISING up from the burning debris, Baalphegor-Moabites shrugged off the effects of the explosion, ready to continue the battle.

The demon peered through the thick, black smoke and fire, unfazed by the hellish conditions. *It's just like home*, he thought, taking in a lungful of dirty, searing heat, *only much, much milder.*

To say that he was angry was an understatement. When he'd first been approached by the mysterious gathering of hellions, spouting their fearsome knowledge of the Devourer's coming, he saw their offer as the perfect opportunity. Here was the chance to survive when so many would perish, and all he need do was harvest the collected life experiences of his spawn littered across the forbidden planes, save one.

In exchange for one humanity sack, from a changeling left upon the earthly plane, the hellions would provide him an opportunity to flee the coming devastation, to travel to pristine dimensions where the demonic had yet to tread.

It was an opportunity he could not afford to lose, and now it had gone horribly awry.

Baalphegor heard the wails of sirens piercing the night, the puny creatures that thrived upon this world attempting to extinguish what his rage had wrought. In his anger he decided that he would kill them all. He began to move through the gathering of humanity, just outside the perimeter of smoke and fire, longing to vent his anger and frustration in an explosion of slaughter.

The demon paused.

There is still a chance that this can be salvaged, he thought, searching the rubble around him for signs of life. If his offspring still lived—and if even only recently slain—the organ could be harvested, the exchange could still occur.

Ignoring the temptation of wanton death and murder, Baalphegor extended his senses, searching for his son within the burning debris of the ruined home. And, stronger than the pungent odor of blood upon the air, he found the scent.

With a shriek of victory, Baalphegor dug deeply into the wreckage, past the shattered wood, crumbled plaster, and brick and found what he so desperately sought.

"There you are," the demon hissed, extracting the limp body of Daniel Ferrick from the smoking remains of his home.

The changeling moaned, and Baalphegor smiled, a warm trickle of saliva dribbling from his widening grin to spatter down onto his spawn's face. Danny sputtered and coughed, arms waving in the air as he regained some semblance of consciousness.

"So good to see you alive," Baalphegor said, attempting to disguise the excitement in his voice. "Now let's get down to business."

EVE opened her eyes, gazing up at the nighttime sky through thick billowing clouds of smoke. She attempted to move, feeling broken bones grinding painfully together as they attempted to heal.

The pain was pretty bad, but she'd get over it. She always did.

She remembered the flash of arcane energy, the explosion decimating Julia's home and tossing her like a rag doll through the air. It usually took quite a bit, but Eve guessed that she must have lost consciousness. Pushing herself into an upright position she heard the chatter of humanity outside, drawn to the disaster like moths to flame.

Not good. Just more lives to be lost in collateral damage.

Willing herself to heal faster, Eve rolled over and struggled to her feet, not *even* wanting to think about the condition of the outfit she had just bought at Copley. Briefly she considered talking to Conan Doyle about a clothing allowance. The number of outfits that were ruined while working for him was a crime, and she didn't see why she should have to foot the bill.

"What the fuck?" she grumbled, almost losing her footing as wreckage shifted under her. She threw herself forward and landed on the roof of a UPS truck that had been parked outside of the Ferrick house.

Eve stood and surveyed the destruction caused by the demon's spell. The Ferrick house was toast. There was nothing much left of the Colonial but burned piles of wood, brick, and rubble. The smoke and fire seemed to be keeping the spectators at a distance, but that wasn't going to last much longer. She could already hear the wail of fire engines and police cars.

Glancing to her left, Eve saw something that caught her

eye in a nearby tree. Walking to the edge of the truck's roof, she found Ceridwen nestled within the oak tree, its branches having reshaped themselves as if to comfort her. She didn't appear to be injured too badly, but there was the slight tang of Fey blood spiking the air.

"Hey, Ceri," Eve called. "You all right?"

The sorceress's eyes opened. Her staff had fallen to the ground far below. Now it shot up into the air, straight to her grasp. The moment her fingers closed around it, the moisture in the air collected around the top of the staff and formed a frozen sphere of ice. Flames flickered inside the sphere.

"Daniel," she said, eyes darting about.

"Yeah," Eve said, jumping down to the ground. "I was just thinking the same thing."

Ceridwen joined her, lowered to the ground by the limbs of the oak.

"Can't see shit with all this smoke," Eve said, prompting Ceridwen to raise her staff, summoning a wind to clear the obstruction.

"Oh, shit," Eve said, her gaze falling upon the large pile of rubble across from them.

Baalphegor stood atop the wreckage, a beaten and bloody Danny Ferrick on his knees before the demon. The boy was clutching a jagged piece of glass, the edge of the makeshift blade about to cut into the thick tendril of flesh the connected the swollen sack to his body.

A clatter of bricks behind her startled Eve, and she whirled around ready for a fight, but pulled back when she saw that it was Squire and Shuck, emerging from shadows cast by a burning sofa. The animal appeared injured, but alive, dragging a dead, eel-like creature behind it. The beast plopped down among the rubble with a sigh, and started to eat its prize. Shuck was done with fighting, she guessed, and that was all right with her.

"What'd I miss?" the hobgoblin asked, brushing soot from the arms of his leather jacket, attempting to ignore the fact that he'd recently riddled her with bullets blessed by the Pope.

That was an issue for another time.

Squire's eyes bulged as he saw what was about to happen.

"This is not good."

DANNY saw his friends emerge from the rubble of his house, desperate to reach him, to prevent him from doing what he was about to do. He wanted to apologize to them, to tell them that he'd tried to fight it, but it was just too strong. The monster inside him wanted to be free, and it had showed him every horrible thing that he'd done over the last few days—every bloody detail in order to prove to him that his humanity was already dead, that the Danny Ferrick he remembered had died a long time ago, and he just had never realized it.

The cool breeze summoned by Ceridwen's magic caressed his face, carrying her lovely voice within it as she begged him to stop. Squire was screaming, as was Eve, bounding across the wreckage of his home—of his life, really.

Eve. Deep down he thought she would be the one to understand. She had hinted at a time in her life long ago when the monster had dominated, and he had to wonder, had it ever really gone away? Or was it still inside her, locked away.

Is there a chance for me? Danny wondered. If he did what he was about to do, cutting away his humanity, embracing the monster, would there be an opportunity to regain what he'd lost?

If completely a monster, would he care?

Baalphegor roared, casting a spell that acted as a concussive blast, hurtling Danny's friends back to where they had started. His demon sire looked back to him, large, golden eyes beckoning him to take that next step—to begin the journey toward his special destiny.

The touch of the glass was excruciating, a single spurt of blood shooting out as his makeshift knife bit into the thick flesh. It wouldn't be long now, he thought, starting to saw, hands sticky with the blood of his humanity.

Soon he wouldn't care; soon he would feel nothing.

The air grew deathly still, the world seeming to slow and then completely stop. Danny couldn't move, and no matter how hard he tried, he was unable to complete his task.

His father tossed back his head and roared his rage at the night sky. Seemingly unaffected by whatever had occurred, the demon spun around, arcane energies leaking from its fingertips, ready to confront whatever had denied him his prize.

Frozen, Danny watched two figures—a man and a woman—passing through the stationary plumes of smoke on their way toward him.

"Doyle!" Baalphegor shrieked, his screams echoing strangely about the stilled air.

Yes, it was Conan Doyle.

And my mother.

C O N A N Doyle was so furious that the spell required to bend time to his will—something that normally would have winded him at the very least—actually fueled the fires of his rage.

This never should have been allowed to get this far, he thought as he walked down the debris-strewn Newton Street. He remembered when he had first encountered Baalphegor during the war in the Faerie realm, where the fates of all realities were hanging in the balance. That is where their association should have ended. He ought to have killed the demon, then. None of this would have happened.

But such recriminations were useless. The past was past. Tonight concerned the future.

Julia stumbled by his side, almost falling to her knees.

It was as if she were in a trance, mesmerized by the sight of her home, now only a smoldering pile of rubble, and her monstrous son perched with his demon sire atop the ruins.

Even from this distance, Conan Doyle could see what the boy was about to do—giving up his humanity, handing it over to the hungry predator—and he had put a stop to it, momentarily. The spell around Danny would not last for long.

And there was something else lingering in the smoky nighttime air.

A hint of Hell.

The demon screamed his name, the shrill cry cutting through the thickening stillness of the frozen moment.

It had been toward the end of the Twilight Wars, sick and exhausted from the years of battle, that he had encountered Baalphegor at the edge of a clearing where the walls of reality had grown incredibly thin. The beast had been but a shadow of itself, its dark, leathery skin covered in bleeding sores as it squatted on the brink of death, attempting to manipulate magicks too complicated for its current condition. It was attempting to open a portal, to escape the death that would surely claim it in the realm of Faerie.

So lost in its misery, the collector demon hadn't even heard Conan Doyle and his patrol as they approached.

The armored guard, many of them having fashioned garb from creatures such as this, had prepared to slay the demon. But Conan Doyle had stayed their hands. The wretched creature had not been one of their enemies. Baalphegor was merely a scavenger, a parasite, hoping to benefit from the conflict. His presence alone was enough to condemn him, but Conan Doyle had been so tired of all the killing—of all the death—that he had allowed the pathetic beast to flee, even lending him a bit of his own magic to momentarily peel back the veil of reality to one of the lesser realms.

The guilt weighed upon him now, added to all of the other mistakes he had made in his long life.

"Stay your hand, mage," Baalphegor screeched from his

perch atop the rubble. "All I wish is to leave this realm and the realms that surround it. You know as well as I that soon, no matter how hard you fight, they will be no more."

Guilt gnawed at him. Unaccustomed to admitting his faults, or even that he had any, Conan Doyle's anger surged.

"How dare you," he growled, conjuring a spell from deep within him to strike the filthy beast down.

A sphere of copper-gold magic pulsed and churned in his hand, surging with such power that he could not have held it back had he wished to. Conan Doyle hurled it at the demon, and the explosion of raw magic blasted Baalphegor from his perch.

His body seething with all of the magic he could summon, Conan Doyle looked to Julia, who still stood beside him.

"Go to him," he said, pointing toward the changeling that she still believed to be her son. "See if there is anything left of the child you remember."

He turned away, striding toward the place where he'd seen the demon fall. Squire, Eve, and Ceridwen joined him, and he was reminded of a time long ago when he'd stood with a patrol at the edge of a forest dark and deep and had encountered an evil too pathetic to kill.

Conan Doyle waved them away, needing to do this on his own.

The spell that he had woven on time was unraveling, things flowing again as they should. The wails of police cars and fire engines were very close, adding to the urgency of the situation.

Careful with his footing, the mage climbed over the wreckage of the once quaint home to where he'd seen the demon tumble. Conan Doyle was at the ready, body tensed, defensive magic at his lips, as he steeled himself to deal with a threat that should have been vanquished long ago.

He found Baalphegor cowering in the shadow of what looked to be the only section of wall left standing. The demon's body smoldered, the magic he had thrown at it having charred and torn its leathery flesh.

The demon shivered as if cold, hugging itself as it cowered.

And Conan Doyle was again reminded of a time, long ago.

"I just want to get away," Baalphegor whispered. "Just as before. You're a merciful creature. Let me live . . . allow me to leave this plane, and I will share with you what I know about the boy."

Conan Doyle was taken aback. The magic of his latest spell ran the length of his arm to leak from his finger tips. It ached for release, the power of the hex surging painfully. His whole body shook, but he held the magic at bay.

"What about the boy?"

The effect of his first attack upon the pitiful demon seemed to be spreading. The tears in its flesh oozed, and threads of oily smoke rose from those wounds as Baalphegor continued to shiver and shake.

"Do we have a deal?"

Slowly, Conan Doyle nodded.

"The Hellions that approached me . . ."

"Hellions?" the mage asked, right arm shuddering with a spell uncast, a dark hex that began to form a churning cloud around his fist.

Baalphegor recoiled from the searing light, nodding. "They approached me, knowing all about the boy, whispering of some dark destiny for him. They told me of the Demogorgon, of its coming, and what it will mean to your species."

Conan Doyle considered this, both curious and confused. He knew well of the Demogorgon's coming, but this was the first he'd heard of Hellions acting against their cause behind the scenes, before the Devourer even arrived, and the first whisper he'd heard of some strange destiny for Daniel Ferrick. The dimensions truly were spinning out of control, entropy taking hold even before the Demogorgon arrived.

The words of the poet Yeats now seemed prophetic.

> *Turning and turning in the widening gyre*
> *The falcon cannot hear the falconer*
> *Things fall apart: the center cannot hold*
> *Mere anarchy is loosed upon the world.*

Conan Doyle looked down upon the demon. Already the shivering wretch had begun the process of conjuring a dimensional portal, the air around its wavering hands beginning to shimmer. Baalphegor turned its horrid face to him, its piss-yellow eyes searching for the same compassion that it had found from the mage so long ago.

And Conan Doyle unleashed his mercy, the hex that had built up in him bursting from him, searing his marrow as it arced from the tips of his fingers, reducing the creature to so much ash.

JULIA stood amidst the wreckage of her home beside the monster that was her son. She could feel something changing in the air, Conan Doyle's magic leaving perhaps, the flow of time returning to normal. Danny held the piece of glass tightly in his grip, the edge of the jagged blade biting into the thick strip of flesh, which she now knew connected the boy to his humanity.

Confusion whirled in her mind. She was not sure how she was supposed to feel at the moment. Staring at her son, she felt new pangs of fear, different from the terror she had felt before. The memory that had been stolen from her was the very foundation of her love for Danny. Had the thieving Hellion destroyed that love?

No, it remained. Even without that memory, there were so many others. Love abided. Yet she stared now at her boy, her Danny, and wondered if all that remained of him was a monster.

Time started to flow fully again, and she gasped as the razor-sharp glass continued to bite into the cord of flesh.

Instinctively she reached out, taking hold of Danny's hand, preventing the shard from cutting any further. Danny turned his face to her, and for the briefest of moments she did not recognize him. The hatred and fear in his eyes made her fear for her own life, and for her own soul.

His eyes flashed, and he bared his fangs at her, but she held his gaze, and the demon's stare softened. Julia shook as she reached out and pulled him close, though with love or fear she did not know. *Maybe both*, she thought, as she took him into her arms.

Kneeling in the broken remains of their home, the two of them began to rock. Julia closed her eyes, rubbing her hand along his back lovingly, as she had done so often when he was an infant and would wake up crying in the night. It had been the only thing that would comfort him so that he could go back to sleep. Julia would rock with him in the rocking chair, softly singing to him.

Julia wanted to sing to her son now, as they rocked together.

But she couldn't remember the words.

16

NIGHT in Florence was a celebration of light and music. Clay had always considered it one of the most beautiful cities in the Western world. The architecture and city design made it a fairy tale place, where art and beauty were venerated above all else. True or not—and history proved it both true *and* not—whatever blood and intrigue existed in the city's past, its beauty endured.

Clay and the ghost of Dr. Graves had visited the Pitti Palace earlier in the day and wandered the Boboli Gardens, where the symphony had been playing on that night in 1943 when Graves had been murdered. A lovely spot, the gardens held nothing else of interest. Neither of them sensed any resonance of the violence that had occurred there so long ago, and when Graves slipped into the spirit world he returned to report finding the place nearly barren of spectral activity.

They ought to have been despondent. No discussion had occurred as to what they expected to find in Florence, but both of them had arrived in this city with growing anticipation. Ever since they had begun looking into the murder of Dr. Graves, the mystery had broadened and deepened. Zarin had been savagely killed by his own pet. The FBI forensics team had revealed the connection between Graves's murder and the Whisper, and the link to the murder of Roger Alton Bennett.

After hours spent meandering about the Boboli Gardens in fruitless search of some bit of its haunted past, some echo or clue, they should have been at the least disappointed. Conversation ought to have ensued as to what their next step would be, though they were both well aware that there was no logical next step from here. If the visit to Florence turned up nothing they would have to start from scratch and come up with entirely new angles and theories regarding Graves's murder.

Yet neither Clay nor Dr. Graves mentioned the possibility of departure. There lingered in Clay a dreadful certainty that they had come to the right place. It might have been just a feeling in his own heart, but there also seemed a strange frisson in the air that had affected him the very moment they had stepped off of the plane in Florence. His skin prickled, and the small hairs on the back of his neck stood up.

After their visit to the Boboli Gardens he had stopped in an outdoor café for a cappuccino. A sudden shudder went through him. Clay glanced around, attempting to make the reaction appear to be natural.

The ghost of Dr. Graves had been seated in the chair beside him, and in that moment Clay was sure he saw an odd ripple pass through the ethereal substance of the specter.

"What is it?" the ghost asked.

"Do you feel it?"

Graves stared at him for a long moment before nodding. "*Focus*. Like someone is watching us."

Clay tapped the edge of the table. Whichever way he turned he felt the spiderlike skittering of—Graves had called it focus—up his spine. "Someone," he agreed. "Or something."

The waiter brought Clay's bill. Only after he had set it down and walked away did Clay notice that there was a folded promotional flyer beneath it. The slick, full-color piece was a tourist-targeted plug for the Teatro del Maggio Musicale Fiorentino, where the city's great symphony was in residence.

"Graves," Clay said, and unfolded the flyer. He almost expected to find something written inside, but there was nothing.

The ghost rose from the chair, passing right through the table as he drifted up behind Clay to read over his shoulder.

"The symphony performs tonight," Graves said.

Clay had already noticed. He pushed back his chair with a scrape of metal on stone and started after the waiter. The man was standing by another table taking an order from two elderly women whose mouths were twisted into twin permanent sour expressions.

"Scusi, signore," he said, but his grip on the waiter's arm was anything but polite.

The man flashed him a confused, angry, and somehow dismissive look. "I will come to you in a moment—"

Clay flashed the Teatro del Maggio flyer in front of his eyes. "This. Why did you give me this?"

He knew the answer before the waiter could even open his mouth. The man's eyes said it all. He had never seen the flyer before. And yet Clay had seen him set the bill down in its small leather folder himself, and the flyer had been inside.

"I did not. You are mistaken."

Clay wished he could argue, but there was no lie in the waiter's expression or his tone. Someone had either slipped the flyer in with the bill without his knowing it, or he had been compelled to do so himself by some outside force and now had no memory of it. In a world of dark magic, this latter would have been simple enough.

"I'm sorry. Excuse me," Clay said.

He returned to the table and paid the bill, tipping generously. The ghost of Dr. Graves stood behind him, watching closely but saying nothing. Only when Clay strode away from the café and turned into a narrow, cobblestoned street that would lead to his hotel did Graves speak up.

"Someone is playing games with us."

"No doubt."

"I take it we now have plans for this evening?"

"Yeah," Clay replied. "The symphony."

THE theater resounded with rapturous applause. In the glow of the stage lights, the faces in the audience beamed, enchanted. From his seat in the box nearest to stage right, Clay could see both the orchestra and those held in their sway. The audience seemed composed both of well dressed Firenze natives in suits and gowns and tourists clad in whatever remained clean and neat from their luggage.

Golden horns gleamed in the bright lights on the stage. Violin bows glided across strings, eliciting sweet and somber notes in turn. The conductor stood before the symphony orchestra with his back to the audience, baton dancing in his grasp, guiding his musicians into Debussy's *Prelude to the Afternoon of a Faun*, which had been one of Clay's favorite pieces since he had first seen it performed in 1920. The butchery done to his memory in the twentieth century made it difficult for him to recall the circumstances, but the music was a memory unto itself.

In the cacophony of applause that followed the tune, Clay clapped as loudly as anyone. As he did, he surveyed the audience again and leaned slightly to his right, to the space at the edge of the box where the ghost of Dr. Graves hovered beside him, the merest suggestion of a silhouette. The ghost's insubstantial legs passed right through the floor of the box as though he'd been severed below the torso.

"What are we looking for?" Clay muttered low, the words inaudible to anyone else, thanks to the thunderous applause.

As the clapping died down, the symphony launched into a Mozart concerto. Graves rose several inches and gusted forward so that he hung out over the audience. Just when Clay had begun to doubt that the ghost had heard him, Graves floated back toward him.

"I don't know. For the moment, I suppose we simply enjoy the music. But be on guard."

As if Clay had to be told to be wary. More than ever, his guard was up. He had rarely felt so on edge. Though he attempted to portray a sense of easy calm and he applauded in all of the right places, he could no sooner relax into the music than he could have in a viper's den. An almost tangible sense of trouble . . . of malice . . . pervaded the theater, overriding the elegance of the orchestra and the enthusiasm of the crowd.

So they waited.

Long minutes passed. Clay remained as still as possible despite the electric tension running through him. Wave of applause followed wave of applause, and soon nearly a full hour had passed. The symphony was not the best he had ever heard, but there were moments when their performance reached the sublime.

Halfway through Ravel's *Alborada del Gracioso*, the orchestra simply halted.

The pause took the audience by surprise, and for several awkward moments they stared and coughed and fidgeted. At last someone began to applaud, slowly at first, and was joined by an uncertain ripple of audience accord.

"What is this?" Clay whispered.

The ghost of Dr. Graves did not turn. Yet even from behind him, gazing at the orchestra through his transparent, gauzy form, Clay could hear his words.

"Perhaps it's what we've been waiting for."

As if on cue, the conductor raised his baton and the orchestra started again, launching into a piece of music unfamiliar to Clay. The melody was both sweet and sorrowful, but it was nearly ruined by the performance of the musicians. There was a jerky, stunted quality to their playing that still allowed the tune to come through but added enough discord that it was nearly wretched.

The ghost of Dr. Graves seemed to billow and flew backward as though blown by some unseen wind. Clay shifted in his seat and started to stand, brow furrowed in concern. No one in the box bothered to admonish him, so startled were they by the unpleasant turn the music had taken.

"Graves—" he whispered.

Eyes a churning gray abyss, the ghost turned to stare at him. "This is it, Joe. They were playing this song that night, when I was shot. When I died."

The lights in the theater dimmed. The musicians moved like marionettes. The cello player lost his grip on his bow and did not seem to notice, his elbow still jerking back and forth as though drawing music from his instrument.

In the midst of this, only the conductor continued to move smoothly. The music became more and more jarring, a savaged interpretation of a piece of beautiful music, the ghost sonata that Graves had so often heard when he traveled into the spirit world. What had he said, that he thought it was the spirit of his wife, letting him know that she was waiting for him?

There was nothing so romantic about this.

The conductor turned, very purposefully, and looked up at the box where Clay sat. For a moment, Clay felt certain the man's strange, silver eyes were staring straight at him. He held his breath, staring back, knowing there was little he could do in such a public place.

Then he realized the conductor's gaze was not locked on him, but on the space next to him. The man with his dancing baton and his wild gray hair was not looking at Clay, but at the spectral form of Dr. Graves hovering in the air beside him. No one else in the theater could see the ghost, but the conductor stared right at him.

And rather than reacting with fright, the conductor smiled.

"Joe," Graves began.

Clay nodded, but he could not tear his gaze away from

the spectacle unfolding on the stage. Members of the audience began to boo, even as others tried to shush them.

The conductor raised his baton and pointed it at a violinist, a young, slender, olive-skinned woman. As though on an invisible string, the woman rose from her seat, playing as she walked like some country fiddler. She went to the stairs and descended toward the audience. A rotund man with wisps of white hair sat in the front row, dressed like nobility but behaving like rabble. He shouted at the woman and at the conductor.

As the violinist approached the round man, Clay saw it at last. In the dim light it had not been immediately obvious. His eyes saw the world on several spectrums, and he had not as yet been focused enough to notice the tendril of soul energy that ran back up onto the stage, a ribbon of silver mist that connected her to the conductor, even as he directed her movements.

"What the hell is this?" Clay muttered.

For it was not merely the violist who was affected. Soul tethers linked the conductor to the entire orchestra the same way he had always seen murderers linked to their victims. Yet the members of the orchestra were not dead, only under the influence of the conductor.

The lithe, beautiful violinist stopped playing. She smiled down at the confused, disapproving fat man in the front row, and then she stabbed him through the left eye with her violin bow.

"Move!" the ghost shouted at Clay.

The shapeshifter was already in motion.

People began to scream, some to get up from their seats and run toward the violinist, others to flee for the exits. Clay ignored them all. His entire focus was on the violence unfolding in the front row.

The violinist raised her instrument and brought it down with both hands, shattering it and the man's skull in a single blow.

"No!" Clay screamed as he leaped over the railing of the box. He dropped from the mezzanine down to the aisle below, perhaps forty feet from the violinist and the dying man.

A new soul tether shimmered into existence, connected the murdered man to his murderer . . . yet it did not attach the old man to the girl responsible for the violin bow jutting from his raw, red wound of an eye socket. Instead, the soul tether led back to the conductor, the one truly responsible for this horrid murder.

Clay raced toward the violinist. A woman, perhaps the dead man's daughter, attacked her and began to slap her, screaming hysterically. The violinist stabbed her in the throat with the jagged, splintered remains of her instrument. Others began to approach her now. A man grabbed hold of her, and she spun, lunged in, and bit into his cheek, tearing away a ragged flap of bloody flesh.

The orchestra continued to play its hideous tune.

Clay grabbed hold of the violinist, pushing away others who might have helped. More people were screaming and heading for the exits now. The woman tried to attack him but could not escape his grasp.

Something struck him on the back of the head. Clay staggered, lost his grip on the violinist, and she was on him. He looked past her and saw a thin musician in a tuxedo wielding a bloodied trumpet. Other members of the symphony were coming down off of the stage now. The conductor's baton danced, but now it was not the music he commanded. He played the soul tethers that connected the orchestra to him as though they were puppets and that spiritual link their strings.

The trumpet crashed toward Clay's face. He reached up and stopped the blow from falling.

The conductor looked into his eyes from atop his pulpit and laughed.

Then he stopped laughing. The ghost of Dr. Graves moved through the musicians like a rolling cloud of smoke. The phantom darted across the theater and struck the conductor.

The man sagged, his baton lowering. It continued to

dance, but now listlessly, as though only half of his attention was focused there. The light had gone out of the conductor's eyes, and his smile faded. He moved now only like a sleepwalker.

And the ghost of Dr. Graves was nowhere to be seen.

He had *vanished* inside the conductor.

DR. *Graves is lost in thick, roiling mist. Shapes move in the swirling gray; features coalesce that might be faces. He feels solid ground beneath his feet, and the mist brushes damply against his face.* The spirit realm, *he thinks.* The otherworld . . . but it's never felt like this, so substantial.

And how did he get here? He had seen a strange, doubling effect around the conductor, a kind of phantom silhouette that surrounded him, creating a ghost halo. Graves had understood immediately that whatever power the conductor held, whatever he was doing to the orchestra, it was not his own. The man had been inhabited by a ghost. Yet this is no ordinary specter. This spirit has the strength of will and the focus to slip inside a living human and take over the body. It is an ability Graves has only encountered twice before in other ghosts. He is capable of it himself, but avoids such violations at all costs.

He has entered the conductor not to control him, but to drive out the intrusive spirit. Instead, he has been dragged into the spirit world, or some semblance of it.

The mist thins, and the gray around him resolves into buildings and cars and lampposts. The soulstuff coalesces into a street corner in New York City. Across the busy square in front of him is the Flatiron Building, and he knows now that he is looking south. A car rattles by, all smoke and fog, but its shape and style makes it easily identifiable for Graves. Once, he had owned this very car. It is a 1936 Nash Ambassador with whitewall tires and a wide running board. His had been powder blue. This one is only the gray of the mists.

Its tires sluice through the soulstream, which runs shal-

lowly along the street. Graves can feel its tug inside of him, and as he watches the Nash Ambassador disappear into the ghost buildings, he longs to be inside it; to travel into the past and join Gabriella forever.

"Beautiful automobile," says a voice.

Graves spins, hands reaching for the holsters beneath his arms. He freezes when he sees the dark figure on the opposite corner and the familiar hat and scarf of the Whisper.

"Broderick," he rasps.

The Whisper laughs, and the sound is as much a part of the past as that car and this nostalgia city, this New York, circa 1940. His pistol is already drawn and aimed at Graves.

"You're going to shoot me?" the Whisper asks as he crosses the street. An old Hudson sedan rumbles through the ghost city and passes right through him. "What good will that do?"

"You might be surprised," Graves says, fingers touching the grips of his guns but not pulling them. The Whisper has the drop on him.

"Would I? I quite doubt that, Doctor Graves. What do you think I have been doing, wandering this place of lost souls all of this time? Why, the very same thing I did in life. I've been experimenting."

"So I see. Your control of the orchestra is impressive."

"I've kept busy. I couldn't spend all of eternity nursing my hatred for you. Though, and you'll have to trust me on this, it has taken up a great deal of my afterlife."

The laughter comes again, that susurrus of soft, mocking chuckles that Graves never quite understood the trick of, even in life. The effect is unsettling, a distant echo.

The Whisper comes to within ten feet—if distance can be measured here—but Graves does not move. In life, he had survived many bullet wounds, but if Broderick's pistol is anything like his own gun, it could tear at his very soul.

"Lower your hands, please, Doctor."

Graves complies.

As though bursting into instant reality, people surround them. Spirits of this era stroll along through the soul-stream, across streets, and along sidewalks. Gray swathes of humanity in fedoras and suits, the women in jaunty hats and the modern dresses of prewar New York. Laughing lovers walk arm in arm. More cars growl by, convertibles with rumble seats and boxy new models. Soon, the war will stop all automobile production in America, the metal needed for tanks and airplanes.

"All of this," Graves says, forcing himself not to reveal how much this taste of the past has affected him. "This is you?"

The Whisper does a curt bow, his eyes locked on Graves, the barrel of his pistol unwavering. "Practice. There are so many souls, so much spirit just lingering here. It isn't hard to shape it, if you've the will. Like sculpting with clouds.

"Here," the Whisper says, gesturing dramatically with his unfettered hand. "Let's have a look at another familiar setting. You might remember this."

A wave passes through the spirit world, rippling through this ghost New York, and the landscape changes. New York is washed away and replaced by gardens, by the milling aristocracy of Florence in the waning days of the war. The Boboli Gardens, in the shadow of the Pitti Palace.

And the music starts to play.

Graves glances at the Whisper and sees that he is bobbing his pistol along to the tune like the conductor's baton.

"Beautiful tune, isn't it?"

Graves's fingers itch to pull his guns, to jerk the triggers and fire phantom bullets into the ghost of the Whisper, the ghost of Simon Broderick.

"You recognize the place?"

He has managed to maintain a strange calm that surprises even himself, but now Graves feels a hatred rising in him unlike anything he has ever known. In the flesh-and-blood world, Clay is dealing with whatever horror the Whisper has unleashed there. But the real battle is here.

He knows that. Whatever it takes, the Whisper must be stopped.

But not without answers.

"You know I do."

In life he had been disgusted by the crimes of Simon Broderick, and shamed by the way the man had tainted all of the efforts of the other heroic private adventurers of the day. He had felt disdain and pity, but never hatred.

Now it fills him like poison.

Graves glances around, taking in the lampposts, the beautiful Italian women in their gauzy gowns, the orchestra, and he turns his back on the Whisper. As he does, his right hand crosses his chest, reaching for the gun holstered under his left arm.

"Do you think I'm a fool?" *the Whisper asks, and there is a click as he cocks his pistol.*

Graves lowers his hands to his sides, jaw set with fury.

"I don't know what you are," *he admits.*

"Savage, you called me once. Madman, too, I believe."

"Those things, certainly," *Graves replies.* "But I won't pretend I understand any of this. You were dead. I saw you throw yourself from the cathedral roof. I saw your body strike the ground. I was there when they removed your corpse. Your skull was shattered, your organs exploded. You cannot have—"

The Whisper's laugh fills his ears, but already Graves understands.

The conductor. The weakness of certain souls, not only in the spirit world, but in the realm of flesh and blood as well. If Broderick can control the conductor . . .

"You possessed someone."

Beneath his wide-brimmed hat, the Whisper's eyes shine with glee. "Ironic, isn't it? In life, you excoriated me for my claims that I could control the minds of men, and as nothing more than a shade of life, the whisper of my former self, at last I can do precisely that.*

"You have no idea how much I have enjoyed watching you torment yourself trying to unravel the mystery of your *demise. But now comes the pièce de résistance, my old friend. You think that this was the place, don't you? You were murdered here?"*

Graves is unfazed. "I thought so for a very long time," he says, over the music from the symphony, the sweet music that had filled the air on that golden night when he had stood here in the gardens with . . .

He searches the crowd for her face, for Gabriella's face, but cannot see her in the gray, misty tableau that the Whisper has crafted around them.

"But I didn't die here," Dr. Graves continues. "I know that now. The impact must have been real. The memory is too powerful, too detailed, to be merely hypnotic suggestion or some influence of yours. Some sort of tranquilizer dart, I presume."

The Whisper nods. "Bravo." He raises the pistol; aims it directly at Graves's face. "Watch."

And now the gray mist coalesces again. The soulstream rushes around his feet, and the tug feels more powerful than before, as though they have drifted closer to the Ivory Gate. It flows past the ghosts who reenact this terrible scene, and he stands and watches himself come across the lawn of the gardens, growing anxious, then frantic as he tries to reach the conductor and the orchestra beyond.

A loud pop fills the air. Something strikes him in the back and he falls. People rush around him, kneeling by him. Gabriella is there, shrieking in anguish, dropping down beside him. She cradles his head in her lap and bends to kiss his forehead, sobbing, shoulders rocking with grief.

Graves frowns. This makes no sense. If he wasn't shot, if it truly was only a tranquilizer dart, then how is it Gabriella could be so close to him and not see that there is no bullet wound? No blood?

"This isn't the way it happened," he says. "This is nothing but theater, a fiction of your own creation."

"You'd like to think so, but ask yourself, how else could

*it have happened? Would anything have kept your beloved
from your side when you fell?"*

The Whisper strolls toward the horrid scene and the
soulstream alters around him. The Boboli Gardens meta-
morphose once more into New York City. Cars roll by, but
there are fewer people on the street. The mist swirls and
roils all around them, and now the city is nearly dark,
shades of black and gray, late at night.

"Walk with me," the Whisper says.

"I think not."

The muzzle of the pistol rises, gestures northward.
"Walk."

Graves hesitates only a moment before he starts north.
Every block is familiar, rendered in loving detail. All of this
from the Whisper's mind, under his control. He sculpts the
soulstuff of the wandering dead around him as they pass
through the spirit world. Even though they are the wisps,
not the conscious ghosts like Graves himself, it is unsettling to see the remnants of human souls used so callously.

And beautiful. He cannot deny it.

"You've figured out most of it by now, Doctor. Puppet-
ing a weak-willed Florentine surgeon, I paid several others to rush to your aid when you fell. That soon after my
own demise I had not yet built up the concentration to control more than one person at a time. But coin is the best
puppeteer of all. You were brought to the surgeon's office,
and there I performed upon you the same surgery I had on
so many others. I altered your mind. I changed you, made
you docile, and with the mesmerism I had always em-
ployed to assist in that transformation, I turned you to a
task that I had set out for you."

Graves understands. He sees the truth coming before
the words are spoken, and already he is shaking his head
in denial.

"Oh, yes. Docile you might have been, but your skills
remained. Your strength and your stealth were all I needed.
The rest of you was malleable enough. I arranged a clan-
destine meeting for you with Mayor Bennett, the son of a

bitch who'd crucified me in the newspapers. You gave him the nails, Doctor, and good old Roger hammered them home. Oh, how pleased he was when he learned you were still alive, that your death in Florence had been a ruse. You were the only man in the world Bennett would have trusted enough to let down his guard so completely."

Again the spirit world convulses around them, mist churning and choking, and the pull of the soulstream becomes even more powerful. Graves feels like simply surrendering to it. After all of this, what is the point of remaining here? Yet he finds himself unable to let go without seeing what else the Whisper has to show him.

Though he knows what is to come.

Some part of him has begun to remember. The recollection is dull and shrouded in fog even thicker than the mist of the spirit world, but it is there.

The landscape shifts. They are on the observation deck of the Empire State Building. Roger Alton Bennett gazes out across the city . . . his city. He takes out a cigarette and lights it. There is a scuffing noise behind him, and the mayor turns.

He grins. "Damn, Leonard, but it's good to see you."

The ghost of Dr. Graves watches himself step out from the shadows, face slack and expressionless, and grab hold of Mayor Bennett.

The murder is brutal and ugly and—as he hurls the man from the observation deck to twist and tumble down eighty-six stories to the street—spectacular.

The venom of hatred burns so hot in him now that Graves feels as though he will burst into flames.

"And afterward?" he asks without looking at the Whisper, staring out across the city, not looking down.

"Oh, I killed you." The words are followed by that soft, insinuating laughter. "I wasn't worried about being discovered. What could they do to a man already dead? But I so relished the pleasure of strangling you to death, just as I'd done to all of the other men whose minds I'd altered.

Your bones cracked in my grasp. I chose a strong host for that. I wanted to feel your neck crack."

Graves shakes his head. *"No. Something still doesn't fit."* He turns to look at the Whisper. *"They matched the DNA of the remains in the crypt with mine. Those were my bones. Why would you bother to put me there?"*

Beneath the brim of that hat, the devil smiles. *"I'm a man of my word, Doctor. When you were dead, I turned you over to Gabriella. I'd promised her, after all—"*

"You're insane."

"True. But it changes nothing."

"I died in her arms. She was at the funeral. There were photographs in the newspapers, entire articles—"

The ether ripples around them, and now it is the featureless spirit realm at last. Wisps and ghosts pass around them like a thunderstorm rolling across the ground. The soulstream is deep here, and its pull grips both specters with such force that they must set their feet firmly to avoid being dragged into the current.

"She was my creature by then," the Whisper says, and the pleasure he takes in those words drips from his lips. *"I had haunted her for the better part of a year, whispering to her. It wouldn't be enough for me just to control her body. Vengeance demanded her mind. I was her ghost, the voice in her head, in her dreams. I went to bed with her every night, and so often you were not there—"*

"I was—"

"You were a celebrity," Simon Broderick spits, and the muzzle of the pistol twitches with the word. *"Do you have any idea how easy it was to convince her that you didn't love her, that you only loved the world and your ambitions for the future? That you lived not for her but for the spotlight?"*

"Lies!"

"She was bitter and lonely, and she knew that eventually she would be forgotten completely, instead of merely going to bed alone. She gave you so much love, but she was so afraid that she could never be enough for you. I whis-

pered into her mind the truth, that the only way to keep you to herself was if you died before you could alienate her completely. She wept and screamed when she held you in her arms not because you were dead, but because by then she hated you as much as she loved you."

"No—"

"The only condition she gave for helping to hide the truth was that when you died, she would claim your body and bury you in that damned crypt."

Graves shakes with hatred. He flexes his fingers. The Whisper narrows his eyes and watches his hands warily.

"You said it yourself, she was your creature. You mesmerized her. You put all of those thoughts in her mind, twisted her thinking."

"Some, perhaps," the Whisper says, with a wide, Cheshire cat grin that seems brighter than all of the gray otherworld, and darker than night. "But I only nurtured what was already there. And you'll never know how much of her betrayal was my influence, and how much your own negligence.

"One, last thing, Doctor. You should know that she was miserable forever after that day. Wracked with guilt. When she died, she took it as a mercy, and as she breathed her last, she did it wishing she had never met you."

The scream that tears its way out of Graves is pure anguish. Grief has overridden his hate.

He throws himself backward into the soulstream. Even as he falls he draws his guns.

17

THE Teatro del Maggio echoed with screams and discordant notes that could no longer be called music. Clay couldn't worry about Graves. He was a ghost. The people who were still breathing had to be his main concern.

Crowds rushed the exits, shoving and jostling and cursing each other. But some of the members of the audience had decided to intervene. Either they had not seen the bloodshed that had already taken place—the violinist murdering two people in the front row—or they thought themselves heroes. The last thing Clay needed right now was anyone playing hero while he was trying to keep everyone else from dying.

The musicians had slowed down a little, and that was helpful, but even if Graves was distracting the conductor, they were still following whatever commands he'd already given them, and they were still influenced by the soul tethers that linked them to him. There were dozens of them and only one of Clay. A tuba player and a fat man with a French horn kept playing, as did the cellist who went through the motions without a bow to draw music from the instrument. The others carried their instruments off the stage with dull, lifeless eyes and a homicidal urge.

"Back off!" Clay barked as the violinist grappled with him again. He backhanded her so hard she flew out of her shoes and hit the floor, rolling into the first row of seats. She lay unconscious, and he hoped she would wake up eventually.

Each of the members of the symphony was linked to the conductor with a soul tether. Somehow he—or whatever was inside of him—was controlling them all. Things would have been much easier if they were just mindless zombies. But the musicians were alive, and he wanted to try to keep them that way; not an easy task, given that they were trying to kill him and anyone else within reach.

A quartet of angry looking men ran out from back stage. One might have been some kind of manager, because he started shouting in Italian, directing the others. They ran at the musicians who were piling down off of the stage. A flutist grabbed a fistful of hair and dragged one of the men over the edge, then leaped on him as he struck the ground. The flute rose and fell, and blood spattered with each blow.

"Damn it!" Clay shouted.

He tried to push past the musicians around him, but there were just too many of them now.

The trumpet player swung his horn again. Clay snatched it out of his hand and flung it into the balcony. The trumpeter and a tall, wiry, white-haired woman grabbed his arms. Thick hands reached up from behind him and grabbed his head, clawing for his eyes. One finger found his right eye socket and plunged in.

Clay roared in pain as his eye popped, spouting blood and vitreous fluid that dripped down his face.

With his single intact eye he saw a fourth musician coming at him. The man held a golden cymbal in both hands, and as the others held Clay steady, he swung it toward his neck like a guillotine blade.

Enough.

Clay had held off this long because there were so many civilians still in the theater. It didn't matter anymore. With a single thought, he willed his body to change. His flesh flowed, and bone grew, a new eye replaced the ruined one. In a heartbeat he had shed his human guise and taken on his true form, the massive creature of hardened clay. The cymbal struck his chest with a hollow clang, gouging the earthen substance of his body.

With a shrug, he knocked away the trumpeter and the white-haired woman. He grabbed hold of the thick wrist of the large musician behind him, even as the man tried to hang on to his towering, monstrous form, fingers digging into hard clay.

In the thrall of the conductor, the man did not even cry out as Clay snapped his wrist. Other musicians started toward him. He slammed his fist into the trumpeter's face, shattering his nose, causing a spray of bright red blood. The man's eyes cleared, and even as Clay watched, the soul tether connecting him to the conductor dissipated.

The man began to scream in pain.

Finally, Clay thought. The conductor's control was weakening. Whatever Graves was doing inside of the man must have been having an effect. The musicians were becoming more sluggish, their eyes duller than before. The conductor slumped across his podium, baton still lazily bobbing in his hand, head lolled onto his chest.

Several musicians started up the center aisle in pursuit of audience members who had not yet escaped. No one was still trying to interfere. Once they had seen Clay in his true, golem-like form, even the bravest among them had decided to quit the place. But even as he glanced toward the crowd pushing and trying not to be last out the door, a tuxedoed musician staggered after them, swinging a trombone like it was a club.

Clay plowed through a pair of musicians as if they were children and leaped a row of seats to get to the aisle. The trombone player had begun to beat at the departing crowd. He struck a young dark-haired woman in the temple, and she crashed to the ground. The horn swung again and a well-groomed, handsome man put up his arm to block it.

The impact broke bone, and he clutched his arm, screamed, and staggered backward.

The trombone player swung again, but by then Clay had arrived. His patience had run out. He gripped the man by the head and hurled him back down the aisle. The audience members still inside the theater screamed louder than ever, more terrified of him than of the murderous musicians.

The orchestra stalked through the theater, soul tethers still linking them to the conductor. They prowled along the seats, streaming toward the central aisle, moving toward Clay. The dark-haired woman lay unconscious at his feet, and no one was stopping to worry about whether she would reach safety. He wasn't going to wait here for her to be killed.

Cracked, dry clay flesh shifted again. Black fur sprouted, and he hunched over, massive fists pounding the carpet. A mountain gorilla, he charged down the aisle at the musicians. As a wave they lunged at him. Instruments swung and stabbed at him. The gorilla batted a viola and a saxophone away. Hands twisted in his fur.

Clay backhanded one man. His foot shot out, and he kicked another in the chest hard enough to send him tumbling back down the aisle to collide with the stage. Then he was just fighting on instinct. Bones broke and blood spurted, but he did his best to make sure the injuries were not fatal.

There were too many of them.

Soon, he would kill someone, and he could not allow that to happen. As they piled on top of him, he shifted again, from gorilla to python. The huge snake coiled around three musicians in seconds, crushing them, cutting off their oxygen. With his serpent's eyes, he saw all three of their soul tethers dissipate.

It would help, but not enough. If he couldn't free them all, and soon, he would end up killing them.

•   •   •

THE Whisper fires, phantom bullets punching through the swirling wisps and ghosts all around them. Souls cry out in pain they never imagined feeling again. One of the bullets strikes Graves in the left shoulder, and his roar of anguish turns into a snarl of pain as it tears away a piece of his soul, a bit of his spirit that is destroyed forever.

Then he is in the soulstream and the current takes him, sweeping him toward the Whisper. Graves thrusts his arms up out of the churning ectoplasm and fires both guns, pulling the triggers again and again.

Broderick fires one last time before the first phantom bullet strikes his chest. A second and third hit his torso. One creases his temple. A fifth hits his right shoulder, and he drops his pistol. It lands in the soulstream and is swept away, another piece of his soul gone for eternity.

He splashes into the soulstream, arms and legs moving, struggling to force himself to stand against the current. His hat is swept off and sails away toward the Ivory Gate. Graves does not turn but knows that those twin spires must be visible in the distance by now.

The ghosts all around them begin to whisper, a hiss of white noise like a rainstorm on a tin roof.

But the Whisper is the most focused spirit Graves has ever seen. Even with bits of his soul torn away, he thrusts himself out of the stream as Graves rushes by, carried on the current. He could manifest another gun, but that would take moments he does not have.

Broderick lunges. Graves pulls both triggers again. One phantom bullet strikes the Whisper in the throat but the other goes wide. And then the ghost is upon him, and Graves feels his true strength at last. The Whisper clutches him around the throat with one hand, and with the other grabs his right wrist. Graves drops one of his guns.

He raises the other, but the Whisper drives him down, submerging him completely in the soulstream . . .

A strange calm envelops him. This is how it was always

supposed to be. Why has he fought so long to avoid this peace, this cradle of comfort and tranquility? This rest.

His hands open, and the other gun falls from his grasp, bits of his soul sucked away by the current. He could manifest the guns again, but for what purpose? He is traveling at last to the gate and beyond, to whatever awaits there. A smile touches his lips. Gabriella waits.

He hears the music again, the ghost sonata.

Gabriella.

Isn't waiting.

His eyes open, and Graves looks up through the surface of the ectoplasmic river flowing around him and over him and he sees the face of the Whisper staring down at him with those laughing, glittering eyes.

He thrusts his free hand up and clutches Broderick's throat. His legs drive downward, find solid footing, and even as he fights the current he pistons himself up out of the soulstream.

"That's right!" Broderick sneers. "Fight it, Doctor. I want to carve your soul to shreds so that you're nothing but a wisp when you finally pass through the gate."

Thrashing against one another, they stumble together, slipping deeper and deeper into the spirit world. Graves hammers the Whisper with his fist, over and over. Broderick clutches his throat, hate burning in his eyes. Any trace of sanity has departed, and now he is only the lunatic Graves watched leap to his death from the roof of St. Patrick's Cathedral.

Wisps and ghosts swirl above them, the gray storm clouds of the spirit realm attracted to the furious emotion roiling between them. The soulstream rushes around them, and their brawl twists them off balance. Together, they splash into the soulstream once more, and now the current has them.

Faces gaze down. As the Whisper strangles him, the ghost of Dr. Graves stares up at the specters hovering above them. He catches sight of the twin spires of the Ivory Gate, looming larger than he has ever seen them before.

The sight fills him with longing, and now the soulstream tugs at his heart as much as it does the ethereal substance of his spirit. Peace awaits.

His final reward.

But the Whisper does not deserve to pass through those gates.

With his forearm, he forces Broderick back and twists around. His upper body is above the rushing stream of souls now, and he gazes at the Ivory Gate ahead and the current churning between the spires. Ghosts mass on either side of the soulstream, lingering on this side of the gate, gray mist figures, some only wisps, but some so distinct they look almost solid.

Some of them look familiar.

They are nearly at the Ivory Gate when Graves sees Hank Reinhardt's ghost standing beside the soulstream. The substance of his spirit streaks and runs in the air from the pull of the gate, but the hulking killer does not move.

"Mister Whisper!" Reinhardt shouts, pointing.

And he understands. As powerful a specter as Broderick has been, he has avoided those phantoms that would have pursued him even into the afterlife. But they have waited for him, knowing that some day he will pass through the Ivory Gate. Perhaps they sensed his nearness or perhaps they've been waiting all along. What matters is that they're here.

"Yes!" Graves calls, tearing the Whisper's hands from this throat. He drives his feet down, dragging his enemy toward the edge of the stream, fighting the current. "Take him, Reinhardt!"

"Damn you, Graves!" Broderick snarls, trying to tear at the very substance of his soul.

"It's not me that damnation awaits," Graves replies . . . Graves whispers.

He summons up all of the strength of his soul, musters the courage and endurance of his heart, and he fights the current of the soulstream. The Whisper fights him, but

Graves drives them both out of the deepest, most powerful current, off to one side of the gate.

Where Reinhardt is waiting.

And the killer isn't alone.

"Simon Broderick!" Graves shouts, striking the Whisper again and again. He holds him down, twisting his ethereal substance, and now the Whisper tries to escape. Broderick's spirit grows less substantial, attempts to slip into the soulstream, to ease himself from the grip of Dr. Graves.

"I think not, Whisper," Graves says darkly. "We're all ghosts here. You've nowhere to run."

They come for him then, dread specters darting through the mists, the lost souls of every one of the criminals whose brains the Whisper had mutilated and rewired, these men whom Simon Broderick had then murdered.

They fall upon him like ravenous animals.

The Whisper screams, and all Graves can do is step back and watch as they tear his soul to shreds. In tatters, his spirit cannot hold. If there is a final rest for Simon Broderick, it will be anything but peaceful.

One by one, the ghosts of those tainted men slip into the soulstream, their spirits blurring and stretching until they merge with the current and are carried through the Ivory Gate.

Reinhardt is the last to go. He nods, clutching the Whisper's scarf in his massive fist. Graves nods in return, and then Reinhardt gives his soul over to the pull of the gate. He is lost no more. His wandering spirit is at rest. If there is a hell awaiting him on the other side of the gate, he has surrendered his soul to fate, having lingered in the world between life and death long enough to take his own vengeance.

His specter elongates until he is only a wisp, and then he too is gone.

The ghost of Dr. Graves stands alone, and he gazes down at his hands and sees that he too has begun to blur.

The soulstream has him in its grasp. Peace calls to him, and he yearns to surrender.

The mystery is solved. Whatever awaits—Heaven, Nirvana, or nothing at all—surely he has earned it.

He glances up at the Ivory Gate, and between those twin spires, he sees the silhouette of a familiar figure standing on the other side.

"Gabriella?"

CLAY could have transformed himself into a lion or tiger, into a bull or a stag, but in any of those forms merely fighting the possessed musicians would likely have ended up with some of them dead. His only choice was his true form, and he wore it now, the towering golem of cracked, dry clay. Musicians attacked him from all sides, now. Men in tuxedoes beat him with stools and instruments; women in elegant uniforms clawed at him and stabbed him with whatever they could lay their hands on.

He shouted his frustration, and it echoed off of the perfect acoustics of the theater. He could leave. Just get the hell out of here and try to keep the musicians inside. But even as he considered this option he discarded it. Soon the police would arrive. They were probably already outside the building, trying to get through the panicked crowd. If Clay just left, the musicians would be free to go as well. They might continue their homicidal rampage outside, and surely that would end up with many of them being shot.

"Damn it!"

A tall, thin scarecrow of a man lifted the double bass above his head, face impassive, eyes dull, and prepared to bring it down on top of Clay's skull.

With a snarl, Clay reached out a massive, earthen hand and grabbed the huge instrument by the neck, snatching it away. He raised it, anger boiling over in him, and began to swing it at the man, thinking to knock him away, and broken bones be damned.

In the last instant before impact, he saw the man's eyes

clear and widen with sudden awareness. The bassist saw him and screamed in terror, and then Clay hit him with the heavy double bass, unable to stop his swing. Something broke inside the man, and he was tossed into a row of seats where he struck painfully, tried to rise, and then slumped into unconsciousness.

"Shit," Clay whispered.

All of the musicians had stopped. Some of them staggered as if drunk, and others collapsed onto the ground. A woman shrieked, pointing at him and screaming in Italian. The soul tethers connecting them to the conductor evaporated, slipping away as if on an errant breeze and dissipating completely. Even the strange, ghostly halo around the conductor was gone, and the man slipped from his podium and collapsed to the ground, moaning.

"Graves!" Clay called, and he started for the stage.

The musicians who were conscious and aware shouted and fled for the exits.

At any moment, others would regain consciousness even as the police arrived, and so he shifted his form again, his mercurial flesh altered in an instant, and the golem was gone. Only handsome, ordinary Joe Clay remained.

He leaped up onto the stage and ran to the conductor. The man's eyes were rolled back and the lids fluttered as he mumbled something.

"Doctor Graves," Clay said, lifting him up, talking to the conductor in a low voice. "Are you in there, Leonard? What the hell's going on?"

"I waited," Gabriella says.

Graves touches the Ivory Gate, bracing himself so that the soulstream—almost impossible to resist so close to the gate—will not drag him through. On the other side of the gate is an image of the only woman he had ever loved while he walked the Earth. She is barely a wisp, a specter haunting the afterlife, an apparition even to ghosts. But her eyes, that face . . . it can be no one else.

For the second time, he says her name.

The sorrow in her gaze tears at his heart, and she beckons to him. The soulstream does not seem to affect her, and perhaps it is because she has already passed through the gate.

"I waited here," she repeats. "At first I was so confused . . . nothing seemed real. But when I passed through the gate it was like waking up from a terrible dream, and I knew . . . I knew what I'd done. I held on. The music calls me, Leonard. My heart is torn. I should be at peace here, on this side . . . but I waited."

Graves cannot speak. How long has he waited for this moment? Eternity and more, or so it seems. His business in the world of flesh and blood is complete at last. He can rest. And here Gabriella is, awaiting him.

And yet . . .

"You helped him. The Whisper."

Those lovely eyes are downcast. "You don't understand."

"No."

As if struck, Gabriella's ghost flinches, and she fades ever so slightly. She lifts her gaze.

"He was there, all the time. He was with me, saying the most frightening things. I felt him in my head, don't you see?" she pleads, and her voice is wracked with anguish. "I'm so sorry, darling. So very sorry."

Graves never imagined that a dead man could feel such heartbreak, never imagined that a ghost could be torn so completely apart. The Ivory Gate feels warm to his touch, and there is comfort there. He longs to pass through, where he will never feel such sadness again.

"But you knew, didn't you, Gabriella? It wasn't all the Whisper. How much did you fight him?"

She shakes her head, this insubstantial phantom of the woman he had once loved. "I only wanted you to love me, to marry me and be the husband you always promised that you would be."

The Whisper's bullet had torn pieces of his soul away

forever, fragments of his spirit lost to the ether for all eternity. The loss of his guns had done the same. But still he had felt whole and strong, had felt that he would endure. This loss is far greater. Whatever piece of his soul is ripped from him now, Dr. Graves knows he will feel its absence for as long as his consciousness endures.

"Our time is here, don't you see?" Gabriella says. "Come to me, now, Leonard. Please, my love. Our time at last, to be together the way we always dreamed."

The longing in him almost destroys him. He wishes he could surrender to her pleas and to the pull of the soulstream. Her eyes are full of guilt and repentance, but also love and hope.

Graves uses the spire of the Ivory Gate to brace himself, and he turns his back on Gabriella's ghost. Bending low to fight the current, he starts back through the soulstream, back across the spirit world. He can hear Gabriella calling to him, but her voice becomes fainter with every step, until even that is nothing but a ghost . . . and then the rush of other spirits around him takes over, and he hears only white noise.

With a thought, he manifests new phantom guns in the holsters under his arms.

Perhaps there is still business for him to tend to in the world of flesh and blood.

EPILOGUE

THE fireplace in the front parlor at the brownstone in Louisburg Square crackled with dancing flames. Somehow the warmth from the blaze did not seem to reach all the way into the room. The curtains were drawn aside, but the afternoon was so gray it seemed night had arrived prematurely. A cold, November rain fell.

Arthur Conan Doyle felt the chill in his bones.

He stood by the fireplace, leaning with one elbow on the mantel, his pipe held loosely in his hand. It was unlit, the tobacco tamped down inside, waiting for him to enjoy it, but for some reason he had not yet set it to burn.

Ceridwen sat on the floral loveseat with Julia Ferrick, holding the shattered woman's hand. Dark circles hung beneath Julia's eyes. Her clothes were wrinkled, and her hair was tied back in a ponytail. For the past two nights she had slept—though slept little—in a guest room in Conan Doyle's home. They had all needed time to recover from the events set in motion by Baalphegor, and Julia needed to be close to Danny.

Conan Doyle had let it go on as long as he dared without interference. This morning that had changed.

He caught Ceridwen's eye. She smiled wanly at him, doing her best to comfort Julia and, somehow, to comfort Conan Doyle as well. Ceri had taken to wearing the clothes that Eve had helped her choose to blend better in the human world—the Blight. It astonished him to see how comfortable she looked in the navy skirt and light blue cashmere sweater she wore today. Even while sitting there with Julia, sharing the woman's fear and grief for her son, Ceridwen remained elegant, her presence powerful.

Conan Doyle had to tear his gaze away from her. Impatiently he withdrew his pocket watch and opened it, sighing at the time.

"Don't get your knickers in a twist. I'm here."

He glanced up to see Eve standing in the arched doorway and nodded his approval.

"What of Squire?"

Eve glanced regretfully at Julia, then looked at Conan Doyle and shook her head. "He's not in the mood. He and Shuck are watching his *Knight Rider* DVDs downstairs, eating chili dogs and ice cream."

"Ah," Conan Doyle said. "I wondered what that smell was."

Ceridwen smoothed her skirt, tightened her grip on Julia's hand, and looked up at Eve.

"He's going to keep the beast, then? Here in the house?" She glanced at Conan Doyle in surprise.

"Might not be a bad idea to have a guard dog around," Eve replied.

Conan Doyle frowned. He'd not have expected Eve to support the idea of having the slobbering shuck around the house. As far as he knew, she hated the beast and had no use for pets in general.

"We shall see," he said, and then he looked around at the three women. "All right. It's only the four of us, then. Shall we discuss the reason for this gathering?"

Julia took a deep breath and sat up a bit straighter. "My son, you mean?"

Conan Doyle narrowed his gaze, perturbed by the edge

in her voice. "Yes, Julia. Your son. More particularly, what's to become of him after the events we all witnessed this week."

Ceridwen placed her free hand on Julia's back.

Eve entered the room and slid into a high-backed chair. "I take it you've made a decision."

Conan Doyle stepped away from the fireplace, regretting the diminishing warmth on such a raw day in his drafty old house. He clutched his pipe in one hand as he strode over to the windows to peer out at the gray day. The one benefit of a day as dark as this one was that Eve did not have to hide away.

"I have."

"What are you going to do?" Julia asked tersely.

He turned, tapping the bottom of the pipe's bowl in his open palm, idly packing it further.

"The sack that had formed on his chest has disappeared. His humanity, the accumulation of everything about him that might be considered a soul, has been reabsorbed into his body. I've examined him closely, much to his displeasure, and all that remains as evidence of this episode is a round patch of hard, callouslike tissue that had been the sack, and a scar where Daniel cut himself."

Conan Doyle saw the hope in Julia's eyes and glanced away. He looked at Ceridwen, and then at the doubtful expression on Eve's face. Of all of them, she was the most cautious about Danny. He wondered at her cynicism. If anyone could provide the example the boy needed, it would be her.

"That's . . . that's wonderful news, Mr. Doyle . . . Arthur," Julia said. "But I'm more concerned right now with what's going on inside of him than outside."

He nodded. "Agreed. But in this case you cannot separate the two. Danny's been through a great deal. He is a confused young man. He has been presented with awful truths and terrible choices, and I worry that he made the wrong ones. Had Eve and Squire not been there to interfere, on two separate occasions, and myself on a third, I fear that Danny would have taken a path from which he could never return."

Ceridwen gazed at him with those violet eyes, full of love and compassion. "Surely, Arthur, we've saved him from that."

"We did," Julia agreed. "We stopped him."

Eve leaned forward, staring at the other two women. "Yeah. For now. I'm sorry, Julia, but there's no way to know where his head is at. He's hardly talked to anyone since we brought him home. We all want to think that now that he's got all of that humanity back inside of him that he'll be all right, but with it comes the guilt and the doubt surrounding the things he did. He's never going to know what he would really have done at the end, because the choice wasn't his. And it doesn't help that Doyle incinerated his father right in front of him."

Conan Doyle glared at her. "You won't make me regret that, Eve. Baalphegor deserved no mercy and received none. Had I allowed him to live he would only have plagued this world and others even further, and he would have returned for Danny again and again until he had what he wanted."

She threw up her hands. "I agree. I'd have toasted the son of a bitch myself, given the chance. But Danny was torn, Arthur. I could see it. We all could. The fact remains that this particular hellspawn was his *father*. He has to live with that. And he has to live under the roof of the man who killed him."

The room went silent. After a moment Eve sighed and looked around at them all. "What? I'm only saying what we're all thinking."

Julia looked at Conan Doyle and then turned to Ceridwen. "What about you? Do you think he'll be all right? I know you have a sense of people, an empathy."

Ceridwen turned her violet eyes upon her lover again, and for several seconds they just stared at one another. Then the elemental sorceress looked at Julia again.

"I do. He's in pain. A great deal of pain. And Eve is not

wrong about his guilt. Danny is profoundly confused and afraid, of and for himself. But he loves you, Julia. And he feels a sense of safety here. That much I know. What the future will hold for him, though, none of us can predict."

Conan Doyle cleared his throat. He was cold by the window, but he remained where he was. "Ah," he said, "but Baalphegor made a prediction. Or was aware of one. He indicated that some seer or another had prophesied some great destiny for Daniel."

"That's . . . that's got to be good, yes?" Julia asked, eyes imploring.

"We can't know that," Eve said. "He'll play a role in something huge. In my mind, that's got to be the fight against the Demogorgon, but we don't know. Just like we have no idea who'll benefit from the role Danny plays. The light . . . or the darkness."

Again they all fell silent. Eve had a talent for quieting a room.

"So, what now?" Julia asked at last.

Ceridwen smiled softly. "Now, we wait. We continue our fight and our preparations for the coming of the Demogorgon, and we watch Danny very closely. All of us. We become his family, and we take care of him, and we make sure that when the time comes that he must make a decision at last, that he chooses the light."

"And we are going to need your help with that, Julia," Conan Doyle continued. "Which is why I hoped you would move your things in here."

"What?" she asked, brows knitted. "Live here?"

He spread his hands, pipe still clutched in one. "Temporarily, if you wish. But, yes, I do think it would be greatly beneficial to your son. For his sake, and possibly for the world's, he needs you here."

She shook her head. "I couldn't just live here. I'm a grown woman. I'm capable of taking care of myself. I'm hardly a charity case—"

"Stop it," Eve snapped.

Julia flinched and stared at her.

"This isn't charity. Put aside your pride. You're thinking like you're still some suburban mommy whose kid is at boarding school or something. Danny is a part of something greater than himself, now, and like it or not, that means that you're a part of it, too. Now, you can walk away from your son if that's your choice. But if not, then snap out of it. You can live as much of your normal life from here as is possible. Otherwise, things like the mortgage and the electric bill aren't that important anymore."

She smiled. "And besides, Doyle's got embarrassing amounts of money. Why not live here and let him worry about the grocery bill? He won't even notice. And then you can focus on Danny."

Ceridwen gave Julia's hand a little shake. "You really are welcome here."

Julia nodded slowly. "All right. Let me think about it awhile. I do appreciate your offer. I'm . . . I'm just very afraid for him right now."

"We all are," Eve said.

Conan Doyle crossed back to the fireplace, the chill from outside having crept into his bones. He set the pipe down on the mantel and let the heat of the flames warm him.

"I've been afraid for him from the beginning. I always feared something like this."

"You knew this would happen, didn't you?"

Conan Doyle did not turn to face her. "Demons do not leave their changeling offspring in this world for no reason. I knew that one day, Danny's sire would come for him, though the circumstances I could only guess at."

"Why didn't you tell me?" Julia asked. "You came to see me when he was just a boy. You could have warned me, then."

At the fireplace, Conan Doyle hesitated. He was very poor at explaining himself and his decisions. How to tell the woman that a warning would only have destroyed the happiness of the years she had with her son before it all had become so horribly wrong?

"That's what he's good at," said a familiar voice, deep and rich and full of simmering anger. "Keeping secrets."

Conan Doyle turned, eyebrow raised, to see the ghost of Dr. Graves shimmering in the center of the room, the gray day and the firelight conspiring to give him more dimension and gravity than he normally manifested.

The ghost had his arms crossed and was staring at him.

"Arthur always knows more than he says," the ghost went on. "That's how he maintains control. Or, at least, the illusion of control."

Conan Doyle gazed at Graves, his expression neutral. "Welcome back, Leonard."

Even as he spoke, he saw Clay enter through the arched doorway from the hall. He wore a thick, brown leather jacket, spattered with rain, and faded blue jeans. His close-cropped salt-and-pepper hair glistened with raindrops.

"And welcome back to you, Joe," Conan Doyle added.

Clay gave a small wave and leaned against the door frame. "Yeah. From the update Squire just gave us, it sounds like we missed quite a bit."

"You might say that," Eve muttered, and Conan Doyle saw her exchange a meaningful look with Clay. The two had been bonding quite a bit in recent months, and how could they not? Clay was perhaps the only creature alive with whom Eve shared any real kinship, save the filthy vampire hordes.

The ghost of Dr. Graves went over and pretended to sit on the arm of the loveseat beside Julia.

"Are you all right?"

"I will be," she said, brightening with his presence. "We really could have used you, Leonard. I'm so glad you're back."

"I'm sorry," the ghost replied. "Had I any idea, I would have put off my search."

"I know," Julia said. It was as though she and the ghost were alone in the room. The warmth and caring between them was unmistakable. "Did you find the answers you were looking for?"

Graves cast a baleful glance at Conan Doyle. "I did."

Julia smiled. "Yet you're still here."

The ghost nodded, reaching out to touch her hair. His hand passed through her, but she went to touch him as well, grasping only smoke.

"I've solved my own mystery," Graves said. "But there are so many threats to the world, now. The darkness is coming nearer, and I thought I should stay and do my best to help. And I made a promise to you, to help Danny adjust to his life. I've done a poor job of that, obviously. I'll do what I can to make it up to you."

Julia smiled even more broadly. "Thank you. You can't imagine what that means to me."

Graves did not reply, save to smile. Then he turned toward Conan Doyle, and the smile faded.

"We're pleased to have you back, Leonard," Conan Doyle said. "You and Joe both."

The ghost drifted toward him, not bothering to mimic the rhythm of walking. He simply floated across the room, his spectral substance wavering in the November gloom.

"One of the reasons I stayed, Arthur, was to keep an eye on you."

Conan Doyle stiffened and crossed his arms. "I'm not sure I like your tone, old friend."

"How are you my friend, Arthur? Honestly?"

"I have always been your friend."

Ceridwen and Julia looked taken aback, staring at the two in surprise and concern. Eve shot a curious glance at Clay, but his expression was unreadable. Conan Doyle took this all in and then focused his attention on Graves again.

"From this point on," the ghost replied, "don't think of me as your friend. Think of me as your conscience. I will be watching you, Arthur. You, with your arrogance and your manipulations. You think so damned much of yourself that it blinds you. You always know best, don't you? Or you think so, anyway. Your genius, your cunning, your wisdom. Only you can save the world from the darkness, and from itself. And you gather us around you not as friends or comrades or even respected allies, but as pieces on a chessboard.

"Your Menagerie.

"And you think that only you can save *us* from the darkness, and from *our*selves. So you keep secrets, the way you kept them from Julia and Danny. And the way you kept them from me!"

In a fury that Conan Doyle had never seen from him before, the ghost lost all cohesion and surged forward like a crashing ocean wave. His face coalesced from the ethereal mist just inches from Conan Doyle's own.

"You knew, you bastard!" the specter, his visage terrifyingly inhuman, roared. "I thought you were ignoring me, or that you were not the detective I had been led to believe. But all along, you knew, didn't you?"

Conan Doyle stared at him, jaw set. "You don't understand."

"Damn you, Arthur! You left me lost! You let me wander all this time!"

"It wasn't . . ." Conan Doyle began. Then he lowered his eyes. "An examination of your remains made certain conclusions inevitable. I planned to tell you about the Whisper, but when I realized you hadn't been shot, it was not difficult to follow the logic to the additional conclusion that Gabriella had been involved—"

Julia gasped. "Oh, my God," she whispered, covering her mouth in horror.

Conan Doyle raised his eyes and looked at the churning, furious apparition before him. "I knew the truth would destroy you, Leonard."

Slowly, the spirit of Dr. Graves coalesced again. His expression was stoic, his spectral clothing neat and his manner nothing less than civilized. He stared at Conan Doyle with disdain.

"And, quite obviously, you were mistaken," Graves said. He glanced at Julia and Ceridwen, over at Clay, and finally at Eve. "All of you, take note. Arthur Conan Doyle is fallible. He makes mistakes."

The ghost wavered in the air. Through his transparent form, Conan Doyle could see all of the others staring at him.

"I will stand by your side, Arthur. The darkness that rises now is too great for us to be anything but allies. But from this point on, I warn you never to underestimate me or attempt to deceive me again. If you expect any of us to survive the coming of the Demogorgon, if you expect the world to survive, you have to start taking us into your confidence, treating us like your friends instead of your pawns. Otherwise, the darkness will claim us all, and our fight is hopeless."

Graves extended one spectral finger, pointing at him. "If I think, for even a moment, that your arrogance is jeopardizing our chances of survival in all of this . . . I will remove you from the fight."

Conan Doyle glared at the ghost, spine stiffening, a cold anger rising inside of him. He nodded. "As it should be. And rest assured, old friend, that I will do the same for you."

As chilly as the room had been before, it had become far colder still. The fire burned low in the fireplace, as though the oxygen that fed it had been stolen away.

The ghost stared at Conan Doyle a moment longer and then turned to Julia.

"With your permission, I'd like to see Danny now."

"Please," she said, nodding. "I think it will do him good. If he'll talk to anyone, he'll talk to you."

The ghost drifted from the room. He paused to nod toward Clay, who still stood leaning against the door frame. Clay nodded in return, and then the ghost of Dr. Graves was gone, disappearing into the darkness of the corridor.

Within the parlor, the only sound was the crackling of the fire, the howling of the wind, and the patter of icy rain upon the windows.

•   •   •

DANNY lay curled on his bed, ancient Pearl Jam playing low through the ear buds of his ipod. He stared at a spot on the wall, focused on the feeling of his chest rising and falling with each breath. Just breathing. That was what it was to be alive.

The room stank badly of teenager and demon. There was no pretending to himself anymore that the smell was anything else. Despite the chill outside, his window was open a few inches. The cold breeze that whipped through that gap felt good, and it took some of the stink away. At some point, he was going to have to clean his room and do laundry.

A shower wouldn't be a bad idea either.

At some point.

But not now. He couldn't bring himself to get up. His stomach rumbled hungrily, but even that was too much trouble. And it brought too many ugly thoughts into his head. What, exactly, was he hungry for?

So he lay there, letting the battery of his ipod run down, smelling his own stink, staring at that spot on the wall, and feeling himself breathe.

He realized he was not alone. He shifted his gaze away from the spot on the wall for the first time in hours and looked up at the ghost of Dr. Graves, hovering beside his bed.

A spark of something ignited within him, and at first he mistook it for anger. Graves had abandoned him. The ghost had promised to help him, to keep an eye out for him, and when Danny had needed him the most, Graves had been nowhere to be found.

But even those thoughts seemed dull. The spark in him wasn't anger, and he wouldn't allow himself to think it was anything like hope or relief, so he ignored it.

Danny pulled the headphone buds out of his ears.

"You never heard of knocking?" he asked, his throat a growl from going too long without speaking.

Graves mustered a sad sort of smile. "Hello to you, too."

"You're back."

The ghost nodded, his expression all seriousness now. "I won't be leaving again."

Danny frowned in confusion. "But you were going to go . . . to go on."

"Change of plans. I'm here. And I won't be leaving again."

A maelstrom of convoluted thoughts and questions entered Danny's mind. He wanted to talk, but he did not know what to say.

"Maybe you're not ready yet," the ghost said. "To talk about what happened."

Danny nodded slowly. He still had to work things over in his own head awhile before he could talk to anyone, even Dr. Graves. He stared at the transparent figure, could see the mess of his room right through him.

"All right," Graves said. "That's all right. I'm going to go, now. But I'll be here in the house, when you want to find me. Before I go, though, I wanted to give you something."

"Okay."

The ghost reached into the pocket of his jacket—a piece of clothing that was just as much a phantom as he was—and withdrew a scrap of thick paper. He offered it, and Danny took it from him. The paper was no ghost, but real and rough like parchment.

"What is it?" Danny asked, glancing at the scrap and at the writing scribbled on it.

"Something to think about," Dr. Graves said.

Then the ghost faded away, vanishing in increments, from figure to silhouette to nothing, and Danny was alone again. He looked down at the scrap of parchment. Upon it was written a quote from *Dr. Jekyll and Mr. Hyde*, by Robert Louis Stevenson.

•   •   •

"I N each of us, two natures are at war—the good and the evil. All our lives the fight goes on between them, and one of them must conquer. But in our hands lies the power to choose—what we want most to be, we are."

Danny stared at it for a long time, read it over and over again, and eventually simply focused on the final line. He felt a strange, cool, dampness on his cheeks, but only when he reached up and touched the moisture there, put it to his tongue and tasted salt, did he realize that he was crying.

And then he cried all the harder, and he smiled.

He could cry.

THE ULTIMATE IN
SCIENCE FICTION AND FANTASY!

From magical tales of distant worlds to stories of
technological advances beyond the grasp of man, Penguin has
everything you need to stretch your imagination to its limits.

penguin.com

ACE

Get the latest information on favorites like
William Gibson, T.A. Barron, Brian Jacques,
Ursula Le Guin, Sharon Shinn, and Charlaine Harris,
as well as updates on the best new authors.

ROC

Escape with Harry Turtledove, Anne Bishop,
S.M. Stirling, Simon Green, Chris Bunch, Jim Butcher,
E.E. Knight, and many others—plus news on the
latest and hottest in science fiction and fantasy.

DAW

Mercedes Lackey, Kristen Britain, Tanya Huff,
Tad Williams, C.J. Cherryh, and many more—
DAW has something to satisfy the cravings of any
science fiction and fantasy lover.
Also visit dawbooks.com.

Get the best of science fiction and fantasy
at your fingertips!